INTO THE BLUE

COASTAL FURY BOOK 3

MATT LINCOLN

PROLOGUE

ONE OF THE benefits of living-legend status is that it was easy to bribe a crew of Navy kids on shore leave to help at my first outdoor live-band event. Waive the cover charge and give them a little responsibility, and it was like they'd always worked my bar. The girls on my staff also appreciated help from familiar faces.

"Hey, Charlie, that speaker's getting in the way over there." My manager, Rhoda, had everything so coordinated that all I had to do was check IDs and collect the cover at the door. "Nadia's bumping into that thing every time she goes out the side door."

"Got it!" Charlie waved over one of the guys to handle it.

Charlie, or Ensign Charlie Sheets, had taken the

unacknowledged lead in this little band of young sailors. They reminded me of the pilots in *Top Gun*, so enthusiastic and full of life. Hell, Charlie looked kind of like Anthony Edwards, Goose. Sometimes that comparison gave me the chills, though. I liked the kid.

"Do I need to show my ID?"

I looked up from my little table and laughed. Mike Birch, the former owner of my bar, back when it was Mike's Tropical Tango Hut, stood at the door with a wistful smile. Even in his sixties, the guy was a strong presence, and nobody would mess with him unless they had a few loose screws.

"Hey, buddy." I stood and offered him my hand. "Thanks for the assist."

"I wouldn't miss it," Mike said with a grin. "As long as the girls don't mind an old fool like me bumbling around their bar, we'll be fine."

"Mike!" Rhoda ran up and gave him a hug. "We're ready for you. Ethan got that old stool out for you."

They'd become fast friends in the months since I opened Rolling Thunder. This was the first time Mike was in to help tend bar, and I almost couldn't convince him. Retirement was a great thing, but this was special.

"Rhoda, cover the door, will ya?" I asked. "I gotta show Mike around the patio."

"Copy that," she answered with a wink. "The band's finished with sound checks. Charlie and his Merry Sailors got all the tables and chairs re-situated. We're ready to go." She looked at her phone even though there was a perfectly good ship's clock mounted above the entrance. "Two hours until showtime, boss."

Mike and I started toward the new section of the bar when a mighty crash rolled in through the wide double doors outside. We sprinted out to the source and found one of Charlie's crew tangled up with a stack of folding chairs.

"Mackenzie, you okay?" I passed a few chairs off to Mike and then one of the other kids.

"Yes, sir." Charlie's newest tagalong, Mackenzie, pushed the rest of the chairs away and glared at the rack that loomed above her. "One of the wheels went out, and it dumped chairs everywhere."

I helped her to her feet, but she couldn't put weight on her left ankle. Her cheeks reddened. I got it. Female sailors had a shit-ton more to prove than their male peers. Weakness was not allowed.

"Can you move it?" I asked as the guys cleaned up the chairs behind her.

"I'll be fine with an ice pack," she informed everyone. Her grimace wasn't convincing. "I just rolled it is all. No blood, no foul."

"Charlie, get her other arm," I ordered. A small crowd of early regulars, sailors, and the band had already gathered around us. "Everyone else, as you were. Someone, get that chair rack stabilized and out of here."

Mike met us at the bar. Even though the labels were different and countertop new, he was perfectly at home. He dug out a bag of ice from his vintage ice maker I'd gotten rehabbed, added a dash of vodka to make it stay cold, and then handed it to the walking... er, limping wounded.

Charlie and I got Mackenzie onto one of the new stools. Someone found a sweatshirt and used it to prop her leg up on the next seat. Her ankle was swelling, and the bruise didn't look good. I laid a dish towel over her skin and then set the ice on her ankle.

"You oughta get that x-rayed," I told her. Yeah, my liability insurance would take a hit for this, but I didn't care. "Don't mess around with ankle injuries, kiddo."

"I've been waiting a month to see this band, Mr. Marston," she admitted. "They have some sick guitar work in their YouTube videos. I do not plan to miss this."

"C'mon, Mac," Charlie pleaded. "I'll take you in. We'll catch these guys some other time."

Speaking of the band, three of the members walked up at that moment, and one had a folded shirt in hand.

"We feel bad you got hurt," the lead singer said. "Your buddy Jeff said you're a fan. This ain't much, but I got the guys and Claire to sign this for you." He offered the shirt with a sheepish grin. "I'll make sure you get in to see us next time we're around."

"I love your original stuff," Mackenzie blurted out. "The cover stuff is great, but I just know you're going to do great with your own work."

She and the singer... damned if I can remember his name... met each other's eyes. Now, I'm not the kind of guy to believe in that whole "zing" thing, but I swear to God something zapped between those two.

"I'll get it looked at after the show," Mackenzie promised. "A few hours won't make much of a difference."

I wasn't so sure about that, but hey, it was her choice.

"Hey, man." The singer grinned at me. Uh-oh. "I

heard you were some badass secret agent or something. That's cool."

"Oh, dude!" another band member cried out. "You're that guy who tells those stories!"

Mike laughed his ass off behind the bar where he had happily occupied his old stool. I glared at him. He started the whole story-telling thing, but hey, it got Rolling Thunder some attention. I was tempted to go hide that stool of his after all.

"I wasn't a *secret* agent," I explained to the musicians and early customers who'd wandered up. "More like an investigator, a special agent."

Charlie, dear Ensign Charlie, wagged his brows and grinned. Uh-huh. I had an idea of how the band found out about the stories. Sneaky kid.

"Mr. Marston, we have some time," Mackenzie pointed out. "I haven't heard any of your stories yet." She pointed at a pair of scuba masks that hung on the wall with their straps intertwined with a yellow ribbon. "Ty said you were going to tell us about those masks sometime."

I realized I wasn't getting out of it this time. With a sigh, I eased into my usual seat, the one next to the only remaining stool from Mike's days as owner. The RESERVED sign had a little dust on it, and I blew that off.

"Hey, Mike, a little Mango Fest, huh?"

With a quiet nod, he poured me a shot and delivered an empty one, upside down, to Robbie's seat. He set the rum bottle next to the shot glass. By now, the kids and regulars knew the routine, and they quietly respected it.

"About those scuba masks," I began. "Well, folks, it's not every day you meet your murder victims before they die."

1

Bridget and Darrel "Dare" Lemon had dived the Great Blue Hole a half dozen times to prepare for this trip. It was only forty-odd miles from the coast of Belize, which made it convenient to test the gear their niece helped engineer. Divers rarely went four hundred feet deep due to cold and pressure, and the new suits were built for warmth. The extra insulation plus other modifications were also intended to make it safer for divers to linger in hydrogen sulfide zones. The acidic water could eat through metal and cause burns and sickness in divers.

Bridget was proud of Haley for her innovation, and it was exciting to test at a site which had depth *and* the acidic water. The Great Blue Hole had both. It was one of the very few scuba dives ever made to the bottom of the hole, and if they got to the bottom, they'd go for a record of time safely spent at the bottom. Decompression was going to be a bitch on the way up, but it was totally worth it.

"How's the mask?" she asked her husband as they hovered at the no-go zone. They had full face masks to prevent burning from the hydrogen sulfide and to allow them to talk. "Any fogging today?"

"Nah, it's good." Dare gave a double-okay and then clicked on his Sola Dive light. "Booty check."

Bridget laughed as he played the dive light across the visible seams in her gear. She noticed that light lingering on her chest. Dare was such a tease, and that was just one of the things she loved about him. When he pronounced her equipment intact, she did the same check for him.

"Aunt Bridget, Uncle Dare, how do you copy?"

"Looking great down here, Haley," Dare radioed back to the boat. "Still sounding crystal clear from down here. How are you receiving?"

"Like you're standing next to me," Haley answered. "Next mic check in five."

The radio was rated up to six hundred feet, but Bridget knew not to count on it. The Hole went down to four hundred seven feet, but the dead zone started at around two-ninety, which was already a deep dive.

Bridget squashed a thrill of anxiety that ran down her back as she and Dare stopped kicking and allowed their bodies to sink below the usual hundred thirty-foot depth limit for Hole divers. As much as she wished to explore the deeper reef life that few divers got to witness, the day's job was to test the gear, not do research.

Their tanks and dive suits were designed to not only work at greater depths on compressed air but also to block out hydrogen sulfide, a noxious layer created from decaying matter in areas that got little circulation. Exposure through the skin could cause burning, nausea, and other symptoms. Divers could usually pass through these zones with little trouble as long as they didn't linger. They could stay a bit longer if they didn't have exposed skin, but with this specialized gear, they hoped to extend that safe time greatly. If this worked well, Haley hoped to adapt it to better tech for hazmat crews.

"There's the cloud," Dare announced in a tone of reverence. "Haley, mic check before entering the dreaded acid layer."

"Copy loud and clear," their niece responded. "Aunt Bridget, how's the GoPro?"

Bridget tapped the device on her diving helmet. "Nice and secure."

The camera was literally out of her hands, and she was happy for it. A hundred-plus feet remained to their descent, and she liked having her hands free in murky, unfamiliar locations. She swung her dive light across the side of the Hole they'd chosen to be close to for the duration. Above the hydrogen sulfide layer, life along the wall was typical of the depth. At the top of the cloud, however, the die-off was complete. Nothing survived below that level.

Dare swam over in front of her. "Second thoughts?"

"No. Just... nerves." Bridget gave him their traditional double-okay signal. "We're doing something no one else has."

"Let's get to it, then, woman!" He paddled backward a few feet and then sank. "Come on in. The water's poison!"

She watched his light go from white to yellow in the cloud. That alone was eerie, but that's all it was. She took his cue and stilled her body to let gravity take over. The clear water turned murky and took on a brown hue, nothing she couldn't handle. The two of them had been a technical dive team for two decades. And yet, she couldn't shake a sense of unease.

"Almost at the bottom." Dare's voice crackled over the radio, which was a bit unsettling. His light was still close by. "Sonar's pinging pretty good."

"Roger that," she answered.

Bridget started kicking to slow her descent. Even with the suit's modifications, she felt the pressure of being four hundred feet down. Their deepest dive ever was four hundred thirty a few months earlier in another location. Like then, she and Dare wouldn't have long to explore before they had to start ascending, even with extra tanks and specialized air mixes.

"Silt ahoy." Dare's announcement was followed by a sound of disgust.

"What's wrong?" Bridget started toward him, but his hazy silhouette waved her off.

"Trash," he sighed.

"Gross." There went the feeling of joy at their accomplishment. "We'll bring a garbage net next time."

"Yeah. Look around over there. Maybe you'll have better luck."

Bridget spent a while picking through lumps under the silt and scanning the area with her dive light. They were the first divers but not the first visitors to make it to the bottom. Richard Branson worked with Fabien Cousteau and went to the bottom less than a year earlier with a submersible operator. They'd mapped the area and found a few things, including two of the three bodies they expected to find, a soda bottle, and a GoPro. Remembering that made her touch hers again. Yep, it was still safe and sound in its special case.

Something unusual poked up through the silt. Bridget swam over and poked at what looked like a thin towel. It was blue or teal, but it was hard to tell within the puff of silt she disturbed to pull it out. Unsurprising, maybe, but it was still disappointing to see everyday things in a seemingly untouched area.

"Shit..."

Bridget froze with towel in her hand. "Are you okay?" she asked.

Dare was slow to answer. "I have a leak in the suit..."

The connection crackled worse than before. Alarmed, she looked around for the telltale glow of his light. Everything was dark, and only her light penetrated the poison cloud.

"I don't see you," she ventured as she grabbed for her personal sonar. "Flash me, baby."

He didn't laugh, but she finally saw a dim spot a little way off. She pointed her sonar and was relieved when it pinged right where she'd seen the tiny glow.

"Coming." Bridget kicked over to where she found Dare bent over and holding his gut. She played her light across his suit and possible areas for the hydrogen sulfide to penetrate but saw nothing out of the ordinary. "Where's the leak?"

"Dunno," he muttered. "My hands are burning, an' m' head hurts."

His gloves appeared to be intact as she took a closer look. The little towel she'd found kept floating in the way, so she dropped it. Whatever was going on, she needed both hands free to help Dare.

"Haley, we're starting ascent," Bridget radioed. There was no reply. "Haley, do you copy?"

"Soundin' crackly," Dare said.

"You, too. Let's get kicking," she ordered. As she gave him her left hand, she could've sworn she felt a tingle, as well. She dismissed it as psychosomatic. "Think about tonight on the beach. It'll make you feel better."

"Aye-aye, ma'am."

Bridget rolled her eyes. How she loved that man... and worried about him. This was the wrong time and place for something to go wrong.

Deep dives like this were for the best of the best only. The deeper a person dove, the more often and longer their stops on the way up. Barring an extreme emergency, decompression came first, and symptoms of poisoning came last. For Bridget and Dare, it was the most miserable ascent of their diving careers.

They got Haley back on the radio by the time they hit the first stop.

"I was getting worried," the younger woman told them. "Did you forget mic checks?"

"We were fine talking with each other, but I guess we got distracted," Bridget confessed. "Your uncle is having some issues with the H2S. I think it's breached his gloves."

"No way! Okay, I'll have his bunk ready when you all get up here."

After that, they maintained their check-ins. Halfway up, Bridget decided her hand really *was* burning, and her head and stomach didn't feel so hot, either. Dare was in worse shape, though. He kept groaning, but he was able to stick to the planned stops. By the time they surfaced, both were ready for a good night's sleep.

Haley helped the boat captain lug both of them out of the water, and then she tended to her uncle while Bridget rested at the back of the boat. Nausea came and went, but the headache and burning skin on her hand wouldn't ease up. She got her gloves off and rinsed her hands several times to be sure there wasn't any lingering poison. A thorough inspection showed no tears in her left glove.

"He's out like a light," Haley announced when she climbed up from the cabin. She crouched next to Bridget. "You don't look much better."

"I can't figure how it got through," Bridget told her.

Haley shook her head. "I'll have to get a closer look back home. We're running late already."

The sun was low, and Bridget realized she and Dare were going to miss their usual post-dive beach date.

"You want us to stay another day or two?" she offered. "We can take a later flight and help examine the suits."

Haley made a face. "I love you and Uncle Dare, but you two have *got* to get home."

"And out of your condo?" Bridget asked with a laugh. She accepted Haley's help with getting her gear off. "Got some hot university student waiting for us to clear out?"

Haley snorted. "I'll take care of this stuff. There's some broth down there if you want it."

Bridget did find it, and the broth did ease her stomach. When they reached the condo later that night, she and Dare both felt better but not well enough to sneak out to the beach like when they were kids. Instead, they passed out for the night and made it to the airport with time to spare in the morning.

At bag check-in, Bridget noticed Dare still seemed a little pale.

"Do you want to wait a day?" She checked for a fever, but his cheeks were nice and cool. "If you're not up to flying—"

"Let's just go," he snapped. He caught himself. "Sorry, love. Hey, I'll feel better once we're home."

As they made their way through the metal detectors, a security person quietly took them aside.

"I apologize for the inconvenience, but I have a question for you," the young man said. "One of your bags set off a radiation detector the first time it went through. When we sent it again, nothing happened." He looked between them as if hoping they'd have answers. "Did you happen to go anywhere unusual?"

"We went on a few dives," Bridget answered. "Last I checked, there weren't any power stations down there." She tried to keep a sense of humor in her tone, but she was so very tired that she wasn't sure it sounded right. "No, honey, I don't think so."

"Okay. Well, we'll send it through once more," he decided. "If it's clear, we'll send it onto your plane."

"Thank you," Bridget said.

The bag sailed on through, and they boarded shortly after. Dare took the window seat, and Bridget used his upper arm for a pillow. She dozed off shortly after they hit cruising altitude.

Bridget woke up to someone placing an oxygen mask to her face. She didn't remember getting out of her seat, but now she was on her back underneath the harsh sun and being rolled somewhere. Between the thunder of passenger planes coming and going and the wing they passed under, she realized she was on the tarmac of an airport far busier than in Belize City.

"Mrs. Lemon, can you hear me?" someone yelled over the noise of a jet engine. "Do you know where you are?"

Her throat hurt too much to speak, so she mouthed the word "airport."

They reached an ambulance and loaded her in. One medic spoke on the radio while the other checked her vitals and talked with her.

"Do you know which airport?"

That seemed important, but the answer eluded her. All she recalled was snuggling into Dare's shoulder on a plane. She shook her head. She didn't know where she was, and she didn't know where her husband was.

"Mrs. Lemon, you and your husband appear to be very ill and are going to the hospital," the paramedic told her. "Welcome to Miami."

2

———

My siren ripped through the late night, and my dashboard lights threw reds and blues against buildings as we raced past. The black Mustang ahead swerved around traffic and almost hit someone trying to cross the street.

"He's gonna kill someone," I growled. "Where's air support?"

Holm checked the tracking app on his tablet and shook his head. "Too far out. We gotta stop this."

A Miami Metro squad car dropped in behind us. Pretty soon, there'd be a posse of police cars out only making the situation worse. They had no idea we were chasing a human trafficker we'd been hunting for months. Calling them off wasn't an option, though.

The car juked left, down a side street. He almost hit the oncoming cars, but the drivers stopped in time. As I turned and sped past, I heard the crunch of someone getting rear-ended.

"Robbie, get on the horn to that Metro guy. Have him stop for that collision." That'd get one squad car out of the way. "How's CGIS looking?"

"Parker's almost caught up with us," Holm reported. "He's two blocks back. Why hasn't TJ hacked this guy's car yet?"

"It doesn't work that way, partner. Not yet."

The brake lights glowed for a second on the Mustang, but the driver decided to charge forward. Water splashed into the air as he hit a flooded street.

"Shit, shit, shit," I swore as I floored it down the submerged road. "Robbie, is the tide coming or going?"

"High, and it gets deep in this neighborhood."

"He better hope it doesn't drown my car." I followed the black muscle car around a corner, and the water didn't get any better. "I'm gonna make him clean every damned inch of it!"

Holm's dry laugh didn't help. "Yeah, I'm sure that's allowed."

The Mustang dropped speed and lost control about the time my Charger's engine sucked in water and died. Inertia kicked in, and we kept going forward as the car took to floating, like hydroplaning, only worse. My feet felt wet a second later.

I slammed the car into park, not that it'd do much good at that point, and grabbed my tactical helmet and rifle from the backseat as Holm kept an eye on the Mustang, and then we switched so Holm could gear up.

"He's trying to restart it," I laughed. "That's not happening."

I opened my door. Water crashed in, and the Charger dropped the two inches back to the ground. I jumped into the knee-deep slew of water and sewage and crouched behind my door with the rifle. The streetlights were patchy in that area, and our suspect, Grundy Walsh, was a tricky son of a bitch. Tricky other than not knowing how to deal with Miami's streets at high tide.

"Hands out the window, Walsh," I shouted over my car's speaker.

The Mustang rocked around, which was never a good sign. A scream echoed across the stilled water and off the houses.

"Come on," Holm tried. "Make a good choice here. Give it up."

The Mustang bumped into an SUV parked at the

edge of the street and came to a rest. The passenger door was trapped against the larger vehicle, which only left the driver's door, and we couldn't see through the heavy window tint. Fortunately, the steady whomp-whomp of the CGIS chopper announced the arrival of the ultra-bright spotlight.

"You're not going anywhere, Walsh." At that point, I wasn't sure if the trafficker could hear me, but I needed to try. He had at least one hostage, maybe two.

As if on cue, the driver's side door eased open. A young woman emerged first, but her right arm was clenched by our suspect. He exited the car while holding a handgun to her head.

"Back off, or she's dead!" Walsh looked around with a wild set about his eyes. "Let me go, and you can have her."

I leaned into my car to get Holm's attention from his position behind the other door on the Charger.

"Robbie, have CGIS back the chopper off. Get Parker to go around a block away if he can. That Jeep'll give him some cover."

"On it."

As the chopper backed off a little with the spotlight, I saw a shadow in the yard behind the Jeep.

Then another. Looked like Parker and his partner, Yvonne Bell, were on my wavelength already.

Walsh shoved his hostage forward and surveyed the growing police and Fed presences in the area. This wasn't going to end well for him, not if he didn't drop it. SWAT would take his ass out if we didn't first.

"There's no way out, buddy," I shouted over the commotion. "Work with us, and the prosecution might go lighter on you."

"You assholes are supposed to negotiate!" Walsh pointed his gun in my direction and then waved it around. No one dared to fire and possibly hit the girl. "I swear I'll kill her."

"Do that, and you die," I told him.

Something launched out of the car and into Walsh's back. At first, I could've sworn it was a wildcat, but it was another girl, this one all fury and dressed in black. She slammed Walsh face-first into the floodwater, which shocked him into letting go of the first hostage and his gun.

I winced but didn't feel bad for the goon as we rushed him. The girl in black screamed in at least two languages and had to be pulled off of his back before she drowned him. Not that I would have minded. Walsh was one of the traffickers we'd chased down since breaking up the Trader's organization a few weeks earlier.

Our shadowy backup stayed on the dry lawn behind the Jeep, of course. Parker stepped into a streetlamp's glow as I cuffed the drenched suspect.

"Is this your new thing, Marston?" Parker called out. "I heard you smelled like all sorts of roses on the first night of your last big case."

I flipped him a friendly gesture as we dragged Walsh up to the grassy area. Bell rolled her eyes and turned away toward the trafficking survivors.

"This'll take a couple of extra showers," I admitted, but then I frowned. "These folks don't get to wash it out of their neighborhood, though." I nodded toward the growing crowd of onlookers.

Parker rubbed the back of his neck. "True. Anyway, I got word we're taking Walsh. Some weird jurisdictional stuff." He grinned. "I'll see if my boss will buy you some new shoes for your trouble."

I gladly handed Walsh over to the CGIS agents. My agency had more than enough work taking down the Trader's trafficking network, thanks to a database our people recovered. Women and girls were being rescued almost every day throughout the Caribbean and southern East Coast.

"Get ATF on this guy," Holm said as he walked up from the Mustang. "He has a friggin' armory in the trunk."

"And yet he turned his back on one girl. One. Girl." I shook my head at Walsh, who looked away. "Guess you didn't break that one's spirit, after all. What a shame we had to stop her from drowning ya."

The intense system of breaking their victims' spirits and remolding them into perfectly obedient Stepford slaves had been a hardcore part of the Trader's process, as was the branding process. The trident and flower tattoo was plainly visible on both of the survivors we rescued that night. One on the calf, and one on an upper arm.

My phone buzzed in my pocket. The boss, Miami MBLIS Director Diane Ramsey, was ringing. I stepped away.

"What's up, Diane?"

"Ethan, we have a sensitive situation at Miami-Dade General," she told me in a strained tone. "You and Robbie need to get over there. I'll message you the details."

I went over and told Holm about our new instructions.

"'Sensitive situation'?" he echoed. "I hate when she says that."

"Yeah. I got a bad feeling about it, partner."

Little did I know it'd be more than a bad feeling in no time flat.

3

WE ARRIVED at the hospital after quick showers at our MBLIS field office. I doubted I'd ever get the reek of raw sewage out of my skin, but a thorough scrubbing worked for the time being. I was less happy about having to sign out a pool car to replace my Charger.

The Lemons shared a private room in a quiet section of Miami-Dade General. The hospital had only been open two years, but it had become the state-of-the-art lead in Southern Florida in no time. Holm and I followed Doctor Schvalla Hill to an empty waiting room near our living victims. Living for now. Dr. Hill closed the door to the room and leaned back against it.

"Bridget and Darrel Lemon are suffering from

acute radiation poisoning," Dr. Hill informed us. "We have an idea of how they were exposed, but we can't rule out other possibilities. They started showing symptoms during their flight home to Miami from a diving trip in Belize. Possibly earlier, but their memories are hazy, especially Mr. Lemon."

I blinked, and my breath caught in my throat. That's what Diane meant by "sensitive situation."

"As in exposure to radioactive materials?" I asked in disbelief. "What about other passengers and people they were in contact with?"

"Everyone on the plane has gone through decontamination," she told me. "The Lemons' niece is going through it now in Belize. People are being quiet for now, but it's going to get out."

Next to me, Holm looked as lost as I felt. "How does this even happen?"

"That's why we called you," Dr. Hill answered. "They've been decontaminated, so it's safe for you to go in." Her stern brows and the set of her mouth made me feel like I was in the principal's office. "Speak quietly and don't turn up the lights. Mrs. Lemon will speak with you. Mr. Lemon... he may sleep through it."

I shook Dr. Hill's hand. Her vice-like grip served as a warning.

"I expect your agency to protect my patients better than the last time I met you."

"Yes, ma'am," I answered with as much sincerity as I could summon. Although we did our best to prevent a tragedy a few weeks earlier at Miami-Dade, tragedy came calling anyway when a witness-survivor was kidnapped and staff shot. "We're doing everything we can." Like before.

Dr. Hill gave a sharp nod and then led us into the room.

"Mrs. Lemon, Special Agents Marston and Holm are here to speak with you. They're with MBLIS."

The woman in the bed closest to us was sitting up with a book. She laid the book on her lap and offered a slight smile. She looked over to the other bed and took a deep breath.

"He's everything to me," Mrs. Lemon said as she watched her husband's sleeping form. "I don't know what I'll do without him."

"How long have you been married?" I noticed a white circle on her empty left ring finger. She absently rubbed at it.

"Seventeen years." Mrs. Lemon turned her gaze toward us. "I hear you're divers, too. What's your agency?"

"MBLIS," I answered. "We investigate crimes that

occur in or involving international waters. Holm and I were SEALs before this, so we know a few things about diving." I winked and grinned.

"Darrel wanted to be a SEAL," Mrs. Lemon said with a laugh. "Turned out that he couldn't stand guns. He got kicked out of boot camp when he couldn't get over it."

"It's not for everyone, Mrs. Lemon," Holm admitted with a gentle smile. "We need more people who can't stand guns." I gave him a side-eye. He wasn't wrong, but I hadn't heard him say anything like that before. "It says a lot that he even tried."

She nodded. "Please, agents, call me 'Bridget.'" She pointed to her husband. "Darrel goes by 'Dare' in the diving world."

"Oh!" My jaw dropped. "Dare Dives! I'm slow today. Robbie, this is the couple who does all those technical dives and equipment tests. The ones I followed on YouTube."

Holm's eyes widened, and he stared at Dare's bed. These two were well known in the diving world. They'd been pushing deep dives for the past two decades and helped with a lot of innovations in that field.

"Our niece designs a lot of our gear now," Bridget said with pride. "We've been so busy educating that she's taken over most of the engineering." Her smile faltered, and she looked down at her hands. "I mean... we *were* educating. I... I guess that's over now."

"May I sit next to you, Bridget?" I asked. At her nod, I pulled a visitor chair close. "What's his prognosis?"

She shrugged her shoulders. "Days. Weeks. Hours. Nobody really knows, but the best guess is a few days. The way the doctor explained was that he got close to something really, really hot." Bridget looked to the ceiling and bit her lower lip. A tear ran down the side of her face and toward her ear. "The only thing we know for sure is that he's dying."

"I'm so sorry," I said. Near the curtain, Holm pinched the bridge of his nose. "And you, how are you doing?"

"Rattled. Scared." She met my gaze. Her hazel eyes reflected the green tones of her hospital gown, and her salt-and-pepper hair wisped around her face. "They're pretty sure I'll live, but I'm going to have a high risk of cancer for the rest of my life."

"So, tell me about your trip to Belize," I prompted.

"We went to test equipment to make deep dives safer." She reached over to the bedside table and picked up a phone. "More and more recreational divers are pushing their luck, and we're looking out for them. Technical divers always like pushing things, too." A smile slipped out at that.

"You went to the Blue Hole, then?" Holm asked with no little hint of wistfulness. That was a bucket-list dive for both of us. We just hadn't made time for it. "How deep did you go?"

Bridget frowned. "We went all the way down..." Her hands grabbed at the blanket as if clawing at a memory. "My GoPro caught the footage, but I don't remember much of it." She shook her head. "We ascended safely, but I barely remember it."

She handed me her phone, where a video was primed to play.

"We used full face masks, and my niece recorded our radio transmissions, but they cut out by the time we reached the bottom."

"That's four hundred feet," I told Holm, and he nodded. "If anyone knows how to pull off a dive like that, it's you and Dare." Yeah, there was a reason the Lemons were heroes in the diving world. Their expertise was off the charts. "So there's no recording of what you said at the bottom?"

She pointed to her temple. "It's here, but it's

fuzzy. I got so sick later that, I don't know, I forgot stuff."

Holm came over and watched the video with me. Bridget must have had a great case for the GoPro because the best of them were rated at maybe two hundred feet. I pushed play and couldn't stop an appreciative sigh. The water in Belize's Great Blue Hole was clear, and she'd descended near the reef wall.

In the upper zones, the reef life was as mind-blowingly gorgeous as it got. The shallows had the sandy floor and the saturated colors of fish, coral polyps of every shape and size, living rock every-where, sea turtles... everything.

Further in, the floor dropped off into a sapphire abyss. The Lemons kept close to the wall, and the camera caught images of the cave system that existed long before the ocean rose to take over dry land. Stalactites and stalagmites, some larger than small houses, that could've only formed before the caves were submerged were now covered in algae.

At the point labeled one-hundred-and-thirty feet, they did a check.

"*How's the mask?*" Bridget's voice came over the radio. The camera focused on Dare treading above the layer. He made the extra air tanks he carried look like no big deal. "*Any fogging today?*"

"*Nah, it's good.*" Dare tapped his full-face mask. His mellow voice was familiar from his YouTube channel as he swung his light toward his wife and momentarily blinded the screen. "*Booty check.*"

Holm snorted and then cleared his throat. "Sorry, ma'am."

"He's always had a great sense of humor," Bridget waved off the concern. "It's how we did equipment checks."

Her use of the past tense hit me in the gut. She was a practical person and knew she'd gone on the last dive her husband would ever make. I wondered if she'd ever dive again.

The video skipped ahead to a point labeled two-hundred-and-eighty-five feet.

It was like looking at clouds from a mountaintop. The misty layer was barely visible in the dim daylight. Bridget's flashlight showed the still, eerie barrier to the bottom of the Hole. That mic and equipment check was more serious.

Dare came into view. "*Second thoughts?*"

"*No. Just... nerves.*" Bridget's voice sounded tense. I looked up and saw her gazing at Dare's bed. "*We're doing something no one else has.*"

"Let's get to it, then, woman! Come on in. The water's poison!"

A slight laugh got the best of me. I wasn't into watching a lot of media, but Dare's sense of humor had me hooked for a couple of years. My career took priority, and I'd lost track of his channel, but I'd always appreciate the man's immense knowledge and terrible jokes.

The couple descended into the hydrogen sulfide cloud. Bridget's clear blue view turned caramel as visibility dropped to a few feet. Dare's flashlight sometimes flickered across the screen. The mic checks with their niece were more subdued and developed a crackle until the radio cut out altogether at around three-hundred-and-ninety feet, according to text on the screen.

Following that, the only audio bits were occasional murmurs of the couple speaking with each other, the parts which weren't recorded from the boat. I kept wondering if they were experiencing interference.

"Radioactivity?" Holm suggested as I paused the video.

"Dunno. Water's a hell of an insulator." I frowned. "It could be several issues. Bridget, do you remember anything about the radio?"

She gave a slow shake of her head. "Just vague moments. Sometimes I think I remember it breaking up, but it might only be because I know we lost contact with the boat." She tapped her fingers on her book.

I resumed the playback. Bridget's GoPro caught clear images of the detritus and silt. The water had a bluish-brown cast to it, and the floor seemed to reflect it. Her gloved hand poked at uneven points in the silt to reveal dead conchs of different sizes, a few crustaceans that were just as dead, and, eventually, some sort of blue fabric.

"I wish I'd brought that up," she told me as she held out her left hand.

I paused again. In the picture, Bridget had wrapped the fabric around her hand along the same margins as the fading burns on her hand now. Damn.

"Was that a towel?" I asked. "A radioactive towel?"

Holm's brow wrinkled and then cleared. "It could be medical waste. Or maybe it got exposed at a power plant or..." His face paled and chose not to finish that sentence.

"Dare started feeling sick around then," Bridge told us. She blinked. "I do remember that. The first symptoms made us think it was hydrogen sulfide getting in through the seams of his suit." She sighed. "That's what we told Haley, anyway."

The next part of the video showed Dare doubled over, and I winced. It was hard to see divers in distress, let alone in those conditions. The rest of the video had been edited to show their ascent with decompression stops. They used an advanced technique technical divers had been employing in the past few years, a technique developed with Dare's input.

"And that's it," Bridget said. "We felt better enough to get on the plane the next morning." She shrugged. "Over-the-counter stuff for nausea and headache, and hydrocortisone for the burns."

"What do you remember about your flight?" Holm asked as he stood. He walked over to Dare's bed.

"We were exhausted," Bridget answered. "I think I drifted off pretty soon after we were in the air."

"I think he's waking up," Holm quietly called.

Bridget swung her legs out from under the blanket and tugged her gown tight. Even layered front and back, nobody liked hospital gowns. Holm stepped away as Bridget padded over to Dare's side.

She pulled a heavily bandaged hand from under the blanket and stroked his arm above the gauze.

"Hey, you," she whispered. "We have visitors."

Dare looked up to Holm, who nodded. "Special Agent Robbie Holm, sir." He started to hold out his hand to Dare, but he caught himself and gestured to me instead. "That's my partner, Special Agent Ethan Marston."

Dare's reddened eyes met mine.

"Not a pleasure... to meet you," he rasped. A hint of his mischievous nature touched the corners of his mouth. "Bet you don't... don't meet many murder victims before... before they die."

"Well, it's a first for my partner and me," I answered. "You've made a hell of a difference in the diving world. You'll be missed."

"Plan a... a big funeral reception," he told Bridget. "Got the divers goin'."

She squeezed his shoulder and nodded. Her jaw muscles tensed, and she blinked several times. Damn, that woman was strong.

"Ashes to the sea, baby," she whispered. "These men will find the motherfu—," she cleared her throat and blushed. "They'll get the bastard who did this to you."

"I have one question, and then we'll leave you

folks some privacy," I gently announced. Dare's barely perceptible nod angered me. Nobody should have to go through what was happening to him. "Do you remember anything that you might have touched or handled on the bottom of the Blue Hole?"

"Yes."

I waited, and Bridget groaned. "He's being obnoxious as usual," she told us. "Dare, what do you remember?"

A weak smile reached those waning eyes. "It's my nature." The rasp was a little worse, and I wondered how much longer he'd be able to speak. "The Blue Hole... it is spectacular... Someone violated it. I... didn't realize what I had." He stopped to take several shuddering breaths. "Small, empty canisters... towels... Felt something hard, tubelike, under..." He lifted a hand, flinched, and laid it down. "The silt. Felt burning when I picked it up... thought H2S."

Bridget caressed his upper arm. "That's all," she said for him. "It's the most he's said today."

Dare's eyelids were getting heavy.

"Thank you for your time." I shook Bridget's hand. "We'll do our best to get to the bottom of this."

A shaky laugh came from Dare's direction. "'Bottom' of this."

"Bottom of the Blue Hole." Holm laughed. "Good one, Dare." He touched the foot of the bed. "It's been an honor to meet you."

"Are you going to dive the Blue Hole?" Bridget asked before we left the room. "Make sure it's safe for the tourists?"

"Any excuse to get my fins wet, ma'am." I grinned. "We're going to Belize, and we'll make it right."

"Do that." Dare's voice was barely audible now. "Dive safe... and go find my killer."

4

THE NEXT MORNING, the conference table was, for the first time in memory, full. Everyone on my immediate team under Director Diane Ramsey was present, and she, Holm, and I were the only ones who knew the seriousness of the case.

We even had the new member who'd joined us less than a week earlier. Diane stole him... *acquired* his talents... from Cyber now that we were getting more digital crime.

I'd barely had a chance to meet the guy before now. As I prepared the slides on the laptop at the front of the room, the new guy wandered in last, found an empty seat next to Special Agent Lamarr Birn, and sat. Everyone turned to face me.

"First big briefing," TJ Warner said with a

nervous laugh. He ran his hand through the curly mop that was his hair and rocked back in his chair. "Um, go team?"

Birn covered a laugh that shook his shoulders but stayed mercifully silent so that Warner totally missed it.

"Sure, go team." I nodded to the kid. "May as well start out big with this case."

I surveyed the assembled team. To my left was Diane. Although she was the boss, she used to be one of us, Birn's partner. We had all become good friends, and it sometimes felt strange to answer to her. Holm and Birn were there, of course, as well as Birn's latest partner, Sylvia Muñoz.

"Bonnie and Clyde" sat toward the back of the room, as they tended to hyper-focus on the scientific angles to our cases. Bonnie had some badass computer skills, but she'd lost lab time trying to catch some tech load our unit often dumped on Cyber. That was why Warner joined us. He'd take the load and would sometimes bring Bonnie in to help.

Finally was Ethel Dumas, our outspoken medical examiner who scared away every assistant MBLIS tried to assign her. Speaking of Ethel...

"Explain to me again why I'm here," she

complained from the chair she'd dragged to the door. Ethel hated group settings, so for here, there was nothing like access to a quick exit. "We don't have a body, I don't have a report."

"You will soon enough," I informed her. "Our victim is still alive. Barely."

People sat straighter as I pulled up one of the Dare Dive videos on mute. He was demonstrating techniques to equalize ear pressure and moved on to remove his regulator long enough to show the camera what it looked like when working underwater. If I unmuted it, we'd hear a quirky narration aimed, in this case, at novice divers.

"He's our vic?" Birn exclaimed. Yeah, he was another fan. "Well, hell, what happened?"

"What I'm about to tell you does *not* leave this office," I stressed to the group. "It'll get out to the media soon enough, and when that happens, the closer we are to solving it, the better."

"You're not inspiring confidence, Marston," Muñoz pointed out.

"Darrel Lemon is dying of acute radiation sickness," I announced to shocked silence. "He and his wife, Bridget Lemon, dove to the bottom of the Great Blue Hole in Belize, and they encountered radioactive materials at approximately four hundred feet deep. Mrs. Lemon's exposure was less intense, and she's expected to make a full recovery. Our job is to find out what they were exposed to and who put it there."

"Woah," Warner breathed.

"Yeah, 'woah' indeed," I echoed. "The Hole is shut down until the approved diving areas are cleared of radiation. Holm, Birn, Muñoz, and I are going to help with some of this while we look for any evidence that might show in the normal dive zones. We have something in the works for exploring the bottom."

An old friend often worked the area, and I'd reached out on the way to the briefing that morning. I'd hear by noon if his involvement were a go.

"Do we have any theories?" Rosa "Bonnie" Bonci asked.

"We're leaning toward medical waste based on what was filmed." I advanced the presentation to a still of the towel-like fabric Bridget Lemon had found in the silt. "This could be from a nuclear medicine department. That would jive with what Dare said about finding canisters."

I posted a slide with images ranging from vials and tiny canisters with the yellow radioactivity labels to larger canisters for storage and containment. In tiny doses, the particles saved lives by making it possible to image parts of the body that otherwise aren't able to be seen on scans.

"The good news is that water, especially saltwater, is an excellent insulator," Bonnie told the group from her seat. "The diving hole is probably safe, but I get the need to make sure."

"The bad news is that Dare Lemon was in contact long enough to receive a deadly dose," I added. "What's strange is that even though the exposure was bad, it shouldn't have been lethal, if the doctors are right about time and type of exposure. Something's not adding up."

Joe "Clyde" Clime tapped and swiped on his tablet in a sudden burst. His brow furrowed, and he frowned.

"Do you have something, Joe?" Diane asked.

He froze and looked up. "This reminds me of something I heard about a while back. There are rumors that it could be possible to... to condense radioactive particles, so to speak, to make stronger materials." He shook his head. "There isn't much online, just a few hints that it could be a thing. It shouldn't be a thing, though, because even if it is possible to do that with used medical waste, it would be a lot of expensive work."

Although we'd been focused on medical waste, more nefarious purposes had occurred to me. I hated to consider the implications of Clyde's revelation. If there was someone out there making radioactive materials stronger, a lot of people could get hurt.

Diane stood and smoothed her pants. Ethel turned the lights on, as my presentation was clearly over.

"You are all flying to Belize City," Diane ordered. "Now you get the nature of the threat. Even without Cly—Joe's information, this is serious. The public gets antsy when there's anything about radioactivity in the news. Something like this has the potential to create panic, especially if it turns out someone is trying to weaponize medical waste." She pinched the bridge of her nose. "The other complication is that Belize tourism depends on the Blue Hole, and they are begging us to get it open." Diane folded her arms. "Get it done. Dismissed."

Everyone dispersed except for Warner. I cocked an eyebrow.

"Problem?" I demanded.

"Um, no, sir, not exactly." He clutched his laptop to his chest and looked at the floor. "I just... I didn't know I'd be traveling. I thought I'd work everything from here."

"Are you or are you not capable of going into any system you access?" Diane asked him. "I was given to understand you're one of the best and can hack damned near anything."

"True..." He straightened and lowered the laptop to the table. "I've only had to be on-site twice, though. As long as a system is connected to the internet, I can get in."

"We run into closed networks once in a while," I informed him. "It's better to have an expert with us than have to wait several hours to fly them in. This didn't occur to you when you accepted the job?"

"I made it clear that some travel would be required," Diane reminded Warner. "You indicated it wouldn't be a problem."

Warner opened his mouth to say something and then shut it. He stood and kept his gaze on the floor.

"I'll go get ready, ma'am, sir." He started toward the door, but I stepped in front of him. He finally looked up with wide eyes. "Seriously, it won't be a problem, Agent Marston. I... I just thought I'd have more time before I had to fly somewhere. That's all."

"You're afraid of flying?" I guessed.

"Yes, sir." He forced a smile that looked more like a grimace. "A little Xanax should do the trick, as long as you don't need me right after we land."

I stepped out of his way. "We'll be in Belize City for at least two days," I told him. "Pack accordingly. And, uh, don't forget your Xanax."

After he left, I gave Diane a long look. She shrugged.

"He said it wouldn't be a problem," she repeated. "We give him a chance, see how he does. Seriously, Ethan, this kid is brilliant."

"As long as he does his job, we're good," I assured her, and then I winked. "I promise not to give him too much shit about it."

"Ethan, don't you dare—"

"Hey, my flight's leaving in a little while," I told her. "I better go before my boss gets on my case."

My phone buzzed when I was halfway down to my temporary car. I smiled when I saw who was calling.

"Hi, Tessa."

5

Tessa Bleu knocked on her uncle's office door frame. Donald Farr, the editor of the *National EcoStar*, looked up and waved her in. Behind him, floor-to-ceiling windows showcased New York City's skyline in a display she never got used to seeing.

"Shut that door behind you," he ordered.

She did as he said and then joined him at his desk. The seats on the guest, or audience, side of the desk were made of stiff, new leather stained a coffee hue that complemented the wood trim in the office. He waited in his throne of a desk chair, the penultimate editor-in-chief, part Perry White, part J. Jonah Jameson. His graying walrus mustache twitched the way she often saw it do when he was agitated.

"I have an assignment for you." He slid a manila

folder across the desk in a manner she suspected he'd gotten used to when he commanded the naval fleet. "Something's going on at the Great Blue Hole in Belize. MBLIS is investigating, and I want you to cover the story."

She gasped and grabbed the folder. "I'll be working with Ethan?"

"I want you embedded in with the team." He stood and pointed at her. "And by 'embedded,' I mean you keep out of trouble. Stay back, take pictures, ask questions."

The stern look couldn't hide the twinkle in his eye, which made her think of Sam Elliott for about the thousandth time.

"Why is this so important, Donald?" She leaned forward, and her hand itched for a notepad and pen. "Did someone die at the Blue Hole?"

"Meet Marston and his team in Belize City," Donald instructed, brushing aside her questions. "Sign whatever you need to sign to get in on the case. Our official angle is how MBLIS investigations affect the ocean and coasts."

"'Official angle'? What's the unofficial angle?"

"Go see Marston, sign some papers, and you'll find out," he gruffed. "Take your underwater camera.

There's a lot of coral and some amazing caves in the Blue Hole."

"Okay. So, something happened *in* the Blue Hole...?" She tried to fish more out of him, but he didn't take the bait.

"Your flight is midday tomorrow. That'll give you time to get ready." Donald returned to his seat. "Be careful, Tessa. I don't know what direction this'll go."

This was a change from his overprotective nature. Before, he would've sent her home at a hint of danger, but he'd relaxed somewhat since she got caught up in a case involving the notorious Caribbean drug king, Cobra Jon. It'd been the better part of a year, but the memories were sharp, especially her memories of Ethan Marston.

"I'll get packed," she promised. "Anything else I should know?"

Donald grunted and gestured toward the door in dismissal. Since the Cobra Jon incident, Tessa had learned how to recognize when her honorary uncle was withholding information, and she was certain the man was holding back now.

Back at her desk, where she'd been working on a feature about threats coastal cities faced from rising sea levels, she pulled out her phone. She had to make the call, but she decided to procrastinate by looking through the manila folder Donald had given her.

She opened it to find a photo of an older YouTuber she somewhat recognized. Although she enjoyed diving and kept up on her certifications, she'd never developed the unquenchable passion others did, so this vlogger wasn't as familiar to her as, say, some famous nature photographers.

The next page was a summary of the situation.

Dare and Bridget Lemon were hospitalized following a minor illness on a flight from Belize today. Other passengers were checked for infection and released. The Lemons, stars of "Dare Dives" on YouTube are technical divers known for pushing the limits of deep dives when not educating divers of all levels on various diving topics. Dare Lemon remains in critical condition while Bridget Lemon is reportedly in stable condition.

Behind the report was a one-way ticket from Laguardia to Belize City. The one-way ticket suggested he didn't know how long she was staying, which meant he really *didn't* know everything about the case.

Tessa neatly packed the materials she'd been working on for her rising waters story and slipped them into her desk's locking file drawer. She stared at her phone for a few minutes before giving in and finding an entry in her contact list. She dialed before she could stop herself. He answered on the second ring.

"Hi, Tessa."

The smooth sound of his voice brought a smile to her lips.

"Hi, Ethan. I have some news for you."

"Are you moving to Miami?" He sounded a little too hopeful, which didn't offend her in the least.

"Not in the foreseeable future," she answered, "but I found out I'll be seeing you tomorrow."

"Geez, I'm sorry." The soft tone of his voice was belied by a hint of frustration. "I'm not going to be in town for a few days."

"Yeah, I know... my uncle Donald is sending me to meet you in Belize."

The line went quiet, and Tessa was afraid the call had dropped. She took it away from her ear to find the call still active.

"What does he know about Belize?" Ethan's guarded tone put Tessa's journalism senses on alert.

"He's sending me to take underwater photos at the Great Blue Hole," she told Ethan. "And that I'm to talk with you when I get there."

"The Hole is closed right now."

She laughed. "You don't just put a lid over the Hole and shut it down."

"Seriously, civilian divers aren't going to be allowed in for two or three days at least. It's not the time for a photoshoot." Ethan's exasperated sigh came through the phone loud and clear. "I really wish I could see you, but there's no point in you flying down if you can't go diving."

"Donald said I'm going to be embedded with the team," she blurted out. "Whatever you're investigating, I'm going to document it. I think he already has it arranged."

"Like hell, you are!" Ethan's vehemence startled her. "Any other time, I'd take you diving there myself, but with this case? No."

Tessa ground her teeth. "I'm a grown woman, Ethan, and I have an assignment from my boss. My risks are my own to take."

"Your risks become my team's risks. If we're responsible for your safety, the overall unit's safety is compromised the moment things go sideways."

"It's not my call," she informed him. "I'm flying in tomorrow. Either meet me at the airport or don't, but I'm going."

"I'm going to see what's going on with this embedding thing," Ethan said with a slight growl.

"As much as I'd kill to see you, this case has bad news written all over, through, and under it."

"I'll message you my arrival time," she stated. "Figure out if you'll be there or not."

She ended the call and pushed back from her desk. The casters on her chair allowed her to roll a foot or two away before colliding into the desk behind her.

Whatever caught Donald's attention had Ethan worried. That alone made Tessa determined to bust the story wide open

6

THE KING AIR 350 our department recently acquired looked different from the last time I saw it. The engines and tail had been painted Caribbean blue to match a nose-to-tail swooping stripe. Back toward the tail, "MBLIS" was printed in small white letters just before the blue stripe tapered to a point.

"It's kind of cool," Holm said as we approached. "I like it."

"I thought we liked to keep a low profile," I grumped. Still, as much as I didn't like to admit it, it was a nice paint job.

The cargo area was packed to the brim with not only our standard raid gear but also Bonnie and Clyde's mobile lab and several suitcases. Some people packed heavier than others.

Warner lugged a laptop bag over one shoulder, wore a backpack, and dragged a carry-on sized suitcase. His Hawaiian shirt fluttered in the breeze, and... I kid you not... he wore sandals with white tube socks. His round straw hat had a button pinned to it that showed a scrawny anime kid wearing a similar hat.

"Are you moving to Belize?" Muñoz asked. She crossed her arms and raised a finely shaped brow. "Should we get you another ride?"

"I just didn't wanna forget anything," Warner mumbled. "Um, too much?"

Muñoz laughed. "I'm messing with you. Yes, it's a bit much, but it'll fit this time."

I shook my head. Muñoz was one of those types who could be dead serious or deadpan, and unsuspecting targets never knew what to expect. She was the smallest person in the office, but she had tactical skills that'd make most SWAT units jealous.

"I... I'll do better next time, Agent Muñoz," Warner promised. "This is just, like, way out of my comfort zone." He scratched at his Imagine Dragons tee under the Hawaiian shirt and attempted a smile. "I'm used to sitting in the dark and punching code."

I walked over and picked up the bags he'd set

down. "Let's get you situated. It's going to be fine. Muñoz and Birn have flown with the best. If we go down, you'll at least know that nothing could've saved us."

"Ethan!" Muñoz barked. "Not helping."

I flinched. The kid had gone snow white. Sometimes I really put my foot in my damned mouth.

"It was a joke," I told him in a softer tone. I led him onto the plane and pointed into the cargo area. "They really are the best, and they don't take unnecessary risks. Did you bring your anxiety meds?"

"Y-yes, sir." Warner was getting his color back. I hadn't seen flight anxiety that bad in years, and I felt for the guy. "I took it when I got in the Lyft car."

We stowed two of his bags. He clung to his laptop carrier and plopped into the back, forward-facing row. I went back out and stowed my bag in the wing locker. Muñoz was in the middle of the exterior flight check, but she found time to corner me.

"That Warner guy worries me," she said. "If he starts getting sick, I'm not cleaning it up."

"I'll keep an eye on him," I promised. "How's the weather looking?"

She shrugged. "Not bad. There's a little blow up in the middle of the Gulf, but it's tracking north.

Birn's a little concerned about it, so we're keeping a close eye."

Birn was former Navy, like Holm and me. We learned to never trust clear skies over open water. Muñoz knew, too, but Air Force pilots had different experiences. She could read topography like nobody's business. The Air Force was lucky she just barely made minimum height for her piloting roles.

We finished loading up and balancing out the weight on the plane. I chose the seat across the aisle from Warner, and Holm sat in the rear-facing seat across from me. Bonnie and Clyde sat up front.

The smooth takeoff and relatively quiet cabin seemed to ease Warner's fears. Either that or the Xanax had kicked in. He watched southern Florida pass below his window and give way to the Keys and the Gulf of Mexico. On my side, I glimpsed a dark smudge on the horizon that was almost certainly Andros Island in the Bahamas.

Holm pulled out a tablet and keyboard to work on some reports. My partner was a fairly organized person, but he always seemed to put reports off until the last minute. When he put his earbuds in, I let him be and watched the endless sea below.

Our flight rounded the north side of Cuba. From

the air, the island nation looked like any other lush tropical island. Bright, full of potential. Memories of visits to Guantanamo, however, whispered of darker stories. I didn't see the southeast coast of the island, but maybe that was a good thing. I leaned back in my seat and tried to think of better things... like Tessa meeting us in Belize.

Maybe it wasn't ideal, and yeah, I didn't like the idea of involving her in the case, but I'd be lying if I said I didn't look forward to seeing her. Our time together had been too short, as far as I was concerned, and other than a few calls and emails, we hadn't been in touch in months.

"We'll be landing soon. Get those belts on and all that fun stuff," Muñoz announced from the cockpit.

I looked over at Warner. He'd relaxed midway through the flight and looked out the window the entire time, but he never let go of his laptop bag. At Muñoz's news, he stiffened and clutched the bag to his chest.

Holm stowed his work and put his earbuds away. "Hey, do you want us to call you 'Warner' or 'TJ'?" he asked the younger man. "I don't think we asked."

Warner looked over. Sweat beaded along his bristly upper lip as he answered. "Either one works, sir. Most people just say 'hey, you,' so hearing my name is a bit of a novelty."

"We'll start with 'Warner,' then," I suggested. "Anyway, Warner, remember to breathe. Oxygen is your friend."

The airport north of Belize City set us on a holding pattern that took us over the coastal city and gave us beautiful views of the jungle terrain to the west and the nearest Caribbean atolls to the east. When it was time to descend, the engines changed pitch, which startled Warner until he realized it wasn't going to kill us.

"There's some shear," Birn told us over the intercom. "The landing might be a bit bumpy. Make sure nothing's loose, and we're all good."

I had nothing to check, and Holm had his tablet secured. Warner continued to clutch his bag. He saw me glance over and made a show of taking a calm breath.

Outside the window, the ground got closer and closer. As our tires began to touch down, the plane jolted to the left, lifted several feet, and then slammed the back tires down on the runway. Warner's laptop bag flew into his face and bounced off of his nose. It dropped to the floor.

"Shid, shid!" Warner yelled. He held his hands

over his nose and stomped the floor with his left foot. Blood seeped through his fingers and onto his t-shirt. "Oh God, id hurds!"

Bonnie unbuckled as we taxied and knelt next to him. I grabbed towels from the tiny cubby where a regular seat concealed a small toilet. Bonnie took the towels and helped get the bleeding under control.

"Hate to tell you this, but I think you broke it," she informed him. "We'll get it taped up after we get off the plane."

"It'll be half an hour before we can deplane," Muñoz announced over the intercom. "Everybody alive back there?"

I keyed our side of the intercom. "It's all good. There's only a *little* blood on the floor."

The cockpit door slammed open, which was impressive, considering she'd reached around from her pilot seat.

"Who dares bleed in my plane?" she hollered.

"S-sorry, ma'am," Warner stammered. "Id was an accidend."

"Oh, Warner, you okay?" Muñoz's tone went soft just like that. It was like she went out and adopted a little brother and dumped him on us. "I'll take a look once we park."

We didn't have a hangar to rent, so we joined a

motley collection of private jets, other turbo-props, and a handful of smaller craft. A small tram with a smaller trailer parked outside the rear hatch door as our engines cooled off.

I hopped out to meet the driver, a tall, lean man with a dark complexion and kindly eyes, who extended his hand.

"Special Agent Marston?"

"That's me." I took his hand, and we shook. "Are you our liaison?"

"That I am," he answered. "Anders Tozin at your service. You may place your baggage and equipment on the trailer, and I'll give you a ride to the cars my government is lending you."

"Better not get into any chases that end in the water," Holm said with a laugh.

Tozin's eyebrows lifted at that.

"My partner is giving me shit," I told the liaison. "I killed my car when a suspect went down a flooded street last night."

Tozin's faced smoothed. "Ah. Right, then. I shall hope for the best."

He went over to the trailer and helped load cases and bags as they were brought to him. Warner lingered and began chatting despite the face full of towels. Holm and I went back on the plane to help get the last few pieces.

"Looks like someone made a friend," I observed as Holm dug out a large box labeled for the mobile lab. "Tell you what, I thought the kid was going to puke. I did not see the bloody nose coming."

"I wouldn't have bet against you," Holm admitted. He stopped at the exit and looked out at Warner and Tozin. "Seems to me like he needs to get out more." He glanced at me with his trademark grin and eye sparkle of mischief. "He *is* over twenty-one, right?"

"Legal age in Belize is eighteen," I pointed out. "But yeah. You have to be at least twenty-one to work for MBLIS."

"We'll need to take him out tomorrow night, get him to relax, and realize we aren't going to torture him," Holm insisted.

"Unless that *is* torture to him." I leaned around Holm to see Warner getting on the tram with Tozin. "Take it easy with the kid. He spooks easy."

"Yeah, I can see that."

We got the rest of the cargo area unloaded, and the trailer looked ready to tip over. Holm and I took the tram's back row, just in case.

Tozin got us to a trio of matching black Audi A8s. Not bad, not bad at all. Once everyone and everything was loaded in, Tozin took the lead and escorted our little caravan to a large villa near the beach in Belize City. We parked in a four-car garage and gathered at the door into the house.

"We took the liberty of providing you access to one of the houses we keep for visiting dignitaries," Tozin said with a grin. "Encrypted internet, security system, fully stocked kitchen, briefing room, everything you need."

"I like how you slipped 'fully stocked kitchen' in there," Birn pointed out. "A man's gotta eat." At a side-eye from Muñoz, he corrected himself. "We all gotta eat." He patted his belly. "Some of us more than others."

Tozin showed us the essentials and then made ready to go. We were gathered at the open kitchen, and I had claimed one of the sturdy metal and wood bar stools at the counter overlooking the living room.

"As you might imagine, I have many anxious persons to soothe over the closing of our favorite tourist location." Tozin wrote his cell number on a sticky note and stuck it to the kitchen counter on the way out. "Call me if there is anything you need. Anything at all."

Before settling in, we worked together to sweep the house and cars for hidden surveillance. The only bugs we found were defunct models that had probably sat in vents for years.

"They seem to be playing fair," Clyde said after we clear the interior of the house. "Still, to be safe, Bonnie and Warner are setting jammers in the meeting room."

"So, we're ready for tomorrow," I observed. "The Lemons' dive captain and niece will be available first thing in the morning, and then we go to the Blue Hole."

Clyde scratched at his chin and shifted his weight. "Warner and I have been talking. It would probably be a good idea for us to go set up in the lab the government opened for us. If you find anything radioactive, we need to be ready to process and measure it."

Over in the living room, Warner had made himself at home in a plush recliner with his laptop on his, well, lap and a bowl of chips at his side. His nose was swollen, but Bonnie had stabilized it with some tape. A "They Might Be Giants" shirt replaced the other band tee that had been stained from his bloody nose. Now, he perked up at the mention of his name.

"Oh yeah," he agreed. "Joe and I can handle all that stuff while you guys go out on the water."

Clyde's shoulders relaxed a little, and I sensed a bit of collaboration there. His propensity toward seasickness was well known among our team, so we generally avoided putting him on boats, at least not without Dramamine. I couldn't help wondering if Warner's fear of travel extended from planes to boats. If so, how did he end up with us?

"Have you two played 'rock-paper-scissors' on who gets to drive a fancy-pants Audi to the lab?" Holm teased. At Clyde's sudden flush, I think we both realized that was exactly what had taken place. "Okay, who won?"

Clyde tried to deny it, but Warner's hand shot in the air without him looking up from his screen.

Holm and I left the new buddy crew to bond and went up to choose rooms. Ours ended up being across the hall from each other. He lingered at his door with his tablet in one hand and overnight bag in the other.

"Something on your mind, partner?" I asked. The guy had been preoccupied for a few days, it seemed, but it hadn't stopped him from doing his job as well as ever. "I'm here."

Holm's faraway expression turned to a smile. "It's all good, but hey, I think Bonnie better watch out that Warner doesn't steal her lab partner."

I waved off the notion. "I think the three of them will form a nerd squad and hold the office's good toys hostage for better coffee."

"They wouldn't be wrong to do that."

I cocked an eyebrow. "This is true. Maybe we should warn Diane."

Holm snorted. "Nah. I wanna see her face if and when it happens." He stepped inside his room. "Well, I have to catch up on more reports. It turns out they don't fill in themselves on their own."

"Procrastination will get ya every time. See you at the butt crack of dawn, Robbie."

"Night."

He went in and shut the door. I wandered into my room and kicked back onto the king-sized bed. Surely Holm hadn't gotten that far behind in his reports. Then again, this *was* Robbie Holm I was thinking about. My best friend and work partner usually did get his part of the paperwork in at the last minute.

Even so, I had a feeling that reports weren't all he

was writing. I smiled because I'd witnessed this before. There were some things my buddy was sensitive about and liked to wait before telling anyway, but I was his oldest friend and recognized it.

Holm was showing all the signs that he was in love. What I didn't know was with who.

7

WE MET Haley Lemon and the captain of the boat who took the family out to the Blue Hole the next morning at the marina where the boat in question was docked. The *Maria's Lace* was a simple dive yacht large enough to make the trip and back and maybe stay overnight.

Haley brought a heavy three-ring binder and tossed it onto the table in the yacht's galley. Her eyes were red and puffy, and her clothes were wrinkled as if she had worn them to bed. She slid onto the bench and rested her elbows on the table.

"I designed their gear from top to bottom," she told us. "Uncle Dare and I went through every millimeter of the material to prevent H2S saturation. We tested and retested the deep dive tanks and air mixes." She blinked as she met my gaze. "Did you know that they were each carrying one less tank than normal? It's because of the new compression and mixes we developed. And you know what? It worked. All of it worked. But it didn't do them a bit of good."

I glanced at Holm. He was better at calming witnesses who bordered on hysterical. I was better at fetching water and tissues, so I got up and walked a whole two steps to the sink and cabinet to do just that.

"Haley, it *did* do them good," Holm soothed. "Imagine going through all they are now plus having the bends or H2S poisoning. Nobody could've done better."

I set the water glass and a tissue box next to her binder. She pushed the thick stack of documentation over for us to look at. Those were trade secrets. She was putting a lot of trust in us to give us a peek. I paged through and pretended to be absorbed in it while listening. The pretending part got more difficult the deeper I got into the diagrams and notes. The Lemons really were a brilliant team, and they came up with stuff that would've taken me decades to figure out. I finally had to close it to do my job and listen.

"No, but I'm glad," Haley was saying. "If she'd brought that towel up, Captain Crane and I could've gotten sick, too. We have to go back for yearly scans after handling the contaminated..." She blinked several times, and I handed her a tissue. "We both had a little exposure, but the doctors aren't worried."

"Did you see anything out of the ordinary that morning?" I ventured. "Even with the water insulating the particles, they couldn't have been down there long."

Haley shook her head. "I was too busy doing last-minute safety checks. That's not something you mess around with by getting distracted."

Holm looked at me and smirked.

"What?" I demanded.

"Aruba, and that's all I'm saying."

I wanted to punch him, but we had a witness. It would've been a friendly punch. Probably. He had to know I'd get him back for that one.

"What happened in Aruba?" Haley asked me.

"Nothing," I grunted.

"A girl." Holm laughed. "My partner almost drowned because he got distracted by a girl."

"The less said, the better," I growled. "And that was before the SEALs. It doesn't count, so shut up."

The corner of Haley's mouth twitched. That was an improvement, even if it came at my expense.

"You know what I'm talking about, then," was all she said to that point. "You can ask Captain Crane whether he noticed anything. I'd think he would've said something by now if he had."

I nudged the binder back over to Haley.

"This is remarkable work, and it's going to save lives," I told her. "I can see applications for recreational divers that your uncle was probably going to push to have incorporated into mainstream diving. This is a legacy thing."

Her cheeks colored as she accepted the binder back. She cradled it a little and took a deep breath.

"You're right, of course." She nodded to Holm and then me. "Thank you. I'm flying to Miami in a few hours to... to say goodbye. I'll tell him what you said. It'll mean a lot."

A few minutes later, Captain Derrick Crane joined us in the below deck. The old sea dog's leathery skin damned near creaked as he moved about the cabin. He joined us at his little galley table.

"I know you're going to ask if I saw or heard anything," he started off. His rural American accent got me wondering where he hailed from. "Truth is, I told everyone I didn't, but I got to thinkin', maybe what I saw wasn't what I *thought* I saw if y'know what I mean."

"Pretend I don't." I wasn't so sure I did. "Explain it from the beginning."

"We got to the dive site a little after sunrise." Crane looked past my shoulder as he spoke, almost like he was watching it on replay. "Divers get out there early if they can, and those Lemons weren't no different. There's always boats out at the atolls, so that's normal." He crossed his arms and put his elbows on the edge of the table. "I didn't think much of it except that he was toward the middle, further out than he should'a been. Not my business 'coz I was helping those nice folks with their testing and all that."

"Tell us about that boat," Holm interjected. "What did it look like? What was he doing?"

"I thought he was pushing divers off the boat." He mimicked a shoving motion. "Me, I like divers to step off themselves, but others like doin' other things, and that's their p'rogative. I figured that's all that was going on until after talking to government types. After that, I had a dream where I was seein' it again, only it wasn't people, it was barrels. But it could'a been just a dream." He thought for a moment. "The boat looked like a center console. Somethin' real simple-like, but it was pretty friggin' far, and I was helping those folks on my own boat."

"You still are helping," Holm told him. They shook hands, and Holm gave him a card. "Thank you for your time. If you think of anything else, call."

We left the *Maria's Lace* and walked to a different, quieter area of the marina. I couldn't help grinning as we met up with the three other team members going on the dive trip that day. Bonnie wasn't a diver, but she was always up for collecting samples and doing basic work with the mini-lab. Muñoz and Birn were our equals in diving, though.

"An old friend of mine is taking us out," I told everyone, including Holm. It felt good to be able to drop a good surprise on people. "He and some friends custom-built his boat, and they use it to go after pirates and traffickers. Bounties, if they come across them. Remember that old *Airwolf* show? Think of that concept on the water."

Holm's eyes widened, and then Birn's.

"No way," the big guy rumbled. Birn wasn't easily impressed, so it was cool to get one up on him. "Not him."

Muñoz looked at each of us like we were crazy.

Sometimes I forgot she'd come in from the West Coast less than a year earlier. Some rumors didn't seem to make it out there, and this was one. For her part, Bonnie frowned as if trying to remember something.

"Hey, guys."

I turned to see a tall guy with black hair and green eyes approach. He had a few years on me, but with the shape he was in, he looked no older than thirty.

"Team, meet Jake Header," I announced. "Former SEAL, former so-secret-he-can't-tell-you stuff that's still classified, and now a pirate hunter."

Holm shook his head in amazement. I'd always felt bad that I got to work with someone he'd looked up to and was never allowed to tell him about it. It was during the only time we were sent on different assignments during our careers. It was also one of the most challenging times of my life.

"It's an honor, sir," Holm gushed.

I allowed them a few minutes to get the hero worship out of the way. Birn and Bonnie joined Holm as they chatted with the swarthy modern-day buccaneer.

"You sure this is on the up and up?" Muñoz asked in a low voice as she approached me. "I just

Googled the guy, and there's some heavy stuff about his boat and crew."

I sighed with a nod. "I got special clearance, Sylvia. As much as I love the guy, he walks the edge. The deal was only him, and we're his crew for the duration. As far as we know, there are no international warrants for his arrest."

"And I suppose we aren't checking for local warrants."

"No, ma'am."

Once the hubbub eased, we followed Header to a plain-looking catamaran that had been backed into its slip. It was equipped with generic dive equipment that even Muñoz wrinkled her nose at.

There was just enough space to stow our gear and seat everyone besides. The crestfallen looks on Holm's and Birn's faces were more fun for me. These were badass adults who looked like they were promised bullet train rides and ended up with Thomas the Tank Engine. I got some dirty looks sent my way as I took one of the seats along the hull.

Header winked at me.

"There's more to her than it seems," he promised. This, I suspected, was true, but not in the way he teased. "Welcome aboard. Sit your asses down and hold on tight."

Header trawled out of the slip and through the marina. By the time we reached open water, my teammates looked, for the most part, annoyed. Holm gave me his "you gotta be kidding me" look about the same time I grabbed the front edge of my seat.

See, Captain Jake Header loved to mess with people, even friends and allies. It was in his nature, and you had to be *really* sure you wanted to hang around him for any length of time. It'd been a few years in my case, and I thought I was ready.

"Ethan, is something wrong?" Jake called out in a pleasant tone.

I narrowed my eyes, sure he was up to something. "Why do you ask, Jake?"

"Oh, no reason other than you looked like you were ready to take a shit on my boat."

"I guess I thought—"

Jake slammed the throttle open, and the catamaran lurched forward. The engines fully kicked in, and hell if that bastard didn't catch me off guard, anyway. Like everyone else, I fell sideways and had to grab something to keep from hitting the deck. God, I loved to hate that man.

"What the hell is going on?" Holm yelled over the roaring engines and splashing water. "I thought he had something a little more... advanced."

"Give him a few minutes. You won't be disappointed," I replied.

Header took us north and then to a property with a wide boathouse. A gray tarp hung across the front, and Header docked along the structure's outside wall.

"What you all really want to see is in there," Header announced. "Go on in. As long as you don't break anything, I won't have to break you." He kept me back as the others went to check out their big surprise.

"We got leads on more of those traffickers," he reported. "Some of them aren't looking so good, Ethan. My team is working on an inland rescue right now, and I don't like the chances of what they'll find."

"Do you need to go?"

He shook his head. "I'm a frogman, brother. I'm more useful at sea. My people got it, I just think they're gonna be too late."

"Damn."

"Yeah, but y'know, we've recovered a lot of people so far."

"True that." I jumped onto the dock. "Not to change the subject..."

"Not at all," Header laughed.

"How's it going to feel to run her in the open with a free pass for the week?"

"Christmas, man, Christmas." Header's infectious grin reminded me of some not-so-nightmarish days. "Ready to meet her?"

It was quiet inside the boathouse. Holm and Birn couldn't take their eyes off the sleek, black hull that rode low in the water. She was about the size of her sister, the Ghost that our team took to take down Cobra Jon, but a little smaller. The hull was partitioned into radar-deflecting angles, and a gun turret laid flat across the top. The hydrofoil wings barely fit inside the boathouse which looked like it could berth a decent-sized yacht.

"Ladies and gentlemen," Header said with pride, "meet *Wraith*."

8

HEADER WALKED up to the aft section and put his palm on an inconspicuous section of the hull. A hatch opened to reveal the interior, with cargo netting and fold-out seating. The front looked like an airplane cockpit and even had pilot and copilot-type seats. In the ceiling was a retractable turret which I'd only heard him talk about when it was still a concept.

"This is a supercavitating boat," he explained. "Once we get moving, you'll be amazed at how smooth and quiet we run. It's the same idea as to how the Ghost runs. We have added value in ways you won't get to see because, frankly, your guys like to chase my guys. Those systems are locked down, so don't even try."

"Then what's the point in you working with us?" Muñoz demanded. "This is a military-grade weapon. We're diving at a tourist trap and looking for evidence. We could've taken a regular dive boat, one with more amenities."

"Two reasons," I answered. "First, we don't know who's behind this. If bullets start flying, this is the place to be. Just because we can't access weapons doesn't mean Jake can't."

"Plus *Wraith* is small and fast enough to get in and out of the area with minimal fuss," Header added. "If someone takes exception to our presence, I can handle it."

"What's the other reason?" Birn wanted to know.

"Scuttlebutt is that this boat is equipped to detect radiation at surface levels." I smiled at Header. "Not that I know anything about that. But if it happened to be true, it wouldn't be a bad tool in our war chest."

"I'm thinking there's one more reason," Bonnie spoke up for the first time. "It rhymes with 'ducking pool.'"

"Maybe," I said. "That doesn't make the other points less valid."

Header clapped his hands in a single, sharp note. "Enough gabbing, people. As you'll see in the back, there is scuba equipment here, and you don't need to move all those secondhand tanks and fins over here. Get whatever else you need, like those underwater Geiger counters you brought." He stepped over to me and stage whispered, "Those are pretty damned cool, and if one happened to get 'lost' in the Hole, I'm sure your boss would forgive you, right?"

"I am sure she would not," I said with utmost sincerity.

He winked. "Had to try."

Wraith had plenty of space for all we needed. I took the copilot seat while everyone strapped into the foldout seats. That baby had sonar, radar, and other capabilities besides weaponry. It was a view few law enforcement types would ever get to see, and I conveniently forgot a lot of it when grilled later.

"The Ghost cruises at about thirty knots," Header told us as he warmed the engines. "Her top speed is about fifty. I'm not going to tell you *Wraith's* top speed, but I don't mind telling you that we're going to *cruise* at fifty today."

Wraith's engine quietly whirred, and we crept forward. The tarp was no longer anchored at the sides of the boathouse, only the top. I didn't ask who might've been around to release it... rumors had it that he didn't go anywhere without his mysterious copilot.

"Supercavitation, friends, is a cool thing," Header informed everyone. We slid out from under the tarp. "Depending on the setup, the craft shoots out bubbles or vapor from the front of the hydrofoil's pontoons and washes all the way aft. The difference in pressure between vapor and water propels us forward."

He opened the throttle through an easy acceleration, and I felt the hull rise from the water. The elementary operation of a hydrofoil was to get the hull off the surface and reduce drag. With supercavitation, the pontoons sliced through the water faster than any normal hydrofoil.

"Are we getting to the site or just showing off?" Muñoz complained. "I think we all know how this stuff works."

"Spoilsport." Header laughed. "I don't get to show off to the good guys."

"She actually does have a sense of humor," I told him with a grin. "Well, as long as you're one of the good guys."

"Damned right," she chirped. "Vigilantes are no better than pirates."

"Not today," I reminded her with a long side-eye. She was a great team member, but she had a hard and fast view of right and wrong. I suddenly worried that I'd made a mistake. "We're friends this week. Officially."

"Oh, come on, Syl, enjoy it while we can," Birn suggested.

Muñoz crossed her arms and kept the frown right-side up.

"Right then," Header said in an even tone. "Time to fly."

We'd been cruising at about twenty knots for a couple of minutes. Header opened her up, and the boat surged forward, pressing me back into my seat until we topped out at fifty knots. We veered north to go around the numerous cays and sandbars. While piloting, Header was dead serious. He let me watch him work the controls, but he kept my side locked out. Fair enough.

At the speed we were going, we reached the Lighthouse Reef in a relatively short time. The namesake lighthouse was several miles north at Sandbore Caye. The reef was the second-largest barrier reef in the world, next to the Great Barrier Reef in Australia. Sometimes it amazed me that so many Americans had never heard of such a great spot in our own hemisphere.

We approached the Great Blue Hole at low speed, and the hull settled into the water. A small handful of small military boats from both Belize and the States had gathered in the area, and we saw smaller dive boats dispatched by the military units at the areas where recreational divers were allowed to explore when the Blue Hole was open. The coordinates for our dive were at a location where the naval types were not. Whether by accident or design, it was appreciated. This was a crime scene.

"Gear up, people," I called out as Header opened the hatch. The lower door was a couple of feet above the water, which provided a great dive platform. "Bonnie, get that mini lab open. You never know what we'll find."

While she got to work, Muñoz, Birn, Holm, and I suited up. Each of us carried underwater Geiger counters, and Birn and I carried lead-shielded cylinders in case we found anything radioactive.

We stepped off the *Wraith* into the crystal-clear shallows. Rainbows of reef fish, coral, and anemones surrounded us, and most of the life was oblivious to our presence. Thousands of visitors every year probably had that effect. Even the reef shark who passed by at a distance seemed unconcerned.

We separated into two teams with our usual partners. Muñoz and Birn went east, and Holm and I went west. The local teams were responsible for clearing the shallows, and more experienced divers like us had the sides of the Blue Hole. The tourist areas were getting cleared first so tourists could be allowed back in... and so Belize City could stop losing money from the closure.

We kicked over to the edge of the shallows. I hovered a moment to appreciate the drop-off. Unlike other locations, this drop-off was protected by some unique circumstances. A long, long time ago, during the last Ice Age, this was dry land with caves and maybe even a steady population. All that changed when too much stone was worn away by water and the structure collapsed. It filled with seawater when the ice caps melted and the ocean levels rose.

Holm gave me an okay, and I answered with my own. The Geiger counters had a range severely limited by the fact that they had to be almost on top radiation sources in order to detect them when in water. According to the Lemons' coordinates, we were now on the vertical where they'd been the day of their exposure.

Reef life faded out and changed as we worked our way down and swept back and forth, looking for traces of medical waste. Everything looked clean, and Holm didn't seem to find anything, either. At almost a hundred feet down, the cliff face opened into an enormous cave with the massive stalactites and stalagmites I'd read about. It was one thing to see photos of the algae-covered monstrosity, and a whole other thing to see them for myself. Some were larger than small houses. Others were the size of cars.

I felt the itch to explore and knew I'd have to return for some rest and relaxation. Soon. This system called my name, but it'd have to wait.

As we neared the floor of the cave where it met the drop-off, something white caught in my flashlight. This was as far down as we'd planned to dive, and it was getting cold. I flashed my light toward Holm to get his attention. When he turned toward me, I pointed. He flashed his okay and followed as I made for the item.

For all I knew, it could be random junk that fell from a boat... I was sure there had to be plenty of that in the Hole itself... but when we got within a foot and a half, my Geiger counter started picking up traces of radiation. I handed the counter to Holm and opened my shielded canister.

The item appeared to be some sort of tag. It was small, and I was lucky to have spotted it. I unclipped a grabber tool from my gear. Since the radiation level was low, I made do by scooping it up with the canister and then screwing the cap on right away.

Holm handed my Geiger counter back, and we finished our sweep. It was more than time to return to the top. Ascending often seemed to take more time than the dive. Even though we'd taken extra tanks and had technical diver certifications, a hundred forty feet was deeper than we usually went. It was definitely deeper than most recreational dives.

We surfaced to find Muñoz and Birn had returned empty-handed, which was not a bad thing. Bonnie was happily playing around in her lab, though, and I checked in with her after getting the diving equipment off. Her short black hair was wet, and her floral shirt and shorts were damp, but she didn't seem to care in the least.

"Did you dive?" I asked.

"Yes," she said. "Yes, I did. I took some small coral polyps and rock, just to check the health of the reef, of course." She glanced at me over her shoulder. "Before you ask, I got a permit fast-tracked. I couldn't pass it up."

"You went alone?" I cut a sharp look to Header. Bonnie didn't have enough dive hours to be out there on her own, not at this location.

"Jake went with me," she answered without looking up. "We weren't down for long."

I blinked at Header. "It's great that you took her, but what about *Wraith*? I'm surprised you left her alone in front of all those military types who would've loved to get a look inside."

Muñoz snorted. I'm sure she would've liked to get a better look herself.

"They wouldn't have gotten far," Header assured me. "Even if they broke the agreement and got close, *Wraith* would've dodged around until I called her back." He pointed to an oversized watch face on his wrist. "And she would've alerted me, as well."

"What else does that smartwatch do?" Birn asked with more than a slight sheen of interest.

Header grinned and shook his head. "If I told ya…"

I rolled my eyes. "Yeah, yeah."

"Ethan, you're burying the lead," Holm told me. To the others, he said, "We found something."

I held up the canister which now weighed

several pounds more than it had when we dove in. The tag and whatever seawater went it with it was staying put until we got to the lab onshore. There, Bonnie and Clyde had access to the kind of tools they needed to examine the tag safely.

"Wait," Header said as he gave Bonnie a strange look. "You have a lab in the city, but you brought a mobile lab on my boat for something you aren't even studying?"

Bonnie looked over to him, shrugged, and then went back to examining her samples. She even hummed.

"Yeah," Holm laughed. "She doesn't leave home without it."

"Yes, I do," she corrected, "but I wanted it with me in case I got a chance to dive for these samples. They need to be preserved as quickly as possible." She went back to humming in her happy place.

"Wrap it up," I told her. "We're done here for the day."

She tucked a small specimen bottle with a handful of others like it into a box and then stowed them in a padded case. It took her less than five minutes to wipe down her tools, return them to their notches, and then fold the mobile lab up into two easy to carry cases.

That woman could hustle when she wanted to.

Everyone buckled in, and we got underway. During the ride back to the hidden berth north of Belize City, my thoughts kept returning to the one thing I'd managed not to think about so far that day. Well, not a thing so much as a person.

Tessa was flying in that evening, and I had no idea what to expect.

9

HEADER LOANED us the boat he'd used to take us to the *Wraith*. We had at least one more dive, and it was looking more like we'd be taking a submersible out to the site.

"I have something that might work for you," Header told me as he backed the *Wraith* in the boathouse. "We recently acquired a four-person sub. It just barely fits into *Wraith*, but we've made it work. If you find something at the bottom of the Hole, we should be able to collect enough to help your case."

"I like how he used 'acquired,'" Birn rumbled.

"Right?" Muñoz responded.

I rubbed the bridge of my nose. This wasn't supposed to get contentious, but Header had more fun rubbing my teammates' noses in his vigilante, highly illegal, activities than I'd expected. Then again, I should've expected as much. Even during the few months that we served together, he made a sport out of flaunting authority, especially if he just knew he was right.

"Look, I'm not going to ask questions." I spoke loud enough for everyone to get the message. "We're allies for this mission. Jake's helping us cut corners that would've cost us time. That radiation only persists for a week or so before it fades out." I pointed to the canister. "We're damned lucky I picked that up."

"Not really." Bonnie shook her head. "Ethan, Dare Lemon's exposure was too intense for normal medical waste. Yes, we needed to get out here as soon as possible, but that radiation is bad news." To my raised eyebrow, she added, "Extra bad news. You said that was a little tag. It should've been clean by now, even after a couple of days."

Muñoz gave me a pointed look. I had a feeling I was going to hear it back at the hotel. The truth was, I'd wanted an excuse to team up with Header. That didn't mean I was going to be stupid about it. This case really did get a step up with his help, and as long as he and his crew didn't do anything completely idiotic, we might get to again someday.

Technically, I should arrest his ass, but it was hard to look down on an old friend for playing Batman out on the water when most authorities wanted to avoid it.

"Let me know the plan as soon as you have one," Header said. "I assume more diving tomorrow to finish clearing that section?"

"Yeah." I cleared my throat. "And uh, there'll be one more passenger." Until that moment, I hadn't decided, but this was a case of asking permission was better than forgiveness. "We're going to be working with a photojournalist…"

"No." Jake lost all the humor in his face. "Absolutely not."

"She's a friend." I kept my tone patient. He didn't know Tessa, but I did. "MBLIS made a deal to let her cover our investigation. The Great Blue Hole is a World Heritage Site, and that's on her beat. She won't say a word about your boat."

Header glared at me. He gestured out the back hatch where the others were unloading personal gear. Header was going to get the dive tanks refilled himself, since they belonged to his group, so those were being unloaded separately on the dock. He and I walked up the artfully manicured lawn above the shoreline.

"What the hell, Ethan?" he seethed. "That wasn't part of the deal."

"Hey, man, it's Tessa Bleu. Her uncle is Donald Farr."

"Fleet Admiral Farr?" Header's eyes widened a bit, but he narrowed them again. "He retired, didn't he?"

"He's the editor-in-chief of the *National EcoStar*," I explained. "The guy has agendas, but Tessa is her own person."

"You know her personally?"

"Remember the Cobra Jon thing?" I knew full well that he did. Everyone did. I looked over Header's shoulder rather than meet his eye. "She was a witness in the case."

He leaned into my line of sight and then rubbed his eyes. "You had a thing with her, didn't you?"

"That has nothing to do with this case."

"Like hell, it doesn't!" Header's shout carried across the lawn and to the dock where the others stopped for a moment and stared. He waited until they carried on. "Ethan, a journalist is a journalist. They go after stories, and the *Wraith* is a story. She is not going." He turned and started walking away.

Oh boy. I didn't want to pull the card, but I had to... not because I wanted to be with Tessa, which I did, but because not taking her would cause trouble. Diane had taken me aside before we got on the plane to give me a special order, too late to do anything to argue against it.

"Jake," I said in a soft voice, "we have to take her. It's not my call on this one." Farr's connections had made damned sure of that. I didn't know if Tessa realized how much control that man exerted. "There's a clause in the contract they whipped up for this mission."

Header stilled. "I'm listening."

"I'm not supposed to tell you about it, but I am because you're a friend." I was betting on a lot of things to go right just by telling him. "They want you to think you have a loose leash. You do, mostly, but if you don't achieve mission objectives, I have orders to get you into custody."

He spun, and the full force of his glare hit me worse than a fist would have. Betrayal and fury reddened his face.

"You're breaking orders to warn me that you'll enforce orders?" he growled. "That's a fine line you're walking, *brother*."

"Tessa is coming with us," I told him. "Take her camera before she sees the boat, give it back for the dive. I swear to God she won't screw you over."

Header stepped close and jabbed his forefinger into my chest. "She better not, Marston. It'll be your hide if she does."

He stalked off toward the boathouse. I couldn't help wondering if we'd still be friends after this mission was over. Telling him about the order meant he could vanish as soon as we were out of sight. I blew out a long breath and ran my hand through my hair.

Bonnie waved at me from the boathouse door with a grand smile. She clutched the shielded canister in her other arm. I summoned a cheerful face... or a grimace. It was hard to tell at the moment.

"What's up?" I asked.

"I called Joe and TJ," she informed me. "They have a specialist from the university coming in to help look at the tag you found. We're also going to play with the water that came in the container, see if there's a difference between finding something like that in the open ocean with currents and everything versus the stillness of the Blue Hole."

"Go for it," I told her. "The thing I need, though, is information about what that tag is and where it's from. After that, you can do whatever you want with it."

Her toothy grin was hard to ignore, and I relaxed a little. Until that grin turned evil, and she rubbed her hands like a mad scientist.

"Uh, or maybe dispose of it…"

"Uh-uh." She laughed. "You said. Seriously, though, it'll be a good sample for university students."

"After the case is closed, Bonnie."

"Yes, of course." She held the canister out before her. "This baby will be studied with joy." I shook my head and started toward the *Wraith*. "With joy, Ethan!"

"With multitudes of joy, Bonnie," I chuckled. "No mutant species, okay?"

"You never know what will happen with *science*."

With that, I excused myself and popped into the boathouse. There wasn't much left to move from the *Wraith*, and Header leaned back against the pilot seat with his arms crossed.

"I'll give you this, Ethan. Your people didn't pry into my systems when we stepped away."

I raised a brow. "Of course not. Each of us stands by their word." I glanced around and saw that our gear was cleared out, but then I looked back to Header. "How do you know they didn't try to get into your systems?"

The frown lifted a little. "Everything's on lockdown. If someone messes with something they shouldn't, they get tased." Now the frown quirked upward. "I got a guy who wanted the deterrents to be a little more lethal, but we don't play with lives."

"A little tasing in the morning won't hurt most people." I grinned. "At least not once it wears off."

"If that girl of yours tries anything, she'll be the one shaking it off," he warned. "You tell her to stay out of my way and not to pull any shit. We clear?"

"Copy that," I answered. A little twinge hit me when I thought of Tessa arriving in a little while. "Once she signs the NDAs and everything, I'll brief her on the need for secrecy. To be honest, I think she'll like what you're doing... but don't tell her I said that."

"She doesn't tell, I won't tell." Normally, Header would laugh, but he still looked more like a grumpy old seadog. "I *will* make sure there are no images of my boat on her camera."

"Totally fair, man."

"We're ready to move out," Holm called from the rear of the boathouse. "Header, you sure you don't want us to get your tanks filled?"

"I'm sure. I only trust... I only trust certain people." Pain flashed through his expression. I wondered about it, but he didn't elaborate. "It'll be handled, and they'll be ready for tomorrow's dive."

We had cleared two of the main vertical sections of the area around the last dive the Lemons made. There was one last area, and then local teams could take over from outside that area. Our answers were going to be on this side and maybe the bottom.

"What about the submersible?" I asked. Branson and Cousteau's trip last winter mapped the floor of the Hole, but it was still a large area. "We'll need an operator."

Header shook his head. "I'm running it. I can take you and one other person, but it's gonna take a couple of days to get it here." At my look, he shrugged. "I don't carry it everywhere I go. Like I said earlier, it just barely fits in the *Wraith*. So if we find a lot of garbage, I'm leaving it. We only pick up what you need for your investigation and that I can carry back."

"That'll have to work," I agreed. "I'm looking for evidence and photos of whatever's down there. There has to be some way to trace this stuff." I started toward the back hatch and stopped. "Jake, I don't want you getting hurt after this. Be careful. Catch some bad guys."

"Only the worst, brother," he promised. "Innocent types don't have anything to worry about from my people." He gave a short wave. "See you tomorrow. And this Tessa of yours."

I left the *Wraith* and wondered whether I'd ever see it again.

10

A T HER INSISTENCE, Tessa rode in coach for the flight to Belize. Donald had wanted to put her in business class, but since learning that she was the only one on staff he spoiled, she'd made sure he treated her the same. She had a feeling that the long flight with connections was a passive-aggressive move on his part, but she was determined to move on from it.

As the 747 made a lazy circle around the international airport north of Belize City, she appreciated the jungle toward the western part of the small country and Guatemala. Mexico's Yucatan Peninsula stretched up north. Off the coast, the Atlantic provided a home to an incredible amount of biodiversity, with the Belize Barrier Reef being second only to the one off Australia's northeastern coast.

The pilot and flight attendants announced their imminent landing. Tessa watched the land grow closer. Small neighborhoods lay north and east of the airport, many of which were in the building phases with lots and streets but no houses yet.

They touched down and made their way to the small terminal with little fuss. Belize was not a large nation, and tourism was its primary industry. Although they exported a lot of bananas, citrus, and sugar, they needed to keep the tourists flowing through. She was dying to know why the Great Blue Hole was mysteriously closed to tourism, inasmuch as one could close a feature in the ocean.

Going over the economic facts allowed her a minute not to dwell on meeting Ethan Marston outside the terminal. A minute. It had been months since she got pulled into a case his agency was investigating and eventually into his arms and bed. She had no regrets other than they lived so far apart. Now that she was about to see him, though, she felt a spike of anxiety.

She entered the terminal and collected her bags and checked her phone for messages. There was one, and it was from Donald.

Good luck and be safe.

Tessa had a feeling that any time she spent with Ethan was going to involve an element of danger, at least in this case. For that matter, would they ever meet under normal circumstances? She took a deep breath and adjusted her camera bag on top of her wheeled suitcase. All she had to do was play it calm and cool and see how it went from there.

She left the terminal with head high and posture straight... only to trip over something outside the doors. A strong pair of arms caught her and stopped her bags from flying forward.

"Hey, you okay?"

Oh God, it was Ethan. She felt her cheeks reddening.

"Yeah, yeah. My toe caught on something."

A look down revealed an ugly, uneven crack in the sidewalk. One of the terminal workers rushed to her side.

"I'm so sorry, miss," the young woman said. "That was supposed to be marked, but the cone got moved."

"I'm fine." Tessa smiled and made a show of dusting off her perfectly clean khaki Capris. "No harm, no foul."

The attendant's shoulders dropped in relief.

Ethan's did not. His left arm was still around her, not that she minded. She looked up and realized that her memory of those crystal blue eyes did not do them justice.

"Hi, I'm okay," she blurted out. Ethan's easy grin was easily contagious. "Thanks for giving me a ride."

"My pleasure," he said. "You want me to carry something?"

She picked up the camera bag and put the strap over her shoulder. The humid air smelled of the sea, jungle, and jet fuel. The sun was sinking to the west, and she was more than ready to get busy. On the case. Yes, busy on the case, she reminded herself as she caught a whiff of the light cologne Ethan wore. The same cologne she'd noticed that night at his houseboat.

"You can get the suitcase," she told him. "Um, thank you."

"I parked in one of the police spots," he confessed only loud enough for her to hear.

"I think those are for local police." She stifled a chuckle. "Couldn't you get in trouble for that?"

"Nah. I'm an international cop. More or less."

She followed him to a small parking area with signs promising to tow violators. When Ethan walked up to a slick-looking Audi, she couldn't tell how it was supposed to be a police car. She rolled her eyes and got in. Soon, they headed south on a coastal road.

"I wasn't sure I'd see you again," he said in a soft tone. "We should meet when I'm not investigating a case."

They lived on the same coast yet over a thousand miles apart. Over the past several months, Tessa had imagined being able to reach down all those miles to touch his hand, his cheek. The few times they'd spoken over the phone had been like wrapping a favorite blanket around her shoulders.

"And call when it's not about those pirate coins," she added with a slight smile. "I heard they auctioned off well."

He nodded. "I kept one, though. Gramps would've liked that I held on to at least one." He glanced over with a mischievous grin. "I keep it in my wallet. I'll kick myself if I ever lose it, but it's like he's close by." He looked back to the road and switched on the headlights in the deepening twilight.

"I'm glad you did that," she said. "What did you do with the cannonball and those silver coins you found down in Barbados?"

He'd emailed her about finding proof of a story

about a man forced to walk the plank from the *Dragon's Rogue*, a pirate ship he'd been searching for his whole life.

"I loaned the cannonball to a traveling exhibit on the Golden Age of Pirating in the Caribbean." He sounded happy, and she liked that, but then he hesitated. "I gave the coins to the man who helped me auction the gold ones you and I found. They're too fragile to do much with, sale or display, but he loves them."

Tessa almost told him the news she was working on, but she bit her tongue. She had a good feeling about a lead she might have on his pirate ship from a historian she was working with in Charleston, but she didn't want to get Ethan's hopes up. The timing couldn't be better, because she expected an email any time now, and it would be far more satisfying to give him the news in person.

The twinkling lights of Belize City came into view as she searched for the right way to ask about the case. Tessa knew full well that her assignment was not going to be a popular decision. Donald had warned her as much, and Ethan's initial reaction confirmed it. Considering how well she got along with the MBLIS people last time, she hoped they'd work through the discomfort and come to trust her not to get in the way or make them look bad.

"Ethan, about—"

He held a hand up. "We have some planning to do with the team," he said in a gruff tone that stung a little. "Hang on until we're situated."

"Okay..."

She folded her arms across her chest and stared out the window. If Ethan thought of her as an interloper, there might not be a place for them to rekindle things. On the other hand, she didn't know if it was a good idea. She snuck a glance at his face. It lit up as they passed streetlights, and all she saw was a man intent on finding answers in an unforgiving world.

The drive took them through parts of the city that she doubted most tourists got to see. Like much of Central America and the Caribbean, Belize had its share of crime and poverty. Sagging houses with discolored siding looked like orange ghouls in the glow of sodium-vapor streetlights. Makeshift fencing cobbled together out of old doors, and sheet metal surrounded many of the homes they saw. Pedestrians gave odd looks to the expensive car that rolled through their neighborhoods.

"This place gets hit hard by hurricanes," Ethan quietly told her as he rolled through the neighborhood. "The storms have gotten worse over the years. The Barrier Reef does a lot to protect the coast. In the States, we don't hear about it as much as we do about the one in Australia, but we should. These people depend on it during storms but also for the tourism dollars."

"I read that." She watched as a young, barefoot child ran after a dog. "The government is doing a lot to help the people." She looked over at Ethan. "You want me to get this part of the story, too, don't you?"

He nodded. "If you're going to tell this story, tell about what happens when a few selfish actions can cause a chain of repercussions."

"It's a good perspective," she admitted. "When you tell me more about the case, I'll know how to frame it."

"We're almost at the house." He turned down a side road and then got onto one of the main roads. "Funny thing," he went on. "This is considered one of the most dangerous countries in the region. As long as people aren't reminded of the slums, they conveniently forget the crime and poverty."

"True." How many cities and nations had she covered with similar situations? Too many.

Ethan pulled in to a large villa. The property was well kept, and lights shone from most of the windows. He parked in a large garage with two identical Audis. He started to get out.

"Huh," she murmured.

He held up. "What?"

"It's interesting that you told me about the poverty and everything, and yet here we are at an expensive house with expensive cars." She lifted a brow. "It seems a little on the nose."

"Yeah, that is interesting, isn't it?" He motioned for her to get out as he popped the trunk. "We're here on government business, so they're loaning us these cars and the house while we're here."

He held his finger up to his lips as she stepped out of the car. Now that she was out of the air conditioning and not at the airport, the humid air carried the scent of lush blooms, the sea, and no jet fuel.

"Is something going on?" she asked.

"At the moment? No." He lifted her suitcase out of the trunk and set it on the ground. "I just didn't want the others to notice I'm back yet."

"Why—"

His eyes, those blue eyes, felt like they were burrowing into her soul, and she lost the ability to form words. Ethan seemed to have the same problem. Well, maybe not a problem. Not really. She touched his hand, and they laced their fingers together for a moment. Her heart thrilled at the contact.

"I missed you," he rasped.

"Me too." She leaned in and wrapped her arms around him. "I wanted to visit, but I never had time."

Ethan curved one arm around her back and used the other hand to tip her chin up toward him. When their eyes met again, he used both his arms to pull her in tight.

"You're here now."

His lips brushed hers when the door to the house creaked open.

"Marston's back," someone yelled. "And, oh, boy..."

The door slammed shut. Ethan said something under his breath and let her go. Her body hummed, and she wanted to do anything but let go, but it was too late.

"Sorry, Tessa." He grabbed her suitcase. "Let's get you settled in, introduce you to our two new people, and then I'll fill you in on the case details."

His jaw muscles flexed as if he wanted to say more... or do more. Instead, he shook his head and led her inside. As she followed, she had the sudden feeling that this trip would make or break their relationship forever.

11

AFTER I HELPED Tessa get her things into the last open bedroom, I took her to the small conference room and introduced her to the team. Even though Muñoz and Warner were the only ones who hadn't met her before, it was good form... and it was a reminder that we had to act in a professional capacity. Mostly.

"Tessa has signed a non-disclosure agreement about what she's going to see and hear over the next few days," I informed everyone. "It lays out what she may and may not include in the piece the *EcoStar* is going to publish about our department."

"What I don't understand," Muñoz said, "is why a *retired* fleet admiral gets to have a say in our case. No offense, Miss Bleu, but I don't care if he was also one of the Joint Chiefs, retired is retired. What does he have to gain from manipulating us?"

"Muñoz—"

"No, Ethan, I got it." Tessa's emerald eyes flashed in my direction as she pushed some of her chestnut brown hair back from her face. Damn, I was in trouble now that she was back. "Agent Muñoz, believe me, I'm trying to figure it out, too. What I do know is that I take my job seriously. The Great Blue Hole is in peril. Something about this case has threatened the entire ecosystem of the Hole, not to mention tourism in a struggling nation. Given the secrecy, I'm guessing it goes deeper than that. My job is to do what I can to educate our readers about these threats. Part of that is also showing our audience how agencies like MBLIS have an impact."

Birn leaned back, and Muñoz crossed her arms.

"How do you mean, 'have an impact'?" she demanded.

Tessa frowned. "How do you not? Maybe not every case, but in this situation, something has closed down tourism. Whatever happened here could happen again somewhere else. A few weeks ago, you shut down the largest human trafficking operation in this hemisphere. The Trader didn't care about human beings, and they had no trouble scuttling a ship in a fragile ecosystem. Cobra Jon was no better."

"So you see us as helping the environment, in a way?" Holm ventured. He leaned back in his chair. "That's kinda cool."

"I don't like everyone knowing who we are," Birn told us. "Meaning no offense, Tessa, but we do our jobs best playing under the public radar."

"We can't hide forever," I countered. "Given all the internet coverage of, well, everything, it's surprising that we aren't mentioned more often in the media."

"I suspect some of that has to do with the excellent work of your cybercrimes unit." Tessa nodded toward Warner. "Donald suggested that the unit's skill at manipulating the web had included watching for MBLIS mentions and removing them."

Warner's eyes widened as he looked over at me, and I nodded.

"It's true," he said. "It actually uses a lot of our resources."

Holm sat up. "Does this article mean we're outing ourselves? That sounds way less cool."

"The agency," I clarified in an even tone. I hated the idea myself, but it went way over my pay grade, which wasn't low. "Our identities and likenesses will in no way be part of the story. Tessa is only covering the investigation and how we operate."

"Um, Ethan?" Bonnie leaned forward on her elbows. "What about you-know-who?"

"What?" I frowned until she mouthed Header's name. "Oh, my old friend. Yeah, part of the deal is keeping that out of the coverage also."

Tessa gave me a sharp look. "I missed something."

"Yeah." I scanned the team's faces and found varying amounts of discomfort. Dammit, Farr. "Now that nobody's happy, let's start at the beginning. Bonnie and Clyde, you stick around to give your updates. Everyone else, unless you wanna hear everything a second or third time, call it a night. We're diving tomorrow morning."

I walked Tessa through the case from meeting the Lemons all the way through that day's dive. The only part I left out was the *Wraith*.

"Dare Lemon." She sighed. "Wow. Uncle Donald made me watch his videos when I was learning to dive. He still sends links when they release... released new episodes. Did his niece take you out to the dive site?"

"No," I hedged. "She's flying up to be with family." At Tessa's understanding nod, I plunged in and hoped for the best. "An old friend of mine is helping us out, but there's a catch. You can go with us, but you have to hand over your camera before you get on his boat."

"I don't think so!" She stood, and her cheeks flared. "What's the point of me going if I don't have my camera?"

"You'll have it for the dive, and you'll get it back after we're ashore," I promised. I might have been too hasty to call those eyes emerald. They were more like fire. "His boat is... you could say it's top secret."

Her brow smoothed. "Like the Ghost you took after Cobra Jon?"

"Sort of. Maybe a little less legal."

Bonnie laughed behind her hand, which did not help.

"Just tell me," Tessa ordered. "You had no trouble being direct the last time we were together."

That was because I hadn't missed her for over six months back then. Now that we were in the same room, I didn't want her to leave. If she couldn't handle the thing with Header, she'd be on the first flight home.

"We're working with a guy named Jake Header," I told her. "He has a boat a lot like Ghost, and in return for his help, we don't arrest him for the week."

"That's all?" she asked. "I've heard of this guy. A buccaneer type who takes the bad guys out by doing it his way. So he's doing this out of the goodness of his heart?"

"He's a former SEAL, and we served together for a while."

"And?"

That's why Tessa was a journalist and the other part of the reason why Header had objected to her presence. Not even my team knew the deeper reason. To win Tessa over on this, though, I had to tell her.

"Bonnie and Clyde, I need you to turn off your ears for a minute," I said.

Bonnie tapped her lab partner on the shoulder. He pulled out a pair of earbuds and looked around.

"What?" he asked.

"Don't listen to Marston."

"I wasn't." He put his earbuds back in and went back to whatever he was doing or listening to. I could not figure that guy out sometimes.

"Jake told me, by the way," Bonnie announced. "I kind of wouldn't shut up about why and all that, so he shut me up by promising to take me for a dive if I promised not to tell everyone else why he was helping."

"Oh." I chuckled, but Tessa wasn't smiling. "So yeah. Dare Lemon is Jake Header's half brother. He's risking a hell of a lot by trusting the US and Belize governments not to go back on our promises. They'd all kill their mothers *and* grandmothers to get their hands on his tech."

Tessa crossed her arms. "You thought I wouldn't get that?" The hurt in her voice sliced through whatever good feelings had built up with her return. "Of course I won't betray someone like him."

I didn't think it would be wise to question her use of the phrase "someone like him."

"As much as you mean to me, I have to do my job," I told her. "You're a journalist. Header doesn't want journalists near his boat, but he's making an exception on the condition that nothing about him or his boat make it into your story."

"Next time, just tell me what I need to know." Tessa stood and turned to Bonnie. "Is this an update I need to hear right now? I've had a long day."

"Nah, it can wait. Ethan's the one I really need to brief. I'll give you the nutshell in the morning."

"Thanks, Rosa."

Tessa left the room, and I slumped in my chair.

"Hey, she remembered my name," Bonnie pointed out.

"I just reintroduced you."

"Right, as 'Bonnie.' That woman, she pays attention to things."

"Am I getting a lecture?"

"Do you need one?" She kicked Clyde's chair. He appeared to be asleep sitting up. "I mean, I could do the whole don't-assume-things speech, but we know how that one ends." She pulled out one of the buds and blew in his ear. He jolted to his feet. "Then there's the 'trust-the-people-you-care-about' diatribe. Or the 'you-should-be-kissing-her-up-not-pissing-her-off' address. If you want a lecture, Ethan, let me know which one."

"I think I just got one," I muttered.

"If you say so," Bonnie answered.

"Huh? What'd you get?" Clyde asked in a sleepy voice. "Sorry, nodded off there." A sheepish grin spread across his face. "Turns out TJ and I have the same taste in PC games. We stayed up a little too late."

Bonnie made a noise and pushed the tablet in front of Clyde.

"Tell me what you got on that tag." I dropped into a seat. "Anything useful from the lab?"

"There's a string of numbers," Clyde said with a yawn. "We're trying to figure out what they mean. Hopefully by tomorrow." He glanced at the screen for a second. "There's some pretty intense gamma radiation clinging to that tag. Alone, it's not enough to hurt a person if they don't hold on to it for long, but if there were a box or even barrel full of that stuff, it would be bad news."

"I think a Hulk joke would be bad taste here," I observed. Neither of them laughed. "What makes this one special?"

Bonnie took the lead this time. "Medical science uses materials with short half-lives. It clears out quicker. Therefore, there's less exposure. Beta rays are easily blocked by something as simple as fabric or cardboard. Gamma rays can go through things a lot easier, but lead and water are good blockers."

"*These* gamma rays have a long half-life," Bonnie added. "The seawater is insulating whatever's down there. About half the radiation is gone at fifteen centimeters, and then half again at thirty. Dare Lemon had to be on top of a significant amount of radiation to get that much exposure."

"That kind of exposure went right through the wetsuit." Clyde rocked back and forth in his meeting chair. It squeaked. He didn't seem to notice. "So we're looking for a cluster or pile of material that wouldn't have screamed 'radiation' at a couple of risk-taker divers."

"Bridget Lemon said the floor was covered in silt." I stood and paced the length of the table. Pacing was more Holm's thing than mine, but this made less and less sense. "If the stuff was dumped less than a day earlier, how did it get covered so quickly?"

Clyde shrugged, but Bonnie tapped her lips with her forefinger. Then, her eyes widened.

"It's possible that the Hole had a larger sandfall than usual," she suggested with a downward scooping motion. "Maybe the container with the waste disrupted a ledge or something that held back a lot of sand. By the time everything settled, the debris was covered up."

I nodded. "Makes sense. Kind of like triggering an avalanche."

"I'm going to do some research tomorrow, but I don't know of any medical waste that involves radiation to that intensity." Clyde stood and yawned again. "Something's off about it."

"I agree." Bonnie stood, as well. "I think the only way we'll figure it out is if we recover all the debris or find out from the person responsible."

"Tomorrow morning, we're sweeping another section near the Lemons' dive site," I reminded them. "It looks like we'll be able to take a small sub out in three days."

It was a decent plan, as long as Header didn't bail on me.

12

THE BOAT RIDE north from Belize City felt like it took longer than my diving watch showed. I hadn't told the others that Header might vanish. There would've been more questions than I was willing to answer. As long as I kept my yap shut, I had plausible deniability. In theory.

Header's catamaran bounced through the early morning chop as I steered it toward the estate where the boathouse hid the *Wraith*. My stomach sank as we came round the last forest outcropping. The boathouse was empty behind the flapping tarp. I eased off the throttle and scanned the area and then behind us. Nothing.

"Where's your buddy, Marston?" Muñoz hollered over the engine and surf. "Did he spook and run?"

I ignored her as I studied the scene. Because of the tarp, I couldn't see to the rear of the boathouse, so I brought us to the opening for a better look.

"They lit out in a hurry," Holm said. He pointed to the one side of the tarp. "It's still lashed along this side." He pointed to the other side. "And over there, you see where the lines were cut?"

Scraps of nylon rope littered the dock. Whatever happened, they didn't have time to untie the secured tarp.

"Some of the tie-downs are pulled out," Tess said.

She was right. The more I studied it, the more it looked like the boat rammed through the tarp. That was some rush.

I cranked the catamaran's wheel to park it on the other side of the dock. We weren't leaving until we inspected what we could. I owed MBLIS and the Belize government that much, at least.

"Hang on." Birn stood with his hand over his aviator glasses. "Lookie who's here."

The *Wraith* glided in and gently bumped against the dock. Header didn't bother putting her in the boathouse. He maneuvered her until the hatch was even with the dock. The door lowered two feet or so below the dock's underside, and Header appeared with a rope. My old friend was covered head to toe in black smudges and was bleeding in several areas. Holm jumped onto the dock from the catamaran, caught the line, and secured the boat.

Header moved slowly and accepted Holm's hand as he stepped up to the dock. Birn helped me secure the catamaran as the others hopped out to see the rogue captain. I kept an eye on Header as he shuffled toward the boathouse without talking to anyone.

"I got this," Holm told me in a quiet tone. "He's your buddy."

I nodded and ran after Header.

"Jake, what happened?"

He shook his head and held up a hand. The guy needed a moment. I walked with him around the rear of the structure. As soon as he was out of sight of my team, he leaned against the siding and slid to sit on the ground. I signaled them to stay back before I went over to sit next to him.

"What happened?" I asked, softer this time.

He sniffed with one of those smiles that people used when they were trying to process bad shit. His fists clenched and released.

"Remember that mission near Somalia?" His voice was rough, unsteady. "The one with the family? No bad guys, just damned bad luck."

"Engine fire?" I leaned my head back against the wall and looked to the sky.

"It came over the horn a couple hours ago. Boat on fire and rescuers were at least an hour away. I was twenty minutes, tops."

"Sorry, Jake. You did your best. You always do."

"No." He met my eyes. "It was like being on that other boat. I froze, Ethan. The girl was screaming, and I froze."

Oh hell…

"I—"

"And don't give me some bullshit about PTSD!" he yelled. He swallowed and got his voice under control. "I got the girl out, but she saw her parents suffer, man. She's gonna live with that, and she's gonna have some bad scars."

There wasn't anything I could say to help. People tend to think of SEALs and former SEALs as unfeeling badasses. We *were* badasses when we had to be, but that kind of thing ate at a person's soul, especially once the battle was over. That's the side the public rarely saw.

"I noticed the shower in the boathouse," I told him. "We'll start loading and give you some time to clean up. I'll just tell them it was a rough rescue. They'll leave you alone about it."

"Thanks." The corner of his mouth twitched. "Keep that Muñoz character away from the controls. She's too curious."

I chuckled. "I'll make sure of that." I stood and dusted off my shorts as Tessa's laugh rang out from down the dock. "And I'll hold on to Tessa's camera until you're ready to go."

"You sure you trust her?" Header asked.

"With my life," I promised.

"Don't let me down, Ethan."

I returned to the group at the end of the dock. They had most of our gear in place. The refilled tanks from the day before were neatly stacked, as well as all the other dive equipment.

"How bad was it?" Holm asked when I walked up.

"Bad." I glanced at everyone. "Cut him some slack today. He did a good thing, but it didn't end well. He's getting a shower and will be ready to go when we are."

Muñoz met my eye the longest. I started to say something, but she gave a sharp nod and walked off to help move another case. Tessa came over with her camera equipment.

"Two bags?" I wondered.

"My camera, underwater housing, and lights."

She gestured toward the boathouse. "I'm not sure where to put the bags. You said he'd hold them until we're at the site."

"I told him I'd take care of it until he gets out here." It was the first chance I had to talk with Tessa in private that morning. I didn't want to waste it. "Look, I'm sorry for not showing enough trust in you last night."

She handed me the straps to both of her bags. "It stung, and I overreacted. We both had long days, so let's call it even." A frown creased her otherwise smooth forehead. "I love Uncle Donald, I really do, but I don't think he's telling me everything he knows."

"As much as I admire him, I gotta agree," I admitted. "Let's take this one step at a time, see how it plays out."

"alright." She looked over my shoulder and cleared her throat. "Captain Header, thank you for allowing me—"

"This the camera rig?" He nodded at the bags I held.

"Yes," Tessa hedged.

"I'll hold on to it while you're on my vessel." Header's gruff tone rubbed me the wrong way, but I held my tongue. "I still don't know that I want you going along."

"Jake..." I wasn't sure what to say at the moment.

Tessa's jaw dropped, and she looked to me. Header looked between us and laughed.

"I'm just messing with you." He took the straps from me and handed them back to Tessa. "Ethan vouches for you. His word is gold, Miss Bleu. All I care about is that you don't take any photos, from any angle, of my boat. Too many agencies want intel on the *Wraith*. I'm putting a hell of a lot of trust in these folks just letting them near her. MBLIS and other groups might not agree with the way I operate, but the truth is, we're on the same side."

From inside the hatch, Muñoz narrowed her eyes at Header but didn't say anything. She joined Birn and Bonnie on the bench seats and fastened her harness. Tessa and I went in, and Header untied *Wraith* from the dock and closed the door. He was acting like himself, but there was a slump to his shoulders and a dullness in his eyes that weren't there the day before.

After getting Tessa situated, I joined him at the front. A hint of oily smoke lingered about, but I couldn't tell if it was from him or traces left on his seat. He goosed the engines, and the boat jolted forward. In the back, the only conversation was held in low voices once we hit cruising speed. Header pushed harder than the day before, hitting sixty knots with little effort. I pretended not to notice. If anyone else noticed, they didn't say anything.

A small part of me wanted to ride with him on the open sea someday, maybe even chase down modern pirates. The larger part of me didn't want to throw my career away and end up in prison.

"Here we are, folks," Header announced as we slowed up to the Lighthouse Reef Atoll. "Miss Bleu, you can join us up at the front if you'd like to see the approach."

"Are we chopped liver?" Holm complained good-naturedly.

"You're the so-called enemy," Header answered in a flat tone that settled any further joking. "I prefer days like this, when we're allies."

I did, too. On most days, a run-in with Header would mean a fight or, more likely, a chase to apprehend him. Neither idea appealed to me, and I hoped I never had to engage against him.

13

TESSA WATCHED Ethan's team prep their Geiger counters and lead-shielded canisters. The enormity of the case hit her stronger than before as she got into her dive gear and readied her photography rig. Even though she was perfectly safe from the mysterious radiation at the bottom of the Great Blue Hole, the thought of being anywhere close to it made her skin crawl.

At the moment, she wasn't sure she would thank Donald for pushing her to get the certifications she was using for this particular dive. Reef and wreck diving was fun, and she didn't mind more technical dives, but she didn't live for it the way others did. Others like Ethan.

She noticed him steal glances in her direction.

He seemed as conflicted about her presence in Belize as she was. The first MBLIS case she was involved in opened both their eyes about the level of control her honorary uncle could choose to wield their lives.

"You ready?" Captain Header asked as he took the seat next to her.

Tessa looked up from where she was putting on her flippers.

"Yeah." She patted her camera with a smile. "This will be different from my usual underwater photography."

"Marston is a great dive partner," he said with a smile. "He saved my ass once or twice." A shadow crossed his face. "One of the best guys I ever worked with. I'd steal him from the agency if I could." He winked and stood. "Get some photos of the cave formations while you're down there. Nothing like it, as far as I've seen."

"I'll do that." She raised a brow. "I'd be happy to email you some copies."

The captain laughed. "Nice try, paparazzi."

"Had to try." She grinned and then lowered her voice. "For what it's worth, if you ever want me to tell your story without compromising your group, get in touch." He pulled back slightly. "I understand your hesitation, that's why I'm only saying it once. I promise."

He nodded. "Journalists aren't in the habit of asking my permission before trying to do a feature. You're a different breed."

"I'm an environmental reporter, and a lot of my work involves the ocean." She felt eyes on her and saw Ethan watching her speak with Header. He wore a neutral expression, and she couldn't help wondering about his thoughts. "I'm covering this investigation because it directly involves one of the World Heritage Sites and because a lot of what MBLIS does has an effect on the Caribbean ecosystem."

"Is that the entire reason?" He grinned toward Ethan.

"I'll leave you to speculate," she told him with an eye roll. "Thank you, Captain Header."

He stuck his hand out. "Call me 'Jake.' All my friends do."

She shook his hand, surprised at the quick turn-around. "Thank you, Jake. Call me 'Tessa.'"

"I'm gonna call you 'Late to Entry' if you don't get moving, woman," Ethan laughed. Behind him, Birn and Muñoz stepped into the water. Robbie had his mask in place and stood at the edge of the hatch door. Ethan turned toward the *Wraith's* captain. "Thanks, Jake. You can talk to Bonnie if you need to vent some air."

"Have a safe dive!" Bonnie waved from where she was setting her mobile lab. "I might collect more specimens, Ethan, but we'll be back before you so the *Wraith* won't eat anyone."

"Thaaanks." Ethan turned toward Tessa. "Remember the plan?"

"You take point, Robbie goes left, and I stay close. If I see something that's not regular trash, I'll let you know." She'd elected to carry a mesh bag in case she did find trash, even though it was unlikely. It was her thing. "Let's do it."

The guys went in ahead of her. She followed and itched to explore the reef that stretched behind and ahead of them. The drop-off, however, loomed to her left. Beyond the bright, sandy floor was the Great Blue Hole's cerulean abyss. A group of hammerhead sharks passed near the surface above the Hole, and a delightful thrill passed through her body. Most people feared sharks, but smart divers rarely had to worry.

Ethan and Robbie led her to where they said they'd left off the day before. Wall dives, especially deep ones like this, weren't her favorite. She quelled the wave of anxiety that always accompanied such a dive, and she focused on her camera and even breaths.

As they descended, she took a few shots from behind as they swept the Geiger counters along the wall. About sixty feet down, they hit the thermocline where the tropical water met with the cold layer below. The layer looked like mist on a cool morning. She took some shots of the cloud-like formations and then sank through with a shiver. Well, several shivers, until she acclimated to the colder water. That was her least favorite part of deep diving. Even with a thicker suit, the chill always worked its way to her bones.

The water cleared again, and they descended with no issues. Tessa spied an interesting, if small, ledge nearby. She got Ethan's attention and pointed to it with her camera. He gave an okay signal. It was an easy few kicks over, and she spied what looked like a patch of algae hanging on its far side. She took a few photos as she approached, but something seemed off about it.

Once on the far side, she shined her dive light on the object. It was some sort of blue fabric, maybe a hand towel that fell from a boat. It didn't look like anything special, but they had a protocol. She flashed her light at the other two, and they responded by flashing back. As they swam over, she snapped a few more photos.

Robbie reached her first, and she backed off to photograph him checking it out. He gave a sudden kick backward and gestured at Ethan and then the Geiger counter.

Tessa's stomach tightened as Robbie waved her close to get a picture of the readout. A red light pulsed next to the number to warn of danger. She captured the device's face and then moved back. Logic dictated that it was unlikely she got any exposure worth caring about. Anxiety spat in the face of logic, and her chest tightened. To keep her breathing even, she visualized one of her favorite tide pools and its peaceful biodiversity. Her heart calmed, and she settled.

Even as she dealt with her fears, she documented the collection process. Robbie used a grabber to move the towel from its perch and into the container Ethan had attached to a lift bag. It was at the end of a tether that was out of range of his body, but he still had to bring it close to twist the cap onto it. He finished and gave her an okay signal. As if nothing happened, he and Robbie went back to the section of the wall that they were scanning before working their way back. Their grid approach was thorough and, given their extensive diving experience, quick.

Soon, they were to the bottom of her certification level. The upper portion of the massive cave was accessible and oh, so tempting. Stalactites... the largest she'd ever seen on land or underwater... stood guard narrowly within range of her ability to photograph them. There was a chance the photos wouldn't come out, but she'd be damned if she didn't try. Hauntingly beautiful scenery like this was a rare find. While it'd been photographed by hundreds of visitors, she was there, in the moment, and it was hers to try.

Ethan and Robbie made quick work of checking the last section of the cave entrance before rejoining her with an all-clear. They'd never left visual contact with her, even though they went deeper than she was allowed.

The cold water was starting to get to her, and she was more than happy to ascend. They couldn't get to the warmer upper levels fast enough. Patience wasn't her best trait, but she always followed dive plans. That didn't mean she loved the dive stops to avoid the bends. She just wanted to chase the chill from her body.

Tessa managed not to think about the find of the

day until they surfaced near the *Wraith*. Ethan set the container on the hatch door before getting out of the water. He took Tessa's camera rig and then gave her a hand. She didn't need it, but she wasn't going to say "no." When she grabbed his hand, she didn't want to let go. That wasn't an option, so she gave his hand a squeeze and then moved on to get her gear off. Robbie was the last out of the water.

Jake took the lined canister and set it in a mesh cargo space on the wall. Tessa took a seat on the other side of the boat. Birn passed his Geiger counter over the canister.

"Signed, sealed, delivered," he declared. Tessa stared at him. "Well, not SSD, but it will be in a couple hours. The radiation's contained."

Tessa kept her thoughts to herself as she stripped down to her swimsuit and then put her shorts and shirt from earlier back on.

"You okay?" Ethan sat next to her like Jake had earlier. The difference was Ethan's nearness sparked a light in her heart. "It looked like you had a hard time for a minute down there."

So he'd noticed. The anxiety attacks were embarrassing but manageable.

"I handled it. The reading on that cloth surprised me is all."

He kept his voice low, below the clatter of the others removing and storing dive gear. "Has this happened before?"

She met those sapphire eyes. Sometimes, they were lighter, she'd noticed, depending on the surroundings. A little like hazel eyes, but blue.

"Not that often," she insisted. "I have an instructor who has helped me through it. Seriously, I'm fine."

Ethan's brow wrinkled, but he spoke no more of it. Since he had the pull to get her certification revoked, she chose not to admit the extent of the problem. Yes, it was dangerous to dive with anxiety, but like she said, she knew how to handle it.

When it was time to go, she strapped into her seat next to Robbie. Ethan had all the luck in getting to sit in the co-pilot seat next to Jake. Maybe, if she were lucky, she'd get to ride up front someday and be able to tell a tall tale from the sea.

14

ALTHOUGH SHE TRIED to hide it, I saw Tessa was shaken by her close encounter with the fabric she'd found. She shot backward after taking a photo of the Geiger numbers, and she breathed fast and unevenly while Holm and I collected the item. When she lowered the camera between shots, her widened eyes spelled trouble.

My heart quickened, and I made a hand sign to Holm to indicate the situation. He paused as he used the grabber, took a quick look, and nodded. We couldn't call the dive until the fabric was contained, which meant we'd have to dive again later after getting her to the surface to clear the rest of the area.

As soon as I got the lid in place, Holm went to check on her in a subtle move to avoid making the situation worse. I kept the canister on its lift-bagged tether far away from her.

I had to give her a ton of credit. By the time Holm reached her side, Tessa had calmed down. Her breathing was regular, and her movements were more fluid. The cave floor was the last area to check. It was twenty feet below her cert. Holm only went about ten feet below where she hovered and kept an eye while she took pictures of the top part of the cave. I made quick work of the job and rejoined them.

I'll never know if she realized how close we watched her that day. It scared the ever-living shit out of me. She handled the ascent like a pro, but once on the boat, she got skittish around the canister. For some people, the very idea of being close to radiation approached phobic levels. Tessa appeared to be one of those people. To overcome her panic down there spoke to her courage.

Still, I kept an eye on her while we checked in with Muñoz and Birn. They'd returned about fifteen minutes before we did.

"We didn't find anything, but it was a beautiful dive," Muñoz reported. "It got a little cold down there, though. My partner didn't like that part so much."

"Hey, you're the one who signaled she was cold," he protested. At my raised brow, he waved off the concern. "It was on the ascent, and she warmed up pretty quickly."

"Noted," I said.

I also noted her indignation. Fortunately, we didn't need to perform deep dives that often. Muñoz was a hell of an agent and a badass in a fight, but that didn't change that fact that her petite size made it easier for her to get hypothermic.

Before we left the dive site, I sat next to Tessa.

"You okay?" I asked in a low voice. Even though I didn't want anyone to hear, I had to check in with her. "It looked like you had a hard time for a minute down there."

"I handled it." Something about the look in her eyes worried me. "The reading on that cloth surprised me is all."

"Has this happened before?"

If so, Farr needed to know before sending her on underwater assignments. Assuming he didn't know.

"Not that often." Her cheeks reddened. "I have an instructor who has helped me through it. Seriously, I'm fine."

No, she wasn't fine. She had no business diving with us that day. By all rights, I should've reamed her out for it, but I didn't have the heart... not in front of everyone else. It was Farr who encouraged her to push her luck and Farr who knew she could be in danger due to anything from radioactive debris to being present if we faced down a suspect. I planned to call Farr as soon as we got back to the Villa, if not sooner.

On the ride back, Header appeared more relaxed, and he kept *Wraith* to the fifty-knot cruising speed of the day before. In the back, I noticed Bonnie chatting as animated as usual. Her hair and clothes were dry, so if they'd gone diving, it would've been quick.

"Did Bonnie take samples or anything today?" I casually asked Header. "She was stoked about what she brought back yesterday."

"*Rosa* took water samples. She said she wants to test for, uh, stuff." He chuckled. "I took her word for it. As long as the water's good, I'm happy. Why do you keep calling her 'Bonnie,' anyway?"

"You haven't met Clyde. Those two barely leave the lab, it seems like. Their last names are Bonci and Clime. Since they work together so well, the office joke became nicknames, something they've embraced."

"Joe designed a new Lab Rats shirt with Bonnie

and Clyde rats," Bonnie said from her seat. I hadn't realized she was listening. "They're supposed to be delivered to headquarters next week." She grinned. "We ordered enough shirts for the entire unit."

Birn groaned. "I'm so glad."

Muñoz elbowed him. "It's cute. I'll be happy to take a shirt," she told Bonnie, who blinked.

"It's a gag gift, but if you like it, I'll give you two."

Header looked over at me with a confused expression.

"Jake, Sylvia Muñoz is a many-faceted jewel," I informed him. From her seat, she crossed her arms and gave me her patented death glare. "You, she will not like, because you *allegedly* break international law. When she does like someone, she's quite friendly."

"And if I like you and you piss me off, I drag you to a surprise training session to teach you respect." She pointed to her eyes and then to either Header or me, I couldn't tell which. "You boys better watch yourselves."

"Ma'am, yes, ma'am!" Header said through an appreciative laugh.

Muñoz ignored him after that, but she radiated less anger toward my friend, the lawbreaker. I wish I could tell her about Header's connection to Dare

Lemon, but limiting it to need-to-know was part of the deal.

Back at the boathouse, Header disappeared for a few minutes. When he returned, he had news.

"My submersible will be here tomorrow night," he told me. "That's the earliest I could do. It was in use."

I didn't ask for details that could incriminate him. It was easier not to think about the reality that put us on opposite sides of the fence except for this one short week.

"See you in two days, then," I said.

My team was waiting for me on the catamaran. I tossed a salute at Header, which only served to annoy Muñoz, and maybe Birn. He wore a frown when I got to the console. Yeah, I was on thin ice just by associating with Header. They didn't know what he and I went through in a few intense months. Not even Holm knew, and he was my best friend. Header was a damned hero, and nobody would ever know.

I was agitated as we left the boathouse behind. Sometimes to do good in the world, real good, a guy had to break the rules. God knows, I broke a few rules to get things done during my career. But because I had the veneer of my service and special agent status, and because I got results, those moments got overlooked. A guy like Header wasn't much worse. The difference was that he had pissed off the wrong people, and that got him where he was.

The others chatted and enjoyed the uncharacteristically mild weather as we approached the marina in Belize City. Two figures stood near the slip during our approach. It turned out to be Clyde and Warner. They had big grins as they helped tie the catamaran to the dock.

"What are you two so excited about?" Holm asked with a smile. "Win some huge gaming competition?"

Clyde shook his head, and Warner's grin widened.

"It took a couple of hours, but we figured out the numerical code on that tag," Clyde told us. "It was a serial number for, get this, radioactive isotopes used in medical imaging. Not bad in the right doses, but yeah, they can be awful in the wrong setting."

"Are you saying it was a label?" I asked.

Warner nodded. "Sort of. It was a tag attached to the vial. We tracked it to the hospital where it was delivered." He interlocked his fingers and then stretched his hands palm out, which made his knuckles crack loud enough for even Bonnie to cringe. And she was a master cracker of knuckles. "I did a little poking and prodding to trace its route." He shook his arms out. "It went to Cliffside General Hospital in Tampa, Florida."

"The place that built a hill to make a 'cliff' a few years ago?" I laughed. Tampa didn't do cliffs. "Who handles their medical waste?"

"MediWaste Removal Services," Clyde told me. "The CEO is Devon Cole, and they have contracts with several hospitals and medical centers."

Muñoz walked up while holding half of Bonnie's mobile lab. "Hey, you gonna stand around shooting your mouth, or are you gonna help us unload the boat?"

"Uh, sure..." Warner eyed the catamaran and grimaced. "I mean, I'll carry stuff to the cars from the dock, but I am not stepping on that boat."

"So, why did you two come out here to report the big news?" I picked up a case and pushed it into Warner's chest. "You could've called."

Clyde rubbed the back of his head. "I needed to get out of that lab."

Everyone but Tessa looked at him in various states of shock.

"Hey, I don't live in our lab at HQ," he insisted. "I like it down there, but this one smells like Lysol and dirty clothes, and it's too warm in there. The air conditioning is weak. I don't like it."

Bonnie brought her water sample case off the boat and handed it over to Clyde. He raised his brows.

"Tessa found something," Bonnie told him. "I'll take it and relieve you at the lab. Go do something not-boring." A wicked grin spread across her face. "Like using my mobile lab to test the twenty water samples I brought back from the Hole. Good times, buddy!"

Clyde stared at the carefully packed case in his arms. The stricken look on his face should've been caught on camera. He was wearing the first version of his Lab Rats shirt, with anime-style caricatures of both he and Bonnie. That, with the box and his face with the look of shocked misery, would have made a great meme for their Facebook Page.

Yes. Bonnie and Clyde had a Facebook Page. I wasn't on social media often, and even I heard of their posts.

Just like that, I heard a click. I looked to my left and saw Tessa snap a photo of the priceless moment. She'd removed her camera from the diving rig, and it now hung around her neck.

Clyde mouthed something along the lines of "why?"

"I'll blur your face, if we use it," Tessa told him.

Bonnie set a metal case on the dock next to Clyde's feet. "I kid, Joe. We're going in together." She pointed at Warner. "You, too. We have another find to inspect. If we can discover its origin by tonight, they can do something about it tomorrow."

I cocked my head at Bonnie. "Yeah. Make sure to get the location so we can plan a trip if it's not too far from Cliffside."

Clyde made no complaint when he accepted the metal case with the radioactive fabric. He set it in the trunk of one of the borrowed Audis. Soon, he, Bonnie, and Warner left for their temporary lab in a seldom-used military building.

"We'll have a briefing in the morning," I updated everyone. "Robbie and Tessa, I'm going to see if Director Ramsey can get us a mid-morning flight to Tampa to interview MediWaste's CEO. Unless something comes up, everyone has tonight off."

"Well, I'm going to go work on reports," Holm said with a fake yawn. "I'm going to head back to the house and work on that." That was not the guy I knew, and I wasn't the only one to give him a funny look. "How about you, Lamarr, Sylvia?"

"I saw some artist gallery or another when we drove through the other day," Birn mused. "It looked familiar, and I want to check it out tomorrow."

"While he's doing that, I'm going to do a little shopping at the market," Muñoz admitted. "I have nieces and nephews who complain that I don't bring them souvenirs from my worldly travels."

"Both of you watch your sixes," I warned. "Belize City isn't the safest port in the world, and we still don't know who we're after."

"Don't need to remind me," Muñoz muttered. "I'll go wait in the car. I'm ready for dinner. You all decide what you're doing."

Birn went to the parking lot ahead of us, and Muñoz followed in his wake.

"I'll eat in so I can get to those reports," Holm said.

"You okay, Robbie?" I stepped closer and spoke in a quiet tone.

He wagged his eyebrows at me, ignoring my question. "What are you two going to do?"

"Us?" Tessa's voice squeaked a little. I didn't blame her. It felt like the team was manipulating us into talking. "I don't... We don't have plans, as far as I know."

"How about we change that?" I suggested. "Let's

find a quiet place where we can talk and eat. Have you ever tried chimole?"

"I've heard of it." She tapped her lower lip and smiled. "I'd be happy to go try it with you."

As Holm chuckled and left for the cars, I held out a hand. Tessa grasped it with both of hers.

"So, date night in a couple hours?" I asked.

"You better believe it."

She kept my hand in hers as we left the dock. The evening was looking up.

15

TESSA AND ETHAN only stopped at the villa long enough to change into casual evening wear. She chose an off-white shift with a jade floral scarf around her waist. Her sandals were new, with a slight wedge and cream straps that went with her outfit.

Most of the team went out for dinner, but Robbie sat in his room with the door open. On her way to meet Ethan, Tessa knocked on the doorframe. He looked up as he closed his laptop.

"Going out now?" he guessed. "Have fun."

"Why aren't you out with the others?" Tessa asked.

He shrugged as he tapped a finger next to his laptop. "I had a lot of paperwork that I put off until the last minute. Which was about a week ago. The brass are getting pissed that I haven't caught up yet."

Tessa had a feeling there was more to his story than late reports. Call it reporter's intuition. She thought about asking more about it, but it wasn't her place. He was Ethan's partner and friend, not hers. That didn't stop her from wondering, though. Instead of pushing, she smiled and moved back into the hallway.

"Good luck, then. I'll bring your partner back before the car turns into a pumpkin."

Robbie chuckled. "Cool. See you later."

As she went down the hall to the stairs, she heard his door shut. He was definitely up to something. Had he told Ethan what he was doing other than finishing overdue reports? She shook her head to clear it. No, it wasn't her business. Ethan trusted the guy, so she did, as well.

The villa's teak handrail and stairs gently curved from the second to the first floor. The stairs landed in the living room, across from where they'd entered through the garage's mudroom. Ethan occupied a barstool at the open kitchen's counter that looked into said living room.

"Wow," he breathed. "You look great."

He didn't look so bad himself. His khaki slacks

moved freer than the usual pleated, heavier material he wore. The pale blue button-up shirt was short-sleeved, casual yet dressy. Ethan looked every inch the sharp-dressed man.

Tessa took a deep breath and held a spike of anxiety in check. On the way to Belize, she'd worried that either she or Ethan might not feel the same as they did when they were together for such a short time all those months ago. Those doubts dissolved as she was caught up in those eyes. Damn, those eyes could carry a mountain on a feather, they were so clear and blue. His hands were warm and firm as he wrapped them around hers.

"There's a little place by the beach I want to take you to." His voice was rough, as though he was holding something back. "They tell me their chimole is the best in the city."

She gently extracted her hands. "That sounds like a plan." Her stomach growled in agreement. "I might be a little hungry."

"Chimole it is," he said with a laugh.

The short drive took them a little out from the city where there were fewer lights, and the waxing moon shone off the water. He parked in a small lot with cracking asphalt. As she got out, she spotted dolphins playing and leaping in the moonlight. She itched for her camera, but this was one of the rare times she hadn't brought it along.

"It's not fancy, but when Robbie and I had business here last, the people were good and the food even better."

The restaurant was small, and the siding had the appearance of, well, a small restaurant that faced a sea that could punish coastlines and beyond. Colorful light strands invited them to the front where several tables were arranged on a tidy patio surrounded by a wrought iron fence.

They entered through a screen door that screeched as screen doors were wont to do. Aromas surrounded Tessa, teasing her with cumin, cinnamon, annatto, and garlic. Other wonderful scents mingled into a warm invitation to dinner.

Tessa's mouth watered as they entered and were shown to the patio where all the tables were empty. It appeared to be a slow night, but it was in the middle of the week, so that fact spoke nothing about the restaurant's quality. A soft breeze teased at her hair, which she'd left down for the night. Ethan must have noticed because he reached over to tuck her hair behind her ear before they took their seats. Their server lit a candle that rested in a hurricane glass at the center of the table and then left them with menus.

"Bring many girls here?" Tessa teased.

The corners of his eyes crinkled. "Only the one. I'll see what she says after dinner is over." He nodded toward the inside. "During the day, it's beer and chimole or beer and fry jacks. They have great tamales, too."

"You're stuck on the chimole," she observed. "Must be good stuff."

"It's different, but yeah, it's good." He shrugged. "If you don't enjoy it, order anything else off the menu. These folks know how to cook."

Their server returned a few minutes later. Ethan placed his order, and Tessa decided to try the chimole as well. When they were alone, Ethan's smile faded, and he caught her gaze with a sense of concern.

"What's wrong?" she asked. Considering what happened during the dive, she had a feeling of what was coming.

"I don't know that 'wrong' is the right word." He looked out at the sea, where lightning flashed across clouds far to the east, and then back at her. "You know we have to talk about the dive, right?"

There it was. It'd been naïve to hope Ethan wouldn't bring it up again.

"Yeah." She fiddled with the napkin at her place setting. "I should've said something, but if I had, Donald wouldn't have sent me here." Her chest tightened at the very thought. "It was the only excuse I've had since the Cobra Jon thing to see you."

Ethan reached across the table and cupped her hands in his. She hated that it made her feel warm and protected. Modern women were supposed to be above needing big, strong men to make them feel better, but she wasn't above it. She was strong in her own ways, but he was strong in ways that made her feel safe.

"You never need an excuse to see me," he promised with a gentle squeeze of her hands. "Tessa, the last thing I want is to lose you like that. When you started to freak out, it scared me far more than collecting radioactive evidence. I've seen divers panic, and it doesn't always end well."

She looked at their hands, her smaller ones clasped within his larger palms and fingers. Calluses roughened his fingertips, and tiny scars laced his knuckles and palms. She ran her fingers over the marks as she thought about what he'd said.

"You're right." She shook her head a little. "It was stupid to go diving today. I pretended it wasn't a problem, but I lied to myself."

"It wasn't stupid. Reckless, maybe, but not stupid. You're trying to do your job, and you got scared." A smile touched his lips. "Whatever you've been learning to handle, it worked." The smile faded. "It worked today, Tessa. You can't go on deep dives like that until the problem is gone."

"If Donald finds out, he won't assign me to any photo dives." Tessa closed her eyes, saw nothing but her uncle's worried face, then opened them again. "I don't live for it the way you do, but I do love finding new ways to frame reef life. My other job is to document how bleaching hits a reef and whether or not it recovers. Some manage it to reclaim areas, some don't."

"Preaching to the choir, sister," he said. "That doesn't change the fact that if you have panic attacks underwater, it could kill you. I don't want that to happen. I like you alive."

His half-hearted smile almost broke her heart.

"I'm sorry I scared you," she whispered around a sudden frog in her throat. "For what it's worth, I scared myself a lot more."

Their server appeared with a tray that contained

two wide bowls of steaming chimole. At first glance, it was a surprise to see the stew was black, but the presentation of the boiled chicken pieces with tomatoes and onions centered around sliced boiled eggs was as inviting as the intricate aroma of the seasonings, only some of which she could identify. A bowl of white rice and a plate of fresh, warm corn tortillas were set between Ethan's and her dishes, next to the candle. Their server produced tall bottles of the house favorite beer, one for each.

"Enjoy," the server told them. "You will be able to wave at me through the window, should you need anything before I come back."

Tessa thanked their server and tried not to think about the conversation she and Ethan had been having about her diving situation. When she said earlier that she was working with an instructor, she'd been telling the truth. The man was doing all he could think of to help with the semi-random panic attacks when she was diving.

"We don't have more dives planned for this trip," Ethan told her. "If we had, I wouldn't have allowed you to go."

"I wouldn't, either." Eye contact would have helped, but she wasn't so sure she spoke the truth. "That's not a position I'll ever put you in again."

She sipped at her stew, at first to avoid speaking, and then because it was a fabulous dish. The light lager added a crisp note to the recado flavoring, which also gave the dish its distinctive black coloration.

"I have good news," Ethan said as he smiled and handed her a napkin to catch a dribble that tickled at her chin. "The day after tomorrow, we're going to have a small sub to take to the bottom. It's allowed up to four passengers, but there'll only be three. Since it's not a dive per se, I thought maybe you'd like to go with us. You can take your camera and get footage of anything we find."

A chill trickled through her body. "Will we be exposed if we get too close to some of that material?"

"Unlikely. We're not lifting anything out. Jake made clear that the sub can only pick up a few things. Once we find ground zero for the debris, we'll mark it for the military to clean."

Tessa held a spoonful of broth halfway to her mouth. "So we might find something, but you don't know what or how much?"

Ethan snorted. "That's the sum of it. Any new information is worthwhile, especially if we confirm the site as a dumping ground."

Tessa nodded and worked on her stew. She

wanted to be as comfortable around the evidence as Ethan, but the images she'd seen and stories of acute radiation poisoning terrified her. Cancer patients she'd know had gotten cancer from the radiation used to treat their first cancers.

"I'm scared to go," she blurted out. "Maybe if I understood nuclear science, it wouldn't be so frightening." It wasn't that she was ignorant, but that she had excelled at the fine arts more than the advanced sciences when she was in school. "I want to understand this stuff, but it's not how my brain works."

Ethan cocked his head and smiled. "It's okay, really. We all have strengths and weaknesses. I couldn't write a great book if my life depended on it, but I can teach you how to dive, fight, and tie knots. Honestly, I only understand what I need to work this case. That's why we have Bonnie and Clyde. They break the science down so we can use it in our investigations."

"I need to walk," Tessa said as she put her spoon down. "This food is good, really it is, but I can't eat."

Ethan paid their bill and led her down to the beach. The moment they reached the sand, she removed her sandals. Her toes sank in, and she wiggled them in contentment. Without saying anything, she made her way to the water and let it wash over her feet. The surf was gentle, as the coast was protected by a series of atolls and caves that broke up the larger waves.

Ethan removed his shoes and rolled up his slacks to walk with her. He gave her time to collect herself. It meant everything just to have him there, next to her.

"I'm sorry," she eventually said. "I didn't mean to ruin dinner."

"Hey, you've had a difficult day." He stepped in front of her, and she looked up. "You're doing your best in a situation you didn't ask for. It's not ideal, but I'm glad you're here."

"I am, too."

She leaned her forehead into his chest. This assignment was supposed to be exciting and reunite her with Ethan. Well, that was how she had seen it. Donald wanted more, a headline that would generate readership while keeping true to the magazine's ethos of preserving the environment.

"We could talk about something fun," Ethan suggested. "Name something."

Tessa straightened and felt a smile beam right out of her.

"I want to know everything you ever learned about the *Dragon's Rogue*," she told him. "You said there's an old woman who has records that actually go back that far in time?"

Ethan laughed. "Yes, and you'd love her. We learned to call her 'Aunt Esme' while working that trafficking case a few weeks ago. There was a young woman we helped during that case. She ended up moving in with Esme in exchange for helping her to preserve the files before they disintegrate."

"And she had information about the ship?"

"Yeah. There was an old log entry that led us to the location of the cannonball and silver coins we found." He found her hand and gave it a squeeze. "If we're lucky, there may be more pages in that house somewhere."

"That's terrific!"

Tessa considered telling him about the contact she had in Charleston. As of his last email, the man who Tessa was paying to search records believed he was close to what he was looking for. No, she'd wait until she had confirmation before breathing a word to Ethan.

She glanced up and caught him staring at her. "What?"

He smoothed her hair away from her face and then traced his finger down her jawline. His callused fingertip felt like a thousand hot little stars shooting off along the trail. She took a shuddering breath and reached up to pull him close to her face. It had been too long since they were this close, without people everywhere.

Their kiss was brought in with an explosion. They both whirled to see orange flames shoot into the sky from outside the restaurant. Tessa wanted to believe it was some kind of fireworks display, but she knew better, and so did Ethan. He immediately launched into a sprint while holding onto her hand.

Without warning, he flung her to the ground. She was ready to yell at him, but he signed at her to be quiet. A rifle's loud crack echoed down the beach and out to sea. The next crack sent a bullet into the sand near her elbow. Ethan pointed to a patch of tall grass. She nodded and started a long, slow crawl toward the spot where he'd pointed.

More shots rang through the night, but they ended as Ethan got close to the restaurant's walkway. People shouted from inside the building, and a man barreled out with a shotgun.

By the time the chaos died down, the shooter had fled.

16

THE INVESTIGATION into the shooting and explosions ran late into the night and required several agencies' involvement, no thanks to the potential link to our investigation.

Anders Tozin showed up within twenty minutes. I'd just finished my statement to the police and was leaning against the trunk of one of the squad cars. Tessa was giving her account inside the restaurant where they were cleaning glass from a window that was shattered by the concussion and debris from the car bomb. The owners and employees were lucky that the damage wasn't worse.

"Are you injured?" Tozin asked as soon as he found me.

"Tessa and I are fine." I shook his hand. "Thank you for coming."

"Do you think the person who caused the, er, situation is responsible for the attack tonight?"

Tozin caught himself from saying exactly what we were investigating. God knew we didn't need word getting out about the radiation at the Hole. Tourists were clamoring for access, and I heard at least six dive boats were turned away while we were inspecting the underwater wall.

"Yeah, it could be the perp," I conceded after a little thought. "The question is how would they know who and where to attack?"

Tessa left the restaurant, and I waved her over.

"Mr. Tozin, this is Tessa Bleu. She's our embedded journalist during this investigation. Tessa, Anders Tozin. He's our liaison with the Belize Government."

"Pleasure to meet you," Tozin said. "And please, call me 'Anders.' I'm not one for formality, especially after the bullets fly."

They shook hands, and a wry smile touched Tessa's face. "Violence is an occupational hazard around this guy." She jabbed her thumb at me. "I'm glad your government is providing so much support."

"It's our mission to keep the tourist industry profitable," Anders told us. "I know you understand this, but it cannot be stressed enough. Tourism is our bread and butter, as they say."

Tessa leaned against the car with me. I wanted to put my arm around her, but I held back. If our perp truly was watching us, they already had us pegged as being together. If not, well, there might still be a chance to keep her safe.

It was the middle of the night by the time we got back to the villa. One of the local police gave us a ride back since our Audi had gone up like an M80 in a mailbox. While we were at the scene, a message came in from Diane. Our flight to Tampa would take off mid-morning. The CEO of MediWaste, Devon Cole, was in town, and Diane would arrange the meeting.

"You're going, too," I told Tessa as we were driven to the villa in the back seat of a Belize City police vehicle.

"Why aren't we taking your plane?" she wanted to know. "Wouldn't it have been easier?"

"It would if Lamarr and Sylvia were available to fly it." I leaned my head against the back of the seat. "They're staying to look out for Bonnie, Clyde, and Warner. Whoever went after us could go after them."

I looked over at Tessa. Sand still clung to her dress and calves. She'd crossed her arms and leaned her head against the car window. If Farr hadn't sent her on this assignment, she wouldn't have been in danger. Again.

"You should go home," I suggested in a gentle tone. "It wasn't fair for Admiral Farr to push you on this case."

She straightened and narrowed her eyes at me. "I'm a big girl, Ethan. If I didn't want to come to Belize, I wouldn't have. Uncle Donald has never forced me to do anything."

Maybe not, but he sure as hell manipulated her. Even though I damned near worshipped the man, his constant interference whenever Tessa was around rubbed me the wrong way.

"Look, I'm glad he got me assigned to the case when you found that dead gangster," I continued, "but since then, he's poked his nose in everything you're involved in when I see you."

She glanced up at the cop who was driving us. We were near the villa, so the ride was almost over.

"We'll talk when we get inside," she told me. She smiled at our captive audience. "I'm sure you're tired of hearing us bicker."

The officer waved it off while keeping his eyes on

the road. "Don't worry. I've heard worse. You aren't kicking my seat and calling me names."

"Fair enough," I laughed.

I recognized two unmarked government cars parked on the street outside of the villa as our officer pulled into the gated courtyard. It was nice to work with a responsive administration for once.

Birn met us in the garage. The front entrance was too open for my taste and had been from the start. I hit the button to close the door Birn had opened to let us in.

"Get everyone in the conference room," I told him. "This is our guy, and we need to know how he tracked us. I'll be there in fifteen. I have a call to make."

"It's two in the morning..."

"Don't care," I snapped. "Look, someone came after Tessa and me. There's a leak because nobody is supposed to know we're here on this case."

Birn nodded with a frown. "We'll be there." He marched back into the house.

"That was harsh," Tessa said. "What's a meeting going to do in the middle of the night?"

I pinched the bridge of my nose. She was right. My team was used to me addressing them better than that. Birn hadn't done anything, and he'd asked a valid question.

"If our target knew we were at that beach, it's a safe bet that he knows we are here, in this house," I said in a calmer voice. "We don't know jack. I'm sick of waiting around for answers."

Tessa put her hand on my arm. "Breathe. I'm okay. I'll go sit in on the meeting, no camera. Go make your call."

"Okay. Let's get busy."

Tessa laughed as I heard the words leave my mouth.

"Maybe, if you're lucky." She snorted. "I think we both need caffeine. I'll go make coffee."

She went inside. I stayed in the garage and closed the door to the house for a little privacy and pulled up Farr's number. My anger surged, but it felt wrong to call a retired Fleet Admiral and Joint Chief to dress him down. I shook my head. Thinking like that would get me into trouble. Dammit, Farr.

It was three in the morning in New York, and Farr's phone rang five times before he picked up.

"What's wrong, Ethan?" he answered in a groggy voice. "You don't do social calls in the middle of the night."

"No, sir, I don't." My jaw tightened. "Tessa shouldn't be here. We got shot at tonight."

"That means you're getting close to figuring out who dumped the materials." Farr sounded more awake. "You're making progress on the case, and you kept Tessa from getting hurt."

"Why are you so intent on putting her in danger?" I demanded. "Last time, you couldn't protect her enough. Did she piss you off? Did I?"

Something rustled in the background from his end.

"I assigned my best photojournalist to document the investigation of a threat to the second largest barrier reef in the world." His words felt like knives. "Your job is to protect her while you go after the son of a bitch who dumped that waste."

I stilled. That information was close to the vest, and Tessa had promised not to share it with anyone, not even her late dad's best friend. Farr had eyes everywhere.

"Any chance you know who's involved?" I kept my tone casual, not that my sudden calm would fool anyone. "We'll take any leads you might have."

"Ethan, there are some things I am not to discuss, even now. We're talking about classified information."

"Oh, come on!" I burst out. "With all due respect, sir, you're bullshitting me."

"Watch your step, son," Farr growled. That voice still sent chills down my spine. "You're lucky I helped get Header involved. You two were among the best SEALs I worked with, but that doesn't give you carte blanche."

I clenched my teeth. Retirement apparently meant next to nothing for one of the most powerful men in the Navy.

"Understood. Sir."

"That said, Ethan, I do have something for you. It was going to wait until morning." Farr's voice seemed to reverberate as if he had gone into a small room. "Scuttlebutt is that there has been radioactive medical waste found at other sites. There's no official report, mind you, just rumors." He cleared his throat. "Before dumping hot waste into the oceans was made illegal in ninety-three, there was a list of approved sites. What people don't realize is that there was a list of secondary sites that were denied."

"The Great Blue Hole," I mused. "That's on the secondary list, isn't it?"

"Yes. There are a handful of sites in the Caribbean, mostly places that don't have the kind of tourism the Blue Hole has."

"Do you have access to the list?"

Farr laughed. "Remember who you're speaking with. I can get you the list ASAP."

"I appreciate that." I took a breath. "What I don't get is why you insist on having Tessa embedded with our team. She's putting an environmental spin on the story, but we both know it's not about the environment."

"You may not believe it, but she had a great angle on the eco spin for this story, and I'm a thousand percent behind her on it."

"I get it. Radiation, the reef, waste disposal in the ocean," I admitted. "What are you looking to gain by having Tessa cover this story?"

"Environmental awareness, first and foremost." Farr yawned. "Furthermore, your work needs to be recognized. There are people in Congress who barely know you exist, let alone the importance of your work. Your funding is in trouble, Ethan. I'm helping you."

This was the first I heard of funding issues. It'd never been a problem before. I made a mental note to look into it later.

"I suppose having Tessa here gets you the scoop on the story," I said in a flat tone. "And we're the stars for stopping someone from irradiating fragile marine ecosystems."

"Someone who committed murder," Farr added.

"Dare Lemon isn't dead yet," I reminded him. "I know it's coming, but he's still alive, sir."

"By the time the feature goes to print, it'll be murder." Farr's voice brooked no argument. "Show Tessa your best work. Get this traitor and deal with him. And Ethan?"

"Sir?"

"Do not let anything happen to Tessa. If she gets so much as a scratch, it's your ass."

"We'll do our best to protect our embedded journalist, Admiral," I answered as if I was still under his direct command. At that point, I may as well have been. "I will discuss arrangements for increased security with Director Ramsey in the morning."

"You do that."

Farr ended the call, and I was left staring at my phone. Had he changed, or had I?

17

It was the first time all of us were in the villa's meeting room at once. The conference table was packed with people in various states of sleepwear and daytime clothes.

Tessa sat near the head of the table, next to an empty seat. Her dress still had grains of sand caught in the folds near the scarf she wore around her waist. A bruise was forming on her upper arm, and her forearm had a scrape that paramedics treated at the scene. I had saved her life when I pushed her down at the beach, but that didn't make me feel any better about it.

"Is everyone up to date?" I asked as I dropped into the empty chair.

"Wait." Muñoz stood. She wore, of all things, Hello Kitty shorts with an Air Force tank top. Her hair was in a loose braid over her shoulder. This was not a side we got to see of her. The look, however, took none of the edge from her personality. "Before we discuss the case, we need to talk about Miss Bleu."

Tessa straightened in her chair. "What about me, Agent Muñoz?"

"I have nothing against you personally," Muñoz told her and then looked me in the eye. "We work under the radar, and that's how we get things done. If she writes us up in a story, we get attention. If we get attention, we get closer scrutiny." Muñoz frowned at Tessa. "Sometimes, scrutiny gets in the way of justice. We may act within the law, but not everything we do is palatable to John Q. Public."

"What are you suggesting, Sylvia?" I demanded. "Our orders are to deal with it and keep her as safe as possible."

"Send her home." Muñoz spread her hands. "Send Tessa home. It's more than her reporting that's a threat. You're distracted by her being here. Everyone knows you were a thing for a while." She sent an apologetic glance toward Tessa. "Seriously, you're a nice person, and I like you, but it's true.

Ethan has a thing for you, and you for him. It's dangerous. That's why they don't send teams of significant others out in the field together."

"I can't send her home," I said in a quiet tone. "Believe me, I want to, and for all the reasons you just said."

"What?" Tessa blurted out. "I thought we were going to work together."

"We are. It's not that I don't want to, but, well, I don't. Sylvia is right. You could get hurt, and we could get hurt protecting you." I leaned my elbows on the table. "I'm going to tell you something, and we will keep it among this team, and this team only. Understood?"

A series of nods and "yes sirs" came from each side of the table.

"I spoke with Retired Fleet Admiral Donald Farr a few minutes ago. Many of you know his connections to Tessa." Next to me, she shifted in her seat. "I'm sorry, you have to hear this also," I told her.

"I know," she sighed. "It still... It's not comfortable."

"Understandable." I stood. "Farr is the editor-in-chief at the *EcoStar*, therefore Tessa's boss. He also is something of an adopted uncle to her. Her father and Farr were best friends. That's why Tessa is here and not some other reporter. Farr pulled strings. He's retired, but he was also one of the Joint Chiefs of Staff. This man is powerful, and for the most part, I believe in his good intentions toward us."

"What do you mean by 'for the most part'?" Birn asked in a stiff tone.

"I'll get to that, but this is the part every one of you needs to wrap your heads around." Farr would have me for lunch if he found out I was telling them this part of the call. "He wants to use this case to take us mainstream because we're going to look like heroes for stopping a bad guy who is endangering the ocean environment. Furthermore, he claims that he's doing this because our funding is in danger."

"What?"

"Are you kidding me?"

"Oh, my God."

The reactions from around the room were as much as I expected. Even Tessa's jaw dropped. So she hadn't known.

Holm frowned. "They cleared *Bette's* purchase."

I blinked. "Whose?"

Clyde flushed and raised his hand. "Um, the plane. The blue stripe on the side made me think of that song, 'Bette Davis Eyes.' It was stupid, and I said it out loud."

"That's not stupid," Tessa protested. "It's sweet."

Clyde's flush deepened, and he sank deep into his chair while nursing a bottle of Mountain Dew.

Holm rubbed the back of his head. "It got stuck in my head."

"Okay, '*Bette*.'" I didn't hate the potential name for the King Air, to be honest. "Anyway, Robbie, our purchase of *Bette* occurred to me, too. Honestly, I don't know. Maybe Farr has an inside track that we don't, or maybe he has bad intel. Given everything I know about him, though, bad intel isn't likely."

"He never told me anything about funding for MBLIS," Tessa said. Her brow wrinkled, and she frowned. "I guess it makes sense, in a way, but he should've told me."

I nodded. "Agreed."

Warner cleared his throat and stared at a point on the table. "Um, Agent Marston?"

"This isn't school, Warner. Speak."

"I can try to find out if we have money problems. They gave me access to the Pentagon a while back." He fidgeted. "I can still get into the network... but only if you want."

He continued to fidget without looking up, and he tapped his fingers on his chair's armrests.

Someone looked a little guilty. Maybe there *was* more to the kid than it seemed.

"Tread lightly," I warned. "Don't snoop anywhere you aren't supposed to. Try not to leave any trails."

"You want to let him poke around the Pentagon's network?" Muñoz stared at me. "Do you know how much shit that could cause?"

"Yeah, Sylvia, I do, but if Farr is right, then something's coming up. Besides, I told him not to snoop anywhere he's not supposed to. Warner can follow orders. Right?"

"Y-Yes, sir." He nodded so hard I thought he might give himself whiplash. "Absolutely. I'm only going to look at budgets and stuff. It shouldn't be a big deal. Promise."

"Wasn't there another part you wanted to tell us?" Bonnie asked. She looked no sleepier than her caffeinated counterpart.

"Farr reminded me of some history about nuclear waste disposal," I told them. "It's fairly common knowledge that radioactive materials used to be dumped into the ocean. They started in the forties, and it went until ninety-three. There was a list of approved sites where this was allowed."

"I didn't know that," Holm said.

"Okay, maybe not common knowledge, but it's

not a secret." I returned to my seat. "What's available but not advertised is that there was a list of potential sites that were denied. These secondary sites could've been revisited if they ever felt the need. Since the whole thing's been shut down for decades, people haven't worried about it, but according to Farr, there are rumors that this kind of waste has been found at some of the other secondary sites."

The varying levels of shock and disgust around the table reflected how I felt about it as well. Tessa watched with an intensity that I couldn't read.

"If they know about the secondary sites, the culprit could have military or government experience," she pointed out.

"Or they could know how to use Google," Warner suggested. He tapped the edge of the laptop he'd brought to the meeting. "I found it, no problem. Some of these locations are a little vague, but it wouldn't take much to find them."

"Find them," I ordered. "Okay, that's what I got from talking to Farr." They didn't need to know every detail. "Are we all updated on the info from the tag I found on the first dive?"

"We briefed these guys on the MediWaste thing before they went to bed," Warner reported. He beamed like a kid with good news. I hoped it was.

"About an hour ago, we got a hit on that towel you found. So, it has a number on its label. They have to do that now so that nothing gets left behind in surgeries. Anyway, we plugged it into the same system as the tag you found, and it was from a hospital in Orlando."

"Any chance they used MediWaste?" Holm asked as he smothered a yawn.

"Bingo!" Warner's smile got bigger. "Better yet, I found out that they subcontract radioactive waste to Sedin Disposal, also out of Tampa. Both hospitals are MediWaste clients but serviced by Sedin Disposal."

"Do we know anything about this business?" I asked.

Warner looked toward Bonnie, and she gestured for him to go ahead. Interesting. They appeared to be working out a system for the tasks that overlapped their roles. It was good to see Bonnie getting more lab time, now that we weren't relying on her to catch tech forensics that didn't require help from Cyber. She had the skills, but her primary duties were in the lab. Such was the curse of the multi-talented. Diane's decision to add Warner to our team looked more and more solid by the moment.

"Sedin Disposal specializes in radioactive waste,"

Warner said. He started to stand, hovered, and sat back in his chair. "The founders are Tim Sedin and Marci Anderson. They got licensed about two years ago, and they're turning a profit."

"How much profit?" Tessa asked. At two or three sharp looks, she shrugged. "Nobody said I couldn't ask questions. Besides, it's relevant."

Warner pointed at her. "Bingo to the lady in white."

"Off-white. Or ecru." She chuckled. "But I'm being pedantic."

"Fair enough, Miss Bleu." Warner turned his laptop around to show us the screen. "Their profits have jumped way up. Their company has even been featured in *Medical Waste Professionals*, the trade publication. I scanned the article, and it doesn't say where they dispose of their waste."

I met Holm's eye. "Guess we're going to have more interviews in Tampa."

He gave a slow, drowsy nod.

"Well, I think we're done now. See you all in the morning," I announced, then I flinched a little. "Later this morning."

Tessa waited with me as the others left the room. Everyone was so eager to get more shuteye that they cleared out with haste. Although I was ready to pass out myself, I was glad Tessa had stayed.

"Did you call Uncle Donald to make him send me home?" Her tone had a bite to it that did not bode well for me.

"I called to see what the hell is going on." I shrugged. "And maybe to suggest he's being unfair to put you in harm's way for the sake of achieving his objectives."

"How did that work for you?"

"Not well, thank you." A wry laugh got the best of me. "I was properly dressed down for my insubordination."

"I don't doubt it." Her stern look melted into the most gorgeous smile. "I'm sorry this has been such a pain, but I'm not sorry to be here."

She stepped closer. I wanted nothing more than to sweep her off her feet and haul her to my room, but I did not want to behave like an ass. Instead, I held my hands out. If she wanted more, it was her move to make.

"I missed you," she said.

"So I've heard," I answered. "The feeling is mutual."

"I may have gotten that idea." She held out her hands, and I welcomed them into my own. "It might be nice to remember why we miss each other."

I took a deep breath and caught the scent of apples from her hair. She pulled her hands from mine and wrapped her arms around my waist. I encircled her with my own arms and kissed her on the top of her head. Her arms moved up, and she locked her fingers behind my neck and looked up. Our lips met right as my phone buzzed the long, short, short pattern I'd assigned to Diane's number.

"Gotta take that," I mumbled. Tessa nodded but kept her arms around me. God, it'd been so long since we were together. I answered the call. "Yeah?"

"I just got word." Diane sounded no more than half awake. "Dare Lemon passed away half an hour ago. I'm sorry, Ethan."

My stomach tightened. It wasn't like I knew the man personally, but he was one of the few celebrities I remotely cared about, and he meant more to Jake Header.

"Thanks," I muttered.

"There's something else," Diane told me. "I got an email that your flight was moved up to eight in the morning. Get some sleep. You have a long day ahead of you."

"Thanks, boss."

"Think you'll be able to sleep?" Tessa asked. She laid her head on my chest, and my heart pounded as hard as ever. "If you need some help…"

"Oh yeah," I told her. "I need a lot of help getting to sleep tonight."

18

Tessa and I found Holm in the kitchen the next morning. Everyone else had left for the day, even Warner. I'd figured the guy would be up late and sleep in like most gamer types I'd met. It turned out that he played hard and worked hard in his own way.

Tessa went straight for the cappuccino machine, and I went for orange juice. Holm leaned against the counter next to the sink with a smug grin.

"Get any sleep?" he asked.

Tessa's cheeks reddened. "None of your business."

I chose not to answer, which would only encourage Holm to pick on me. The truth was that Tessa and I didn't get much sleep in the past few hours, and that was just fine. I hoped to get another late night once we got back from Florida that evening. It depended on how long it took to handle things in Tampa.

"Where is everyone else?" I asked.

"Bonnie and Clyde took Warner to the lab half an hour ago," Holm informed me. "Sylvia and Lamarr are going to hang out in the neighborhood and take turns guarding them while we're gone."

"You ready to fly commercial?" I laughed at his flinch. "Come on, Tozin should have our clearance through Customs ready."

Before our department got the King Air... Bette, we usually hopped Navy or Air Force flights to avoid commercial airlines. Flying with the military allowed us to remain armed. Neither of us enjoyed stowing our sidearms for the duration of a commercial flight, but it was a necessary evil.

"At least you get to carry your camera," Holm complained to Tessa.

"When I shoot something, it generally lives," she said with an arched brow and a slight grin. She grabbed her camera bag and strolled out to the garage.

We were airborne an hour and a half later. The flight was packed, many who were tourists who'd given up on visiting the Blue Hole. I ended up between Tessa and one of the disappointed tourists, someone who talked the entire time.

"I saw you two got on the plane together," the young woman said. She looked over at Tessa, who'd chosen the window seat and had her camera out once the seatbelt light was off. "Were you in Belize for a vacation?"

"Work," I answered as I unbuckled the lap belt.

"Cool. What do you do?"

I pulled out the dive magazine I'd stashed in the pouch of the seat before me. Tessa couldn't stop a soft snort that muffled a laugh, probably at my discomfort at being questioned. My career wasn't one I advertised, and I liked it that way. People noticed when law enforcement was present.

"This and that," I told the girl. The dive magazine had an article that looked interesting about insulated wetsuits. "It's not that interesting."

She took a look at what I was reading. "You're a diver?"

I sighed. "Yeah."

"Cool. I always wanted to try diving, but I'm scared of swimming in deep water." She smiled at me with her crooked teeth and pushed her glasses up on her nose. "My friends dragged me down here to go on a boat to the Great Blue Hole so they could dive it, but they closed it to tourists the other day. We explored some of the atolls instead. I waded around on some beaches and got cool shells."

"Sounds like you had fun." I didn't look up from the page I couldn't read with Chatty Cathy blathering in my ear. "You said your friends were with you. Why didn't they seat you together?"

Tessa nudged me with her elbow. I looked over, and she mouthed, "*Be nice.*" I rolled my eyes at her and looked back at my article.

She shrugged with an exaggerated sigh. "I flew on stand by, so I ended up on a different flight." Cathy looked at my magazine again. "The news was talking about that famous diver who died last night. Did you hear?"

I swallowed and nodded. That was not something I wished to discuss with an overcurious stranger.

"It's really sad, and they won't say why, just that he got sick at the Great Blue Hole." She pulled her phone out of her bag and opened a browser. "I got the wifi package," she explained as she scrolled. "Here. Darrel 'Dare' Lemon. That's his name. There are lots of theories about how he got sick."

"I'm sure." I turned to the next page in my magazine. "Sometimes, that happens."

"He and his wife dove to the bottom of the Blue Hole," Cathy went on. "Some people on their airplane felt ill after being around him and his wife. Did you know she's in the hospital, too?"

"Is that so? I don't watch the news." Why, oh why hadn't they assigned Holm to our row? He was in the front, lucky bastard. There was no business class on this flight, and I was missing it more than a little at the moment.

"People are trying to figure out what happened," Cathy said in a stage whisper as if she were sharing some great conspiracy. Which wasn't entirely wrong. "They go diving in the Blue Hole, get sick on the airplane, and then the people sitting around them get detained after feeling a little sick. Doesn't that seem strange?"

I laid the magazine on my lap and looked her in the eye.

"Things happen all the time," I said diplomatically. "Don't believe what the media says right after something happens. The reports are almost never accurate. Just wait until they know for sure."

Chatty Cathy turned off her phone and laid it on her lap.

"The authorities will bury the truth," she told me. "I think something poisoned Dare Lemon, and it got spread. If he got it at the Blue Hole, then people should know."

Tessa leaned forward so the girl could see her around me.

"I wouldn't worry about it for now," she said in a light tone. "I wouldn't be surprised if some great teams are looking for answers as we speak."

Cathy narrowed her eyes at Tessa and then leaned back in her seat. She picked up her phone and dove into reading whatever it was she read. For the rest of the flight, she kept her nose in her own business, but what she'd said lodged in my mind. The public was getting closer to the truth, and we needed to get an answer before the media exploded with it. At best, we had until our medical examiner, Ethel Dumas, filed her autopsy report on Lemon.

I, too, had wifi on the plane. After ensuring my nosy seat neighbor wasn't watching, I sent Ethel an email via our encrypted service.

How long can you put off filing the report re Lemon's autopsy?

Ethel's reply came within a minute.

Funny thing. I have two or three stiffs ahead of Lemon. Guess it'll be tomorrow before his autopsy.

Writeup depends on findings. Get your shit together within three days. Best I can do.

I showed the exchange to Tessa.

"Better work fast," she told me.

No kidding. I tried to pay attention to the article I was reading, now that Cathy decided to leave me alone, but I kept thinking about how and why someone would dump concentrated medical waste in sites on an old list. Nobody could explain to me how those pieces got more radioactive than they ever should be. Farr's news about the finds in other secondary dumping sites complicated everything. How would a disposal crew from Florida manage to dump radioactive materials around the Caribbean without being detected?

We landed in Tampa a little over two hours after we took off in Belize. I didn't visit the Gulf side of Florida that often, but it wasn't for lack of charm. Tampa had a slower pace than Miami, and the Gulf breeze chased off some of the oppressive heat the day we were there.

Holm picked up the keys for the navy-blue Toyota Camry we had for the day. "You and Tessa ride in the back," he said with a wink. "Besides, I know Tampa better than you."

This was true. Holm's family lived south of the

city, and he made the drive up two or three times a year, depending on how our caseload looked.

"Why do you always have to drive?" Tessa asked me as she got in the car.

"Yeah, Ethan, why do you drive all the time?" Holm tossed back at me with a laugh. "I drive just as well as you."

"That's a story that's between Robbie and me," I told her. Nobody needed to know that pile of embarrassment. It'd ruin my image. "Let's go," I grumped.

19

MEDIWASTE REMOVAL SERVICES occupied the first two floors of a mid-rise building downtown, which wasn't far from the airport. The lobby was three stories tall with a wall along the front that had a waterfall made from stone and various tropical flora. Its location next to the building's glass wall seemed to offset some of the heat transferred from the sunlight.

The receptionist's desk at the far end of the lobby was cut from the same white and gold marble as the floor so that it seemed to rise up from the ground. A middle-aged woman in a floral blouse and overly large glasses stood up from her seat behind the desk to greet us.

"We've been expecting you," she said in a

welcoming tone. "Mr. Cole cleared his morning schedule so he can accommodate you in whatever way you need."

I glanced at Holm. This was a change. Most executives at the center of investigations lawyered up faster than I could show my badge.

"Thank you," I ventured. "I'm—"

"We know who you are," she said through a smile. "If you'll follow me, please."

Follow her, we did. She brought us in through a keycard door and led us down a hall that opened into what I'd call a mid-sized cubicle farm. Large enough to fit a bunch of people, but not so large that it was overbearing or loud. We turned down a corridor and then into a small reception area with a hardwood desk.

"Mr. Ames, these folks are here to see Mr. Cole," she told the young man at the desk. "I'm going back to the front unless there's something you need."

The twenty-something straightened his suit jacket and stood. He looked down his nose at the receptionist.

"Mr. Cole wants his lunch delivered today," Ames ordered. His sharp tone didn't make the receptionist flinch, but it wasn't kind. "I need a coffee, black, with a shot of espresso."

"Yes, sir." With that, she scurried away.

"Are you Devon Cole's secretary?" I asked with casual indifference. Some jackasses need to be knocked down a peg or three.

"I am his aide," Ames snapped. "I'm the one who has to reschedule the meetings he canceled this morning."

"Is that so?" I went over to his desk and loomed. "If this is an inconvenience, we could come back with a warrant and discuss this on a busier day."

That shut him up nicely.

Ames leaned over, picked up the phone, and dialed a number. He waited, and then said, "Yes, they're here. Yes, sir." He met my gaze with his own icy blue stare but couldn't maintain it and looked away. "You may go in."

"Thank you." I smiled and resisted the urge to flick his nose. "Pleasure dealing with you."

Devon Cole's office was simple yet elegant. In other words, there wasn't much character. The furniture was typical of an executive office, with black leather-upholstered seats with nailhead trim for visitors on the near side of his desk, and a larger version of the chair behind it.

Cole stood and walked around the desk to meet us. He was shorter than me by a good five inches or so, but the charisma that oozed from his every move-ment made the height difference a non-issue.

"Special Agents Marston and Holm, I take it?" He shook our hands and then turned to Tessa. "And you are?"

"My name is Tessa Bleu. I'm an observer on the case."

"I'm not sure what that means, but welcome." He shook her hand with a little less enthusiasm and then returned to his seat. There were two chairs on our side of the desk, and he gestured toward a pair of seats along the wall.

"Feel free to bring an extra chair over," he offered. "Now, what can I do for you?"

"Your company has been linked to some medical waste that was illegally dumped in a fragile ecosys-tem," I began. I noticed Tessa glance at me. So? I liked the way she'd put it. "It contributed to the death of a person who was exposed."

"That's unfortunate." Cole steepled his hands. "Would this be referring to the incident at the Great Blue Hole in Belize?"

I couldn't say I was surprised he'd figured out that part. "It would." I handed him a printout Clyde had left for me that morning. "This sheet has photos of the items, a tag and a towel, as well as the serial numbers that linked them to two hospitals in Florida."

Cole accepted the page and frowned at it. He opened a laptop and typed in some of the information. His brow furrowed as he clicked and typed for a few minutes.

"Both of these were covered by our subcontractors, Sedin Disposal, but I don't think they've been to Belize on business for us," he told us. "We do handle some radioactive waste in the Caribbean area, but... Wait."

He did some more searching and ultimately shook his head.

"My director of operations, Simon Kelley, can help you with this better than I," he finally said. "I'll call him in if you don't mind waiting for a few minutes. He likes to oversee transport personally, and that's a few blocks away."

"We have the time," I answered. Something about the name rang a bell, but I couldn't put my finger on why.

Cole made the call and hung up. "He's on the way. My secretary can send for some coffee if you'd like."

I stifled a laugh. Not a secretary, eh, Ames? I met Tessa's look and then to Holm.

"You know, we did just get off the plane from Belize," I told him. "But I don't want to bother, you know? His aide is already busy getting his coffee and your lunch."

Cole pinched the bridge of his nose. "Ames is my nephew, and he is a first-rate ass," he confessed. "I'm trying not to fire him, but my sister will give me a hard time if I do."

"I need to stretch my legs," Holm said with a grin. "How about I take that nephew to help me get some lunch while you all talk? Maybe dessert too?"

"As it doesn't involve poor Martha from upfront," Cole answered. "I'll make sure he doesn't try to pass it off on anyone else."

Cole and Holm went out to handle that, and I looked over to Tessa. A slight frown met my gaze.

"What?" I asked.

"I figured you two would stick together for the interviewing," she told me. "Two sets of eyes and ears are better than one."

I shrugged. "We have two sets." I pointed to her and then back at myself. "Seriously, Tessa, we talk with people separately more often than you'd think. We try to go in together, but some situations aren't as risky as others."

"Like here, in the office of a CEO who might be

behind the death of an internationally known diver?"

"I'm not feeling it," I told her. "I want to look at this subcontractor."

Cole returned and left the office door open behind him.

"That should be interesting," he said as he went to his chair. When he sat, he seemed at least my height. Nice chair. "Your partner charmed his way into getting Nick off his lazy butt and out the door with him." He chuckled. "Okay, he charmed, and I threatened."

I nodded. "While we wait for your DOO... What's his name again?"

"Simon Kelley. He's been with my company for twelve years, and he has done more for us than I could have imagined." Cole folded his hands on the desk and leaned forward. "Don't tell him I told you this, but without him, MediWaste would've folded before I took over. He was the single best hire my dad ever made."

A sharp rap at the office door announced Simon Kelley's arrival. He wore jeans, work boots, and a short-sleeved shirt with the MediWaste stylized font logo over the pocket area. He was close to my height, heavily muscled in the arms, and had deep lines that spoke of a life lived hard. I guessed him to be over fifty years old.

"Simon, these are Special Agents Marston and Bleu."

"Observer, please," Tessa reminded with a generous smile. "And Special Agent Holm will be back soon."

Kelley walked to Cole's desk, crossed his arms, and nodded. "Sir. Ma'am. How can I help you?"

When he crossed his arms, the short sleeve slid up on the arm nearest me and revealed some ink.

"Is that a bone frog, Mr. Kelley?" I asked with genuine interest.

He uncrossed his arms and pulled the sleeve the rest of the way up. The tattoo started on his bicep and wrapped up over his shoulder. It was the familiar style of a frog skeleton climbing his arm, and this variation had a scuba tank on its back. I got to my feet and held out my hand.

"My partner and I were SEALs for twelve years," I told him.

Kelley's severe features softened. "Hoo-Yah." He pumped my hand with a grip that would've damned near crushed another person's hand. "Your partner seems a little, no offense, ma'am, but a little feminine to have been a SEAL."

"Oh no, not me," Tessa protested. "His partner's out getting lunch with Mr. Cole's nephew."

Kelley cocked an eyebrow at Cole, and Cole spread his hands.

"Special Agent Holm wouldn't take 'no' for an answer." His smile faded to exasperation. "They saw Nick ordering Martha around. That poor woman is so scared of that little shit that I'm terrified she'll quit."

"Fire his ass," Kelley said bluntly. "Tell Lisa *I* threatened to quit."

Cole leaned back in his chair and stared at the ceiling for a moment. He collected himself and took on the look of a confident CEO once again.

"You caught me in the middle of family drama, Agent Marston. My apologies."

I chose not to tell him how entertaining I found it to see a multi-millionaire dealing with the same shit everyone else did.

"Not a problem, Mr. Cole." I turned to Kelley. "We're here to ask about your subcontractor, Sedin Disposal."

"They handle radioactive waste disposal," Kelley told us. "I imagine you already knew that part."

He grabbed Holm's chair and turned it so that his back was to the wall, and he faced both us and

Cole's desk. Before I sat, I moved my chair, so I could look at him straight on, and Tessa followed suit.

"We did," I said. "We're interested in knowing where they travel to do this work."

"They go to the client locations, collect the waste, and then move on." Kelley leaned forward and put his elbows on his knees. "For part of the week, they work here, between Tampa and Orlando. Over the past year, we helped them get licensed to do collections throughout the Caribbean. Some of those islands don't have great access to these kinds of resources. We provide it through Sedin."

"Do you have clients in Belize?"

Kelley sat up. "Funny you should mention that. We picked up a new client about, oh, three months ago. They're in Belize City."

Cole straightened. "I didn't know that."

"It's in the reports. You got a lot going on, boss."

"When's the last time Sedin Disposal went to Belize?" I asked.

Kelley pulled a phone out of its belt holster and tapped at it a few times.

"Looks like five days ago," he said as he continued to scroll through his phone. He stopped and looked up. "They flew out the next morning on their plane to make the island rounds. It's a Merlin III."

The office door banged open with no warning. Kelley dropped to a knee on the ground, and I stood. Tessa jumped back in her chair, but whether from the sudden opening of the door or Kelley's and my reactions, I couldn't guess.

"Food," Holm announced as he carried in greasy paper bags.

Nick Ames trailed in his wake. Sweat stained through his finely tailored suit at the armpits and upper back, and his coiffed hair now lay flat against his skull. He was laden with two drink caddies, one for soda and one for coffee, another greasy bag, and a white plastic bag with foam containers. The boy set everything on a side table Holm had chosen for their bounty, and then he stalked over to Cole.

"Uncle Devon, this man is insane," Ames complained. "He took me to a food truck and made me carry this... this offal back in through the building and past everyone in the office."

Cole gave his nephew a blank look. "And your point is?"

Ames sputtered. "It was undignified! I'll hear about it for weeks."

"I don't suppose Mrs. Hastings ever feels that

way when you make her run *your* errands." Cole crossed his arms and leaned back in his chair. "We'll take this up later. Your day is over. Go home, take a shower, and speak to your mother."

Ames marched out of the office and slammed the door behind him. Kelley burst into a hearty laugh. What I saw as hard eyes earlier now looked alive and highly amused.

"About time you dressed that kid down, boss," he told Cole.

Cole groaned. "I am going to hear about it before the end of the hour." He cleared his throat. "Thank you, Agent Holm. I don't know how you motivated that boy to follow your instructions, but I do appreciate it."

"I have nieces and nephews, Mr. Cole. I've had practice."

"And more than a few years in the SEALs, I hear," Kelley laughed. "Hoo-Yah, brother. Simon Kelley, SEAL Team Five."

"Robbie Holm. My partner and I were SEAL Team Eight." They shook hands. "Pleasure, sir." Holm went to get another chair and stopped. "Wait, I've heard of you. Ethan, remember the stories about the guy who took out that boatful of smugglers before they could get those guns to ground?"

"What?" Tessa looked from Holm to me, and then to Kelley. "Alone?"

The details came back to me, and I stared at Kelley. No wonder his name rang a bell. "I heard there were ten targets on that boat, all armed. Was that you?"

"Well, damn, it's not something I tell a lot of people," Kelley scoffed.

"Simon?" Cole looked at Kelley as if meeting him for the first time.

"Yeah, that was me." He cleared his throat. "It was over thirty years ago." Cole shook his head, and Tessa shrugged. "There was an operation to stop gun runners from arming terrorists. We landed on a small island after we got intel that a plane was flying guns and all sorts of bad crap into a little spot there. Somebody paid somebody else off, you know the drill."

"Yeah," I muttered. "The story of everywhere."

Kelley pointed at me. "See? You understand. So, a couple of guys and I got separated from the platoon while the smugglers moved the containers to their boat. Might've had something to do with the fact that Americans were not supposed to be there and us having to keep to cover, but I don't know anything about that."

"Hold on." Tess put a hand out. "Are you saying you were involved with military action on foreign soil without that nation's permission?"

"Who are you again?" he asked.

"I'm an observer on this investigation," she firmly told him.

"Then observe when I repeat that I didn't know anything about that." He softened the harsh words with a charming smile. "It was decades ago, and investigations came and went."

I looked at Tessa. Her jaw was tight and body rigid in her seat.

"Hey, he didn't mean anything," I told her. "He's old guard telling a story."

"And I asked a perfectly reasonable question."

"You're right, Miss Bleu." Kelley stood up and walked over. He got down on a knee so that he didn't hover over her. "I apologize." He smiled. "Hey, I remember you. We met a few years ago at a Memorial Day event. Admiral Farr's your uncle, isn't he?"

She relaxed a little. "Honorary. He served with my father, Dean Hawkins. They were like brothers."

"Not Hawkins?" Kelly reeled back as if looking at royalty.

"You heard of him?" she asked.

"Hell yeah. SEAL Team Eight, like you fellas. Did you know him?"

"He was our CO for a while," Holm told him. "The Hawk was one of a kind."

"I'll be damned." Kelley turned to Cole, who was watching this unfold with bemusement. "I never met Hawkins or Farr, but I sure as hell looked up to them." He nodded to Tessa. "Pardon. *Still* look up to Admiral Farr, Miss. He's a patriot through and through."

"That he is," she agreed. "Were you going to finish your story, Mr. Kelley?"

"There are some details that aren't fit for some of this audience," he told us. "The gist is that I barely made it aboard the targets' boat. The other guys weren't fast enough because that vessel was fast. I neutralized the targets. There were only six, but they were more than enough. Some of the stories had me taking out fifteen or twenty. That's bullshit, but if young sailors wanna exaggerate the truth, that's not my problem."

"I had no idea, Simon," Cole said.

"Like I say, I don't exactly advertise," Kelley explained. "Civilians like the idea of a competent military more than the reality."

"Truth," Holm said in a low voice.

"Gentlemen, this was an educational experience." Cole walked around to the front of the desk. "And lady, of course. I'm afraid that I'm out of time. Simon, if you don't mind, go ahead and walk them out and answer any other questions they may have."

"Thank you for your time," I said to Cole. "And, uh, good luck dealing with your sister."

"Don't remind me." Cole shook his head with a wry laugh. "I hope you catch your man and that this nightmare is over quickly."

"Likewise."

Kelley took us out through unoccupied offices and cubicle farms toward the back of the first floor. On the way, we stopped in an empty office. He closed the door.

"I assume you have more questions," he ventured. "Sedin Disposal and MediWaste have been working together for a while, so I've gotten to know them fairly well."

"We need a schedule of when and where they've worked in the past year," I told him. "Locations, transport, where they took the waste, all that."

"Of course. I'll have all that sent over to your office, but I can tell you now is that they take the waste to special landfills that allow the materials.

Everything is very regulated, so whatever they're doing, it's clever."

"What do you know about the owners at Sedin?" Tessa asked.

That was my next question, as well. We were trying to keep Tessa in observational mode, but I didn't begrudge her asking questions.

"Tim and Marci." He crossed his arms. "Until today, I would've said they're good people. They've worked with tough clients and tougher transport regs, and they never go over budget."

"What's the procedure?"

"No matter where they go to pick up the waste, they make sure it's sealed and then bring it to a land-fill southeast of Tampa. It's expensive and only licensed operators are allowed to access it."

"If some of that material goes missing along the way, it gets a lot less expensive," Holm suggested.

"Fact," Kelley affirmed. "If there's a motive, I'd say Sedin is dumping on his way to or from Caribbean locations to save money and pocketing the difference."

"He has to know he'd get caught," Tessa pointed out. "There are so many documentable steps that it'd be difficult to find the cracks to slip through."

"Tim Sedin is a savvy character," Kelley said. "If

there are cracks, he'll find them. The guy is smart as they come. Too bad he isn't using those smarts for the right reasons."

I held up a palm. "Ease up. We don't know for a fact that it's either of the Sedin Disposal owners. What we have is circumstantial evidence, at best."

"Well, that's who I'm betting on." Kelley opened the office door. "The partner, Marci Anderson, she's naïve, trusts everything Sedin says. That woman is innocent as the day she was born." He gestured for us to leave the room. "I'll be sure to get you that information, Agent Marston."

Holm and I left him our cards as he showed us out the side door. When we got out to the car, Holm got a surprise.

"I... I can't find the keys." He patted his pockets and checked the ground around the car. "I had them a few minutes ago."

I calmly walked to the driver's side door and held up the key fob. With a couple of pushes of the unlock button, Tessa and I got into the front. Holm glared.

"How?"

"You sure you want to know?" Tessa teased.

"No." Holm slunk his way to the car. "No, because right there, I assume you had something to do with it. You know, I don't care which of you lifted the keys. I'll wait for karma." He ducked into the seat behind Tessa. "Oh wait, it already did, Ethan, when you flooded your car. I feel no remorse."

"It's a department car," I reminded him.

"One that is dead. Killed by you."

Tessa looked back and forth between us. She threw her hands up in the air and shook her head.

"You two are as bad as kids. Let's focus." She twisted around to see Holm gloat. "What's the next step?"

I backed the car out and then drove away from the parking garage.

"The next two steps are to get a warrant and get a team to stand by," I answered. "We're going to pay a visit to Sedin Disposal."

20

WE IDLED in the Camry as marked and unmarked police cars gathered down the block. I'd parked across the otherwise quiet street from Sedin Disposal. They had a small building with a rock garden and silver saw palmettos, and the entrance was nestled between a pair of Christmas palms.

"How long does it usually take for warrants to come through?" Tessa asked. The air was going full blast, but the sun was shining on her through the passenger window. "Are we going to be here for long?"

"If we were in Miami, it'd be less than an hour. Diane has federal and local judges she can call at any time of the day." I angled vents in the middle of the dashboard toward Tessa. "She has Tampa contacts, but they aren't as familiar with us. Miami is a bigger port city, so we get most of the action there."

"Too bad she couldn't have called my dad," Holm told us. "Some of his friends are sitting benches."

"Yeah, but we're supposed to be keeping this quiet."

"Which is why it's too bad." Holm laughed. "Mom would just yell at me for not stopping in to say hi."

My phone chimed at the same time as Holm's. I opened the message.

"Warrant's in," Holm announced. "Search and seizure, questioning, the whole potluck."

"It's 'shebang,'" Tessa said with a grin.

"Nah, 'potluck.' You haven't seen the size of my family."

I glanced at Holm. He seemed tired, and the way he'd been hunkering down with his laptop at any given chance was unlike him. I'd been thinking he was talking to a girl online, but I started to wonder if something else was going on. He usually told me everything. I decided I'd ask about it later when Tessa wasn't right there.

"Vests are in the trunk," I told Tessa as we got out of the car. "You get that on and your camera ready. Stay back until we clear the building."

"We've gone over this a hundred times, Ethan," she said in a testy tone. "I'm being careful."

Holm touched Tessa's shoulder and then pulled his hand back. "We'll go over it a hundred and one times if needed." He managed a grin. "If anything happens to you, Farr will have our hides."

Tessa rolled her eyes. "Thanks for worrying about me."

"Any time," Holm said.

We geared up and joined the MBLIS, CGIS, and Tampa police who crowded around the sizzling hood of a marked car half a block down. Locals were predictably assembling on the sidewalks to see what the big deal was. I hated that. Even though we didn't expect anything violent in this situation, there were no guarantees. Hence the vests.

I assigned a contingent to cover the back and side doors in case anyone tried to run. If the raid went the way I figured, the response was overkill, but I had to work with it.

Tessa photographed our short meeting to go over all the units' assignments. She received a few side-eyes, but her presence was largely ignored as she hung back out of the way.

I pulled up the warrant copy on my phone, and Holm and I led the way in. Nobody pulled weapons, but we remained alert as we entered the door between the Christmas palms. The small reception area had six seats in the waiting area, and the reception counter had a sliding window in a wall. A door to the left of the window was locked when I tried it.

A young woman sat on the other side of the window. She played a game on her phone and didn't look up as Holm and I approached the window. I tapped on the glass, and she jumped. She looked up, and her eyes went wide. The name badge on her company polo shirt read, "*Hello, my name is CHAR-ITY, and I'm here to help.*"

"How can I... help?" Her voice was muffled through the window.

"We have a warrant to search the premises and interview employees of Sedin Disposal in the matter of a criminal case." I held up the phone to the glass so she could see. "Are Tim Sedin and Marci Anderson here today?"

"Y-yes," Charity stammered. "I... Let me go get them."

She stood and started walking toward the back. I rapped on the window with my knuckle as Tessa joined the squad in the waiting area. Her camera clicks became part of the background of radio traffic and officers and agents speaking to each other.

"I'm getting them for you," Charity told me.

"You're taking me to them. Unlock the door."

The flustered receptionist came to the door and allowed us into a long corridor with several doors.

"I might get in trouble," she said in a small voice. "You have to have special clearance to go in the back because of what we do. I'm not even allowed in some areas, but we can go to their offices."

"I understand that, miss," I told her with a gentle smile. "Trust me that my partner and I have clearance. We're federal agents."

Charity's hands shook, but she kept her chin up and took us down the corridor. She kept looking back as agents tried locked doors. Our warrant was to go through everything in the building, and yeah, we had people with clearance to investigate the secure areas. We even brought specialists to examine the direct handling of radioactive waste.

Marci Anderson's office was second to last on the right side of the hall. Tim Sedin's was the last. There were only two doors on the left, both metal, with heavy bolts and keycard access.

Charity led us into Anderson's office. The co-owner jumped as we entered. She wore a knee-length summer dress and sat at a white computer desk along the side wall, and a traditional hardwood desk sat to the right of the center of the room. A sofa and recliner took the near-wall on either side of the door.

"Oh my gosh!" She took off her glasses and set them next to her keyboard. "What's going on?"

Charity ran up to her. "They want to search us, Mom. I don't know why."

I glanced at Holm. The relationship was interesting, but nepotism was not uncommon. I walked up to Anderson and showed her the warrant on my phone.

"I'm Special Agent Marston with MBLIS, and this is Special Agent Holm," I told her. "This is a warrant to search your building for evidence of illegal dumping in the Caribbean Sea. A paper copy is on the way."

Anderson's jaw dropped, and she put her hands over her mouth. Her daughter stared at us.

"What's 'embliss'?" the elder Anderson asked in a shaking voice.

"Military Border Liaison Investigative Services," Holm said. "We investigate criminal activity that involves open water across international boundaries."

Anderson blinked. "I've never heard of that."

"Are we being pranked? Please tell us we're being

pranked," Charity begged. "Mom would never, ever do something like that."

"You're not being pranked," Holm told them in an even tone. "And we're here to find out if your mom's company *would* do something like that."

"I certainly would not," Anderson promised. "Where's Tim?"

"Here!" A tall, lanky man with shaggy black hair and a slightly pointed nose strode into the room. He wore a casual suit with the top two buttons undone and tie loose. "Where's this warrant, and why are people flooding my office?"

I showed him the warrant. "Your company is being investigated for illegal dumping of radioactive medical waste in open water." He stumbled backward and recovered himself. "Mr. Sedin, we need to question you two and everyone who works here."

"And we need access to the rest of the building," Holm added.

"Oh, wow." Sedin looked around and found a seat. He dropped down with shocked etched all over his face. "We run a clean business and will cooperate in every way you need."

"With a lawyer's advice," Anderson interjected. "Nobody speaks without our attorney present."

"Call him," I told her. "How many employees do you have?"

"Besides Charity, eleven," Sedin answered. "One is off today, but everyone else is here."

"You only have eleven employees?" I imagined more than that. "How do you process all the waste you take in?"

"The waste is already sealed when we pick it up," Sedin explained. He rubbed his palms on his thighs. "We bring it here to ensure it's up to code for drop off at the landfill we use."

Anderson walked over to him and touched his arm. "Tim, we need to wait for Tony. We know we didn't do anything wrong, but they don't. Don't answer any more questions."

A Tampa officer walked into the office and got my attention. "No weapons of any kind. The building's secure."

We settled Anderson and Sedin in separate rooms as we began going through their offices. The employees in the back were taken to the break room to be interviewed one by one by other MBLIS agents. Tessa followed as Holm and I checked in with agents in other rooms and offices.

"Are we going into the area where they get the waste ready?" Tessa wanted to know.

I turned to her. "You aren't cleared, but you wouldn't want to take your camera even if you did get to go in."

"The waste is sealed, so it's perfectly safe." Sedin walked up to us. "I'll answer questions about how our business works. Your photographer's equipment will be fine. Is she with your agency?"

"Hi, my name is Tessa Bleu." She introduced herself before I had a chance. "I'm an observer documenting the investigation."

"There are some areas we don't allow photography," he told her, but then he turned to me. "Warrant aside, we'll have to discuss with our lawyer before your techs take photos of those areas. It's a security issue."

"So you take security seriously," Holm said. "Why did some of the materials you handled end up in the ocean?"

Sedin shook his head. "That shouldn't ever happen. We monitor the process from beginning to end. Come on, I'll show you the steps we take in here."

He escorted us to the second door on the left side of the hall. His keycard tripped the massive bolt with a clank. Sedin took the three of us plus the two nuclear technicians who were brought in by CGIS. He addressed the technicians.

"Sorry, but I need to see your credentials before you go into the hot room," he told them. "We have suits in the next room." He then turned to us. "You can enter the storage and main floor. The direct waste handle happens in a shielded area, but there are leaded windows so you can see what your techs are looking at."

One of Sedin's employees was escorted in by a MBLIS agent.

"This is Kent. He's one of my techs and can take your guys down to the hot room." He smiled. "I'll show you the rest of the facility."

We started toward the door opposite of where the techs had gone, but Tessa didn't move. The color had drained from her face.

"Tessa?"

"I... I don't know if I can go in there." Her knuckles were white where she clenched the sides of her camera. "It's so close to the radiation."

"Hey, you don't have to," I told her, "but it'd be a loss to your project."

"Excuse me," Sedin said. "I have something that should help." He took three small blue devices from a counter and handed them to each of us. "These will squawk if we encounter loose radiation. They clip onto belts or bag straps, so you don't even need to hold them." He held one out to Tessa. "I promise it's safe."

She accepted the device and clipped it to the camera strap she wore about her neck. Some of the color returned to her cheeks, but her eyes stayed wide. Her fear of radiation was worse than I thought, not that panicking underwater was a mild fear.

"If any of the detectors make so much as a squeak, we'll beat it back here to the control room," Sedin said mostly to Tessa.

For being a suspect, he was awfully cooperative. I wondered what Holm thought, but he was too busy looking at the closed-circuit camera monitors for me to catch his eye.

We followed Sedin onto the floor. The roof was about three stories high, and we were at the end of a space that was maybe the length of a football field. Massive shelving units held yellow and black thirty-gallon drums. A forklift was parked by the stacks with a pallet full of half-size yellow drums plastic wrapped together.

"Each drum is labeled with numbers and barcodes to identify where they came from, who handled them, and final intended destination."

Sedin gestured behind us. "And there's the hot room. This is where I ask you not to photograph anything."

We walked over to the thick windows. I unclipped my little detector and held it close to the window. This was as much for my own peace of mind as Tessa's.

"As you can see, it's quite safe," Sedin promised. He pointed to one end of the hot room. "Small shielded containers go in through there. The techs open the containers and use those machine arms to dump the contents into larger drums. Once the drums are sealed, they go through decontamination at the other end and then to the stacks. The smaller containers go through decontamination and can be reused."

"What happens after they go to the stacks?" Holm asked as we watched a small container opened and then grasped by an operator running the machine that dumped the materials into a fifty-five-gallon drum. "There seems to be a lot of waste over there."

Sedin nodded. "There is. Nobody likes to think about it, but this stuff has to go somewhere. We send it to a landfill that handles the material. The drums are buried, and that's that."

"And everything is tracked from start to finish," I

mused. "So the chain is broken somewhere, and nobody's noticed." Or someone was paid not to notice, or to fudge records. The question was at what point in the chain did that occur?

"Let's get back to the office," I told everyone. "If your attorney is here, we'll have more questions."

Sedin looked to the ground. "There's something you should know before we do that."

"What's that?" I studied his furrowed brow and only sensed frustration.

"Look at MediWaste. We contract solely with them." Sedin snorted. "All our eggs are in that basket, so they have us by the balls. I know I didn't dump anything illegally. There's no way Marci would. Please, look at MediWaste."

"I'll take that under advisement," I promised.

We emerged from the storage area to a flurry of activity. The atmosphere was charged with the rush that followed the discovery of damning evidence against a suspect. A familiar face appeared in the mix.

"Parker, over here," I called out.

CGIS Special Agent Will Parker was also based in Miami, but he traveled. I suspected he might show after my last phone call with Diane.

"Marston," Parker said by way of acknowledgment. "Tim Sedin, you're under arrest for illegal dumping and for the murder of Darrel Lemon." He spun his finger. "Turn around."

"Wait, what?" Sedin gasped. "I thought you were just questioning us to see if there was a link."

"What's going on, Parker?" I demanded. I wasn't about to tell him that I'd been close to arresting Sedin myself. "We're not done with him."

"They found a box of papers next to a shredder in one of the storerooms," Parker told me. "It was a list of times Sedin paid off a landfill worker to look the other way while he only paid to dispose of half the refuse."

"That's ridiculous," Sedin exclaimed. "I never did any of that."

Parker narrowed his eyes. "You better shut your pie hole until you talk to your attorney."

Tessa's camera clicked behind me as Parker handcuffed a shell-shocked Sedin. He looked over and saw the camera, and then Tessa.

"Hey, you're the one who found that body in the cave."

Tessa nodded. "I'm back for a project. Pretend I'm not here."

"Oookay." Parker shrugged. "We found a few

other things to incriminate Mr. Sedin here. You'll get the report."

"This is my investigation." I stepped closer to Parker. "Why are you arresting him?"

"Our holding facilities are better for a multi-agency case." He raised a brow. "Unless you want to deal with the local and state charges that Sedin is also facing?"

"Belize may want to extradite," I said in a mild tone. "I'll give you that MBLIS holding isn't as open as yours, but don't you do anything without talking with us first." I glanced at Sedin and felt that I was missing something, but I couldn't put a finger on what it might be. "I want the transcription of your questioning ASAP."

"Absolutely." Parker narrowed his eyes at Sedin. "There's something else that came up about this guy."

Sedin straightened and looked forward as if expecting what came next.

"What?" I asked.

"He was busted in college for dealing Ritalin and opiates." Parker jiggled the handcuffs. "He spent five years in state prison for it."

"Tim?" Anderson burst out of her office. "They said you're being arrested!"

"I am, and I'm not speaking until Tony meets with me."

Anderson's mouth made a small "o" shape.

"That's not possible," she told us. "He's a good man. Our company has flourished under his direction."

"Tell that to the kid who overdosed on prescription drugs he dealt back in college," Parker snapped. "Now he's dumping poison into the sea. Yeah, it's totally possible."

"Tim?" Tears edged Anderson's eyes. "Tell me—"

"The first part is true, and I paid for it," Sedin told her, "but I never dumped anything in the ocean or sea or anywhere. I've put everything into this and have followed the rules to the letter."

Parker handed Sedin over to another CGIS agent. "I'll meet him at holding in a little while. Let me know if the lawyer gets there first."

"Wow," Holm said in a quiet voice. "He had everything going for him, and he threw it away, for what?"

I shook my head. "He served his time and made good. There might be something to his background check for the clearance, though. We'll see."

Tessa clicked a few more photos and then

lowered her camera. "So that's it? We have the suspect?"

"Maybe."

"What are you thinking, Marston?" Parker asked. "I know that look, and it says you aren't convinced."

"That's because I'm not so sure Sedin is our man. This case isn't over."

21

IT WAS LATE by the time we got back to the villa in Belize City. Everyone was still up even though we had an early morning ahead. Muñoz and Birn would be hanging out with the lab team again while they did more testing on the materials we'd found. Holm, Tessa, and I were going to meet Header for the sub trip to the bottom of the Great Blue Hole.

"We heard about the Sedin arrest," Birn said when we walked in.

Holm went straight to the kitchen and made himself a sandwich. Tessa flopped onto the over-stuffed leather couch in the living room. I took one of the bar stools at the counter by the kitchen.

"Yeah, I don't feel it," I announced.

Holm groaned as he poured a rum and Coke to

go with his sandwich. "Would you drop it?" he begged. "They found solid evidence."

We'd had the argument in the Tampa rental car and then the entire way back to the villa from the airport. Tessa hadn't said one way or another, but I had to think we weren't putting out the best example of world-class law enforcement. Whatever was eating at Holm in his personal life sure as hell was bleeding through.

"We need to take another look at MediWaste," I told him. "Let's talk about it tomorrow." Holm shrugged and tore at his sandwich. "Okay, Robbie, I've had it. What is going on with you?"

"Nothing." He took a swig from his drink as everyone else looked anywhere but at him. "I'm fine."

"You suck at lying," I told him. "Come on, let's go out back and talk."

We went out through a door that let us out beneath the party deck. It was quiet, private. A small patio table with plastic chairs sat like a lone wolf under the deck.

"I'm missing my happy-go-lucky partner." I worked to keep the frustration out of my voice. "He vanished a few days ago and left this grouch behind."

"I'm not a kid, Ethan." He set his empty glass on the table with a thunk.

"Fine. Then tell me what's going on. I thought I was your best friend."

Holm let out a long sigh. "I promised my family to keep it to myself."

Well, I got that part right, at least. "You know I won't say anything. This thing, whatever it is, it's eating you up."

"Yeah." Holm was quiet for a few minutes. We sat in the humid night in silence until he put his elbows on the cheap table and swore under his breath. "My sister disappeared two weeks ago. Nobody will go to the police."

"Shit, I'm sorry." His strange joke about his dad and judges suddenly made sense. "Won't they let you help?"

He shook his head. "She's my baby sister, and they don't want my help." He took a deep breath. "Thing is, she's an adult, and she left a letter saying not to follow her. She wants to be left alone for a while."

"So they can't report her missing."

"Nope. There's nothing to point to her leaving involuntarily. She packed her essentials and took her important papers and everything."

"You could have told me," I said softly. "You don't have to go through this alone."

"I should be able to find her, Ethan, but I can't." His humorless laugh didn't fit the guy I knew. "Every chance I get, I search social media, fingerprints, everything I can access, but nothing. I even went to Warner for help finding a 'friend.' He found a polite way to tell me to kiss his ass."

"He was right to do that."

"I know, and I'm not mad at him." Holm sighed. "I just feel so... so helpless. I don't know if she's in trouble or not, and I hate that."

"I'm sorry that's happening, Robbie. I'm here if you need me."

"Thanks, man." He set the now-mangled sandwich on the table. "I'm gonna sit out here for a while. I need to think."

I got up and squeezed his shoulder. "Give me the word. I'm here."

Holm nodded. It killed me to see him hurting like that, but at least I had the truth. Maybe clearing the air would help down the road.

By the time I went inside, everyone but Tessa and Warner had gone up to hit the rack. Warner was talking photography with her, comparing brands and models of cameras.

"Hey," Tessa called out when she saw me. "How's Robbie?"

"He needs some breathing space, but he'll be okay." I wandered into the kitchen. It was my turn for a drink. I was happy to see some Jack Black Label and was happier to take it neat. "Better get some rest for tomorrow. You sure you'll be okay in the sub, Tessa?"

She nodded. "I don't have a problem with small spaces, and radiation shouldn't be an issue while we're down there." With a sheepish grin, she pulled something out of her bag. "I forgot I had this until we got to the airport. I put it in my pocket, and it didn't trip the metal detector."

I saw what she had and burst out laughing. It was the radiation detector that she'd clipped to her camera strap.

"Technically, we should return it," I told her.

"Well, Sedin gave it to her," Warner pointed out. "He didn't ask for it back. I say she gets to keep it."

"Tessa, if that thing helps, take it with you," I said.

"I planned on it." A yawn overcame her, and she got to her feet. "Night, TJ. Try to get some sleep, huh?"

"Eventually." Warner opened his laptop and

started pecking away at his keyboard. "See you all in the morning."

I walked upstairs with Tessa. As much as I wanted her back in my bed, I saw she was ready to drop.

"Need to be tucked in?" I joked. Sort of.

"Nah." A tired smile touched her lips. "I don't think I'd get much sleep if we tried that."

"Probably not." I kissed the top of her head. "Sleep well."

"You, too. Night, Ethan," she said, and then she pushed the door shut with a soft click.

I retreated to my room down the hall and soon found my way to bed. Sleep was a bastard. I'd start to drift off and then jolt awake with thoughts about the case, Holm, and definitely Tessa. At some point, I did drop off, but I was groggy as hell in the morning when I dragged my feet down the stairs.

"Yo, Marston!"

Warner waved at me from the kitchen. I was starting to think the kid might be some sort of tireless mutant as he brought me a steaming cup of coffee. A few sips later, I didn't care about his sleep habits. He sure as hell knew how to make a pot of joe.

"They're waiting for you in the garage," he told

me. "I was supposed to go 'wake the bear' if you didn't show up by the time the coffee was ready."

"More like a shark," I grumbled. "Or barracuda. Whatever. Thanks, Warner."

"No problemo," he said. "I'm gonna stay here and catch up with stuff from work. They shunt extra stuff over when I'm not busy with your cases."

"Sounds fair. Make you earn your keep."

"Good luck out there. I can't wait to see what you find."

As promised, I found Tessa and Holm in the garage. They were leaning against the car and talking in low tones. They heard me come out of the house and looked up.

"Morning, Ethan," Tessa said with a smile. "Did you get some sleep?"

"I got enough. How're you feeling, Robbie?"

"Better." He had shadows under his eyes, but his mood was improved. I wished I knew how to help my friend, but maybe listening to him was all he'd needed.

The trip out on the catamaran that morning felt different with only the three of us. Header had let me know that we could only bring two passengers on the *Wraith* that morning because the sub took so much space in the back.

It was probably a good thing Muñoz wasn't along, consider the hard time as she gave him. I wasn't sure what to expect as it was. Now that Header's brother had died, we were after a murderer, if it wasn't Sedin. I avoided that topic with Holm. If I were right about it, we'd find out soon enough.

When we rounded the tree line that came before the boathouse property, we found a mid-sized yacht anchored offshore. *Wraith* floated next to her, and a peppy little submersible was being raised onto *Wraith's* open hatch door. Header operated the winch that pulled the tiny craft aboard.

I killed the catamaran's motor and checked my watch. We weren't early. My guess was Header's crew was running late, and that they wouldn't appreciate spectators.

"I strongly suggest you hide the camera bag, Tessa," I told her. "If they haven't seen us yet, they probably will in about—"

Shouts rang out, and I heard Header swear as vile as he ever had. He pointed at me and yelled something. The sudden churning of the yacht's engines and rattle of its anchor chain covered what he said. I did, however, get the message to stay the hell back.

I restarted the catamaran's motor and headed up

to the dock. Yeah, I was dying to know who was working with Header, but it wasn't worth antagonizing anyone.

"I don't know about you," Holm said, "but I didn't see a damned thing."

"I have no idea what you're talking about," Tessa answered with a grin.

"We are such hypocrites," I muttered. "If Sylvia were here, she would've kicked me off this boat and gone over there to take everyone into custody."

"She could've done it, too," Holm told Tessa. "I swear she was born on Krypton or something."

I couldn't help but smile. That was more like the old Holm. We tied the catamaran to the dock and kicked back to wait for Header. The boat just happened to be facing so that we looked out to sea, not because we wanted to peek in the window of an illegal, clandestine operation.

The yacht picked up speed out of the small bay. It was so plain that I wouldn't have been able to pick it out of a marina of similar models if I tried. *Wraith* didn't move for a little while. It looked like the sub was caught on the edge of the hatch or something. I was about ready to start up the catamaran again when the *Wraith* swung around and headed in our direction. He pulled into the boathouse nose-first.

I jumped off the catamaran, then Holm, with Tessa last. Header rounded the corner from the door at the back.

"Not yet," he said. He looked over his shoulder. "I... Gimme a minute."

He stormed back, and before getting all the way back there, he made several expressive signs that ended in one we all recognized.

"Wow," Tessa blurted. She lowered her voice. "He was shouting in ASL."

I stared at her. "Seriously?"

She nodded. "I took it as an elective, and then I kept learning. I'm not great at it, but that business? Yeah, he's arguing with someone."

"Huh."

I looked at Holm. "Something else we don't know, right?"

"You know, it's funny to say that now, but if he does something really stupid..."

"Yeah, I know." I didn't want to admit it was a matter of time before we ended up facing Header from opposite sides. "Another day, okay?"

"For sure."

Header's jaw was clenched tight as he marched over to where we waited on the dock. For a brief moment, it seemed that his green eyes reflected

Tessa's, then they went back to her emerald and his jade. It meant nothing but was unsettling, nevertheless.

"Anything we can do to help?" I ventured.

"With my copilot? Nothing. I swear it was a mistake bringing—" He caught himself and took a deep breath. "Now that my copilot has made himself scarce, it's your turn to help get the Bug unstuck."

"The 'bug'?" Tessa raised an eyebrow.

"The sub," Header explained. "It looks like a bug, so I call it the 'Bug.' Also, it's green. The rest of the crew thinks I'm ridiculous."

"You aren't?" I kidded.

"I am if I can't get it into my boat. I measured three times, but it's refusing to go in."

"Whoa." Holm put both hands out. "Are you saying you haven't actually tried this yet?"

One look at Header's face told me all I needed to know.

"Aw crap, Jake," I complained. "You know I could've found something else."

"Not this quickly," he said with forced brightness. "And I swear I measured three times." He looked over at Tessa. "Good morning, by the way. Hey, where's your camera?"

"I put it away when I didn't see something that wasn't there."

He blinked, and then he got it. "Oh, gotcha. Funny how that happens."

"Let's see if we can help you get the Bug unstuck," I suggested. "We'll have to be able to hoist it up in the open water, anyway."

"True," Holm agreed. He took his sandals off, ran, and jumped off the end of the dock.

"Great." I handed Tessa my phone and the catamaran's key. "Get your camera, and I guess wait. Too bad you can't take photos of a bunch of dumbasses trying to get a tiny sub into the back of one of the world's most advanced boats."

Header laughed and then stopped. He brightened. "Not with her camera, she can't. Hang on." He ran into the boathouse and then back out with a phone. "Do not hand it to either of those guys. They'll probably do something to it. All I want you to do is take some pictures that I can show my copilot."

"Got it," Tessa said.

I shook my head and then looked at Header. He looked back and grinned. We exploded into a sprint at the same time and then jumped as far out as we could. We splashed down within inches of each other. It was a thing we did the few times we had R&R while we served together. I held the record for jumping furthest the most often. Header would say *he* did.

Tessa walked to the end of the dock. It extended beyond the boathouse which made it easy for her to take photos of a bunch of dumbasses. Normally, I wouldn't care to have my photo taken with an illegal vessel, but we were legit for a few days. And it wasn't like Header's crew didn't know who Holm and I were. I relaxed and went over to see what we could do.

"I tried the winch, but she kept getting caught." He pointed to the spot on the hatch door that had green paint scraped onto it. "There's a little ridge on the bottom there, but it's rounded. It shouldn't catch."

He pulled himself out of the water and pushed on the sub to lean it over a little. I saw the ridge he was talking about. Holm felt at it and then at the spot on the door.

"Try the winch, slowly," Holm told him. "I wanna see something."

The sub rocked back onto the point of contact and grated to a halt. Header locked the winch into that position, and Holm took a closer look. He shook his head.

"I think it's off center. You're winching it from one side, right?"

"We thought about that." Header sat next to the sub and let his legs hang into the water. "A couple of people tried to keep it even, but it kept tipping over."

"Did you check inside?" I asked. I didn't think it'd be that obvious, but...

"Of course we did. Look." Header opened the door on that side, and a bunch of water splashed out. "Oh."

"Jake."

"Yeah, Ethan?"

"You're an idiot."

"Thanks." Header sighed, went over to the winch, and miracle of miracles, the damned thing loaded. "Guess I'm distracted."

He walked up to the front and disappeared behind the Bug.

"Robbie, go get our things and Tessa. I need a minute with Jake."

Holm gave me a funny look before he swam back to the dock. I climbed onto the hatch door and padded inside barefoot. Header was slouched in his seat, and water dripped everywhere.

"Shit, I'm sorry, Jake." I dropped into the copilot seat. "I forgot. How are you doing?"

"It's not like I knew my brother that well," he said. "He was the older, cooler kid, and I was the secret his family didn't talk about. Our moms hated each other. They didn't want Dare and me to meet, so Dad used to find ways to sneak us out together. That ended when a drunk driver killed him."

"He was still your brother."

Jake nodded. "We had an argument last year about guns and the boat and stuff. I kept meaning to call him back. At first, I was too pissed. Later, I was too busy."

"I'm not going to feed you platitudes," I told him. "All I know is that it's obvious to me how much you cared. He probably knew it, too."

"I'll call Bridget sometime soon." He winced. "If she doesn't hate me."

"Do what you need to do."

He stood. "I'll start by getting towels."

After that, things went smoother, and we got underway. It struck me that I got along with Header so well because he and Holm were so much alike in certain ways. Goofy, smart, serious about doing what they believed to be the right things. And, at that moment, worried about family.

The ride out to the Great Blue Hole took a little longer due to the extra weight of the submersible. As we glided into where we'd been diving, I noticed the absence of naval vessels. A handful of diving boats were moored at various points around the Hole.

"Guess they reopened," I observed. I hadn't heard that, but we had been gone a day. "Are there any divers near our spot?"

Header shook his head. "Nah. Looks like they marked the area, though."

There was a buoy with a sign that read, "*Danger: Sandfalls - Do Not Dive.*"

"Well then," I laughed.

Header anchored *Wraith* and opened the hatch door. Getting the Bug out was far easier than in. It bobbed about on the water but was more stable than I could have guessed. Holm went in first, and then Tessa, as they had the two cramped seats in the back. There was so little space that Tessa had to keep her camera bag on her lap. Header was next, and I was last. I looked down to where my feet were a little damp.

"Are you sure the water was from the door being opened at the wrong time?" I asked him. "I don't want to drown or anything."

"Yeah. That's on me." He tapped at his smartwatch, and the hatch door closed. "I forgot I did that when we unloaded it from the other boat."

"How do you manage your operation like that?" Holm sounded more curious than dismissive. "Mistakes like could take out your whole crew."

I shot Holm a warning look, but Header held up a hand.

"I told Ethan, and since he trusts you two, I'll tell ya." He flipped the switches to start the sub's engines and checked ballast. "I'm feeling off today. See, I lost my brother yesterday. Now we're gonna find what we need to catch his killer."

22

It'd been a while since I rode in a submersible as small as the four-person personal craft in the back of *Wraith*. Even the arm attachment was tiny, but it served Header well.

"We call it the 'Bug' because it's small, cute, and green," Header told us. "The name also bugs a member of my crew." He toggled the attachment, which made a little whir. "This little grabber has snagged some important... er... things for us," he said with a grin as he closed the spherical canopy.

Tessa took what photos she could before darkness enveloped the sub. Header hovered near the caverns and shined the sub's powerful spotlight onto the more impressive stalactites so she could use her low-light settings to get photos without her flash.

"I want to come back someday and shoot this place properly," Tessa told us in a wistful tone.

She had a long way to go before she was ready, but I wasn't about to remind her of that in front of the other two. Until she got a handle on her fears, it wouldn't be safe for her to dive in open water period.

Header used the light to track the wall as we descended. The Hole formed tens of thousands of years earlier when the supporting limestone structure of a dry land area gave way and collapsed. Silt formed from the reef and Atlantic drops like avalanches or waterfalls, sliding down to the bottom and leaving deposits along the way. The lower we went, the more evidence there was of the silt.

"H2S layer," Header announced.

He played the light across the cloudy level that marked the zone where almost no life could survive. I'd been cenote diving before and had seen the clouds before, but this layer went on and on, with nothing else visible even when we turned the light away from the wall.

The descent through the hydrogen sulfide layer felt like driving through heavy fog. The reading on the depth gauge gave us our only indication that we were still moving downwards. I tried to imagine Dare and Bridget Lemon diving through the layer, relying only on the gauges on their wrists. Hundreds of feet below the surface, far from help, the Lemons had only themselves to get each other out of trouble.

It occurred to me that we had no one on the surface anywhere close to the Hole. I glanced at Header. Maybe that wasn't so. That yacht we saw was likely in the area. Once the thought hit me, I watched and noticed that every few minutes, he clicked a button on a cord that led to an earbud that I hadn't noticed earlier. Those were subtle mic checks.

At least if we got into trouble, his crew knew where to find us. Probably not in time, but it was the thought that counted.

We broke through below the cloudy layer into a midnight-dark zone with some of the clearest visibility I'd ever seen. At the bottom, there were dead conchs with their shells.

"Look at that," Tessa said in wonder. "You can see where those conchs fell in and tried to get out."

The conical shell had come to rest at the end of a long, sliding line. About two or three feet away was the scalloped trail from where it likely landed from the original fall that brought it into the oxygenless layer. I saw photos like this from the Branson expedition, but it was cool to see it in person.

Header followed the line from the conch toward the wall but stopped before the rocky wall. He played the light across the silt and then up and down. The conch had gone up a steep incline far before the wall before tumbling again, and there, I could see a cylindrical shaped beneath the silt.

"What do you make of that?" he asked. "It could be a stalactite that fell a while back, but the topline seems a little too even."

"You might be right." I leaned forward. "Robbie, Tessa?"

Tessa used her zoom lens and got a photo for us to look at. She capped the lens, pulled the image up on the display screen on the back of her camera body, and examined what she found.

"There!" She pointed at something on her little screen. "I seriously doubt anything thing down here is supposed to be neon green."

Tessa handed the camera up to me and pointed to a few specks where the silt layer thinned out. I showed it to Header and Holm, as well. Tessa took her camera back as Header scanned the nearby area with the spotlight.

"Holy shit."

His whisper echoed my thoughts as the light

uncovered a pile of neon green barrels about fifteen feet away.

"Guys? Guys!"

Tessa's strained yelp snapped my attention back to her. I twisted in my seat to see her hold up the radiation detector from Sedin Disposal. The reading showed the high side of safe, but the number was going up.

"Jake, get away from that barrel," I barked.

"I know, I know." He moved the little submersible away until her detector went back to normal. "God, that's messed up."

"This could be the one that broke open," Holm said. "Think about it, Sedin dumps too close to the drop-off, one of the barrels hits rock and bursts open. Bam! Radioactive shit goes everywhere."

"Sedin?" Header echoed. "Isn't that the place you checked out in Tampa?"

"Yeah." I met his eye. "CGIS arrested Tim Sedin at the scene, but it doesn't feel right. Something's not right."

"All the evidence points to him, Ethan," Holm insisted. "This is just a formality, and you know it."

"Are you sure?" I shook my head. "We need to see this through, and that's why we're here." I turned to Header. "There should be markings on those barrels to show where they're from. All of them look sealed," I added for Tessa's sake.

"You didn't tell me they arrested someone." Header's frown didn't bode well for me if I didn't convince him of my side. "If they have the bastard, why am I here?"

"That's the thing. I don't think Sedin did it." I pointed in the direction of the barrel pile, which was now hidden by the darkness. "Robbie, Sedin Disposal doesn't use green barrels."

"I think you're right," Tessa said. "Give me a sec. I took photos of the storage area... Here." She held up the camera display for everyone to get a look. "They had yellow and black. No green."

I didn't need to look to know I was right. "If it was Sedin, maybe he paints some barrels to disguise them, but why bother? The bottom hardly ever gets visitors. The Lemons' dive was a fluke."

"It was pretty easy to trace those materials to Sedin," Holm said thoughtfully. "On the off-chance of this happening, I wouldn't want anything to be traceable."

"You think someone is framing him?" Tessa asked.

"Sounds like a setup to me," Header muttered. "I

know a few things about that. Make the perp look so guilty that nobody thinks otherwise."

By the look on Header's face, the idea hit close to home. I hadn't heard of anything other than the vigilante charges. Maybe I'd ask about it later. Maybe not.

"Jake, is there anything close to the hot barrel?" I wondered. "I'm thinking this one broke open and spilled all that waste."

"You and me both," Header answered. Within seconds of maneuvering the sub around, a humorless laugh escaped his lips. "That's the shit that killed my brother. Look."

Silt-covered lumps spread outward in an arc from the covered barrel, as if it spun on the way down. Like the moon's airless environment, the floor here had no circulation other than movement caused by silt falls and human visitors. The last human visitors had been the Lemons, and Dare Lemon had left his mark. A short message was drawn in the silt.

"*Dare was here.*"

Header made a slight choking sound and sniffed before clearing his throat.

"You can see where he poked through the silt to see what made the lumps." He pointed at spots where Dare had brushed silt aside. "I still can't tell what it is."

"Radiation," Tessa warned. "Position us so I can get some shots real quick."

Header did as asked and allowed Tessa a minute to get her photos. We moved close to the barrel pile with no rise in radiation levels. He shined the light across the barrels but found no labels of any kind.

"I see radiation symbols, but that's it," Holm said. "No identifying marks."

Tessa took a series of photos from different angles Header provided by repositioning the sub.

"We have to ascend," Header announced. "I hope you got enough photos, Tessa."

"I think so." She scrolled through the images she'd taken and shook her head. "Ethan, I think you're right. Tim Sedin would be stupid to leave traceable stuff inside these barrels. He was anything but stupid yesterday."

"Yeah, things aren't adding up." I watched the bottom disappear into the dark as we ascended. "Sedin told us to look at MediWaste, but nobody there is licensed to handle radioactive materials. That's why they subcontract."

"So what if no one there is licensed?" Header spoke as he concentrated on the controls and gauges.

"That doesn't mean that they weren't before. Look at whether anyone there has a history of working with radiation."

"MediWaste employs thousands of people," Tessa pointed out.

Holm leaned back and crossed his arms. "Guess we better start narrowing it down." He looked at me. "Like who had access to information about Sedin Disposal."

"And who would have the knowledge to make a bunch of radioactive trash a hell of a lot stronger than it should be." I shook my head. "The other question we need to answer is who benefits from making a bunch of used medical supplies more radioactive."

"Oh my God," Tessa gasped. "Wait, are you suggesting...?"

"That someone's trying to weaponize it?" I ventured. "Yeah. That's exactly what I'm suggesting."

23

WHEN I WAS AN ACTIVE SEAL, I got a lot more battle experience than I care to think about. One of the things that saved my ass more than a few times was when the hairs on my neck prickled just before a surprise attack, kind of like the quiet before a storm.

I started feeling it a few feet before we surfaced. Holm and Header tensed at the same time. The battle sense never left some guys.

"I'm gonna open the hatch first," Header told us through a clenched jaw. "Something ain't right, and I don't wanna screw around when we get up to her."

"Agreed," Holm and I said together.

"What's going on?" Tessa squeaked as she looked around for the unseen threat. "I don't see anything."

"Don't have to see it to know it's there," Header growled.

Some people might argue that there's no such thing as a sixth sense, that a person is picking up on subconscious cues. I never cared as long as it worked. All three of us had the feeling, and with as clear as the water was, we had to pray that nobody had spotted us.

Wraith's hatch lowered above us almost perfectly aligned with where we were stationed beneath her. Header took us above water, and I threw the canopy open. I jumped out onto the open hatch and grabbed Tessa's hand. While Holm got out, I scanned the water and sky for threats. As Header climbed over the passenger seat, I felt the concussion of a rocket-propelled grenade before the blast slammed into *Wraith's* starboard side. The impact stood us on the left hydrofoil, and then we slammed down. The hatch door landed on the Bug and shattered the canopy.

"Jake!" I called out, but I didn't see him anywhere.

As I started to lean out, bullets plinked off *Wraith's* front and starboard side. Holm searched through the cabin for anything he could use as a weapon while Tessa hunkered down between the seating bench and pilot's seat.

"I'm going after Header," I told them as I kicked off my shoes. "He hasn't surfaced yet."

I didn't wait for them to answer. We needed him. Even if he wasn't my friend, we still needed him to run his boat. I slipped into the water on the port side and swam under the boat's body. Header wasn't there. I resurfaced toward the hatch and half expected to see him in the cabin, but a look in showed me only Holm and Tessa.

The Bug was barely afloat, and it had drifted a good ten feet away already. More gunfire rained against *Wraith's* hull, and I ducked out of sight. Another boat's engine revved hard and neared Header's boat. I took a deep breath, dove under, and kicked hard toward the little sub.

A bullet whizzed past me through the water. I pushed on. It wasn't like I'd never swum through gunfire before. I reached the Bug and didn't surface until I was on the other side. There, I found Header draped over the pontoon on the side facing away from the assault. He was barely conscious and had a nasty gash above his eye.

Another RPG boomed into the water next to *Wraith*, and the waves the explosion kicked up pushed us further away on the Bug. Header started to slide into the water, but I propped him back up on the pontoon. If his crew has been listening in like I'd assumed, this would've been a good time for them to show up. And yet, no one did.

I peeked around the front of the crippled sub. An offshore boat charged toward the *Wraith*. The bullet that had just missed me may have ricocheted or simply gone wide of its target. The shooter didn't seem to notice the sub.

"Wake up, Jake," I hissed. "Snap to."

His eyelids fluttered, and he groaned. The noise and Jake's blood were attracting attention underwater. At the first sight of dorsal fins, I ducked under and found a few reef sharks nosing around. With a little prayer, I heaved Jake up and into the cockpit which was full of shattered acrylic that used to be the canopy. Something brushed against my foot, and I damned near flew out of the water myself.

"What the...?" Jake groaned as I crawled over him to get to the controls.

The sub shuddered with an impact from below. Jake touched his wound and stared at the blood on his fingers for a moment before his glazed eyes shifted to me.

"Jake, you gotta wake up, buddy," I told him. "*Wraith* is under attack. We're helpless without you."

"Nah, you have voice c'mmand." Jake leaned over

the side and hurled. "Didn't tell you 'coz emergency only."

"Hell of a time to find out," I grumbled. Granted, I loved the idea of piloting Header's boat, but that made things extra complicated in my role as law enforcement. "I won't need it. Let's get this smashed bit running."

I heard returning gunfire and looked up to find Holm armed and firing at the enemy. If he could hold them off, I might be able to get back intact and with Header.

The Bug started, but the engine thumped in a pulsing beat. Lucky for me, the controls were intuitive, because Header slumped into unconsciousness. I steered the floundering sub toward *Wraith* as Holm leaned out with his own gun and fired at the offshore boat. It swung broadside with its aft facing us. Four engines. That thing was built for speed.

Whoever was at the helm took more shots at us in the Bug and then lit out. The enemy boat was barely out of the Blue Hole's circle when I reached the hatch. Header came to as Holm helped me get him out of the ruined sub.

"Get that bastard," Header mumbled. "Ethan, 'zero-one-three-Marston.' She'll give you limited weapons an' tracking."

Holm looked at me with brows raised. "Seriously?"

I nodded. "Zero-one-three-Marston."

"Identity confirmed," a feminine computer voice said. "Limited access granted to *Wraith* systems."

"Ethan, he needs a hospital," Tessa protested.

"I know, I know." I turned to him. "Jake, how close is your crew?"

He waved me off. "Just dizzy. I'll be fine." His words were a little slurred, but I got the message. He didn't give me access just to get him to the hospital.

"Robbie, take copilot." I guided Header to one of the bench seats. "Tessa, strap him in."

She nodded and did as told. I slapped the six-inch button to close the hatch and then ran to the captain's seat. *Wraith's* controls went live under my touch. Holm pointed to a radar screen that showed a signal beating it out of the area.

"That's him."

"Any chance you saw who it was?" I asked as I pushed the throttle forward. *Wraith* shuddered and jolted. I pulled back.

"Easy," Header complained. "She takes a light touch to get going."

This time, I nudged, and she glided forward. Steering was as responsive as the throttle, and I got the hang of it in no time. We flew over the water after the attacking vessel.

"Go over weapons," I told Holm. "See what you have and how it works. Jake?"

"He's out," Tessa called up to us. "He could have anything from a concussion to a serious brain injury. We should get him to the city."

"It's not just about us," I told her as we sped out of the circular atoll formation. "That boat is heavily armed. We can't afford to let that guy put civilians in danger. Jake knows this."

In the short moments it took to get *Wraith* going, the other vessel was a speck on the open water. I opened her up to fifty knots, and then sixty. Whatever that other boat had, they were fast, and we were only gaining by a little.

"I got it," Holm announced.

He grabbed a joystick and aligned a targeting screen in the middle of the board. It was kind of like my dad's old Atari. Holm fired, and I felt the thud-thud-thud of *Wraith's* main gun through my feet. The other boat pulled hard to port. Holm compensated, and this time, a puff of smoke rose from one of the engines. The boat's speed dropped as I saw the flash of a rocket.

"Hang on," I yelled.

The RPG hit in front of us. The explosion of water acted as a ramp and sent us airborne for a second. The pontoons slammed back onto the water, and we raced on through six-foot swells.

"I have another line on him," Holm reported. "Them. I see two aboard, but I can't make out their faces."

He narrowed his eyes and fired. It was hard to tell if anything hit until another smoke plume whooshed up from the engines. The smoke darkened and spread. Fire.

I pushed us back up to fifty, and *Wraith* cut through the worsening chop like nobody's business.

"Lighthouse Reef Airstrip," Holm told me. "That's where he's going."

He pointed to a growing smudge. The offshore boat had lost speed, but it still had enough of a lead to arrive at the island first.

"He's got to have a plane up there." I opened the throttle. "I'm not letting this bastard get away."

Wraith surged forward. She sliced through the water like a hockey star on ice. Holm worked on taking out the engines, but the guy was good. Even two engines down, he knew how to handle the trim and speed to evade some of our fire.

Another flash and smoke trail from the side of

their boat, and I cut to starboard. The grenade hit the water to port and sent us skittering to the right, but *Wraith's* sturdy hydrofoils and pontoons kept us upright and flying at those assholes.

The airstrip was at the north end of Northern Two Cayes, a small island at the end of the reef. And there were boaters out.

"Shit, shit, shit," I swore. "Civvie boats."

Holm left off the weapons. He swore a blue streak that'd make any sailor proud as bullets pinged off our hull. I flinched when they raked across the forward windshield, but they didn't so much as scratch the view. Whether they were out of grenades or they actually cared about civilians, our attackers didn't fire any more RPGs.

My bet was on the former.

"There's the plane," Holm pointed at a duo-prop Piper on the sand runway. "Someone's already there, and they're spinning up the engines."

"Dammit!"

We were close but not close enough. They ran their boat aground, and I saw flames about the engines. Lucky for them the engines lasted as long as they did. One figure jumped onto the beach, and the other tossed a few things to the other before vaulting off the boat. They grabbed their gear and sprinted toward the airstrip. Halfway there, one turned back to their boat and dropped to a knee.

We were maybe fifteen yards out, and I put *Wraith* into a skidding stop as their boat went up like a volcano. Flaming metal and fiberglass parts rained onto our hull and peppered the water all around. The wake wasn't as bad because of the shallow water, but there were at least two civvie boats in the blast area.

As I nosed *Wraith* up to the nearby dock, the Piper started rolling. Holm fired at the plane after it passed some small structures. Bullet holes appeared behind the boarding door but didn't slow them down. The pilot had mastered the short takeoff and was airborne before we could do a damned thing about it.

"We need to check on those boaters and get them help." I backed *Wraith* off the beach and headed over to where the sailboat I'd seen was now in trouble. A flaming hole in the sail was spreading. The other boat that was in the area was a powerboat, and they approached the sailors. "Robbie, see if there's a way to hail Jake's crew."

"Aye-aye."

I pulled astern of the sailboat, opposite of the

powerboat, and opened the hatch. Holm ran to the back.

"Is anyone hurt?" he called out.

The answer was faint but clear. "Yeah, no thanks to you idiots!"

"We're suing," someone else shouted.

Holm closed the hatch and returned to the copilot seat. "They're fine."

"Wraith, *come in. We're getting distress readings.*" A deep voice came over the speakers.

Holm and I stared at each other. "They're just now getting this?"

"Had... ow... had transmissions off..." Header groaned. "Tell them... bring fuel an' the doc..."

"The wound stopped bleeding a few minutes ago," Tessa reported with a worried edge to her voice. "I've kept him as still as I could."

I steered *Wraith* back toward the dock near the flaming wreckage.

"*Wraith* crew, this is Marston," I transmitted. "The captain has a head injury and gave me limited control. Please bring fuel and a doctor."

"*The* doc," Header rasped.

"'The doc,'" I corrected.

"*We have your coordinates. Header, if you can hear me, I freaking told you so. This was the dumbest—*"

"*We're en route,*" a calm, light voice reported. "*ETA is twenty. Has the vessel taken damage?*"

"Unknown," I answered. "She handled well, but there were some near-hits that rocked us. I don't wanna move Header any more than necessary."

"*Copy that. Stay put. Don't let anyone else aboard. And, uh, discretion is appreciated.*"

"Aye-aye."

The boat we pursued burnt itself out as we laid Header on a row of cushions. Tessa didn't speak other than a few words to Header.

"I don't understand you," she told him. "You're risking your life by not letting us take you to the hospital."

"I've both taken worse," Header told her. "It... it's what we do."

She crossed her arms and didn't talk to either of us for a while. I didn't blame her for not understanding. Civilians didn't get what it meant to get the mission done, whether it was defusing a bomb or chasing down the bad guy, the mission came first. In too many instances, failure led to more death and destruction.

I sat on the hatch and let my feet dip into the water. A chunk of the other boat's hull had landed almost under where we'd parked. Since it would be a while until Header's crew arrived, and I couldn't do more to help him, I decided to check it out. The water was a little over six feet deep and, now that the sand had settled from the chaos, clear.

The hull segment wasn't large, and it was easy enough to get a grip on the fiberglass. I walked the piece out onto the beach. The blast had littered the beach and immediate surroundings with debris. Visitors were probably going to find remnants for years to come. I didn't want to think about how long it was going to take to clean the mess in the first place.

I started down the dock when I saw the yacht from that morning. They blasted their horn as they approached and then weighed anchor far out enough to not run aground. I waved and walked the rest of the way down to the back of *Wraith* and hopped over to the hatch.

A dinghy appeared from behind the yacht. Two people rode it across smaller swells than we faced earlier. As they got closer, I was disappointed to see they wore hats and mirrored aviator sunglasses. My curiosity was in high gear, but I respected my friend too much to make anything of it.

They parked the dinghy at the hatch door. The first crew member brushed past me and then Holm to kneel at Header's side. Both of them wore loose-fitting jackets, but this person had a feminine jawline and long red hair pulled into a braid.

"Yeah, don't mess with her," the other person said with a laugh. This person had the lighter voice from the radio call.

She flipped him the bird and then gently patted Header's cheek. He'd drifted off again but came to. When he saw the half-hidden face above him, a slow grin spread across his face.

"Hey, gorgeous," he said in a woozy tone.

She answered in a flurry of sharp signing. There was a lot of pointing between him and me. Yeah, I didn't think she liked me. Tessa glanced at me, and I gave a slight shake of my head. I didn't want them to know she could read some of the signing.

"Which one of you is the doc?" I asked.

"I am he." The redhead's companion signed something. She made an exasperated raspberry sound and sat back. "Tell me what happened."

I recounted everything from surfacing in the Bug to laying him on the cushions. He checked Header's vitals and responses as I spoke. The redhead paced between the hatch and the copilot's seat.

"Okay, um, I'm not going to tell her about Bug until later." The doc cleared his throat. "She's already pissed that it's not here. That thing's her baby. Was her baby."

I shrugged. "You might be able to salvage it. That's a nice little submersible, and it did a great job." I looked between them.

"We'll contact your team and tell them where to find you," the doc informed me. "The captain is done here, and that's a group decision." He smiled. "You seem like a great guy, but you're a cop first, friend second."

I nodded. "Understood. It was a hell of a ride, though."

"That it is." He watched the redhead go through another series of signs. "Yeah, she wants everyone off, like five minutes ago. We'll take care of the captain. I won't say I'm not worried, but the injury could be a lot worse."

We grabbed our things, which wasn't much compared to the day before, and moved them to the dock. The redhead stopped Tessa and grabbed her camera bag. She signed to the doc.

"She wants the memory card," he told Tessa.

"No!" She pulled back on the bag. "I didn't take pictures of the *Wraith* or Jake or anything like that."

"Let her show you the display," I suggested.

"Leave her alone," Header ordered in a slightly

stronger tone. I noted that he didn't speak directly at her. Interesting. She could hear but not speak? "The camera wasn't even out until we were in the sub."

The redhead released the bag and backed off with her arms spread wide. She marched to the captain's seat and warmed up *Wraith's* engines. I helped the doc load the dinghy into the cabin, and then he closed the hatch. I shook my head as they pulled away from the dock.

"You were quiet," I told Holm as the *Wraith* joined the yacht.

"He's your friend, Ethan." He picked up his bag. "I have concerns. I like the guy, but Muñoz is right. They're vigilantes, and they're going to cross bad lines someday. What are you going to do when that happens?"

Holm shrugged and walked off and toward the small building next to the airstrip.

"I suppose you're upset that I didn't take him straight to the hospital," I said to Tessa in a soft voice. "He didn't want to go."

"I don't know," she admitted. "Header's an adult and gets to make his own choices. Personally, I would've taken him to an emergency room."

"He wanted—"

"It was your choice," she insisted. "Ethan, you

know as well as anyone that people with head injuries don't make great decisions sometimes."

I rubbed the back of my head and watched the other boaters pull into the only other dock on the beach, way down at the other end of the airstrip. Those folks were one stray piece of shrapnel away from getting someone killed that day. Our unsuspected subject could kill someone else at any time. We didn't know if they would go after innocent civilians next.

The fact that I suspected the answer to that question didn't make me feel one damned bit better.

24

TESSA WATCHED Ethan as he helped his MBLIS team pick through the rubble of the boat they'd chased earlier in the *Wraith*. Muñoz had arrived in a single-engine Cessna a couple of hours after Jake Header's crew left. She'd brought Bonnie and Clyde, as they called Rosa and Joe, and their mini-lab. Another hour later, a Belize Coast Guard cutter brought Birn, Warner, and help for the people whose sailboat had been hit by the explosion debris.

A sudden flurry of activity at the wreckage got her attention. She got up from the towel someone had provided to sit on and picked her way across the debris-strewn beach to where Bonnie stood with hands on her hips.

"What's got them all riled up?" Tessa asked the lab tech.

"They think they found a way to trace the boat to its owner." Bonnie waved Tessa over to where she stood ankle-deep in the water. She wore galoshes, whereas Tessa only had her sandals. "The outboard motors were made by a small company in Tampa. Our subjects filed serial numbers and scraped the company name off the motors, but they didn't get to the crankshafts."

Tessa took photos of MBLIS personnel picking over the remains of said boat. She zoomed in on the part Holm held and was discussing with others.

"So you're saying the crankshaft has information that'll lead to where the motors were made?" Tessa stepped around a charred seat cushion.

"Exactly." Bonnie pointed over toward where Ethan poked through another section of the debris. "He can tell you more about it."

Tessa found him ankle-deep in the water. He turned a spark plug around in his hands and looked out to sea. She turned and only saw the water stretching to the horizon.

"What are you looking at?" she asked him.

Ethan shook his head and looked at her. "Nothing. I'm just going over everything that happened. If we hadn't been afraid of hitting civilians, we could've disabled the plane with *Wraith's* weapons. We could've stopped them from getting away."

"We can still catch them," she told him. "They have that information on the motors being made in Tampa."

He nodded. "That points back to Sedin Disposal and MediWaste. If Sedin is at the center of this, that means at least two other people are working with him."

"You said before you aren't sure it's Sedin." She snapped some photos of him reaching into the water for another piece. "Are you still leaning away from him doing all this?"

"I don't know. Maybe." He stood and nudged sand mounds with his foot. One after another was more sand, with a broken conch shell under another one. "I need perspective."

"Or you need to think about something else for a while." Tessa heard Sylvia Muñoz call her name. "I'm going back in the plane. Come with us. Bonnie or Clyde can ride back with the others on the cutter."

"I should help with this mess. I feel responsible."

Tessa took a breath. "You weren't the one who fired the RPG. The bad guys did that."

He glowered at the water for a moment, took a long, deep breath, and then let it go.

"Okay, I'll fly back with you. We'll bring Warner to help ferret out who that boat belonged to." He looked down the beach toward the other boaters. "I should beat it. They won't want me riding back on the cutter with them." He turned the spark plug over a few more times and then walked ashore. "As far as they know, a couple raging assholes shot up their boat. I'd rather get back to the job than deal with that business."

They waded out of the water together, and Ethan handed the spark plug off to one of the technicians.

"Heya, Marston," Sylvia called out as they approached the Cessna. "It's not *Bette Davis*, but it flies straight and safe. Plus, it's not too big for this little bitty runway."

The Cessna only carried four people. Muñoz piloted, Warner sat in the co-pilot seat, and Tessa sat next to Ethan in the back. It was late afternoon when they landed at the smaller airport in Belize City, rather than the international runway north of town. One of the black Audis was parked by the little terminal, and Ethan drove them back to the villa.

On the way, Tessa checked messages and email on her phone. A familiar name stood out in the email, and she opened the message. The news made her feel a little giddy, and she couldn't help smiling.

"What's made your day?" Ethan asked as they pulled into the garage.

Tessa held the phone screen to her chest. "Just some information that'll be helpful for a different project. I'll tell you about it later."

Ethan shrugged as they got out. He, Sylvia, and Warner went to the meeting room to go through the information they had. Tessa grabbed a bag of tortilla chips and a water bottle from the kitchen and then headed up to her room. She went to her email while the daily download from her camera's memory card progressed.

Professor Calvin Parish was an expert in the American South, and she'd quietly asked him if there was anything in late seventeenth-century port town records about the *Dragon's Rogue*. Pirate ships were known to go up the East Coast. Most people had the idea that they stuck to the Caribbean, but that wasn't so. While the warmer seas were more attractive, some pirates hunted in cooler waters at times.

She read and reread the email. Parish had come through and in a big way. Tessa started for the hall, but she hesitated. This was information she wanted to share at a special moment. This was the last night in Belize, and their last date had been ruined. What better way to make the best of things than to present Ethan with the good news at a romantic dinner in the city, without grenades or bullets?

She ran downstairs and found the meeting room open. Ethan was speaking to Warner, and Muñoz was typing away at something. Tessa knocked on the door frame.

"Come on in," Ethan said. He sounded much more relaxed and in charge. "We have some updates, but we're waiting for the rest of the team to get in."

"They're two, no, one block away," Warner reported. He pointed at his laptop screen. "I put this tracking app on everyone's department phones," he explained to Tessa. "That way, we can check in if someone goes silent."

"Or if you want to know how long until we can leave for dinner," Ethan observed. "Or if someone stays out too late."

Warner put his hands up in protest. "No, dude. We only use it when people are on duty. It's a safety thing."

Sylvia raised an eyebrow. "Still creepy, Warner."

"Did you say something about dinner?" Tessa asked Ethan. She tried not to sound disappointed.

"Since it's our last night Belize, we're all going out to a tavern tonight. They have a little of everything, so it should be a hit." Ethan rolled his eyes at Warner. "Even the pickiest ones of us."

Warner pointed at Ethan without looking up from his computer. "Not commenting on that. I will, however, inform you that our party has arrived."

The door to the garage opened at that minute, and the rest of the team dragged in.

"Anything new?" Holm asked as he wandered into the meeting room.

"I'm waiting for everyone to get in here." Ethan waved everyone in.

Sweat and sunblock scents filled the room. Tessa hoped it would be a short briefing. She liked these people, but she didn't care to share a close space with them right then.

"The boat is registered to Sedin Disposal," Ethan announced. "Everyone who works there was accounted for today."

"What about people who were off today?" Birn asked.

Ethan nodded. "We looked at them, especially one who had extensive military service. They all had alibis."

"Could someone from MediWaste have taken the

boat?" Holm rocked back in his chair. Tessa worried that he might fall if he tipped any further. "They would've had to take it and leave it in the area. That's a hell of a haul to get from Tampa and around Cuba."

Ethan shook his head. "I don't have an answer for that. My best guess is they port-hopped. They must have a bigger boat for longer hauls." He pulled something up on the tablet he was using. "These barrels have been found throughout the Caribbean in those secondary dump sites I briefed you all about."

Tessa thought about the connections Ethan had as a former SEAL. If someone else had those kinds of connections but didn't have the ethics he maintained, an operation like this would be doable. She bit her lip. She was an observer, not part of the team.

"Tessa?" Ethan broke through her train of thought.

"Yeah?"

"You look like you had an idea."

All eyes landed on her. She'd spoken in front of audiences of hundreds, maybe thousands, but in this small meeting space, she felt more self-conscious than she had in a while.

"I think you're right to look at people who have

military experience," she told them. "What you aren't saying is that it almost has to be someone who had extensive experience, like special forces. If these people are working with a network, that would explain how they have the resources to get this operator to the dumpsites. Either that, or it's some rich asshole with money to burn."

"It could be a little of both," Warner said. He tapped at his keyboard. "MediWaste has hundreds of employees. Sedin has a couple dozen. I can find out who matches that description."

"And see who was MIA today," Ethan added. "That little plane wouldn't get them all the way to Florida, but they could get to Belize and move from there."

"Yeah, I've been on that." Warner frowned. "Records are spotty here. I think someone's getting paid off to fudge the logs."

"Maybe that's why the Sedin people haven't noticed their boat isn't home," Tessa suggested. "If they only take it out once a month, and if someone knows that schedule, they won't have missed it."

Ethan rubbed both of his palms across his face. "That's it for tonight. Shower, muster in the garage, and we'll get some chow at that tavern."

Tessa slumped in her chair as everyone left the

meeting room. So much for a private date where she could share the news about the *Dragon's Rogue*. Ethan and his grandfather only got so far before the old man passed away, but in the past year, he and Tessa found the body of Ethan's ancestor who owned the ship before it was taken by the pirate, Mad Dog Grendel, and a bag of coins near the remains. More recently, Ethan and others found a cannonball and thirty silver coins from someone made to walk the *Dragon's Rogue's* plank.

"Tessa?" Ethan stopped in front of her. "Are you alright?"

"I'm fine. I'll go get ready."

"Okay. I'll see you in a bit."

Tessa smiled over the disappointment at the lack of privacy, but the message from South Carolina was too important to wait.

25

THE TAVERN in Belize City was a little too much like home, but it seemed to hit the spot for my team. Tessa, I wasn't so sure about. She sat next to me at the long table the waitstaff put together and glanced over the menu.

"Shrimp po'boy and a cola," she ordered almost as an afterthought.

"Okay, what's on your mind?" I asked with a playful jab at her arm.

"Huh?" Tessa shook her head. "I'm trying to think about the best way to tell you something."

My gut sank. Conversations that started out like that rarely ended well, especially if I wasn't the one starting them.

"I'm listening whenever you're ready."

Across the table, Bonnie and Clyde looked at each other and squirmed. This wasn't how I envisioned the last night in Belize City going.

"Oh, it's nothing bad," Tessa told us. Her cheeks reddened. "It's good news. Well, mixed but mostly good. I didn't mean to worry you."

She smiled at me, and my breath caught. Sometimes, those emerald eyes of her took me by surprise and locked me in. For a moment, I thought about running my fingers through her hair. She'd kept it in a ponytail all day, but it was down for the evening.

"I reached out a while back to a history professor who specializes in the American South to Southeast. He's based in Charleston, South Carolina, so he was happy to look up old records relating to piracy in the late seventeen hundreds."

My heart quickened. It'd been a while since I could do any research about the pirate ship my Gramps and I hunted together.

"Is that the news you got tonight?"

I grinned at her nod and saw that Bonnie and Clyde weren't the only ones listening. Holm, Muñoz, and Birn also perked up at the mention of piracy. Warner didn't know anything about the *Dragon's Rogue*, as far as I knew.

Her smile damned near knocked me out, I swear.

"It is." She looked around the table. "We know that pirate crews ranged up the East Coast. Charlestown was brand new at the time, and the records are super rare."

The one time a little delay wouldn't have hurt, our food was delivered at that moment. Tessa dug right into her shrimp po'boy.

"Hey, you're telling a story," I protested even as a monster-sized, double-cheese, smothered-in-all-sorts-of-goodness burger was placed in front of me. "No more suspense for today."

Tessa laughed as the others agreed. Warner perked up as he realized what we were talking about, and Bonnie quietly got him up to speed as Tessa relented.

"Okay, okay," she began. "Professor Parish found records that were scanned in a few months ago. It turns out that less than a year before the *Dragon's Rogue* disappeared in 1692, Captain Grendel was arrested for piracy. It doesn't say how he was captured, just that he escaped a hanging." She looked at me. "Ethan, the students who are scanning records found what may have been pages from Grendel's logs. They would've been confiscated by Charleston officials."

"What'd they talk about?" I had to know, even if it wasn't relevant to finding the wreckage.

"It looks like he had a wife on Grand Bahama Island, somewhere between where West End and Freeport are today." Tessa beamed. "You told me that you and your grandfather narrowed down the wreckage location. Somewhere between Miami and the Bahamas, right?"

I nodded. It would've been great to get this close while Gramps was alive, but I knew he was enjoying the ride from above. Still, I had to take a few swigs of beer to get the lump out of my throat.

"That's fantastic, Tessa," I said for her ears alone. "Thank you."

She nodded and went back to her po'boy, but I did not miss the smug glint in her eye from knowing she did a good thing. Meanwhile, the conversation at the table moved right into talk of pirating throughout the centuries, from the Golden Age through the present day.

After the talk had died down and food and beer were had by all, we beat it back to the villa. Muñoz and Birn had to get their required hours of sleep before flying us home in the morning, and the rest of us had to get our gear packed. It was going to be a tighter fit this time, as Tessa was given the green light to travel with us.

"Want to see some of the photos I've been working on?" she asked when we got upstairs.

"Absolutely."

I hadn't had a chance to see what she'd captured so far. And, if things went well, I might be able to see more than her photos.

"Have a seat while I get my laptop booted." She closed her door and then went to the simple desk she'd been using. I sat in the guest chair by the desk. "I download them from my camera each night and go through to find shots that'll work for the feature."

She went on about the process and how they chose what to publish, but I had a hard time focusing on her words. Her lips moved and curved in the glow of her screen, and the joy of her work touched her eyes. Some photos caught my interest, especially the ones from the dive and when we went down in the sub. Some were downright ethereal, like the look we got when Header shined his spotlight into the cavern with the giant stalactites. That was where she stopped the digital tour.

"You aren't listening, are you?" she teased.

"I gotta confess, I'm a little distracted."

"Yeah?"

"Yeah."

Not the most stellar conversation twist, but the message was sent and received. Funny thing... I never made it to my room that night. Another funny thing was that neither of us remembered to set our morning alarms. We woke to someone pounding on the door.

"Tessa, is Ethan in there?" Bonnie called out. "You better both be in there because we're already running late."

"I'll be out in a few minutes," Tessa answered as she threw off the covers. "Shoot, I forgot to pack before going to sleep."

"I'll go grab my things," I told her. "Let me know if you need help carrying stuff."

By some miracle, we both made it to the garage within ten minutes. Bonnie was in the driver's seat, and from the firm look on her face, it was clear she wasn't giving up the keys for anyone. For all her complaints about our tardiness, it was her slow, over-careful driving that made us late to meet the team at Bette Davis.

"Our phones have these great things called 'apps,' Marston," Muñoz informed me. She only called me by my last name anymore when she was pissed at me. "The alarm clock apps are, surprise, there to wake you in the morning. Wherever you sleep." She winked at Tessa as they loaded Tessa's prized photography equipment into the cargo area.

Tessa and I took facing seats, and Holm sat across the aisle. He took great delight in stretching out and propping his heels up on the seat across from him.

"You're not *that* much taller," I told him.

"Tall enough," he chuckled.

Once we were airborne, Tessa brought up the documents in South Carolina.

"They're hard to read," she told me. "Professor Parish and others are trying different methods to restore what they can. Some may never be readable. For now, they're holding out hope."

"That's incredible," Holm said in a hushed voice. "It's amazing what modern technology can and can't do."

I wished I could say something to help him. We hadn't spoken about his sister since the other night. Unless there was evidence to the contrary, she'd left on her own, and there was little we could do, technically speaking.

"Oh." Tessa grimaced a little. "So, I found out something else yesterday."

I did not like the wrinkled brow and the slight cringe on her face. "That doesn't sound good."

"While he was looking into pirate research, Professor Parish learned that there are attempts to use satellite imagery to search for shipwrecks. Some of the hardcore treasure hunters are comparing possible sites from the images with known information about various wrecks."

"Has anyone actually succeeded in this?" I asked.

"One that I know of. They found something last year, but they aren't releasing many details."

I released my breath. "I'm not going to worry unless they start finding a bunch of wrecks."

"What plans do you have for now?" She leaned forward like a kid eager to hear a new story.

I laughed. "I have to check out that stretch on Grand Bahama as soon as I get a day off." As she grinned, I thought how nice it would be to have her along for that. "When I have some sites to explore, I'll figure it out from there. Right now, I'm thinking about getting a seaplane and getting my pilot's license so I can eyeball some of the areas from above."

Holm sat up. "At least a seaplane wouldn't drown in two feet of water."

I sagged back into my seat. "Don't remind me. Think they'll have a new car ready?"

"Do I want to know?" Tessa leaned back in her seat.

"Yes," I told her. "And someday, maybe you will."

26

WE HAD a whole one hour to report to our office after landing in Miami. It was the noon rush, and I didn't have a car. Tessa rented a convertible on her uncle's dime, and I did not mind one bit as we flew down the highway toward the marina where I lived.

"Serves him right," she shouted over the wind. "If he keeps sticking his nose into the wrong places, it's gonna get bit."

"I won't argue that."

We dropped everything but her camera off at my houseboat, the *Mariah Jean*. I barely got to get changed into my work clothes and shoulder holster before we had to leave for the MBLIS offices. Even though we picked up a bucket of chicken on the way, we were the first to arrive from the airport.

"Sedin is in holding," Diane told me as soon as I found her, "and that smells good. You sharing?"

Tessa held out the chicken bucket. "Director Ramsey, it is my pleasure to share broasted chicken with you."

Diane snagged a leg and pointed at me with it. "That's the kind of respect that'll get you places, Ethan."

"Yes, ma'am," I said with a wink. "I'm also buying drinks at Mike's bar tonight." I knew Diane could go, but I had to rub it in a little.

Holm arrived as Tessa and I finished eating. To my absolute astonishment, he took the largest piece left in the bucket and proceeded to polish it off in less than a minute.

Diane went down to holding to observe with Tessa. Sedin was already in the room and chained to the table. Before we went in, Diane handed me a folder with new information about our suspect.

"Sedin waived his right to an attorney," she told us. "The guy is either innocent or arrogant. Maybe both." She frowned. "The guy got caught dealing Ritalin in college. He was a biomed major, of all things. We haven't contacted Marci Anderson to find out if she knew about this when they started a company together."

"If someone found out, they could blackmail him into cooperating," Holm pointed out. "Or if he discovered something, they could force him to keep quiet."

"I don't see a motive for anyone other than profit," Diane said. "Sedin and Anderson are the only people who would stand to profit. Charge full fees, take some of the materials for legal dumping at exorbitant costs and then transport the rest to sites where they shouldn't be found. It's a pain but still costs less than the legal route."

"That's one of the angles we're looking at," I told her.

"He's not feeling it," Holm said. "I'm not sure I do, either. Someone went through a lot of effort to pull those materials from the chain of custody."

"Not to mention doing something to make the radiation more potent," I added. "And moving it to neon green barrels that Sedin Disposal doesn't use."

Diane looked back and forth between us. "Do you have a theory?"

"Not really," I admitted with a slight head shake. "But I keep coming back to why those materials were stronger than they ever should've been."

"Lemon shouldn't have been hurt, let alone killed, by that exposure," Holm said as he crossed his arms. "It's like whoever did this wanted *someone* to get hurt."

"Not at the Blue Hole." I hooked my thumbs into my pockets as dread seeped into my gut. "That was an accident. I'm sure of it. Yesterday's attack was about trying to mitigate the mess somehow."

"A fat lot of good that did," Holm muttered. "So if Dare Lemon's death was an accident, what are they trying to do on purpose?"

"Let's see what Sedin has to say." I started toward the interview room.

"Lean on him, but not so much that he rescinds the waiver," Diane ordered. "Whether you're feeling it or not, we need to be thorough. The boat used in the attack yesterday belonged to his company. So far, all the evidence leads to him and accomplices."

"Except for the green barrels," I reminded her.

Holm and I pushed through the steel door to face Sedin.

"You're wasting time," Sedin said as soon as we entered. "Look at Devon Cole. MediWaste is the problem, not us."

I grabbed one of the metal chairs, flipped it around backward, and sat. The tactic was cliché because it worked. Holm was all business as he took his seat and set a large-screen tablet on the table. It displayed Sedin's record from when he was busted for selling Ritalin eleven years earlier.

"Right now, the evidence points to you," I informed him and pointed at the tablet. "It's not like you never had trouble with the law."

Sedin looked at the screen and flinched. "That was years ago and a one-time thing," he protested. "I made a stupid mistake and paid for it."

"Does your partner know about that little mistake?" I pressed.

"No." He shook his head and looked down. "I was afraid she'd refuse to work with me. I tried to get in with other investors before, and that always ruined the deals."

"So you hid it from her," Holm stated. "What would've happened if she'd found out?"

"I don't know. Early on, she was stuck with me. There was too much money on the line for it not to work out." He fiddled with the chain between his cuffs. "She would've been angry, but there wasn't much she could've done."

"What about this year?" I rocked forward on my chair. "Say someone threatened to expose your records unless you helped them out here and there.

Loan them a boat, turn your back on missing materials. Order them special barrels."

He shook his head. "No, I wouldn't. I made a bad choice, but it wasn't murder or robbery."

"You're running a successful business, Tim. If word got out that you sold drugs to college students, clients would drop you like a hot coal."

"But it wasn't like that—"

"Wasn't it?" I pressed. "Prescription drug abuse is big news these days, right there with the opiate crisis. Not good, man."

"They'd understand," Sedin protested. "I'm even working with MediWaste to develop a drug education program."

"What?" Holm stilled. "Who are you working with?"

"Devin Cole himself." Sedin licked his chapped lips. "He had issues in high school and college. Last year, when he found out about my record, we started talking about youth drug prevention."

I looked at Holm and then back at Sedin. "Cole didn't tell us about it."

"Would you?" Sedin shrugged. "That would've exposed us both before we were ready. This stuff has to be released on your own terms, so it doesn't look like you're hiding it."

"I don't know," I stated. "Maybe someone else found out, demanded a few favors to keep quiet."

Sedin shook his head. His dark, shaggy hair tumbled like a wave.

"I didn't do anything wrong," he insisted. "I drive the waste to the landfill myself. It's all there when I drop it off."

"Where's that?" Holm asked in a cordial tone.

"Huntington Landfill southeast of Tampa, with no stops between our facility and theirs."

Holm put his elbows on the table. "Can you verify you were the driver and that nobody else came in contact with the waste you transported?"

"Absolutely." He ticked off the ways on his fingers. "I sign out vehicle keys. The truck has GPS that our office tracks. I sign in at the landfill. They unload the barrels, and I sign off on the release."

That sounded like a tight process.

"Our people will check on that," I informed him. "Tell me again how waste gets from clinics to your facility to the back of the transport truck."

"We have weekly pickups at locations between Tampa and Orlando three days a week. The other two days a week, we fly to points throughout the Caribbean." He met my eyes. "Including Belize City."

"That sounds like a lot of extra work for you and expense for them," Holm observed.

"It's cheaper than setting up their own sealed landfills and then licensing their own people to service small populations," Sedin answered. "We own a plane that meets federal requirements for the transport of radioactive materials."

"Tell us about that process." I began to think the missing link had to do with the flights. "Who flies, who rides, who loads and unloads? All of that."

Sedin cocked his head a little. His dark eyes widened in his otherwise pale face. He tried to stand, but the cuff chain only allowed him to stoop. He shook his head and sat.

"What was that about?" I barked.

"Sorry, sorry." He licked his lips again. "I'm used to moving around when I'm thinking. So, I have two different pilots. Devon Cole recommended Frank Wilson. The other is someone I've known since high school. Boring as hell, but Kevin is one of the nicest guys you ever wanna meet."

"One more question," I told him. "Who has access to your boat?"

"What boat?"

I cut a look to Holm.

"The offshore boat registered to your company," I said. "It was found in Belize yesterday."

He shook his head. "The company never bought a boat."

Holm looked through the information on his tablet and then pulled up the registration sheet. He pointed at Sedin's signature.

"This shows you as the purchasing agent for Sedin Disposal," he said as he held it for Sedin to see. "What I don't get is why you'd take a boat this size from Tampa to Belize just to use it to dump some waste. Why not rent something cheap?"

Sedin's brow furrowed. Holm allowed him to scroll up and down the purchase agreement.

"I don't get it," he said at length. "That's not my signature. It's close, but it's not mine. I don't know who bought that boat or with whose money, but it wasn't me."

Holm glanced at me, and I nodded.

"Thank you for your time, Mr. Sedin." Holm turned his tablet off and stood. "That's all we have for today."

Sedin turned his palms up. "Not that I had much choice."

I stood and turned my chair the way it was supposed to face and regarded Sedin for a minute.

He was right about one thing. Selling Ritalin a few times during college was small stakes. The guy had turned his life around and created a future for himself. He took a hell of a risk by speaking to us without an attorney. Nothing he did since we met him spoke to me of guilt, but we had to follow the evidence.

"Hey, have you ever used green barrels?" I asked him.

"For radiation disposal?" He shook his head. "No. Some bright green ones were delivered to us by accident a few months ago, but I sent them back to the company."

"Okay, that's all I needed to know." I started toward the hall.

"Does that mean something?" Sedin frowned. "I mean, that's all I know about green barrels."

"I don't know. I guess we'll find out."

I met the others in the observation room. Diane watched as a guard freed Sedin from the table, cuffed him, and then led him away.

"I want more on Cole and Kelley," I told her. "Someone needs to vet both pilots. One of them is in on the operation. I don't know about you guys, but I'm leaning toward Devon Cole's pilot."

"I agree," Diane said. "Go ahead and look into

MediWaste, but don't stop looking at Sedin or his employees."

"Nobody's off the board." I turned toward Holm and Tessa. "I'm going to get the keys to my new department car. Meet me at my desk in a few minutes. There's someone we need to go see."

27

"Are you sure Mrs. Lemon wants visitors?" Tessa asked us on the way down to the parking garage. "She just got home from the hospital and is planning her husband's funeral."

"She left a message inviting us to stop by," Holm answered. "Sometimes, it helps to hear from the investigating team. We can't tell her much, but at least we can let her know she's not forgotten."

I clicked the key fob for my new department car. As of that week, I wasn't the mechanics' favorite agent. Flooding the silver Charger had got me on their shit list. Well, it moved me up a few spots. Okay, to the top.

"They didn't seem to like you," Tessa said as we

approached the brand-new, navy-blue Dodge Charger. "How many cars have you totaled?"

Holm laughed. "Only one, but they've had to patch his cars up more than a few times."

"And why do they give *me* the car, Robbie?" I gloated.

"Shut up."

Technically, the cars were assigned to both partners, but teams generally fell into patterns. I drove. Holm didn't.

"Why?" Tessa wanted to know. "You do have a license, don't you?"

"I can drive just fine. It's stupid, and I don't talk about it."

I snorted. The truth was that Holm *did* drive fine.

"He got to take the car home one night," I teased. "It was never the same after that."

He glowered at me and held out his hand. "Just for that, I get to drive this one first, and not another word, Marston."

I stage whispered to Tessa, "You know he's angry when he calls me by the last name."

Holm stalked over to the car and jerked the driver's door open. A pail of blue glitter tipped out and spilled all over his pants.

"What the—"

Holm's yell was cut off by a bunch of men laughing behind us. I spun and found the MBLIS mechanics laughing at the glitter cloud. Tessa put her hand over her mouth but couldn't hide her laughter.

"Seriously?" Holm griped. He held his hands out toward me. "Seriously!?"

"I had nothing to do with it." I grinned. "In fact, partner, you saved me by calling dibs."

Holm threw the keys at my chest. As he stalked past, he winked so only Tessa and I could see. He was always up for a little drama, and it was good to see him getting back to his usual self. For a second, I wondered if he'd heard something about his sister.

The mechanics' laughter lit up again as Holm went to the passenger side. He looked up in confusion as he swung the door open.

"Shit!" he yelped.

I went around and looked, and hell if he wasn't glitter-bombed again.

"It wasn't my fault," he yelled in a plaintive tone. "Marston drowned it, not me!"

"Eh, you were there," our chief mechanic hollered back. "Have fun, fellas."

"Good thing I didn't call shotgun," Tessa mused.

"I think I'll sit in the back, but you guys can check it out first."

After a thorough inspection for more glittery mischief, we declared the car fit for law enforcement professionals and their guests. Holm got as much glitter off as he could before we headed out for Bridget Lemon's house, but there was only so much he could do. When we parked in front of her house, he slouched in the seat.

"I can't drag glitter into that poor woman's house," he told me. "I'll stay out here."

"At least go to the door and pay your respects," Tessa suggested. "It'll mean a lot to her."

The choice was lifted from us when Bridget Lemon walked out and waved at us. She came over to the car as we got out. One look at Holm's shimmering pants cracked her up.

"I'm sorry," she giggled. "I suppose that wasn't your idea?"

"No, ma'am." He smiled for her. "Someone's idea of a joke."

"Well, come on inside." She pointed at Holm. "Especially you. I have a lint roller you can use." She turned to Tessa. "I don't believe we've met."

Tessa stepped forward and shook her hand.

"Tessa Bleu. I'm covering this investigation for the *National EcoStar*."

"Oh!" Bridget put her hand to her chest. "Dare enjoyed that magazine. Are you an underwater photographer?"

Tessa glanced at me and bit her lip. "I've done some reef work, yes."

Bridget led us into the house that Dare built. It was a large, two-story home, bright and open. Mementos from their career together were arranged in tasteful displays throughout the living and dining rooms. The simplest, yet most moving piece was a pair of diving masks. Someone had wound their elastic bands together with a yellow ribbon, and they now hung together over the archway to the kitchen.

Bridget noticed me looking at the masks.

"Those were from our wedding." Her wistful smile touched red-rimmed eyes. "We had the church wedding for our families, but the real celebration was during the honeymoon with our diving family. We rented a superyacht in the Bahamas. A friend performed the ceremony, and when we kissed, everyone dove in." She sniffed but continued to smile. "My mother never forgave me for ruining that damned dress."

"That's beautiful, Mrs. Lemon," Tessa said. "I love how you placed it over the entrance to your kitchen. A lot of people say the kitchen—"

"Is the heart of the home." Bridget beamed. "Please, call me Bridget. I keep telling all these people it's okay to use my proper name."

"May I take a photo of the masks over the kitchen?" Tessa somehow made her gentle voice softer. "It'll help readers see your husband as more than an internet celebrity."

"Yes, please do." Bridget took a shaky breath. "I hope it helps your audience see that real people are hurt by crimes like this."

Tessa took several photos from different angles, including a few with Bridget leaning against one side of the arch. Holm and I lingered in the hallway as they went through a few poses and finished up.

"I'll speak with my editor about doing a proper interview at a better time," Tessa said as she packed her camera into its bag.

Bridget happened to look over at Holm and giggled again.

"I promised to bring you a lint roller, didn't I?" She stepped disappeared through the kitchen for a moment and then returned with one of those lint rollers with the sticky layers. "We can talk in here while you work on that."

"Thank you, ma'am."

Holm wasn't one for blushing, but he certainly had a bit of color in his cheeks. I didn't envy his embarrassment as he attacked the glitter. As he went to work, Bridget turned to me.

"How is the investigation going?" Her hazel eyes took on a flinty edge. "I heard you just got back to Miami today."

"We are pursuing some strong leads, but nothing is settled yet." I gestured toward Tessa. "She got some good photos of where you dove in the Great Blue Hole."

Bridget's eyes widened. "You didn't dive to the bottom, did you?"

"We took a small submersible," Tessa assured her. "As soon as they let me, I'll show you the photos from where he dug around in the silt."

"Did you folks figure out where that stuff came from?"

I nodded. "Yes, and where it was supposed to go."

"Good. I have faith that you'll find the person responsible and bring them to justice."

"We'll do our best."

That was the only promise a person in my line of

work could make, and it seemed to be enough for Bridget Lemon. We offered our condolences and made our way back out to the new Charger.

"I left my car at the office," Holm told me. He grinned. "You're not the only one with new wheels."

"Yeah?" I raised an eyebrow. "I didn't know you were looking. What'd you get?"

"You'll see later. Jerry in the garage is finishing something custom." He turned to Tessa. "You want shotgun?"

"Sure, after a glitter check." She winked and opened the door to check out the seat. "Congratulations on your new car. You seem excited about it."

"Oh yeah," Holm said with a grin.

The Lemons' house was only a few minutes away from our office, and we dropped Holm off out front.

"See you at Mike's later," I told him. He gave me a mock salute and ran inside. I shook my head. "So, Tessa, what would you like to do until we all meet up at Mike's? We're meeting at eight."

"Are there any good places along the beach?"

I thought for a minute and then smiled. "Do you like Greek food?"

"I like it a lot, actually." She stretched. "As long as we can get a good walk in after. I've felt cooped up all day."

"Then I have just the thing."

Half an hour later, we parked across from a cheery restaurant right off the Miami Beach Boardwalk. The wait for patio seating was forty-five minutes, and we put in our names.

"Time for that beach walk we didn't get to finish?" I held out my hand, and she took it.

"I will take that offer," she said. Her eyes twinkled in the golden pre-dusk light. "A nice dinner after that will be perfect."

The white sand beach on the other side of the boardwalk was a favorite among tourists for a reason. That day's mild surf and sparse crowd made for a quiet walk. The lifeguards were wrapping up their day, and parents were dragging kids from their sandcastles and moats. Seagulls circled and pecked at sandwiches and snacks left by beachgoers and squawked as we passed them. Eventually, we drifted to the tidal line and let the water ebb and flow over our feet.

"My dad used to take me to the beach," Tessa told me. "We did all the usual things, but it was special because he wasn't home often enough to make it a regular thing."

"I hear that." I kicked at a formless sand hill that the tide was pulling apart. "I ran from my house a lot when I was a kid. Lots of anger issues and all that. The beach was my favorite place." I shook my head. "If I couldn't take a bus, I hitchhiked. The ocean's always called my name, I guess."

"I believe it. You seem born to the water."

I put my arm around her waist and pulled her close. A gentle breeze played at her dark brunette hair, which took on an umber glow from the sun's last rays of the day. A few strands wisped into her face, and I brushed them behind her ear. The softness of her skin was a balm under my roughened fingertips. I leaned in, but she looked out to the water.

"That boater's acting weird." She pointed to a speedboat that sped up, slowed down, and then sped up again, all the while coming closer to shore. "Think they've been drinking?"

As the boat ran parallel to the beach, the passenger turned sideways and lifted something long and dark.

"Run!" I pushed Tessa behind me and drew my gun from my shoulder holster. "Get to the restaurant. I'll meet you there."

Puffs of sand ran a line through the water and to my left. I fired until the boat swung around for another pass, keeping their full attention on me.

That gave Tessa enough time to hit the tree line by then. The boat got closer, and the passenger got above the person running the throttle. I aimed for them, but at that distance, even my skills as a marksman were iffy. They raised their weapon, and I dropped to my knees. The spray of bullets stitched a line through the water, missing again but much closer. I rolled to the right and barely missed getting plugged as gunfire tore up the beach.

"Ethan, get up here before they hit you!" Tessa screamed from the boardwalk. Her voice was almost drowned out by other people screaming and shouting. "Hurry!"

Whoever captained the boat wasn't as skilled at making sharp right turns as they were at opening up the throttle. I took advantage of the slowed movements as the boat turned to track me and sprinted for the boardwalk. Sirens echoed off the hotel and condo buildings, and that was apparently the signal for our attackers to take off, roaring off into the night. I holstered my gun before police swarmed the boardwalk as tourists pointed at me.

"Don't move," I told Tessa quietly. "They don't know that I'm a good guy yet." I held my arms out as guns were drawn on me and raised my voice. "I'm a law enforcement officer."

"On your knees, both of you," a young officer yelled. "Put your hands behind your heads."

"Oh, stow it, kid," a familiar, gruff voice ordered. "I know that guy. He's a Fed. Right, Marston?"

For a moment, I didn't know whether to be relieved or worried. Detective JJ Rucker was not my biggest fan. At least he didn't throw me under the bus.

"I didn't know you were in the neighborhood, Detective." I gave Tessa a hand up as she'd complied halfway through the young cop's order to kneel. "Is anyone after that boat?"

"It got away too fast," Rucker growled. "Coast Guard has a cutter close by, but folks are saying it's a white speedboat with two people aboard."

"That shortens the list of suspects," Tessa said with an eye roll as she brushed off her skirt. She looked around. "Nobody got hurt?"

Rucker shook his head. "No reports of injuries." He looked at me. "This related to any of your cases?"

"I thought we left the swath of destruction in Belize," I told him, "but yeah, I think those are the people we're after. They know we're getting close." I glanced up at the high-rises behind the tree line and boardwalk. "Have your guys see if they can find any video of the boaters. Send it to TJ Warner at my office."

Rucker's long-suffering sigh would've amused me if it wasn't so important to put a finger on our perps. It was interesting that they hadn't done anything to hurt anyone intentionally but me... and Tessa.

"At least they didn't use an RPG today," Tessa noted in a weary tone.

"RPG?" Rucker echoed. His rheumy eyes widened, something that I'd never seen before. "Your subjects have RPGs?"

"They did in Belize." I walked back to the beach where crime scene tape and lights were erected around the area where the bullets hit. Tessa and Rucker followed. "The good news for you is that they haven't targeted civilians other than Tessa so far."

"So far?" Rucker said. "What's the threat level for anyone not you?"

"Probably low, but we're still trying to determine their motive," I admitted. "I'll make sure to alert Metro if we learn of any credible threats."

While waiting to give a statement, I texted my team to let them know we weren't going to Mike's. They shouldn't have been able to track us to that random spot on the beach. Unless they did...

"Rucker, I have to go. We'll send you our statement later." I touched Tessa's arm. "Let's go."

I took her back to my replacement car in the well-lit parking lot. Insects buzzed around the day-bright LED street lights. I had Tessa stand back as I went to the trunk of the car and hoped that the mechanics had moved my things to the new car. Without glitter.

"What are you doing?" she asked with a frown. "Is something wrong with the car?" She backed up and lowered her voice so I barely heard her over the ambient noise of the surf a block away and cars passing on the street in the other direction. "Ethan, is there a bomb on the car?"

"Unlikely, but I want you to stay back all the same." I hoped there wasn't one. I liked my body in one piece. "I think either they put a tracker on my car or hacked my GPS." She drifted closer as I pulled my Mag-Lite out of the duffle the mechanics stashed in there for me. "Seriously, Tessa, if I'm wrong, I don't want you to get hurt."

She relented and walked to the other side of the parking lot and stepped behind a minivan as I checked the grill and under the bumper, all the obvious areas. Next were the wheel wells and under-carriage.

Now, I've never been accused of being fussy about my clothes, but I happened to have a new pair of khakis on that day. My luck was that the parking lot had been recently sealcoated, probably that week. In the Florida heat, that stuff can leave nasty marks on your clothes. To check the wheel wells and undercarriage, I had to get to the ground. By the time I found the unsub's little device, my pants were ruined. When I stood and held the device up, Tessa ran over to see.

"They knew we were here," I told her. "I'm thinking they drove and then stole a boat from the marina over there." I pointed to the west, where there were plenty of boats to jack.

"You just got this car." She frowned and shook her head. "When would they have...?" Her brows lifted, and her mouth formed a perfectly kissable "o" of surprise. "They could've followed us from your office, or maybe they were watching the Lemons' home."

I nodded as I dialed Diane's cell. She picked up right away.

"I just heard about the shooting," she said. "Any leads?"

"They tracked us. I think they're watching the Lemon house."

"Okay. I'll get some of our guys and a uni on it."
She spoke to someone in the background. "I
wouldn't go to Mike's tonight if I were you."

"I canceled. I'm taking Tessa home with me." At
Tessa's longing glance toward the restaurant, I
added, "After we get some take out. The woman is
famished."

"I don't want to ride in that car," Tessa said. "I'll
gladly wait for my takeout with all those officers still
around than be followed again."

"I'll have Birn meet you two over there," Diane
decided. "He's closest, and he can drop you off at the
marina."

"Thanks, boss. Better get this car towed and
inspected," I added. "Just in case."

"They love you in the garage, Ethan." Diane
laughed. "Adore you."

"Ask them about glitter bombs," I told her. "*Then*
say they love me. Or Holm. Definitely Holm."

"What?"

"Ask him. Talk to you soon." I ended the call
before I got anyone in trouble. Let them blame
Holm, not me, for outing their shenanigans.

28

BIRN INVITED himself along when he dropped us off at my houseboat. I appreciated the ride, but I'd hoped for some private time with Tessa, especially after the chaos at the beach. Birn was the kind of guy who could usually take a hint, but he came right in and plopped on my couch.

"I didn't know to order you anything," Tessa told him.

"Not a problem. I had a snack a little while ago." His phone pinged, he checked it, and then he nodded. "Fact is, Director Ramsey asked me to hang around for a bit, make sure you don't have any trouble. We don't know that you weren't followed again. Not that I'd let anyone track my car."

I tossed a dish towel at him as I crossed behind him. "Smartass."

"Just following orders."

That explained it. I wasn't sure that Diane was thrilled to have one of her agents in bed with the embedded journalist who was foisted onto our investigation. Now that said journalist had been endangered multiple times, it made sense to put more agents on her watch.

"Feel free to raid my fridge if you get hungry," I suggested. "Unless you're only staying for a bit?"

"Haven't decided yet." He put his elbow on the back of the couch and turned to face the kitchen. "Are you trying to get me to leave?"

Tessa's cheeks reddened, and she had to muffle a laugh to keep from spitting out a mouthful of her fully loaded gyro. I was about to say something, but someone knocked at my dockside door. Tessa froze, and I reached toward my holster.

Birn held up a hand. "I'll get it." He crossed the room while at ease and checked through the little curtain on my door. "Hey, what do you know?"

He opened the door, and in walked Muñoz, followed by Bonnie and Clyde. They flowed into my tiny living space as if they'd been expected. I looked over at Birn, and he shrugged with a coy smile.

"Lamarr, what's going on?" I asked in my most patient tone. "I don't remember inviting people over here."

"You canceled on Mike's party," Muñoz informed me in a solemn tone. "Getting bullets sprayed at you will do that, but Mike made it clear that this is an unacceptable development."

"Mike...?"

My phone buzzed with a text message from Holm.

Come up to the parking lot.

I excused myself and went ashore. Between houseboaters like me and vacationers on other boats, the parking area was filled in for the evening. It took a minute to find Holm waving under one of the aging light poles. Mike Birch, our friend and the proprietor of Mike's Tropical Tango Hut, stood next to him and gestured for me to move my ass.

I did not quicken my pace if only to annoy my friends. When I got close, I saw Holm's new, blue Mitsubishi Lancer and busted out laughing.

"Are you serious?" I asked between laughs. "Those kids in Barbados really got to you, did they?"

"I told him he's too old for this foolishness." Mike lightly punched Holm in the arm. "He swears it's just for fun."

"It's a 2015 Final Edition Evolution," Holm said with pride. He patted the rear spoiler. "It's an insta-classic because it's the last year they put out the Evo. You have no idea how long it took me to find this."

"Partner, you crack me up, but if it makes you happy, I'm happy," I told him with a shake of my head.

"I'll be happy to get these goodies inside." Mike opened the hatchback and pulled out a box. "Four Roses, superfine sugar, seltzer water, and fresh mint."

"Because we got shot at."

"It's a bad habit, Ethan," he said with a hint of humor that didn't translate to the concern on his face. "I hear our lovely Tessa was there, as well. I owe her a mint julep for each time she's been fired at *this* time."

"Twice," Holm coughed.

"Twice!" Mike blinked. "Damn, boy. What're you into now?"

"Let's walk, and I'll give you the overview."

We couldn't give specifics, but the nutshell version was more than enough for Mike. By the time we got back to my houseboat, he was as caught up as anyone not directly involved. I opened the door and waved him in.

"Tessa Bleu, two mint juleps for you," he bellowed as we went in.

"Mike!"

Tessa jumped from her seat at the table and ran over. Mike set the box down and gave her a bear hug.

"Young lady, I highly recommend you stay away from people with bad intentions." He shook a finger at her in a good-natured way. "I had to call in one of my bartenders to cover so I could come to take care of this crowd."

"Oh, you shouldn't have done that," she cried. "I'm okay, I promise."

He pulled out the bottle of seltzer. "I wasn't feeling the tango tonight, anyway. There's much better company in this room. I swear I'm gonna retire someday."

"Who'd run the Tango Hut?" I protested. "We need you there."

Mike pointed the seltzer bottle at me and then the others in turn. "You youngsters are going to drive me out of business, what with your line of work."

"Aw, Mike," Muñoz smiled at him. Dang, she could fool a person into thinking she was an innocent, but Mike knew better. "We bring in friends who don't get shot at." She gestured toward Bonnie and Clyde, who'd huddled in a corner to talk some geekery. "Those two, for instance. I don't think they've ever been shot at."

Mike ended up making mint juleps for everyone, whether they liked it or not. For Mike, we all liked it, although I noticed Birn discreetly pour his into the water from my little balcony on the back. He saw me looking, and we nodded at each other. He had a story I knew about, but that was his to tell.

Eventually, we all drifted up to my upper deck that served in place of a patio. I got the chairs out from the storage locker and turned on the white holiday lights Gramps had me string up a few months before he passed. It was something of a miracle that the darned things still worked and that the canopy had survived. I shared cigars that I'd brought in from one of our missions. They were only for special times, and the gathering of my team, who were my friends, counted.

"You got the right of it, Ethan," Mike said around his cigar. "It's peaceful here." A burst of laughter from the other side of the marina floated across the water. "Mostly."

"Eh, I get noisy neighbors sometimes, but it's not bad."

"What about hurricanes?" Tessa asked. "I always wondered what people do with houseboats."

I shrugged. "Depends on the storm. I have a guy who tows it inland and tucks it in a smaller marina if there's a bad blow on the way. If I'm in town, bunk with Robbie or Birn." I puffed out a perfect circle the way Gramps showed me way back. "I can stand a Cat Three easy enough. Just loosen the ties for the storm surge, secure everything, pull the shutters on the windows."

"And hope the dock doesn't break away," Clyde spoke up.

"Hey, that only happened once," I protested with a smile.

I ignored the jibes that followed. The *Mariah Jean* was my home, end of story. Gramps left her to me, along with the property inland. The orange grove and the small house were his and my grandmother's dream. I loved it out there, and I couldn't imagine selling. The neighbors were family friends, and they did a little upkeep in exchange for all the oranges they wanted.

Someone knocked at my door. I went over to the rail and looked down to find Warner fidgeting at my threshold.

"I'll be right down," I called out.

Warner jumped and looked up. "Oh, I didn't see you. Sorry, I'm late, but I got some new info."

I went down and then brought him to the upper deck. Clyde was ready to leave and offered his chair to Warner, who accepted. Warner had his laptop in hand and had a hard time sitting still.

"I put in a request for information on this old SEAL guy, Simon Kelley," Warner told us. "There was a shit-ton of red tape, even with secret clearance."

Bonnie gave a long, low whistle. "Wow, that's serious business."

Warner nodded.

"Robbie, wake up." I kicked at his foot. It was late, we'd had a long day, and he'd had a few drinks after Mike promised to get him home safely. I was also tired and dropped into my chair. "Warner has something."

Tessa looked over from where she was talking with Muñoz and Birn. They circled in with the rest of us, and Holm opened his eyes with more than a little reluctance.

"What do you have?" I asked Warner.

"Tessa and Mike can't hear this stuff," he said. "I'm really sorry, but you have to have at least secret level like these guys have."

Tessa stood and waited for Mike, but he didn't move. He let out a deep breath and met my eyes.

"I got clearance," he said in a gruff tone. "I'll prove it if I gotta, but I don't want to talk about it."

I sat up straight. "What level?"

"Ethan—"

"What level?" I didn't know why I had to know, but since getting to know him, that vibe had come and gone, especially when we glossed over cases.

"I'm retired. It doesn't matter anymore." He tilted his head toward Tessa. "But I want to hear about this Kelley guy."

Tessa shrugged. "Okay. I'll wait downstairs." She yawned. "It's late, anyway."

I felt bad sending her downstairs. Then again, maybe it was safer for her. As she left the upper deck, Muñoz turned on a radio just loud enough to cover our discussion should anyone walk by on the dock.

"You could've told us before," Holm told Mike. "What're you, like, former military or something? And why keep active clearance? You really retired?"

Mike shook his head at Holm. "I like you kids." He pointed at me before I could say something. "You're hardened, but in my eyes, you're kids. I'm fifty-nine, and I'm lucky to be that old." He gave Holm a soft smile. "And yeah, I'm retired. The bar is my retirement gift to myself. Keeps me busy."

"Okay, um, guys?" Warner pointed to his laptop. "This shit is Top Secret. You agents and Bonnie got special clearance for this. I-I'm sorry, Mike—"

"For God's sake, TJ, I got clearance," Mike barked. I'd never seen him this way. He leaned back into his chair and rubbed his face. "Look, I heard of this guy, okay? That is all I can say until I hear what TJ has."

To say everyone was stunned would be an understatement. Gentle, convivial Mike had more to him than I ever guessed.

"Okay then. I trust you," I told him. "Everyone in agreement?"

Bonnie, Holm, and Birn nodded, but Muñoz shook her head. "I have to see something to prove it. I want to trust you, Mike, but I don't trust anyone."

He nodded and took out his phone. People with clearance don't carry anything to confirm it. To have that information on his phone, it had to be encrypted like hell.

"This doesn't leave this deck," he told us. "I never wanted to tell you, but this guy you're dealing with, he's bad news."

He scrolled and tapped, and then our phones all beeped and buzzed. Mike sat back and crossed his arms as we checked the notifications. It came from the CIA. And the NSA. Mike had the highest security level short of the president. There were a few things that none of us would say aloud, including his real name.

"Shiiiit," Holm whispered. "You're a damned Bond."

Mike pointed at him. "Never say that again, Robert."

"Yes, sir."

"Don't ever call me 'sir,' either. I'm a retired patriot."

None of us would think of Mike in the same way again, but it explained a few things, and as much as I hated to think of him like it, it made him an excellent connection, if we ever needed it. Besides, based on the list we were sent, it was no wonder he didn't want friends to know. He just wanted to be left alone.

Muñoz put her phone away. "You understand why I had to ask," she said in a sad tone. "If, um, if you ever need to talk..."

He smiled at her. "I know, Sylvia." He reached over and patted her hand. "I wouldn't hang out with you ruffians if I didn't like you. I'm getting old, y'know? Maybe a little camaraderie isn't so bad."

"Thanks, Mike." Warner opened his laptop. He kept glancing over to Mike as he pulled up the files on Kelley. "I, uh, I see why you know who this is." He swallowed.

"Simon Kelley is the guy you heard of, the SEAL who took out the gunrunners on the boat back in the late eighties." Warner took a breath. "But, um, that's not what really happened. He claimed he believed the boat to be carrying guns and drugs." He looked up. "It was the wrong boat. They were a charter carrying tourists to one of the small islands."

A chill settled into my bones. "He killed an innocent crew?"

"When his platoon caught up to him and determined it was the wrong boat," Warner continued, "he claimed the captain fired on him and that everyone aboard was lying about the guns and drugs. They said he... he did some horrible things to those people."

"They buried it so deep I'm surprised you got your hands on it," Mike said. "What else do they have?"

"It doesn't say why he wasn't court-martialed, just that he was disciplined and resumed his duties following the investigation." Warner swallowed. "There's a reference to another incident, but there aren't anymore mentions about excessive force. Just write-ups from people who thought he was a loose cannon. Kelley got several commendations during the next four years and then went off the radar for a long time."

"Shit like this is why a lot of the public doesn't trust the military," Holm grumbled. "Us regular guys..." He looked over at Muñoz. "Us regular guys and gals just want to serve and make the world safer."

I wanted to punch whoever let Kelley off the hook. Rogue actors and their enablers made the rest of us look bad. Most of us, like Holm said, wanted to keep our country safe. Yeah, we got to fight bad guys, and that felt damned good, but when it came down to it, we served out of love of country.

"Mike, what else do you know about Kelley?" I asked.

"Worse than bad news. That time he was off the radar, he was black ops. Wetwork. He didn't get court-martialed for killing the people on that boat because he was given bad intel."

"That wasn't his fault, then," Birn protested. "Why does that make him bad news?"

Mike glared at the floor. "Because he enjoyed it. Toyed with them like a cat. You get the idea. When he learned they were innocent people, he felt no remorse at all."

"You were there, weren't you?" I met his eye as he slowly looked up.

"We were being vetted for certain services. Kelley went one direction, I went another, but we served together more than long enough."

"Why is he being careful now?" Muñoz wanted to know. I wondered the same thing. "I'd think if he enjoyed wetwork so much, there'd be a trail."

"I do not have an answer for that." Mike rubbed his thighs. "As far as I know, he's been clean since leaving the service. Hearing his name tonight brings back things I'd rather not think about."

The thing about individuals like Kelley was that they relished their work. Death was part of our world, and kill counts weren't uncommon, but to find sport in it? That was a whole other level.

"Warner, is there any intel on Kelley in the recent past?" I asked.

"There are mentions that he might be connected to some paramilitary groups in the States." He looked up from his laptop. "Like, the more extreme militias."

"Doesn't surprise me," Mike said. "Most of us were diehard patriots. He was on another level."

That's when the pieces started to fall together.

"Did Kelley know anything about using radioactive materials?" I asked.

Mike stilled. "Why?"

"He's in the medical waste business," Holm told him. "One of their subcontractors has been illegally dumping radioactive waste in the sea."

"Oh, hell." Mike stood and went to the rail overlooking the marina. "He loved improvising. Devices, tools, you name it. If he's messing around with that stuff, you can bet he has some bad intentions."

"This changes things." I leaned my head back and stared at the canopy. "We'll need a warrant to get into his office, check financials, etcetera."

"We need to find who's working with him," Bonnie reminded us. "You know, that person could be who is keeping him from killing civilians."

"For now," I muttered. "If he's making weapons with radioactive material, that won't last."

"He'll have targets, or he's selling this stuff," Mike suggested. "Either way, chances are that they'll hit a public space. A dirty bomb like that will scare a lot of people."

"The exposure won't be enough to kill people the way it did with Dare Lemon," Bonnie told us. "He was in contact with it longer than anyone would in a bombing. Well, unless they get hit by something. But a few fragments wouldn't hurt them."

"Bonnie, a few fragments could kill them," Muñoz said in a droll voice.

Bonnie waved it off with a frustrated motion. "I mean the radiation alone. The idea of a dirty bomb is to spread radiation and panic the public. It'd be a pain to clear the area, but in and of itself, the radiation wouldn't be enough to kill anyway, even if fragments are soaked in it." She bounced her knee as she thought. "I still haven't figured out how or why he's made all of it stronger, and I don't know why he'd dump some of it."

"Maybe it was practice material." Holm reached for a glass of water. "If it didn't meet his specs, he'd dump it."

"Or he could have enough and is planning to deliver." I got up and joined Mike at the rail. "I'm sorry you had to out yourself to us, but it'll save lives."

"The job never ends, Ethan." Mike looked at everyone on the deck. "Someday, you'll retire and think it's over. Then something comes up. It doesn't have to be an assignment or action, but your training and knowledge will be called on, and you won't be able to walk away."

I hated to ask the next question, but it had started to bug me.

"Mike, have you ever worked with Admiral Farr?"

His face darkened, and for the first time, I got a sense of a side he'd kept hidden from us. "Ethan, do not invoke his name. Tessa can't help her connection to him, but I do not have to acknowledge his existence so long as I live."

I blew out a long breath and leaned on the rail. There were a lot of coincidences in my life right then, and I didn't believe in coincidence when it piled up like that. I couldn't help wondering what put Mike Birch in my path, but I was damned grateful to count the man as a friend.

29

Tessa turned on Netflix while all the super-secret things were discussed on Ethan's deck. This was the first time she was left out of a conversation, and even though it was about clearance levels, it stung. While waiting for Netflix to load, she did a quick Google search for Simon Kelley. Nothing remarkable surfaced. The first several pages of results were about MediWaste and a disposal place before that.

After three pages of hits, she almost put the phone down. She told herself that one more page of results would be it. The link was halfway down the fourth page. The search description suggested a conspiracy involving Kelley. She clicked on the link, but there was a 404 error, which meant the page wasn't there anymore. She went back to the search page and clicked on the link to see the archived version. That also came back as an error.

Tessa searched for *SEALs, Simon Kelley,* and *conspiracy*. The dead link appeared first. Then, it vanished without her refreshing the page. There were no other results. She tried variations of the search but found nothing more than waste disposal links.

This took less than ten minutes. Other than the occasional sound of someone walking around on the deck above her, it was quiet. Netflix had finally loaded, so she chose something to fill the room's silence. The streaming service had created new episodes of a show about a fallen angel that was canceled on network television, so she sunk into it. She was toward the end of the second episode when she heard people coming down the stairs from the rooftop.

She paused and got up to meet them. Bonnie was first, and even though Tessa didn't know her well, she could tell Bonnie's smile was forced. Lamarr and Robbie didn't look much happier. Sylvia, Ethan, and Mike looked downright grim. Her stomach clenched with worry as Warner appeared and then dropped into Ethan's recliner.

"I'm driving Robbie home," Mike said loud

enough for everyone to hear. "I'll see you when I see you. Be careful."

Tessa went over to see Mike out. "Thank you for coming over. I'll see you again without needing a mint julep, okay?"

They hugged.

"I'd be happy to make you a beach drink sometime. On the house, young lady. I won't even make you tango." His grin was almost back to normal. "May it be happier tidings."

Robbie gave her a fist bump on his way out. The others soon followed suit, leaving Tessa alone with Ethan. Finally. She'd been waiting all evening to have some time alone with him, but the impromptu get together had put that off. Now that everyone was gone, Ethan sat at the kitchen table with an empty coffee mug. He rolled it back and forth between his palms.

"That bad, huh?" she gently asked.

She sat next to him and put her hand on his arm. He set the mug down and put his other hand over hers.

"I've dealt with worse," he told her. "The thing is that he was supposed to be one of the good guys. Kelley is a legend, even in the SEALs." His jaw tightened. "Some people are made from bad stock, Tessa, and this guy is one of them."

"I'm sorry to hear that." She laid her head on his upper arm. "Do you think you'll be able to bring him in alive?"

"I hope so," Ethan growled. "That son of a bitch has a lot to answer for."

Tessa had the feeling that Ethan was talking about more than the illegal dumping that had killed Dare Lemon. She wasn't sure if she ever wanted to know what horrible things Warner had revealed about Simon Kelley.

"When are we going after him?" she asked.

Ethan's arm tensed, and Tessa sat up to look at him. "As soon as we have a location. He has to at least suspect we're onto him by now, and we have no idea where his activities are based."

"You'll have to speak with Devon Cole and their pilot they recommended to Sedin," Tessa surmised. "Is that going to be tomorrow?"

"We don't have it planned yet." He sounded like he was hedging, but he turned on that megawatt smile, and her concerns melted away. "Tomorrow comes early. Ready for some shuteye?"

Tessa exaggerated the stretch she'd already felt

coming and then faked a yawn. By his chuckle, she figured he didn't buy the act for one second.

"Yeah, sleep would be good," she told him. "Know anywhere soft and warm I can go?"

Ethan stood and held out a hand. "I have a pretty good idea. If you come this way, I'll escort you."

She took the proffered hand and allowed him to lead her to his bedroom.

Not enough hours later, Ethan took Tessa past the parking lot to one of the buildings nearby. A parking garage entrance warned there was no entrance without a permit.

"I get one parking permit for the garage," he told her. "That's where I keep my car."

"Wait, you actually do have a car?" Tessa raised a brow. "Why do you always drive your work car?"

Ethan cleared his throat and led her halfway through the garage. He stopped in front of a tarped car and dramatically pulled it away to reveal an old Ford Mustang with a coral-orange hue. If that wasn't flashy enough, the car had a black racing stripe, air scoop, and rear spoiler. It looked like it could've been driven straight off the showroom floor.

"What year is this?" she whispered.

"It's a Mach One from nineteen seventy." He laughed. "She's older than either of us, but damn, she's good. I helped restore her, so I know every inch inside and out." His goofy grin made him look years younger. "I've been so busy that I haven't taken her for a good drive lately. Since I don't have a ride to work, she gets to see some sunshine today."

Tessa slid into the front passenger seat and saw not a single dust mote. She set her camera and laptop bags in the back and settled in. The leather bucket seat was firm and comfortable, and the analog clock on the dash was like stepping back in time. She wasn't a car buff, but she'd been raised to appreciate the classics.

Ethan grinned at her as he started the car. The powerful engine roared to life, and Tessa felt the hum through the floorboards. There was a reason these were called muscle cars.

"I liked the color because it reminds me of some of the prettiest coral I've seen," Ethan noted. "If you ever tell anyone that, I'll deny it."

"I didn't hear a thing," she promised, although she thought there was nothing wrong with the admission. "This is amazing."

He revved the engine a little to get her going and then put it in gear. As they left the garage, he put on his sunglasses and rolled the window down.

"The air conditioning is finicky," he told her. "It's not bad out, so we're going super-vintage for the air."

Tessa watched his face as he peeled out from the marina drive and onto the street. By the time they got to the highway, Ethan looked more relaxed than she'd ever seen him. She took her phone out, snapped a picture, and put it away before he even noticed. Sailing along on the highway with a warm breeze on her face felt good. It felt even better for the company she kept. Or who kept her.

The MBLIS regional headquarters wasn't far from the marina, and Tessa regretted that the drive had been so short. What she wouldn't give for a care-free day with no danger, no pressing cases, just Ethan and her.

The Mustang's throaty engine rumbled in the MBLIS garage as they pulled up to the space where they'd found the new Charger the day before. Mechanics from the service area whistled as Ethan took his time to back the car in. He snuck a glance at Tessa, revved the engine a couple of times, and then turned it off.

"Hey, Marston, you never told us about this sweet ride," one of the guys hooted. "Where have you been hiding her?"

"Not here," he laughed. "Is my duty car ready yet?"

"Yeah, it's clear," the head mechanic told him. "How's the 'Stang's clutch holding?"

"Perfect since you fixed it." Ethan gave him a high-five as the newer mechanics processed that their boss knew about Marston's classic car. "I'll pick up the Charger's keys later today. Thanks, man."

On their way up the elevator, Tessa chuckled. "It's like you were a different person," she told him. "Younger, happier. I liked it. That car is good for you."

Ethan grabbed her around the waist and pulled her in for a quick kiss.

"The car makes me feel younger," he agreed after the kiss. "But the passenger makes me happier." As they got off the elevator, he pointed down the hall toward the conference rooms. "We're having our briefing in a few minutes. You'll have to sit this one out because of the clearance situation. One of the other rooms should be open. You can do some work on your laptop."

Tessa watched Ethan join the rest of the team and close the door behind him. Going with his suggestion, she found a vacant office that had a desk and chair and set up camp. With a sigh, she settled in for the video call she dreaded making.

"Tessa!" Donald Farr's face filled her laptop screen. "I heard about the shooting at the beach last night. Why didn't you call?"

"If I called every time something happened, I'd never get off the phone," she said in a weary tone. "Donald, I need to know, have you ever had dealings with Simon Kelley?"

His lips thinned, and though it was hard to tell on a screen, she thought his face paled ever so slightly. He got up from his webcam, and she heard a door shut in the background. Seconds later, he was back on the screen.

"I was afraid of this," he answered. "There were a few characters I suspected, and he's one of them."

"Why didn't you tell Ethan's team?" She glared at his image. "They had to go through a lot to get the information you had all along."

"Not exactly, Tessa," he corrected. "I didn't know where these dumpings came from or who was involved. The motive is apparent once the name is revealed."

"Why would Simon Kelley's name make his motive apparent to you? It doesn't do that for me."

Donald was silent for a moment. "All I can say is

that I'm familiar with some of his work and proclivities. Leave the rest up to Ethan's team."

Tessa rubbed her temples. "I don't understand your reasons for having me cover this investigation, especially now that it's turned classified or whatever. Wouldn't it have been easier to hit them up with an anonymous tip or something?"

"Karma wants to make Kelley her bitch. They can't get him on classified work, but this case will be public as hell." He smiled through his thick mustache. "Your involvement means we get the big scoop."

"Are you more worried about catching the bad guy or getting the scoop?"

"Both." Donald smiled. "Let's have our cake and eat it, too. Hey, you'll have one of the best features of your career by profiling a little-known agency."

"An agency that likes staying under the radar." She put her hands on the table. "I get the appeal, believe me, I get it, but I'm not comfortable exposing them like this."

"I'm not comfortable seeing MBLIS get defunded just because some freshman congressman from Yuppie-Town, New York, has never heard of it," he countered. "Tessa, why do you think SEAL Team Six is so well funded?"

The answer was obvious to her. "Notoriety."

"Exactly. They're the faces of counterterrorism. Everyone knows they exist, but that doesn't keep them from getting their jobs done. Same with the FBI and CIA. When we present the public with this piece on how MBLIS saved innocent civilians from some dire threat, they'll demand their reps keep them funded."

"I guess that makes sense..." Tessa's reply was guarded.

"It has to," he insisted. "Coastal nations need MBLIS as sure as the world needs INTERPOL. If the Pentagon stops funding our offices, we'll have more than pirates and drug runners to worry about."

"I understand, Uncle Donald. I understand."

But as she ended the video call, she wondered how much of the story she still didn't know.

30

Diane assigned one of the up-and-coming agents to fly Holm and me to Florida. Muñoz and Birn had picked up a new case out in the Virgin Islands and weren't available. Not that a hop to Tampa required *Bette Davis.*

Agent Abbie Stark, who aspired to Special Agent status someday, taxied the Cessna 172 at the Miami Execute Airport. She had been, we heard, recruited by the CIA but had been pressured into leaving after personal differences with a supervisor.

Stark didn't know it, but Diane had her fast-tracked to Special Agent. Similar to Muñoz, Stark was easily underestimated due to her appearance. The redhead was average height and build, but that build was all muscle, and she was highly skilled in three martial arts and at the firing range.

"Agent Marston, do you want to log flying time?" Stark asked over the headset mic as we lined up behind other planes. "I heard you're going for your small craft license." She looked at me with a straight face and quirked an eyebrow. "If you're ready, you can do the takeoff."

"I'm not ready to fly with him," Holm groaned. "God spare us!"

"Thanks, partner." I met Stark's serious look. "Are you an instructor?"

She nodded. "I got my private craft license in high school and instructor cert during college. I keep it renewed and give lessons when I have time."

The runway stretched before us, and then it was our turn. I grinned.

"Hell yes, then." I put on the brakes and revved the throttle.

"Okay, go."

I let off the brake. The Cessna bolted forward. When we hit speed, I pulled back on the yoke. The ground dropped away, and I banked west toward Tampa.

"He didn't kill us," Holm muttered. When Stark looked back, he backpedaled. "Kidding. Well, not kidding, but I'm glad that he didn't mess up. I've been in the car with my partner far too many times."

"Stark, should I practice a stall maneuver?" I suggested with zero seriousness.

"No," Holm yelped. "Seriously, Ethan, I will shut up now."

"Good," Stark said with a slight smile. "No back-seat pilots."

The two-hour flight felt long in a little plane, but it was better than almost five hours driving. Stark landed us at a nice little airport right off the bay. Landings were new to me, still, so I didn't volunteer for that part of the flight. Holm made the wise choice to keep quiet about it.

The local MBLIS field office loaned us an agent and a Chevy Traverse for the day. A fair-skinned man with brown hair and a slight beer belly met us at the Cessna once it was parked.

"Agent Dustin Knightly. You must be Agent Marston."

"Special Agents Marston and Holm," I answered. His damp, weak handshake made me want to wipe my hand on my pants, but I didn't want to be rude. "And this is—"

"Agent Abbie Stark," she told him as she secured the plane.

"Pleasure," he said with a smarmy grin. When she was on the other side of the plane, he turned to us. "Hot little thing."

"Agent Stark can kick anyone's ass," Holm snapped. "Including anyone who makes the mistake of harassing her."

"Chill." Knightly held up his hands. "I was just making an observation."

"That is an observation you will forget and not speak of again," I ordered him. "Is that clear, *Agent* Knightly?"

"Understood," Knightly growled. "I didn't mean anything by it."

God, I hated pervs. I had the pleasure of working with extraordinary female agents over the years, and any one of them could put that asshole in his place. I didn't mind putting a stop to it before it got to them, though.

Stark rounded the tail and rejoined us.

"All set," she reported. She gave Knightly a cool look and then addressed Holm and me. "Acoustics can get weird. It's funny the things you hear when your back is turned." She turned back to Knightly and held her hand out. "Keys."

I turned to Holm and grinned. Diane was right. Stark was going places. Her take-no-shit attitude was beautiful to behold as she stalked away from Knightly. I turned toward the Traverse and expected her to toss me the keys. She did not. Although I was her superior, I decided it would be wisest for us to not challenge her wish to drive. Holm sat in the back and smirked at Knightly.

"We need actionable evidence against Kelley," I reminded everyone as we pulled into MediWaste. "If we can get Cole to cooperate, it'll be that much easier to get a warrant."

When we walked into the building lobby at MediWaste, none other than Devon Cole ran up to us. His face was white as a sheet, and his eyes were wide. At the reception desk, Mrs. Hastings looked almost as pale, and another employee ran down the aisle behind her.

"I just called the police," he gasped. "How did you get here so fast?"

"We were coming in to talk. What happened?"

"It-it's my nephew. Nick." Cole turned toward the receptionist's desk. "My sister is going to kill me."

"Mr. Cole, talk to us." I snapped my fingers to get him focused on me. "Where's Nick?"

He pointed a shaky hand toward the back. "K-Kelley's office. He... Oh, my God." Cole ran to a trash can and threw up. "I c-can't go in there."

A police car screeched to a halt outside the glass doors.

"Mr. Cole." Stark stepped in front of the CEO. "Mr. Cole, I'm so sorry this happened. Where is this office? We'll take care of it from there."

He took a shuddering breath and looked at me. "It's two doors down from mine."

"Okay. I know where that is," I said. "Is Kelley in the building?"

Cole shook his head. "He was leaving when I got back for lunch. H-he acted normal. Said he'd be out for a while."

"Knightly, have the police get a BOLO out on Simon Kelley," I ordered. I did not want that pasty asshole around this. "Tell them MBLIS is on scene."

We drew our weapons and ran to the back as the first cop got into the lobby. Knightly's officious voice followed us back until the door swung shut. Holm led us through the cubicle maze until we reached the executive offices. Blood spatters marked the cube wall across from Kelley's office, and there was a pool of blood leaching from the doorway into the hallway carpet.

I stepped over it and looked in.

"Shit..." Stark said when she saw.

"Woah," Holm said.

"Yeah, Kelley's our guy," I muttered.

Nick Ames's body was left two steps inside the door. Kelley must have worked quick to gut the young man. The blood spray that landed on the cubicle continued inside. It looked like someone had given a combat knife to a wild animal. Maybe that's what Kelley was.

Uniformed cops ran up to the scene with guns drawn.

"Put those away," I ordered. "The suspect is gone."

"Badges, slowly," a corporal snapped. "There's a dead MBLIS agent and stolen vehicle at their garage."

Holm and I looked at each other, and Stark swore.

"Our ride was an imposter," Holm snarled. "Dammit. They were ready for us. How the hell did they find out?"

"Badges," the corporal barked. "Slowly and keep your hands away from your holsters."

We complied, and a few minutes later, a harried detective arrived, out of breath, on the scene. He saw Ames's remains and hit the door frame with the side of his fist.

"Detective Chenowith," he said by way of introduction, and between huge gasps. "I was just at the MBLIS scene. They're a few blocks over. Suspect snapped the agent's neck and took the SUV. We think he came here to pick up your guy and get him out of here."

"So much for not targeting innocents," I growled. "He's still escalating, Detective. I want to know how he got tipped off." I looked at Holm and Stark. "How the hell did they know we were flying in?"

"Detective!" A stocky officer ran up to him. "They found the Traverse. It's on fire at a park. Some kids said a couple of men set it and left in a black car. One of the kids got video, but it's not very good."

"Lock down the airports," I told them. "Kelley is going to try to fly out. Check the Sedin Disposal plane besides the commercial flights at the international airport. He may be working with one of the Sedin pilots."

"And the marinas," Holm added. "He's known to grab boats and get the hell out of Dodge."

"Damn," the detective said. "That's a wide net, fellas. We have a lot of marinas..."

"I know." My jaw muscles wouldn't relax, and I couldn't stop pacing. Kelley could be anywhere. "I need a pair of gloves, Detective. Ames must have said or found something to set him off."

"From what I hear, that kid pissed everyone off," Stark observed. "I'll talk with employees. They went to their shelter-in-place locations when the screams started."

"Alright," I told her as an officer handed me gloves. "More of our local agents should be here soon."

I put on the gloves and stepped wide around the remains. Kelley's desk was spotless, but not in the dumped-everything-off kind of way. The few items that sat on the desk were aligned to perfect angles and parallels. Even the desk phone's cords had been laid in precise measure.

Behind the desk, the leather chair showed little wear, and that was at the front edge alone. Of the desk's drawers, the only one that showed a scuffed handle was on the top right. I nudged the drawer out. It held the usual pens, thumbtacks, and business cards that one might expect, but its bottom looked shallower than it ought. I pulled it the rest of the way out and dumped the contents onto the desk.

"Hey, you're messing up the crime scene," Detective Chenowith complained. "You know better."

"I know this guy is in the wind, and the sooner we're looking in the right place, the sooner we'll find him." I saw the space underneath the drawer and showed it to Chenowith. "He's armed." I pointed to an empty nylon holster that was attached to the drawer bottom. "This was his handgun, and this," I pointed at a slimmer, familiar outline, "is the sheath for his KaBar. I guarantee you he has both weapons with him, if not more."

"Oh, God." The detective shook his head as he stared at the young man. "How old was Ames?"

"Early twenties, I think." I looked to Holm, who shrugged. "Robbie, go look at Ames's desk. See if he had anything about Kelley over there. Maybe he ran across something and went to confront Kelley."

"Or blackmail him," Holm suggested. "That kid thought he had brass balls. He might've tried something stupid."

"Exactly."

While Holm did that, I combed through the other drawers and filing cabinet kept in a corner. The only files to be found were records on employees and timesheets... nothing actionable. Forensics from the local PD and MBLIS arrived and dicked around about who should do what.

"Enough," I barked. "It's a MBLIS case. If you don't like it, call Director Ramsey at the Miami field office."

Once that was settled, I finished my cursory look

around Kelley's office. There was nothing to indicate his involvement in anything but MediWaste's business. He didn't even have a computer in the room. It looked like he barely used the space. I left the office, which was more difficult with the activity now centered around Ames's body.

A couple of doors down, at the CEO's office, Holm was alone in the reception room with a folder spread out on Ames's desktop. Red and green notes covered several sheets of paper. Holm shook his head over what he read and waved me over.

"Nick was smarter than he let on," Holm said in a soft voice. "The other day, when I took him out to get food, I saw it. He was screwing with people because nobody took him seriously. I... Ethan, I didn't think he cared about anything I said."

"Robbie?" I stepped up next to him. "Talk to me, partner."

"I told him that nobody would take him seriously until he started to take himself seriously. That he needed to take what he was good at and find something he liked to do with it." He leaned on the desk. "You know, the standard bullshit we tell kids all the time. Ethan, I don't think anyone ever bothered to tell him that one little thing, but look at this. He took it to heart."

I looked at the paperwork. Ames had printed out financials having to do with Sedin Disposal, the contracted collections, and discrepancies that pointed to Kelley. The worst part of it was that these were discrepancies that not many people would notice.

"He'd be alive if I'd kept my mouth shut," Holm whispered. "Someone else could've told him those things another time."

"This is Kelley's doing, not yours." I looked through the carefully notated sheets. "Damn, kid, you got him." I took a deep breath and blew it out. "This will save other lives, Robbie."

"I know, but dammit, Ethan, when shit like this happens, it's the worst part of the job."

"Excuse me, sirs." A young police officer came into the anteroom. "We just got a call. There's a dead pilot in a hangar at the executive airport, and the plane is gone."

"The executive airport is on the inland side of the city," I said to Holm, and I turned back to the officer. "Did they say whose plane it was?"

"Sedin Disposal's, and it's disappeared."

31

"HOW DID THE SEDIN PLANE DISAPPEAR?" I demanded. "There's radar all over the place."

"I don't know, sir," the officer said with a hint of frustration. "I'm just relaying the message."

The officer left as others came in to process Ames's work area.

"How are we getting over there?" Holm asked. "We don't have a ride."

"Yeah, we do," I told him, "and he just walked in."

"I just walked into what?" Detective Chenowith asked in a wary tone. "I'm headed out to the other crime scene. Meet you there?"

"You're taking us," I told him. "Kelley's guy is who dropped us off here."

Chenowith made a disgusted sound. "They didn't tell me that part."

We collected Stark and then made for the other airport. Chenowith got us there and drove down the tarmac to the hangar in question. The medical examiner's van was already there, as well as police from that precinct.

The sixty-foot-wide hangar's door was halfway open, enough for the active crime scene to be investigated but not let out all the air conditioning in the growing heat. We approached the remains and were stopped by the precinct detective.

"I'm Detective Worth." He shook our hands. "Just a heads up that it's bad," he warned us with a glance over to Stark. "Vic's name is Kevin Jones. He pilots mostly for Sedin Disposal, but he has a couple of side gigs with charter flights. Nobody saw who flew out on the plane. Given the BOLO, well, that's why we had you brought over."

"What do you know about the plane's location?" I looked around at the runway and hangars. "Did anyone catch it on radar or eyeball its direction?"

Worth shook his head. "No. Jones wasn't found until after the plane was gone. Airport regulars are familiar with the plane, and they saw it leave fifteen or twenty minutes earlier than the discovery."

"Who found the remains?" I asked.

"The maintenance guy who cleans their hangar." Worth pointed to a Latino man who sat on a nearby cargo box. "He was late today. Lucky him. He gets to live."

I nodded and turned to Stark. "Get some photos for Dumas to examine. See if she'll fly out to look at both bodies."

"Yes, sir."

Stark opened her phone camera and went behind Worth to begin her task. Her calm, methodical approach showed Worth she was quite capable of handling difficult scenes.

"Was Jones the old friend or the guy suggested by Cole?" Holm asked.

"He was the pilot recommended by Cole," Stark told us as she finished her photos. "You suspected him of collaborating because he was the one linked to MediWaste."

"Sedin's pilot is the one working with Kelley?" Holm frowned and turned to me. "Looks like we're definitely making another stop."

"I wonder how many other people are involved from Sedin." I paced the length of the hangar and then stopped. "Yes, we are going over there right now. Let the local MBLIS crew go over this scene."

"You want to see who isn't on site at Sedin," Stark observed.

"Exactly. It might help us to get our bearings on where he may have gone." I stalked back to the pilot's remains with Holm and Stark on my six. "And it'll help explain how Kelley got the materials." I slowed up for Stark. "You get briefed on the case this morning?"

"Not exactly. I got the case file folder and reviewed it before meeting you at the airport this morning." She shrugged. "It's the job."

"That's better than some people," Holm said with appreciation.

"And that's why some people don't make Special Agent." Stark's smile softened her stern appearance, but it vanished when she glanced at the body. "Hold on…"

The ME was ready to move the remains, but Stark snatched a pair of gloves and poked at a clipboard that lay on the floor near the victim. A fuel receipt was clipped over a flight plan. Stark picked up the board and found a schedule of client stops for the eastern Caribbean.

I called Diane as the ME's team got the okay to remove what was left of Kevin Jones.

"I heard about the murders," Diane said as she

answered. "We have someone dropping off a car at your location. I presume you're going over to Sedin Disposal."

"We are," I confirmed. "I need someone to get Tim Sedin to talk about his old buddy, Frank Wilson. We think he's with Kelley, and..." Holm showed me a photo on his phone. "Well, shit. Wilson is the one who picked us up this morning. That was ballsy. We could've known what he looked like."

"But you didn't. We weren't looking at him that closely."

"Ask Sedin if there's anyone at his company who seemed close to Wilson," I suggested. "I'll message Warner to see what he can find to help track Kelley. The three of us here are going to Sedin Disposal and talk to people."

"Good hunting, Ethan." Diane ended the call.

A white Traverse arrived at the hangar as we finished up. The driver jumped out, looked around, saw us, and headed our way. He was muscular, of average height, with flashing dark eyes.

"Marston and Holm?" he asked. At our nods, he gestured to the Traverse. "Special Agent Hallows with Tampa MBLIS. Show me IDs and then get going." He cleared his throat. "I'm getting a ride back with one of the deputies." Sure enough, a county officer was walking over to meet us.

"We'll get this bastard," I told him as Holm and I showed him our badges and IDs. "This one's personal."

"Someone better," Hallows growled. "The more I hear about Kelley, the more I want to rip his guts out."

"I hear you. Condolences to your office."

Hallows gave a sharp nod. "Appreciated."

"We'll keep you in the loop," I promised Hallows.

The employee parking lot at Sedin Disposal had half as many cars as when we were there the first time. We went in and found a new person at the reception desk. He didn't have a name badge and looked a little harried.

"We're here to see Marci Anderson," I told him.

"She's, uh, indisposed," the man told me.

I showed him my badge. "We are here to see Marci Anderson," I repeated.

"Um, okay." The receptionist cleared his throat. "Just so you know, she's having a family crisis. We kinda all are."

"We know about your pilot, Kevin Jones." I put my badge away. "We were just there."

He reeled back. "What? What happened to Captain Jones?"

"That's not the family crisis?" Holm asked.

"No, sir. Her, um, daughter." He got up and went to open the door to the back. "I'll take you back and let you tell her about Mr. Jones."

"Her daughter. Charity?" Stark stepped forward. She really had read that file through. "Did something happen?"

"I'll let Ms. Anderson tell you." He led us down the hall to her office and knocked on the door. "Ms. Anderson, those agents are back," he announced in a loud voice. "They have something they need to tell you."

A minute later, the door creaked open. Marci Anderson's mascara was smudged, and her eyes and nose were red. She held a crumpled facial tissue to her chest.

"Do you know something about Charity?" Her eyes pleaded for answers.

"No, ma'am," I said in a gentle tone. "What happened to Charity?"

"She was gone when I got up this morning." Anderson sniffled and dabbed at her nose. "There was a note, and some of her things were gone." She swallowed. "You know, toothbrush, clothes, wallet. I found her phone by the back door. I think she forgot it. Now I can't call her."

"What did she say in the note?" Holm asked as he gently led Anderson to a chair.

"She said she's leaving with her boyfriend and not to follow." Anderson choked on a sob. Stark pulled up a seat and put her hand on the woman's shoulder. "That she hated working here, and her boyfriend has an exciting career, and she is going to learn from him."

"Who's her boyfriend?" Stark spoke softer than I'd ever heard from her.

"I don't know." Anderson looked up at me. "I honestly don't know."

"Unfortunately, there's not much we can do," I told her. "Unless there's a reason to believe she didn't go willingly, she's an adult and free to make her own choices."

Anderson nodded, and fresh tears ran down to drip from her chin. "The police told me that when I called. She's over eighteen, so I can't track her."

"Unfortunately, we have more bad news," I informed her. Holm was right about some parts of the job being shit. "Your pilot Kevin Jones was found deceased in your plane's hangar."

"No!" Anderson slumped over, sobbing. "Not Kevin. Oh, my God."

The receptionist, still in the room, backed into a table and sat with his hand over his mouth. He looked down and closed his eyes.

"Ms. Anderson?" I crouched before her. "I'm sorry, but you need to know the rest of the situation. I can give you a few minutes, though."

She shook her head and sat up with her chin trembling.

"Kevin... Kevin and I have been seeing each other," she admitted. "Most of the office knows, and it's okay because he's... he was a good person. We were talking about marriage."

"Oh jeez," Holm breathed. "I'm so sorry, Ms. Anderson."

"Please, just call me 'Marci.' I hate my ex's name." She caught my eye. "How did this happen, Agent Marston?"

"Simon Kelley from MediWaste killed him."

Her brow creased. "Why would he do that?"

I stood and stepped back. "Kelley and your other pilot, Frank Wilson, are the ones responsible for the illegal dumping. They took your company's plane and went off the radar."

Marci got to her feet. "I *knew* that equipment

requisition was off." She went over to her computer and punched at keys so hard I worried they might break. "Frank said we needed communications equipment, but that plane was supposed to have everything already set up, but he wanted more. Kevin said they didn't need it, but Frank convinced Tim to buy it. Kevin told me that was the kind of stuff that could build scramblers for radar or transponders or something."

"Shit," Holm whispered behind me.

"That explains why they lost them so quickly," Stark mused. "It's one of the tricks drug runners and coyotes use to cross the border, but it won't hide them forever."

I rubbed my head. Kelley was a slippery bastard.

"Can you think of anything else?" I asked Marci. "Even if it seems small or stupid, it could be useful."

"I only saw them together a handful of times," she told me, "but one thing stuck out each time. They're both very patriotic. Not that it's bad to love your country, but the one day, I heard them laughing about that girl who got hit by a car at a demonstration. Said they're all communists and should get hit by more cars." She shivered. "I agreed with them about a lot of things, but not that anyone deserved to get hit by a car. I told Tim they made me uncomfortable, but he's been friends with Frank since grade school."

"So he knows about this behavior." I looked at Holm. Either Sedin was involved, or he didn't mind talk that made his co-owner unhappy. "Robbie, call Diane. I want to video chat with Sedin."

Marci looked up. "Is it true that he refused a lawyer?"

"Yes."

"I tried to hire someone, but Tim turned her away." She sighed. "I don't know what he's thinking. No offense to you agents, but it's your job to make him look guilty."

Stark walked over to the door. "Only if they are guilty, ma'am," she said in a frosty tone. "He should know better than to risk another conviction." With that, she left the office.

"He hasn't been tried," Marci protested. "Unless... Agent Marston, did he have a record?"

"He got busted selling Ritalin back in college," I informed her. "He's had a clean record since."

"A lot of people make that mistake." She frowned. "I wish he'd told me, though."

"Thank you for your time, Marci," I told her in a gentle tone. "We can call you a ride home."

The receptionist who had stayed quiet at the table stepped forward.

"I'll make sure she gets home safe," he said. "She's my aunt, and I won't let anything happen to her."

"Charity's your cousin," Holm said. "Did she say anything to you about leaving?"

"No, sir. She barely acknowledges my existence." He shrugged. "Sorry, Aunt Marci. I hope she calls you."

"Thank you, folks, for your time," I said in as kind of a voice as I could manage. "I'm sorry for your worries. We'll do our best."

By the time we reconvened back in the Traverse, I was shaking my head.

"Raise your hand if you think Charity's disappearance this morning is a coincidence," I grumbled. Neither Holm nor Stark raised their hands. "Theories?"

"She went willingly," Stark pointed out. "Kelley or Wilson could be influencing her decisions, courting her."

"Or they made it look like she went willingly," Holm said. "Use the girl to blackmail Marci into helping them."

"She didn't know about Jones." I pulled out of

the lot and drove to the airport where we'd landed. "If that wasn't a real reaction, she's a great actor."

We debated the prevailing theories during the flight back to Miami. While we were in the air, Tessa texted to ask my location. Coverage was spotty over rural areas, so I stuck to text.

I'll tell you about it when I get back. In the air.

I hated being short, but I knew better than to have that particular conversation with Tessa over text. My next text came from Warner.

Merlin III found ditched near Fort Myers. No bodies.

BOLO for Kelley and Wilson esp marinas, I texted him back. *Charity Anderson might be with them. Back soon.*

"They ditched the plane," I reported as I put my phone away and Stark let me back at the yoke. "Kelley must have a base of operations, but where?"

"Could be anywhere," Holm groaned. "If he were going to go to one of the militias, I'd expect him to go north. Unless he flew south to divert us."

"I say he works on an island," Stark told us. "It's easier to cross borders and use the sea to lose themselves. There won't be as many questions."

"We need to figure out when Kelley went on Wilson's flights," Holm said. "That'll give us some starting points to narrow our focus."

"You'd think MediWaste would notice a bigwig like Kelley being completely absent from work." I tapped the yoke with my thumbs. "He worked from two locations, though. My impression is that he went between the office and the processing sites several times a day. He could've used that to his advantage."

"You think he tricked them," Stark said with appreciation. "That makes sense. The workers at the waste processing site think he's at the office, and the office thinks he's on site."

"And if they find he's not at either, it turns out he conveniently had an appointment or errand that suddenly came up." Holm made a rude noise in his headphone mic. "Do you think there's a way to track those days?"

I thought about it and sighed. "I have no idea... Wait. We'll have MediWaste check for attendance, or however they work it, at both locations. Robbie, text Warner to get on that. Abbie, when we get back, I want you to work with Warner," I ordered. "Cross-reference when and where Wilson flew with days Kelley wasn't seen at MediWaste's facilities. He may have faked being in the Tampa area by supervising over his phone."

"Whatever he's doing must be damned important to him," Holm said in a tense tone. "Ethan, it must be big for him to throw his life at it."

"I think he's making weapons for a militia," Stark announced. "Your notes suggested it, and I agree with that assessment. It's what makes the most sense. Dirty bombs, grenades, pipe bombs, you name it. They're going to attack an event, a big one with lots of people. This isn't the usual patriot group. These guys are extreme."

"What events are scheduled that'll have people extremists want to scare?" I wondered.

"Hey, I just remembered one," Holm exclaimed. "There's a demonstration that's meant to protest lobbyist money in politics. All the militias' favorite lobbies will be in their sights."

"Anti-capitalists and social justice warriors are some of their favorite targets." I tightened my jaw muscles. "Yeah, attacking a protest won't help their cause. It'll just kill and maim people."

"That's why these guys are the extremists," Holm reminded me. "They're Kelley's types. Kill now, sort it out later."

"He doesn't care about sorting it out," Stark told us. "Guys like him might have causes, but chaos and devastation are what they live for. Kelley is happiest with blood on his hands."

I glanced over at her rigid posture. "Is this personal, Abbie?"

"Yes and no." She took a deep breath and relaxed a bit, but she kept her eyes on the sky and instrument board. "Not him. The person who murdered my uncle was like this. He tormented people for the fun of it and kept at it until they caught him. It's why I chose this career track."

"Keep your head, and you'll do fine," I told her. "We all have reasons, and we have to face those demons sooner or later."

"Yes, sir," she whispered.

32

TESSA WAITED AT MY DESK, in my seat, with her arms crossed. Her camera bag sat in the middle of the desk as if accusing me of heinous crimes.

"You didn't take me," Tessa said matter-of-factly. "You went after Kelley and didn't take me."

Holm and Stark vanished a little too inconveniently for my taste, and Diane was in a meeting somewhere. I was alone with Tessa, and for once, I did not want to be.

"Kelley's dangerous," I told her. "Besides, you already had photos of the two offices. We had no idea he'd snap today."

My chair creaked as she leaned back a hair.

"You're supposed to take me wherever the case leads." She uncrossed her arms and put her hands on her knees. "I'm an adult, and I'm a professional. Don't treat me like a child."

"Tessa, this guy is the most dangerous person I've ever pursued." I took even breaths. The mere notion of Kelley getting near Tessa drew out a feral feeling I hadn't experienced in years. "It's cliché in every sense of the word, but if you're there when I face him, I *will* be distracted by trying to keep you safe."

She surged to her feet and got in my face.

"I will not allow you to pull the man card." Her voice rose as her cheeks flushed. "My job is to document this case, and that's what I'll do. If you don't like it, let someone else take the lead."

"My jobs are to catch Kelley and to keep you alive," I growled. "I thought I could separate the two, but I can't."

"Then learn how," she hissed, "because I am going from now on, whether you like it or not." She backed off and grabbed her camera bag. "It's almost time for dinner. I'm going to get food and then a hotel for the night."

I felt like she'd kicked me in the gut.

"You don't have to do that," I told her. "If you're that angry, stay in the guest room. I won't bother you."

She shook her head. "You're not getting it, are you?"

"You're angry because I tried to protect you. Right?"

"I'm angry because you didn't give me a choice." She sat on the edge of my desk. "Ethan, I value your opinion, but I have to make my own choices. Some of them could lead to danger, but they are still *my* choices."

"He killed two people today." I sat on the edge of Holm's desk. "Kelley enjoys it. I don't know how he went so many years maintaining his role without slipping up, because today, he was back at it."

Tessa stilled. "What?"

Too late, I realized what I'd said. That was another effect she had on me. My guard was down, and I got careless with information.

"Kelley has a history I can't talk about, but it matches with what he did today. Be glad you didn't have to see either murder scene. It was bad even for people used to crime scenes."

She set her bag on the desk again.

"I didn't realize it was so bad," she admitted. "They told me Kelley killed two and Wilson killed one. I heard it was ugly..."

"It was." I wet my lips. "Let's make a compromise.

I'll tell you about a situation. You decide if you want to go. If you do and then I think you'll be in danger, you stay back someplace safe with an agent as a bodyguard."

"I will stay back *on the scene*." Her piercing glare dared me to argue.

"Within reason," I added. "There are some things you do not want to see, Tessa. And I need to know you'll trust me if I tell you to get out or stay back. I won't abuse that trust again, I promise."

She sighed. "I just don't want you treating me like a helpless maiden. Uncle Donald wouldn't have sent me if he thought I was that fragile."

"Of course not."

"So, what's planned for tomorrow?" Her voice sounded less irritable. That was a start. "I assume you have a plan."

"We're in a holding pattern until we get a lead on their location or locations." I smiled. "That means I have tomorrow off unless we get a hit on where they went."

"The last two times we tried to go have fun, we got shot at," she reminded me with a raised eyebrow.

"I don't think they'll come after us while they're on the run," I told her. "Besides, I just had an idea."

"Oh?"

"Let's go see if we can find anything about the *Dragon's Rogue* on Grand Bahama." Her answering grin loosed a knot in my chest. "We'll take a boat out and rent a car when we get there. Drive around, maybe find something, probably not, but it'd be fun."

"What if they find Kelley or Wilson while we're gone?"

"Worst case scenario is that I'm out of range for a couple of hours while on the boat. We can charter someone to fly us out of Freeport if necessary."

Tessa nibbled at her lower lip. That got me thinking about some nibbling I'd like to do for her, but I had to make sure we were all good first. And that included an impromptu day at sea.

"Okay," she conceded. "It sounds fun, and we both need a break."

I held out a hand. "Do you still need that hotel?"

"I don't think I will, after all." She took my hand and pulled my arm around her. "And I think dinner in will be just fine."

Dinner in turned out to be more than fine.

The next morning, I took her to the other side of the marina where a friend of mine kept a powerboat.

"I'm free to use it in exchange for keeping her fueled and maintained," I told Tessa. "They block out the days they plan to use it, and other than that, open schedule."

The mostly sunny skies and calm sea made for a decent boat ride to Freeport. Tessa and I talked about everything but the case. It was nice to spend downtime with her, and we docked in Freeport before we knew it.

Our first stop was where they stored what few archives remained of the turn of the eighteenth century, the library. Grand Bahama, for all its paradisiacal splendor, was vulnerable to hurricanes, and it seemed that they had to rebuild every few years. Because of this, I didn't hold much hope.

"There's that official archive in Nassau," Tessa reminded me. "You should go check it out sometime."

"Now that I know what to look for, I plan to." I smiled at her as we walked into the grand library's front entrance. "Today, however, I want to stand on the same land that I knew Grendel stood on."

"Definitely."

She tucked her hand into mine and damned near dragged me toward their info desk and then the archives section. Said area was small, both due to hurricane losses and sparse populations throughout the centuries.

"I'll search for Grendel and Finch-Hatton on their database while you look for mentions of the *Dragon's Rogue* in the records."

Tessa's light shone brighter in the realm of research, and I liked this take-charge attitude now that we were in her element. Research and photography were interesting to me, but they weren't my life like they were hers. Still, I enjoyed the moment.

"Sounds like a plan," I answered.

They had a computer station to search for books and documents by keywords, as well as records ordered by year. I went over to the shelves and began poking through. In the years since the mid-twentieth century, the records took multiple volumes. The old histories, however, had nothing until the late seventeen hundreds.

"I found some birth and death records," Tessa told me. "The actual forms are at the Nassau location, but they've put most of it online. Unfortunately, they have very little that far back. If Grendel and his wife had a home here, there aren't surviving records."

"I'm not surprised," I admitted. "There probably won't be anything on the *Dragon's Rogue*, either."

Something rustled behind me, and I spun to face... an old white man holding a newspaper at a nearby desk. He folded it into its original form and set it on his lap.

"The *Dragon's Rogue*, eh?" His baritone voice wavered a little. "What brings you digging into that particular story?"

"You know it?" I asked him.

"I'm the archivist. Not many of us still here since this island became all about the tourist dollars." He stood and hooked his thumbs in his pockets the way I sometimes did while thinking hard on something. "I've heard of many pirate ships, including old 'Mad Dog' Grendel's. Some say the *Rogue* drowned off the shores of this very island."

"That's something I hope to find out," I said with a nod. "For now, I'm looking into some rumors that he may have had a wife living on this island." I held out a hand. "My name's Ethan Marston."

The archivist tilted his head. "Not Toby Lancaster's grandson?"

I stepped back in surprise. "You knew my grandfather?"

"Well, sure. He came here several times over the course of a few years." His smile seemed to look back through time. "Toby brought you in when you were a little thing. Told me all about you growing up. Last I saw him, you were in the Navy." He closed his eyes and nodded. "Word got around when he passed. True gentleman, that Toby."

A memory sparked that I hadn't thought about in years. Gramps had a friend in the Bahamas who liked to help look for the *Dragon's Rogue*.

There weren't many he allowed to hunt with him, but there was one...

"You're the only person allowed to call him 'Toby.' Arnold Palmer, 'not the golfer,'" I burst out. "He used to tell me about you, and how you two spent hours searching for leads and checking out unnamed wrecks in the area."

"Yes, indeed, that is me." Arnold jumped up and held his arms out. He hugged me and pounded my back before letting go. For such a frail-looking old man, he was strong. "It is so good to see you, Ethan."

"Small world," Tessa laughed. "I bet your grandfather hit up all the historians in the Caribbean."

"Not all," Arnold said with a shake of his finger. "Toby knew who to avoid. Some of those historians have the treasure bug as bad as anyone."

I chuckled as I thought of a historian who now lived in Barbados. She and another friend were helping to preserve archives that had survived on the sturdier island down south. They were on the lookout for anything relating to Grendel's story, as well. This was becoming quite the team effort.

"The treasure part is great, but for me, it's about family. Gramps would love the progress we're making."

"Is that so? Well, I wish I could help, but Toby and I searched every page in this archive, and there was nothing about the ship or Grendel." Arnold pursed his lips. "Did you say there was another name?"

"Lord Finch-Hatton. He was the original owner."

"Ah, yes. Hmm." He tapped at his bottom lip. "I do recall that now. There aren't any records on him, either. However, there may be hope." Arnold ambled over to a ten-drawer flat file, each drawer filled with old, dutifully preserved maps. "Would you believe these are replicas? The originals are in Nassau."

"That's incredible." Tessa marveled at each one he pulled out. "May I take photos of this?"

Arnold shrugged. "No skin off my back. Better check with the library board if you want to do anything with those pictures, though. For research only, it's fine."

Tessa was right. The maps really *were* incredible. Whoever replicated them took the time to apply the inks just so and weather the parchments and papers. It would take an expert to tell the difference.

"What does the map have to tell us?" I asked. I wasn't sure what to expect, but a map? Not much.

"Burial plots, cemeteries, that sort of thing." Arnold moved with the swiftness of a sloth, but I didn't have the heart to hurry him along. The man was doing his best, which was more than enough. "If I'd known the family was here, I would've searched the sites. At least, I would have looked more carefully."

He stopped at one of the trays and ran a finger along the edge. Tessa and I remained quiet as he put on a white glove and then traced a route from Freeport to West End.

"Are these places still marked?"

Arnold shrugged a little. "Some yes, some no. Most no, but that doesn't mean you won't find anything." He stopped his trace. "Here. This is the oldest-known burial ground. A mission church stood there a long, long time ago. As far as I know, there isn't much built or remaining in that area, depending on how you want to define it."

"Nature reclaims what's been taken," Tessa mused. "Disasters wipe out human accomplishments, and humans rebuild."

"Until they don't," I said. "Some places need to be left alone, and this stretch of the island, more so. Look at that, Tessa, three old plots along the road, which must have been horse and wagon trails hundreds of years ago."

"We can start at West End and work our way back," Tess suggested. "I know how much I wanted to see West End, even though it's a tourist trap now."

"True that," I answered.

Arnold nodded. "I've lived on this island for a long time. Before that, I vacationed here with family. It's changed. Lost its character in most ways. That's why I sit here. I make sure a few things stay the same."

I put my hand on his shoulder. "It's good to see you again. I'll be sure to stop in the next time I'm in Freeport."

"If I'm still here." Arnold's wink called my attention to his hazy right eye. "It may not be for long, son, but I'll be in good company with that rascal Toby."

He took his seat and picked up the newspaper.

"Thank you, Arnold Palmer, Not-the-Golfer." Tessa made it sound like a royal title, and Arnold beamed. "I'll nag at Ethan to visit you."

"You do that. Cheers!"

A bittersweet tang followed me as we left the library. I'd clean forgotten Arnold lived in Freeport. It was dumb luck to run into him. At least, that's what I told myself. If I were a more spiritual type, I might believe Gramps led me to find Arnold at that library. Some people would say he guided me from the beyond.

"What are you thinking?" Tessa asked.

"I'm thinking I'm hungry," I laughed. "I'm also thinking that we lucked out by finding Arnold. Food and then a graveyard hunt. Sound fun?"

Tessa chuckled. "Let's go."

Between food and driving to West End, it was an hour before we arrived at the small, ritzy tourist location. All along the drive was evidence of new construction going up on streets devastated by past hurricanes. At the furthest tip of the island, however, Old Bahama Bay was a bright destination spot with pastel buildings to welcome resort guests. The marina had slick yachts, fishing boats, and even a few sailboats that day.

"Conch salad?"

Tessa pointed at a small, colorfully striped building. Piles of empty conch shells littered the ground behind, and patrons relaxed with dishes of conch salad and other seafood delights.

"Still hungry?" I asked. "If you want a conch salad, be my guest."

"I will."

While she waited for her styrofoam bowl of chopped conch and veggies, I looked around and tried to imagine how the area looked in the early 1690s, back before there was much settlement in the area. The indigenous people were long gone by then, which left the tropical flora and fauna to take over until the Europeans arrived. Where the resort now stood, I imagined grasses and palm trees, bushes with dozens of birds.

Grendel's wife would have been in near isolation here, at the end of a long island, but a pirate who valued what he saw as his would prefer that to leaving his woman alone among strangers in a strange town, or aboard the *Dragon's Rogue* with his scurrilous pirates. Maybe she lived with or near trusted friends or neighbors. Or guards. We knew very little about Grendel's personal life, but, with luck, the South Carolina team would learn more as they processed the archived documents.

"Ethan, there you are." Tessa walked up and showed me her bowl. "This is pretty good. Want a bite?"

"It's all yours," I told her as I turned away from

the bay. "There's nothing left of the original character of the place. It's all chintz and glamor."

She paused with her plastic fork halfway to her mouth and then put it back in the bowl. I didn't mean to ruin her fun, and I started to say something, but she held up her forefinger in the "hang on a minute" gesture. She turned in a slow circle, much as I had moments earlier, and then back to meet my eye.

"It's true," she said in a sad tone, "but it's the way of the world. My job is to preserve as much of the natural world as I can through photos and words before it disappears. If we're lucky, my work might help protect some of those bits of the world." She took another bite of her salad.

"We can't save everything." I took in the happy and contented faces around us. One couldn't be sad for long here. "I would love to know how this island was before, but things change."

"True." She nodded toward the rental car. "First site?"

"Yeah." I got as much as I could from the visit. Any sense of Grendel's presence was long gone.

The first graveyard was almost two miles down the road. It was near a construction zone and covered in brush. As we got out of the car, I wondered if anything was left. There were no obvious grave markers. The most interesting part to the spot was a collection of beer cans and used condoms.

Tessa stayed by the car while I tramped through the weeds and brush looking for signs of what once was there. All I found were more weeds, a tree stump, and a few rum bottles. We moved on to the second location only to find a home built over the space.

The third site was closer to Freeport than West End, and I didn't hold out much hope. It was a little spit of land sandwiched between two large resorts. Its wild greenery challenged the modern simplicity of the resort style, and I was a little in awe at its existence.

"There's a plaque." Tessa pointed to a wrought-iron fence, where a sealed, wood-burned plank made a proclamation. Tessa read, "'This burial ground is protected by an anonymous trust set forth to honor the Finch name.'"

"It doesn't say to stay out." I looked past the fence and only saw palm trees, bushes, and a few other native island plants. "Come on, let's go look."

There was a gate in the middle of the fence, and it was unlocked. Tessa looked up and down the street before following me in as if she feared being busted right that moment. Given the hideous shriek of the rusty gate hinges, I wouldn't be surprised if the police showed up expecting a group of kids to be torturing a cat.

There was a small clearing in the middle of the plot. Thirteen small headstones, each chipped and worn by centuries of weather, were arranged in two rows. It was as though a cemetery began and ended within the same thought. And yet, someone had cared enough to ensure its protection.

I crouched by the nearest stone. Its simple, nearly erased script had a name and year.

Emile 'Shorty' Collins - 1704

"Tessa, look at this."

"You better see this one first."

She answered so softly I almost couldn't hear what she said. I rushed over to where she knelt at the other end of the back row. Moss and grime covered much of the stone, which was larger than the others. It had scrollwork engraved at the corners and a finer script than the block letters of the first.

Here Lies Eva Finch ~ Fair as the Sea, Sweet as the Songbird ~ 1701

Astonishment rang through my bones. This could not be a coincidence. My ancestor, Lord

Jonathan Finch-Hatton, was the original owner of the *Dragon's Rogue*. Guilford "Mad Dog" Grendel stole the ship on its maiden voyage and used it to terrorize the Caribbean for the next five years.

"I'll take pictures of the stones," Tessa said. She stood and squeezed my shoulder. "We'll make sense of it."

There were any number of possible explanations. The most likely was that Lord Finch-Hatton also took a wife, and she lived with Grendel's wife, as well as a few friends or servants. We knew Grendel hadn't killed my ancestor when he took the ship. I'd discovered good old Jonathan's remains in a cave near where Tessa had discovered a much fresher body back when we first met. The former lord had been dressed as a pirate, shot, and washed up to the cave in a pinnace. That is also where we found the golden coins I'd recently auctioned.

While Tessa worked her photographic magic, I explored the other gravestones. The names included "Pickle Eye" and "Rot Gut McGee," among other colorful forms. The last one, however, was the seventh in the first row, behind the stone I saw first.

Johnny Finch - 1734.

"I wonder if Grendel had his wife take on the

Finch name to protect her from retaliation," Tessa said once she was done taking photos.

"If so, why name their son Johnny?" I shook my head. "Things aren't adding up. I can't imagine wanting to name my child after the man whose ship I stole."

"Unless Grendel befriended Finch-Hatton," Tessa suggested. "You said it looked like Grendel didn't kill him outright."

"We need to find out the name of Grendel's wife," I decided. "If Eva was his wife, then we can expect that Johnny was his kid. If his wife was someone else, then Finch-Hatton took a wife of his own, and she stayed with or near Grendel's family."

The stillness of the moment was broken by a call causing my phone to vibrate. This was one of the downsides of having an international SIM card. I checked the caller ID, and it was Warner.

"We got a location," he told me. "Check that. We almost have a location. Kelley has a few aliases we found since diving in, and one pinged at Ponce, Puerto Rico."

"What the hell is he doing there? I thought he was aiming to supply one of the militias."

"It's anybody's guess," Warner said in a weary tone.

"Do we know if he's alone?"

"No, sir, we don't know yet." Warner spoke in a muffled murmur to someone in the background and then returned to our call. "I have people scrubbing the security footage for the past day at the business where we pinpointed him. By the time you get back, there should be more intel."

"I'll be back in three hours unless you need me sooner," I said.

"Three hours is fine. We're not sure how long this will take. As it is, we got super lucky just to catch this one."

"Good work, TJ. We'll see you in a while."

Tessa quirked a brow as I put my phone away. "Sounds like we found what we needed just in time."

"Hell yeah," I said with a laugh. "Hell to the yes."

33

Tessa buckled into her seat across from me on *Bette Davis*, the King Air 350 MBLIS was using to send my team to Puerto Rico. We'd gotten back to the houseboat so late the night before that we had both fallen asleep as soon as we fell into bed.

"I hope our pilots got more sleep than the rest of us," Tessa told me.

I waved off the concern. "They got their required sleep while the rest of us planned the raid."

"I'm glad Lamarr and Sylvia are coming," Tessa admitted. "I don't understand why you guys don't have a dedicated pilot, though."

I studied her for a moment. While the reason wasn't a secret, it wasn't broadcast everywhere, either.

"Funding," I told her. "The approval for the plane went through, and the deal was done before they found out the Pentagon decided we have two fully licensed pilots who also happened to be special agents. Instead of hiring a pilot as promised, they put that on Muñoz and Birn's shoulders. What a happy coincidence." Only nobody was happy.

"That means fewer cases for them, right?"

Holm snorted from across the aisle. "No such luck. We've been trying to help, but we keep getting pulled out on some crazy cases of our own."

Tessa looked at her hands, which were palms-up on her lap. "Donald is right," she murmured. "You need this story so voting citizens will tell their representatives to keep giving you money. They'll see you keeping our nation safer, stronger, and then they'll want to help."

"That's what it looks like." I could not tell how upfront Farr had been about supposedly wanting to help, but I had no wish to get into an argument over it with Tessa. "For now, we are doing what we can to keep things rolling."

A shadow crossed her face, and I had the feeling its name was Donald.

"We're going out to taxi," Muñoz announced over the speaker. "In four hours, we'll be in Ponce, Puerto

Rico. During the flight, my partner and I will take turns getting briefed on the raid plans."

Those briefings and more discussion on the contingencies were about the only conversation for the entire flight. When we set down in Ponce, we were notified to contact Warner immediately.

"They found video of Charity Anderson in Ponce just last night," he announced over the phone. "It's hard to tell whether or not she was with them willingly. Diane had Tampa MBLIS agents go over to check out the home and this letter that Anderson supposedly left her mom."

"What did they learn?"

"The letter she said Charity left her turns out to be a ransom of sorts," Warner explained. "Kelley and Wilson will keep Charity alive as long as Marci does a few things to help them escape. Marci said she was too afraid to tell you the other day because of their threats."

"Shit." I rubbed the back of my head. "So we have to catch up to them and negotiate the release of a hostage. While we're at it, let's make sure no dirty bombs get into the hands of the more extreme militias. It gets better and better."

"I'll let you know if anything changes," Warner promised.

San Juan MBLIS greeted us with a small caravan of dark Dodge Durangos and Chevy Traverses. As much as I wanted to stash Tessa somewhere safe, I kept her with me in the lead vehicle.

"Tell me the plan," I ordered her.

"We stop at a farm to the south of the property," she recited. "We'll put on body armor, and you all will get your weapons ready. Once we get to the property, I'll stay back with two agents and wait for you to scout it out." She met my eye. "If things get hairy, they're to get me to San Juan. If Kelley and Wilson are on scene, it will almost definitely get violent."

"It *will* get violent," I emphasized. I laid my hands on Tessa's shoulders and spoke in a low voice just for her. "Please, Tessa, be careful. I wouldn't forgive myself if anything happened to you."

"I'll stay away from Kelley, I swear." The sun glinted in those emerald eyes, and she blinked. "I'm more worried about you. Please be okay."

I nodded. "That's the plan."

She tilted her head. "And how often do things go according to plan?" She winced. "Sorry. I'm nervous, but I have faith in you all."

I introduced her to the two agents who were going to stay back with her until we cleared the property we were to storm. Agents Wallace and Greer were in their second and third years with MBLIS in Miami. They showed a lot of promise, and I felt good leaving her with them. The three of them were the last vehicle in the caravan about to descend on the devil's hill.

"Let's roll out," I hollered.

Kelley's compound's existence had been difficult for Warner to ferret out and more of a challenge to locate. Satellite imagery showed a large structure that appeared to be a house. Another structure with a metal roof was about fifty feet away. An access route wound almost a half-mile from the main road through a heavily forested area.

I pulled up to a deep-rutted drive in the middle of a shallow valley. We had to assume Kelley had the property rigged with sensors, cameras, and traps. To combat this, we had a special unit park behind us with a trailer, courtesy of the United States Navy.

"I can't wait to see this guy in action," Holm said with a huge grin as we got out of our vehicle.

"Yeah, this will be the cool part," I agreed. "I'm telling you, Robbie, we lucked out."

Two sailors were already at the back of their unmarked trailer undoing the locks to release Sasquatch, a new robot designed to detect the traps we worried about while sending a short-range jamming signal to derail camera systems and certain types of communications.

"Let's see this bad boy, Captain," I said in a cheerful tone.

"Aye-aye, sir." Captain Renaldo gave a sharp nod to his assistant, who controlled the door to the trailer. The seaman disappeared into the trailer as soon as the door was open enough for him to fit in. "My CO said he got a message from Director Ramsey that I'm supposed to deliver last minute."

"Okay..." I glanced at Holm and then back to Renaldo. "I don't know why she'd do that instead of calling me."

"I only know that I'm supposed to tell you this: 'Don't scratch it, Ethan.'"

Holm bust up into quiet laughter, and I swore a sailor-blue streak. Rumbling laughter from behind announced Birn's arrival, and Muñoz followed with a head shake.

"You sailors are easily entertained," she observed. The scowl broke. "That said, you did scratch my plane." She took a hand off the rifle she wore to point at me. "And if you do that again, I will hurt you." She turned to the Navy Captain. "Come on, I gotta see this baby."

"Yes, ma'am!"

That's what I loved about Muñoz. Some people might think she was tiny, but that woman was fierceness cubed, and nobody better get in her way. Not even long-timers with seniority, like Holm and me.

The assistant emerged with a control board about the size of a tablet and only a little thicker and handed it to Renaldo. I heard a soft whir, and Sasquatch rolled out of the trailer. The five-foot-long robot had six tires with deep treads. It resembled the Mars rover Curiosity, but without the solar collectors. The head-like protrusion on the front had cameras and sensors to detect heat and movement. The back half had four arms, two small and two large. A pneumatic ram was attached to the near side of its body. An antenna rose up from the middle as we watched.

Captain Renaldo and his assistant went through all the checks to ensure all systems were operating. As it finally rolled forward, I saw that someone had painted a bone frog on one of its black fenders. Probably against regs, but who was going to remove it?

"I have it configured to allow our comms to work," the sailor reported. "No guarantees that the target doesn't have our frequencies, but we have new encryption that should help."

I hoped so. Kelley was smart and knowledgeable. We still didn't know how many contacts he had in the military and through whichever militias he might be supplying with weapons. We also had to assume he had conventional weapons at the ready.

Renaldo directed Sasquatch onto the long driveway. The camera feed was sent to a laptop screen as well as the control board so that we could observe its progress. He sent the robot forward at a slow pace, and I watched the robot itself until it disappeared around a curve.

"I keep feeling like we're tipping them off," Holm said in a hushed tone. "I have a bad feeling about this op, but there's nothing I can base it on."

"We got each other's sixes," I told him. "Nuke the worries, and we'll see this through together."

Holm nodded but still frowned. It hit me that I'd spent so much time with Tessa that Holm and I hadn't hung out in our usual bachelor routine that week. I'd also taken his word for it that he was doing okay about his sister's disappearance. Charity's similar disappearance from Tampa couldn't have helped.

I took Holm aside and let others take my place watching the robot's feed. This had to be quick and now.

"Robbie, are you good to go?" I got a good look into his eyes. They were their usual grey-blue, but there was a shadow there that I had not seen before. "If you aren't, you gotta stay back. For you and everyone else."

His eyes flashed, and he stepped back. "I'm fit for duty, Ethan. If I weren't, I wouldn't be here." He stalked back to the small crowd around the screen.

I hung back and looked up the driveway and scanned the forest. Other members of the team had started patrolling the tree line to watch for breaches in the perimeter. The forest was quieter than I liked. Was it because of our presence, or were Kelley and Wilson out in the trees planning a slaughter? If they were, they'd find it more of a challenge than they could handle.

"Cameras," Renaldo said. He focused on the camera and panned and zoomed to examine. "Appears to be wireless."

"Okay, everyone, assume he knows we're on his doorstep," I announced into my throat mic. "Camera blackout will have him on alert even if he thinks he's in the clear." The responding clicks reassured me that our frequency wasn't blocked.

Renaldo sent Sasquatch forward again. There were no tripwires across the drive, but the robot

detected motion sensors, also wireless, at even inter-
vals along the way.

"Fall in," I ordered everyone. "Bot is almost to the
end of the drive."

Vehicle doors opened and slammed as people
got out of their vehicles. Other units, some with
CGIS, had already penetrated the perimeter to the
sides of the property while our caravan sat on our
thumbs. With luck, Sasquatch's jamming would
cover their approach as well. They'd started out as
soon as the jammer went live. They were some of the
best personnel at detecting tripwires and other traps.

On the monitor, Sasquatch showed the edge of
the house in question. It looked like a cabin-style
ranch home. Through the trees, we saw patches of
the blue metal outbuilding. Renaldo made
Sasquatch go in reverse and then crawled up to park
between a couple of trees to await further orders.

We got to the tree line at the end of the drive
without event. Whether it was because Holm was
already spooked or some other cue, that bad feeling
had a hold of me now. The approach felt too easy.
There was no way Kelley would leave his flank
exposed like this. He was too savvy to depend on this
paltry set-up of a few cameras and a line of motion
detectors.

I looked through my binocs. The windows were blacked out, and there were three deadbolts on the front door. A hum from somewhere near the house sounded like an air-conditioning unit and kicked out. The faint strains of classic rock came from an indefinite source. I got a guy with a parabolic microphone to the front. He checked the closest windows and shook his head.

"Radio," he whispered. "That's all."

Check-ins with guys on the other sides of the building came back the same. It was too quiet. Way too quiet. I had Renaldo join us at the tree line with Sasquatch's control board.

"We're going to ease the bot up to the porch and test the door," I directed the captain. "I don't like this, and I want to take it slow."

"Aye, sir."

The robot rolled to the porch and up all three steps. It paused at the top. Everything looked fine, so it rolled toward the door. No traces of trouble. It extended an arm to touch the door. Nothing.

"Sasquatch entering," I announced over the mic.

The robot rolled back several inches so it could deploy the battering ram, and the house went up as if a damned missile hit it. Debris hit like shrapnel in every direction, and the trees swayed back from the

shockwave. My ears rang even through my protective
headset.

"Birn, CGIS Blue, get back from the outbuilding," I shouted. "Everyone else, check in."

Within moments, everyone was accounted for.
We were damned lucky we had that robot, but we
had another building to clear, and clear fast.

"Sassy hit a pressure plate, sir," Captain Renaldo
reported. "She's out of commission."

I turned to the smoking pile that had been a house
moments earlier. The outbuilding was a good hundred
feet from the house, and the siding was pockmarked by
parts of the house that had punched through the metal.
I grabbed Holm and ran toward where Birn's team was
covering the outbuilding. They were along the edge of
the tree line on the opposite side of the property.

"No movement, nothing," Birn informed us.
"Burly dude over there tied a rope onto the sliding
door." At my pointed look, Birn frowned in the guy's
direction. "We'll have words later about following
orders, but he did do us a solid with that door."

The rope was barely long enough for the team to
have cover if the building blew like the other one. A
pair of grunts took up the end and, on my order,
heaved.

The door creaked open. When it did not explode, they pulled a little more, and this went on until they got it all the way open. A whole lot of nothing happened. Holm and I went along as Birn led his team on a cautious approach to the outbuilding. Several neon-green drums were lined along the far wall in the dim, yellow light. Two heavy-duty work tables took up the middle of the building's space. Remnants of lab equipment lay scattered across the tables, and boot and dolly cart tracks led out across the threshold. Whatever they'd been putting together, and however they'd been doing it, all the important stuff was gone.

"Weak radiation," someone reported. "It doesn't go past the door."

"Seal it," I directed. "We'll bring in crews to clear and clean the building."

"Ethan!"

I turned to find Tessa running up the drive with her camera bag bouncing against her hip with every stride. As she darted around the splintered remains of the house's outer walls, I saw that she had dirt all up and down the front of her clothes.

"Tessa?"

"Ethan, they killed Greer and Wallace and then

took off in the Durango." She leaned over to gasp for air.

"Are you okay?" I looked her over for injuries, but all I saw was sweat and dirt.

"I'm fine." She shifted her bag to the other shoulder. "There aren't toilets, so I went behind a tree on the other side of the road. They didn't see me."

"Was Charity there?" There hadn't been signs of her since the video of her in Ponce.

Tessa's brow wrinkled, and she met my eyes.

"Charity is with them," she told me. "She's the one who killed Greer."

34

TESSA'S STOMACH fluttered when she saw the MBLIS and CGIS agents ahead of her gather at the mouth of the access route to the compound, even though the raid hadn't even started yet. Ethan was in there, and she wasn't sure how she felt about that. It wasn't her place, she felt, to have an opinion on his job. Even so, her stomach didn't just flutter. It shook and trembled.

"They'll be fine," Agent Wallace predicted. "These guys do this stuff all the time, and the only people who get hurt are the idiots who resist."

"Dude," Agent Greer responded. "These are the guys who killed the Tampa agent, remember? And that was the 'nice' one of the crew. The other guy gutted two people."

"Yeah, but those people weren't SEALs, man. We have a bunch of badasses up there." Wallace leaned back against the Durango. "Those asshats don't have a chance against our guys."

"Thanks, fellas," Tessa said in a sharper tone than she intended. "I'm aware of all this."

Wallace straightened. "Sorry, ma'am. We were out of line."

Down the road, the mass of people in battle gear moved onto the property. Tessa said a prayer to a god she wasn't sure she believed in. Maybe there was something in the air, but she couldn't shake the feeling of something about to happen. She suddenly wished that she hadn't had that tall coffee on the way to the raid.

"I'll be right back, guys," she said as she grabbed a portable toilet.

Greer saw what she was about to do and pointed across the road. "It'll be safer over there. They scouted it out before going onto Kelley's land."

Since she'd heard a coquí and noticed a small waterfall in the creek they'd parked near, she also took her camera bag. A quick diversion wouldn't hurt.

She finished the first task quickly and got her camera out with the longer zoom lens in hopes of spying a coquí, a melodic frog endemic to the Puerto Rican jungle. They were nocturnal, so she hadn't expected a chance to find one singing during the day.

A loud rustling came from the direction of the road, and then she heard Wallace's voice.

"Who goes there?" he called out. "Hands up and show yourself."

"Please..." A young woman's voice rang out. "Please, I need help."

That sounded like Charity. Tessa made her way back to the tree where she'd left the portable toilet. She wandered further than she'd planned and had to be careful where she stepped to avoid tripping over roots and undergrowth.

"Hey, aren't you Charity Anderson?" Greer asked in a surprised tone.

Tessa reached the wide tree she'd used. She thought about leaving the toilet for a few minutes to go help, but everyone sounded fine, and she was the one who always preached about leaving no traces of your presence in the wild.

"Yes, I am," the girl announced. "These bad men took me from home." The fear left Charity's voice. "Really, really bad men."

Tessa heard a grunt and froze.

"That was amazing," Charity gushed. "I finally did it!"

"Yes, you did." That was Kelley's voice, the one that set Tessa on edge when she first heard it in Tampa. "You could've been quieter. Mine didn't make a sound. Stealth is critical to your operation."

Tessa set her camera to its quietest mode and dared a peek between a thick patch of ferns to the side of the tree. All the agents along the road in front of the Durango must have gone onto the property because Charity and Kelley stood in the middle of the road in broad daylight. They'd pulled the bodies of Greer and Wallace to a slight ditch on her side of the road, and Charity pulled a black knife out of one of the dead men's backs. She wiped it on his clothes and put it into a sheath she wore strapped to her leg.

Tessa zoomed in on the scene and took photos of Kelley and Charity. She swallowed her bile and got images of them standing over their victims. As they chatted, Tessa guessed that they were waiting for Wilson, the pilot.

"Did you see that photographer here?" Kelley asked Charity.

"I thought I did, but she disappeared. She probably went up the road with her boyyyyfriend." Charity made a childish face.

"Do you know who her uncle is?" Kelley snapped.

Charity shook her head. "No, sugar. Is he important?"

"Hell yes. Admiral Farr is a true patriot. He's infiltrated that shit rag *EcoStar*." Kelley's grin sent shivers down Tessa's spine. "It's simple. Gain influence over the enemy's sons," he looked down at Charity, "and their beautiful daughters, and turn them against the traitors that infest the halls of Congress." He held up a finger. "Now, we can't give him specific plans because if he knew and didn't turn us in, he'd be buried. That's okay. He'll be proud when we deploy the weapons in places that'll show those socialists we mean business."

"Hey, isn't that the guy that Frank says sold out?"

Kelley scoffed. "Frank doesn't understand complex strategy like I do. Farr is on our side. When the time comes to oust the enemy, he'll stand on the side of the mighty eagle."

"That'll be so cool." Charity flung her arms out and spun.

The way the girl acted reminded Tessa of Harley Quinn, the Batman character who was the Joker's sycophant. And sicko was right. She was childish and hopelessly devoted to an unabashed psychopath.

Kelley touched a finger to his ear and nodded. "Frank says the invaders are up by the cabin," he told Charity. "They have some kind of fancy robot going in. You want to do the honors, my dear?" He handed her something small and black. It looked like a cell phone.

"This is gonna be so cool," Charity gushed as she caressed the phone. "Is Frank safe?"

"He's on the way." Kelley handed the girl a slip of paper. "Dial this and hit send."

Tessa realized what they were doing only when Charity punched in the numbers. There was no way to warn them up at the property. She clamped her hands over her ears and shrank behind the tree as a massive *boom* shook the ground and slammed through Tessa's body. She curled into a crouch until the subsequent shockwaves passed.

When she was sure it was over, she took a shaky series of breaths and got her equilibrium back and the ringing in her ears receded. She picked up her camera, but the lens was cracked by the concussion. A series of hoots came from the road, and she went back to the fern. Wilson had joined them and removed a headset of some sort.

"That was epic," Charity hollered.

She hugged Kelley, who sneered over her head until she let go and ran to hug Wilson. His face cleared when she no longer touched him. That confirmed one theory to Tessa. Kelley had no real attachment to the girl. Wilson, however, hugged her back and spun her.

Kelley kicked around at Wallace's gutted remains until he found what he wanted. He stooped, retrieved something from Wallace's pocket, and then held it high.

"That nice fella loaned me his keys," Kelley told his crew. "It's a shame that he won't get his keys back, y'know?" He laughed at his own joke. "It's a shame we didn't have time to blow the shed. Oh well, another time."

Charity got into the front passenger seat, and Wilson slipped into the seat behind her. Kelley jumped into the driver's seat with something approaching giddiness. That was the most emotion Tessa had seen the man express.

Kelley put the Durango in gear and backed up over Wallace's body. He then rolled out, once again going over what was left. Tessa thought she heard a crunch, but she did not want to think about it.

CHAPTER 35

"It was a trap," I confirmed to Diane as I walked at the edge of the tree line on Kelley's property. "They knew we were coming, and they got away with the weapons. We're damned lucky nobody got killed."

I felt like shit for letting Kelley slip past. We thought we had everything covered, down to setting up a solid perimeter. Whatever we missed, we'd figure it out after we caught Kelley, Wilson, and Charity Anderson.

"Someone has to talk to Marci Anderson." Diane's sigh came through loud and clear. "That someone is me."

"You could have someone from the Tampa field office tell her in person." I shook my head. "I don't envy whoever ends up telling Marci that her daughter didn't just run away with a psychopath, but that she killed a MBLIS agent."

"There's something else," she told me. I heard a door shut in the background. "Warner found evidence of a mole in Cyber. They've fed intel to Kelley."

"That's how he's kept ahead of us." Even though I'd suspected it, the confirmation ate at my gut. "I think this militia group he's mixed up with has people everywhere. This isn't good, Diane."

A truck trundled up from the access drive. It rocked from side to side as it maneuvered the uneven ground and then stopped outside the taped-off area around the outbuilding. Muñoz and Birn met it while Holm and Tessa waited for me so we could go through Tessa's account from the roadside.

"One thing at a time," Diane told me. "Warner will figure it out. Bonnie's working with him on it. It shouldn't be long."

"You sure it's not Warner himself?"

"Bonnie's working with him," Diane repeated. "That said, I don't think it's TJ. He's worked with Bonnie before, and she trusts him. He's shown no inclination toward extremism."

"Gotta go," I interjected. "They're ready to

inspect the outbuilding, but I don't think there's much left in there."

I ended the call and headed over to the team. As I passed Tessa, she grabbed my hand for a second, squeezed, and let it go. People saw, but there was no point in hiding my connection with her. She had her camera bag, but she'd told me the camera's main lens was cracked by the force of the explosion. I resolved to do something about that as soon as I could. The least the office could do would be to replace it.

The San Juan MBLIS radiation techs were busy putting together a decontamination unit for people to pass through while cleaning up the scene. Their lead tech came over and updated us.

"We're going to process and decon the scene, but our initial look shows you're right." He pointed to a monitor with a grainy image. "We hacked the CCTV already in place. The reception isn't great because of the radiation, but an empty table is an empty table."

"Mostly empty," I muttered. "Looks like the drums that cut loose knocked crushed some of the equipment and knocked the rest on the floor."

"Why bother?" Holm asked with a frown. "They were already running, and they blew the house. What was the point?"

I scanned the scene and swatted at a mosquito that kept flying at my face. Unless Kelley had another safe house, this was all he had for a base of operations. He gave up his access to hot medical waste when he murdered Nick Ames and walked out. The man had brass balls.

"Kelley was done with this place," I said with something approaching certainty. "Whatever he's been working on, it's ready, and he's shipping it to the mainland."

Muñoz had been having a quiet discussion with Birn. She turned when she heard what I said.

"We know he's not working solo, now," she pointed out. "Think about it. Charity helped him make money by skimming off the disposal fees that didn't go to Sedin, but there were bigger pockets to help him get to this point. Charity and Wilson aren't the only people helping."

I didn't like where she was going, but we had to go there.

"Taking Kelley out is only going to be one spoke in the wheel." I looked into the treetops, wished I could find some peace there, but a hot wind blew through. I looked at my team. "Keep focused on Kelley, Wilson, and Anderson. They're the direct threats. With luck, we'll sweep up some key players." I clapped once. "Someone find Stark. We're leaving."

I chose a Suburban that had brought CGIS agents. Their special agent on-scene wasn't happy, but when I quietly told him the situation we had in Cyber, he relented and handed me the keys. Before my team piled in, I took them aside, away from others.

"Keep it to small talk until I say otherwise," I ordered.

The weather was a popular topic as we drove away from the scene. A few miles down the road, I pulled off next to a field and had everyone get out and meet a good twenty yards away.

"What's with all the cloak and dagger?" Holm asked.

"MBLIS has a mole," I announced. "Warner and Bonnie are closing in on them, but right now, I don't trust anything that could be bugged. Like MBLIS vehicles. We took the Suburban because CGIS vehicles are less likely to be bugged, but until we get the all-clear, I'm not taking chances."

"So what's the plan?" Birn wanted to know. "With Kelley knowing what we're going to do, we're screwed until that mole is taken out."

"We're flying back as soon as we rustle up a fresh

pilot and copilot." At Muñoz's scowl, I continued, "We can't wait until morning. The minute we get intel, we gotta be on it. Sorry, Sylvia, but you gotta let someone else fly her."

Tessa shoved her hands in her pockets. I had to admit, I liked the tank-top and cargo pants look on her. It'd be fun to see her dress like that under better circumstances. At the time, however, I saw she was working something over in her mind.

"We know Kelley's working with at least one militia." She kicked at a dirt clod. "He spoke about a coming war, and that he wanted to show my uncle and other people that these patriots are ready to act. Charity said some people think Donald has sold out, but Kelley firmly believes that's not so. He said that Donald is infiltrating 'socialist' spaces."

Stark raised her brows. "Did he say which patriots?"

Tessa shook her head. "Just that they're ready. It's a bunch of extremists, not real patriots."

"Kelley's people are close to doing something," I told them. "That's why the weapons were gone. They're already on the way. The question is whether they're on a plane or boat."

"Or more," Birn said. "This son of a bitch put a

lot of work into this. I'm thinking he's shipped out most of his stuff and is taking the last of it now."

"Let's get back to Miami." I looked at each person in turn. "Don't talk about the case on the plane or until the mole is outed."

On the way back to the Suburban, Tessa caught me by the arm.

"Kelley is crazy, Ethan. Completely delusional." She squeezed her eyes shut and shook her head. "I mean, you know that already, but you don't *know* it until you've seen him." Her eyes opened, and they brimmed with tears. "I'm scared. If he's not stopped—"

"We'll stop him," I promised. "One way or another, that bastard is going to pay for his sins."

THE SUN WAS SETTING as *Bette Davis* landed in Miami. Tessa slept through it, but the others were either awake or woke up with the noise. Holm had stared out the window for the entire flight, and I wondered if he was thinking about his sister again.

A text hit my phone as we taxied to the private terminal. It was from Diane, and another came in from Warner.

Warner wrote, *Mole located and arrested. We're secure now.*

Diane messaged, *Got tip about Kelley. You and Tessa meet me at the office ASAP. Send others home for rest. Need M&B to fly in the morning. Tell Stark she's going. Will email them details now.*

I passed Diane's orders on to the team. Tessa and

I drove over to the office. It was just after dusk when we arrived. The garage's sodium-vapor lights lent an orange cast to the area, and the navy blue Charger looked... unwell in that light. Before we went up to the offices, I went over to where Rudy, the chief mechanic, was closing up for the night. I held the keys over the counter where he was marking a few final notes.

"What now, Marston?" he complained. "I went over it front to back, back to front, and every other way imaginable. The car is fine."

I jingled the keys. "I don't like the color."

Rudy stared at the keys. "Are you shitting me? You want a new car because you don't like this one's color?"

I felt Tessa's eyes on me and could only imagine what she thought of me at the moment. I tried not to care too much as I dropped the keys on the counter.

"It messes with my workflow," I told Rudy. "Seriously, I just don't like that car. Silver's my favorite, but I'll take any other color than that one."

Rudy sighed. "Did you get all your crap outta this one?"

"Didn't put any in there."

He mumbled under his breath, snatched the keys, and went back into his office. I heard the metal key cabinet open and then slam. He came back out and slapped a new key set on the counter.

"I had this one ready to go for someone else. I'll change the name on the paperwork so that it's yours. Sign it in the morning, but you can take the car tonight."

"Knew you loved me," I told him. I picked up the keys. "Thanks, Rudy."

"You tell anyone, and you'll end up with the oldest POS I got."

"My lips are sealed," I promised. "Tessa?" She rolled her eyes and went on toward the elevator. "She won't tell, either."

On the way up, Tessa leaned against the elevator wall. "I just want to get back to your place and get a shower."

"You don't smell bad," I told her. "I could get used to Rugged Tessa."

"You're nose-blind from your own sweat," she informed me with a slight smile as the elevator doors opened. "Maybe we can shower—"

"Tessa!"

"Uncle Donald?" She stumbled out of the elevator and into a hug with the silver-haired former sailor. "When did you get here?"

"An hour ago." He looked at me without any of

the judgment I expect to see. "You're not hurt, are you?"

"No, no. Just shaken." She released him and held a hand out to me. "Please don't blame Ethan for—"

"Not at all."

He waved us into Diane's office. She'd taken one of the guest chairs, and Farr helped himself to the director's seat. It was simple decorum, yet it rubbed me the wrong way. I let it go, though, because this was the man who had led a fleet and sat among the Joint Chiefs. Decorum was all he knew anymore.

"Ethan, Tessa, I'm glad you're back safe and sound," Diane said. "Admiral Farr, if you don't mind, I have updates for Special Agent Marston."

"You can call me 'Donald,'" he told us. "I'm retired, but with permanent clearance."

"In other words, Uncle Donald wants to be a fly on the wall," Tessa said in a droll tone.

"Alright." Diane grabbed a tablet that she'd left on a table next to her. "We got a tip from a militia member. He went into the Charleston field office and asked for protection and immunity." She projected an intake photo of a regular-looking, clean-cut man. "Chad Billings. He said he couldn't get on board with using the dirty bombs, and he represented several people who felt the same as him.

He volunteered to take one for the better good by outing his brothers."

"So these are the people buying from Kelley." I crossed my arms. "It's good to know that not all of them want to hurt innocent people."

Diane met my eye before continuing. "You were right that Kelley got his weapons out before you stormed his property. He had help from this group. They're called the Legion of Patriots, and they've been largely off-radar until now. They're planning to hit a big event with these weapons. Billings gave us the location and time for the delivery."

"Haven't heard of them," I said with a shake of my head.

"I have." Farr put his elbows on Diane's desk and steepled his fingers the way he used to during the time I served under him. "They've been kept mostly off the grid by big money. Donations to the right people, things like that."

"Why do they want to do this, and why to the extreme of using Kelley's weapons?" I stood rather than fidgeting in my seat like a five-year-old. "He's all about chaos in search of restoring the nation to his idea of constitutional. This so-called legion can't think that dirty bombs will win people to their side."

"It will encourage extremists," Farr answered.

"It's not the same as a nuclear warhead hitting a city. This is an inconvenience with a few casualties. People will see the legion as finally doing something more than talk, and they'll rationalize the deaths and injuries as collateral damage."

"Wait." Tessa put up a hand and frowned. "Are you saying this whole thing has been a recruiting tool?"

Farr stood. He walked over to me and put a hand on my shoulder.

"Why did you join the Navy, Ethan?"

"To serve my country, sir."

He nodded. "And?"

"Because I wanted to do something more than sit on my ass all day, bitching about the world going to hell." Farr released my shoulder as the answer hit me square in the face. I turned to Tessa. "A recruiting tool. That's exactly what this is. They can't fight the war on their own, even with this group's resources. People who want to act but feel they don't have outlets will want to join this group."

"It's a better theory than most I've heard," Diane told us. "You're going to South Carolina in the morning, Ethan. Billings said Kelley is scheduled to deliver ordinance to Legion members south of

Charleston tomorrow evening. He'll be taking in one shipment by boat."

"He flew, then," Tessa pointed out. "There's no way he'd get to South Carolina from Puerto Rico in less than a day."

I nodded. "Agreed. My bet is they flew into a small airport and loaded their cargo into a truck. Get that truck to a marina and load the goods on a boat. Probably during the night so people don't see the storage drums."

"If they're in drums," Diane said with a steely tone. "They might be in smaller packages to make distribution easier."

I tried to remember if I'd seen any traces of shielded containers other than the drums. It'd been so fast that I couldn't say either way. It did, however, make sense.

"Either way, they had to get it from the plane to a boat." I paced while thinking. "Kelley has to have onshore contacts. We catch him, we catch his boat, and we just might be able to trace that back to the people supporting his crusade."

"Go get your sleep," Diane said in a weary tone. "Be back at o'six hundred. Wheels up at nine. The drop off is at sunset, so you have most of the day to get ready. We have agents in our Charleston field office getting a plan together, and your team will finalize everything when you get there."

"Sleep sounds good," Tessa admitted. "I'm exhausted, and my arms are killing me."

"I'm going to the hotel for the night," Farr told Tessa. "I can get you a room if you'd like."

She shook her head. "Thank you, but no." She looked up at me with a smile. "I'm going back to the houseboat with Ethan."

Farr nodded. "I thought you might, but it's my prerogative to make the offer." He lowered his thick brows at me. "Try not to let anyone shoot at her tonight, Marston."

"Copy that, sir."

Tessa and I left Farr and Diane to talk in her office. On the way down to the garage, Tessa wrapped her arms around me in a quick hug.

"What was that for?" I asked. "Not that I mind or anything."

She pushed her forehead into my chest. "For being you. For being here. I don't know. I feel safe right now."

I hugged her back and kissed the top of her head. After all that had happened since the beginning of the case, I didn't know how she could feel safe around me. Hell, *I* didn't feel safe around me half the time. I felt like I was a magnet for danger in all its forms.

The elevator dinged at the garage level. Rudy's office door was closed, and the window was dark. I led Tessa to where the department cars were kept and handed her the key fob.

"I don't know which one is mine," I told her. "Wanna do the honors?"

She rolled her eyes but took the keys and held them out. A click on the fob flashed the car's lights, and we went on over. Another click confirmed we had the right one.

This Charger was red, and it had black accents the other cars didn't.

"This is more like it," I said with a grin. We got in, and I found an inventory note signed by the dealership and Rudy. "Oh, wow."

"What?" Tessa leaned over to see the note. "Seriously?"

"'Ready for D. Ramsey.'" I laughed. "Well, what she doesn't know won't hurt her. Besides, they'll get her a new one like it. I just need it sooner."

"You have that backward," Tessa said with a smirk. "What she doesn't know won't hurt *you*."

36

THE LEGION OF PATRIOTS OWNED, through a private trust, a sizable estate on one of South Carolina's sea islands south of Charleston. The area was forested on land, and saltwater marshes ran between inlet rivers and the shores. Many residents kept long docks that took them over the marshy areas to their boats. The Legion estate was one such place. Gathering clouds muted the greenery in the trees, across the lawn, and out through the oddly still marshy area.

My team and I hunkered down on our bellies in the woods we'd infiltrated at the outside edges of this particular estate. Stark was on one side of me, Holm on the other. Muñoz, Birn, and a couple more agents were hidden on the other side of the lawn. A handful of MBLIS agents waited in unmarked vehicles at various points in the neighborhood.

Tessa and Farr were on a Coast Guard cutter out on open water, past the salt marshes. This time, she hadn't argued about staying back. Even had she tried, Farr would have pulled strings to keep her safely away.

We'd been in place since mid-afternoon. Several men had arrived, and they lingered out back while they cleaned guns and barbecued. Fragments of their conversations were audible as their voices rose in excitement and laughter. None of it was intel. The men talked about everything from NASCAR to fishing to beer, but not about their militia activities. Not outdoors where neighbors could potentially overhear. Some wandered inside as the humidity intensified and the sky darkened.

"Boat approaching," a voice said over the radio. "Positive IDs on Kelley and Wilson."

They approached on a flat-bottomed skiff. A black tarp was secured over what looked like stacks of boxes. Their boat skimmed along the length of the dock across the marshy area until they reached the shore. Wilson jumped out to meet a trio of men who approached from the back of the house.

Kelley remained on the boat with his hand on the console.

"Mobile teams, get in place."

That was the cue for the vans and trucks we'd parked through the neighborhood to park in front of the house. There was a risk the men inside the house would notice, but with the windows all blacked out, we might have a chance. No cameras had been observed, but they were likely hidden or small like those new Ring cameras.

The discussion between Wilson and the Legion men was jovial, although the men at the back of the house were casually assembling their cleaned weapons. I didn't dare wait too long.

"Wait for my mark," I said into my throat mic.

I wanted to wait for Kelley to get off the boat so he couldn't jet, but he didn't look to be moving anywhere. We had an inconspicuous boat docked nearby in case he spooked, but it'd be best to get him on the ground.

"Fishing boat on approach," a spotter warned. "Blond female at the helm."

"Is it Anderson?" I whispered.

"We can't tell. Trying to get positive... Wait. Yes, it's her. Positive ID on Charity Anderson. She's stopped the boat."

"What is she doing?" Holm asked.

At the same time, Stark hissed, "She's his ride."

A stocky man brought a duffle bag out from the house and took it to Wilson, who, in turn, walked it over to the boat. Kelley took his hand off the console and checked the bag. He picked up a phone, tapped at it, and then stuffed it in a cargo pocket on his pants.

"Anderson moving in," the spotter reported.

I raised my head enough to get a look at the end of the long dock. Sure enough, a blue and white fishing boat approached. She swung around to face the ocean before aligning with the end of the dock. Kelley and Wilson hopped up to the dock from the skiff.

"Go," I told everyone over the mic. "Go, go, go!"

Agents flooded the house and backyard from every side but the shore. Holm and I sprinted in Kelley's direction. He laughed, walked backward, and gave us the bird with his free hand. Wilson grabbed at Kelley's arm to get him to move faster, and Kelley whipped around, clocked Wilson on the temple, and then jumped into the boat with Charity. Wilson staggered and fell into the water.

Charity opened the throttle and set the fishing boat chugging into the channel before we could get to it. They were almost out of firing range by the time we reached the dock.

"You'll never catch me!" Kelley laughed as we raised our weapons.

We fired at the boat. Charity screamed, and Kelley dropped to the deck. He rose with a surprise of his own, marched up to the rear deck of the fishing boat, and aimed for us.

"Run," I yelled at Holm.

He saw the RPG launcher at the same time, and we busted ass to get out of the way. The grenade hit the side of the dock feet from where Wilson was struggling to get out of the water. The concussion blasted half the dock and sent a wave down the rest that threw Holm and me headlong onto the shore.

"Get the cutter going, and I need the chase boat, now," I ordered over the radio. I ran over to the skiff as gunfire was traded up by the house. Birn had command over that part of the raid should we have to go to water. Bullets plinked into the soft ground as Holm and I flew toward Kelley's delivery boat.

"What are you doing?" he yelled.

"We gotta get out to the chase boat." I looked over and saw help. "Stark, get over here."

She ducked and sprinted toward us. "Sir?"

"You're driving the skiff to get us to our boat," I

shouted over the noise. "Bring it back in one piece. It's full of evidence."

She stared at the tarp-covered boxes and got aboard. Holm and I shoved it into the water and jumped in. The outboard-engine boat we were using waited at the edge of the floating timber shards. A Coast Guard officer was at the helm and waved to acknowledge he saw us. Stark maneuvered the skiff to bump softly against the chase boat. Holm got aboard, and I leaned over to Stark.

"Wait until the shootout is over before you take that shit ashore," I warned her. "You do not want those boxes breached."

"I understand, sir. Good hunting." She gave a salute and gunned the motor as soon as I was clear.

Holm and I reloaded our weapons as the chase boat surged forward in the direction of Kelley and Charity's flight. They were headed toward open water, which wasn't good news. The wind had picked up to create chop through the inlet. It was going to be worse once we were past the islands. Not only that, but there were resorts up and down the way, including Hilton Head to the north. Already, people were running out onto their docks and yards to see what the explosion had been about.

"There they are, sir," the captain alerted me.

"They're going out to sea like you said. Cutter is launching LRI now."

Long-Range Interceptors were the Coast Guard's armed chase boats deployed from the rear of specially designed cutters. Kelley was between our boat coming out from the islands and the LRI in open water. Our outboard motors gave us a speed advantage, and we started catching up.

Kelley's boat cut hard to the south after he cleared the shallows. I saw the Coast Guard's cutter on the horizon, and a tiny speck that had to be the LRI angled toward the target.

"We need Kelley and Anderson alive if at all possible," I reminded them over the radio. "The rest of their weapons have to be located."

"Aye-aye. Doing what we can, sir."

Our boat gained enough so that I saw Kelley stripping down, and he seemed to be shouting at Charity. By her body language, she wasn't having whatever he was saying, but he didn't seem to care as he pulled up a wetsuit.

"He's gonna dive," I yelled to Holm as I stripped down to my undershirt and cargo pants. "We're not going to get there in time."

The boat we were on was used as a dive boat, and we'd made sure it had fresh equipment, just in case.

As I got my gear on, Holm took shots at Kelley's boat to try to slow them down.

"He's holding a gun on the girl," Holm shouted.

I stood in time to see her jerk back and drop, another victim of Kelley's blood thirst. Still, I had a hard time feeling sorry for her after she buried that knife into Greer's back, but that was one less witness to where Kelley stashed his weapons. He pointed the handgun at us, and we ducked. At this distance, effective aim was out the window, but a guy could get a lucky shot.

Holm was pulling fins on, and I was ready with my tanks when Kelley stepped to the platform at the back of his boat with his duffle in hand. He waved and then leapt into the water. I guessed that he planned to lose us by swimming to shore. He knew his boat couldn't get away.

The LRI was almost caught up as we pulled along the escape boat. I was almost ready to dive when I heard crying.

"She's alive," our captain called out.

"That's something." I looked at Holm. He was ready to go. "Let's do this, partner."

"Hoo-yah!" we yelled together.

Due to incoming weather, the water wasn't as bright as I'd have liked. I scanned the area as I equalized. We were near one of the artificial reefs South Carolina had gained attention for creating. I didn't see Kelley in any other direction, so I pointed toward the reef.

We kicked toward the edge of a concrete art installation that had coral polyps growing all over it. Kelley wasn't on the other side. I saw a glint a long way ahead. When the glint faded, I saw Kelley's silhouette. Holm saw it too and waved for me to go with him.

For being in his late fifties, Kelley was damned fit. He swam better than most people half his age, even with towing the duffle. I saw a hint of neon yellow and saw that he'd affixed a lift bag to make it easier, but that didn't make it a cakewalk. Holm and I gained slowly at first, but we crept up after a minor drop-off.

That's when it hit me. Kelley had slowed too fast.

I grabbed at Holm's ankle, but he jerked away as Kelley lunged at him. In a flurry of bubbles, Kelley and Holm grappled against each other. I pulled my Ka-Bar and went behind to go for Kelley's hoses, but he twisted out of reach. He broke cleanly from Holm and stopped kicking to let himself sink into the darkness. The lift bag faded with him.

Holm and I descended after him and managed to

hit Kelley with our dive lights. He hit the bottom, kicked up a sand cloud for cover, and vanished. I traced as much of the cloud as I could with my light, and Holm got the other half. Kelley was gone when the sand settled enough to see, but his duffle was left with its tow line dropped on the floor, the lift bag bobbing in the current.

I scanned as much of the surroundings as I could, and I saw Holm's light beam doing the same... until it dropped toward the bottom in lazy arcs. I spun around and found Kelley all over Holm. Both men had their combat knives out and struggled to disable the other through injury or cut hoses. I kept my light on them and kicked as hard as I had in years. How had Holm gotten that far from me already?

A blood cloud erupted between them. For a second, both continued to battle, but then Kelley drove his arm into Holm's gut, and my partner doubled up with his arms around his middle. Blood billowed into the water worse than I'd ever seen, but Kelley wasn't done. I was less than an arm's reach away when Kelley sliced through Holm's hoses.

Kelley disappeared into the dark as I grabbed Holm and traded out his regulator for my octopus. The hose was long to allow free movement of the diver in trouble, but Holm wasn't in any shape to move on his own. We had to be at least twenty-five feet down, and he was losing blood fast. I adjusted his buoyancy to help him ascend faster.

I broke the surface first. The LRI was nearest, and I shined my emergency strobe at them. They gunned the motor to get over to us, and I saw the clipper was nearly on the scene.

"Holm's hurt," I shouted to the guys on the LRI. "It's bad. Get a chopper out ASAP."

I helped them load him into the LRI with no small amount of swearing on my part. Kelley was going to get away again, but there was no way I was letting my partner die without a fight to get him help.

Before going back under, I got the captain's attention. "I'm gonna take a look a—"

Something locked around my neck and dragged me under. I drove my elbow back into Kelley's side, but his iron grip didn't loosen against my carotid. My vision dimmed from the blood flow being cut off. I grabbed my Ka-Bar and slammed it into Kelley's leg. That got him loose enough for me to break his hold. I kicked up to the surface and got a lungful of air.

"Need more divers," I shouted, but they were

already on it with guys in wetsuits getting their gear on.

By dumb luck, Kelley hadn't cut my hoses, and I dropped under the surface to find him. This time, I had a blood trail to follow. Holm's cloud had dissipated enough that I knew this was Kelley. I was not letting the bastard escape this time. As I searched, I noticed a small pack of lemon sharks roaming about. They wouldn't be attracted to human blood, but I had to watch out. Even the normally chill lemon sharks could be attracted to all the commotion.

I refocused on Kelley. He was angling for his duffle bag. At least he was consistent about the money. Too bad for him that I caught up barely ten feet below the surface. I caught the motion of other divers leaping in, but they weren't close yet. Kelley must have caught my movement out of the corner of his eye as he spun around to face me. He went for a feint at me, but I saw right through it. I blocked his actual attack with my off hand and struck at his middle with my knife. Even so, Kelley twisted aside so that my blade only slid along his belly with no more than a scratch, and his counter-slash made fire lance up my exposed side. God, the man was fast, but he hadn't cut me deep.

Kelley must have wanted to drag this out because

he backed off for a moment. Through his mask, his eyes flashed with hatred, and his legendary calmness was anything but.

Kelley charged, but as I braced for the attack, one of the yellow-gray sharks zeroed in on him and slammed into him from the side. It whisked off in another direction, clearly finding the madman unappetizing, and bubbles swirled everywhere as the water turned scarlet. I swam under the cloud and found Kelley sinking and trailing more blood than Holm had earlier.

I did not want to save Kelley's life, but I also wasn't a cold-blooded killer like him. I sheathed my knife and grabbed his arm to haul him toward the surface. The other divers were only then arriving. They took over and got Kelley to the top quicker than I could've at that point. A diver paced me to the surface while giving me the space I needed to shake off the battle fury and adrenaline drop.

One of the Coast Guard's huge orange choppers took off into the angry sky as I broke the surface this time. God, I hoped Holm was alive in that bird.

Someone screamed my name. It took a few seconds to recognize that it was Tessa from aboard the cutter which had gotten closer in the past few minutes. She was looking at the mess that was Kelley being lifted into the LRI.

"Tessa," I bellowed. She stopped screaming as I flashed my strobe in her direction. "Tessa, I'm over here!"

She saw me and put a hand to her mouth as her loose hair whipped around in the growing wind. I waved to her and then swam for the LRI. They'd loaded Kelley, and I needed a look. The captain gave me an arm up and spoke in my ear.

"I don't know how, but the son of a bitch is conscious. He doesn't have long, though."

"Thanks." I clapped the man on the shoulder.

Kelley lay on the floor of the boat with blood-soaked gauze packed in his middle. The captain started the boat and headed us over to the LRI's hatch at the back of the cutter.

"Well, Marston, you win." Kelley's voice was a shadow of its former self.

"I didn't win shit. I stopped you."

"Me? Yeah." He shivered and frowned. "So that's how it feels..." His eyelids fluttered but then snapped open. "I served a higher purpose. God and country. Real patriots know what it'll take. Ask Farr. He knows." His mouth stretched into a beatific smile. "They'll… they'll burn it down." His voice was no more than a whisper. "You'll see."

"Go to hell," I spat.

A foamy red laughed bubbled up from his throat, and then Simon Kelley stilled forever.

37

Tessa hated being out of visual range of the take-down, but the Coast Guard cutter was far too large to navigate the channels through the salt marshes.

She didn't want to admit to herself that it was a relief to be away from the danger for once, especially when Ethan was in the middle of it. The uncertainty drove a spike into her heart. Yes, he was often involved in dangerous operations, but she rarely knew about them. She tried to imagine knowing about every mission. Her chest hurt just thinking about it.

"They've gone in," a Coastie informed them. "Gunfire reported."

Donald put his hand on her shoulder. "He'll be fine."

"I wish I felt more confident about that," she told him.

He squeezed her shoulder once and let go to cross his arms. Even in his five-figure suit, he looked the epitome of a fleet admiral on the cutter deck. Tessa felt out of place with all the uniformed Coasties now that she was back in civilian wear with her Capri pants and sleeveless blouse.

"Female subject approaching dock in civvie boat," the Coastie updated. "Kelley running for a boat."

Tessa pressed against the rail as if it'd get her that much closer to seeing what was happening. She thought she might hear cracks of gunfire, but the cutter's engines and the general cacophony covered up the noise. She'd give almost anything to be on the scene to know her friends were okay, especially Ethan.

A popping sound came from the estate's direction, and then a boom echoed across the islands and water. Tessa spun to face the Coastie as he got the report.

"Kelley is on a boat," he told them. "He fired an RPG into the dock. Wilson hit. Agents Marston and Holm made it back to shore." He cocked his head and listened. "They're... Hold on."

"Come on, come on," Tessa said under her breath.

"Easy," Donald said in her ear. "They'll get him. Kelley's running out of options."

"Marston, Holm, and Stark are on the arms skiff... Belay that. Marston and Holm are on the chase boat. Stark seems to be taking the skiff out of battle range." The Coastie stepped toward the rail while keeping a hand on his headset. A deep thrum hummed through the deck. "Kelley's boat is coming toward us. Launching LRI."

For a moment, Tessa was torn. She'd never seen the Long Range Interceptor in person, let alone launching from a cutter, but she had a job to do. The job came first, and she pulled out the backup camera she'd left in Miami when they left for Puerto Rico. The cutter was a good distance from shore, and they started chugging in. Ordered shouts rang out from the rear of the cutter as they launched the smaller boat.

Tessa pointed her lens toward the inlet channel. There, barely visible, was a white speck moving faster than a boat ought to in the marshy channels. She lowered the camera and saw the LRI bouncing out of the cutter's wake.

"There's nowhere for him to go," Donald observed. "He's as good as ours."

"What is your deal with this guy?" Tessa asked. She kept her voice low to avoid challenging him in front of the military crew. "You didn't fly in the last time I was kidnapped and almost killed. Why now, why with Kelley?"

Donald looked down his nose at her. For a moment, he seemed like a completely different person. A person with absolute authority, steel resolve, and no tolerance for questioning. Tessa resisted the impulse to shrink away.

"There are some things I cannot and will not discuss with you," he told her in a cold tone. "I love you as if you were my own, Tessa, and I would do anything to protect you. That is why I'm telling you to drop it. Now."

She looked away first. Donald had always had that effect on her, and the more she learned, the more it bothered her. As she lifted her camera to look for photo opportunities, she thought about how nice it might be to live in Miami, where it was summer year-round.

Kelley's boat was just into view of the long lens. She snapped a few shots and then looked for the chase boat Ethan was in. They were still a good distance back but looked to be gaining. Kelley's boat got close enough that she saw someone with blond hair at the wheel. Charity. Tessa took several shots in hopes of getting a clearer view.

The LRI charged in Kelley's direction as Charity took a hard turn south, but Ethan's boat was closer. Kelley stood in the back, exchanging his clothes for a wetsuit as he appeared to be arguing with Charity. As their boat veered south, Tessa got a better view from behind and took pictures. Charity wildly gestured with one hand while she steered with the other.

Kelley zipped his wetsuit and grabbed something from below where Tessa could see. He turned in Ethan and Robbie's direction but raised his arm sideways toward Charity, gun in hand.

"No!" Tessa yelled as her camera clicked away.

Kelley's arm barely kicked back, and Charity dropped out of sight. He pointed toward the white chase boat, and the same minimal kickback happened two or three times. Ethan's boat was closer by then, and Tessa saw he and Holm pull diving tanks on over their undershirts and fatigue pants.

Kelley stepped into the water just before the chase boat pulled alongside. Ethan and Holm finished getting ready, and then they leapt in. The

LRI parked next to both boats as well. Coasties swarmed Kelley's vessel and lashed it to another support boat that had arrived to tow it.

"They're calling for medical rescue," the Coastie behind her announced.

Tessa jumped a little. She'd forgotten his presence since the boats had come into view.

"Medical?" she echoed. "For Charity?"

Tessa thought she'd seen Charity take the shot to her head, but maybe not. With someone like Kelley at the trigger, though, she'd have been dead if he wished it.

"Patient is conscious. Rescue helicopter being called in."

"What if someone else gets hurt and needs to be flown out?" Tessa asked. Her imagination created all sorts of terrible scenarios in which the chopper needed to be close by.

"Charleston isn't far from here," Donald said calmly. "There'd be time."

The inability to do anything to help ate at Tessa. Photography was her forte, but it didn't feel like enough, not when Ethan and Robbie were in so much danger.

Someone broke the surface next to the LRI. Now that the cutter was so close, she could see there were two divers. One diver barely moved, and a dark area spread in the water around them. The Coasties on the LRI hauled the lifeless diver onto their deck. He had on the undershirt and military pants that Ethan and Holm wore. Tessa's knees felt unstable, but she stayed upright. A shock of yellow hair told her it was Holm.

Ethan remained in the water. A shadow came up from behind, and Kelley reared up from the surface to grab Ethan's neck. They went under. Coasties in the LRI piled out of the enclosed troop space. Each wore a wetsuit and grabbed their diving gear. Tessa got shots of them going into the water. She was sure they'd be great, but it was hard to care.

The monstrous beats of a Coast Guard Jayhawk's rotors stole her attention. She took photos of the aircraft's approach while checking in the water for signs of Ethan. It was impossible to see below the surface on such a gray day, with storm clouds gathering in the southwestern skies.

One of the Coasties noticed first.

"Shark," he yelled from the cutter deck. "Whoa, those are lemon sharks. That's weird."

Tessa looked to where he had pointed. Sure enough, a shark fin broke the surface, and the animal had a second dorsal fin. She pointed to it for

Donald, but it went back under. She used the polarizing lens to see just under the surface of the water through her camera. Several lemon sharks circled in the area. She looked up seconds later to see a dark patch spread in the water. Blood, but if it was from a knife wound or a shark bite, she couldn't tell.

Two dark heads surfaced a few moments later, but Tessa couldn't see which diver was who, especially since they ended up on the other side of LRI.

"Ethan!" The scream ripped through her throat before she realized what she was doing. She kept at it. "Ethan!"

A light flashed at her eyes from in the water. She looked, and it was Ethan. Relief boiled through her body, more so when the Jayhawk hovered over the LRI with first one basket and then the other. It began to rain as the LRI headed back to the cutter. Someone offered Tessa an umbrella as she put her camera away, but she shrugged it off. She gave the bag to Donald and ran back to where the LRI was to return.

In no time and yet too long, Ethan made it aboard the cutter via the LRI's recovery into its bay. The soft rain turned into a deluge as Ethan got on deck. Tessa ran to him and gave him the biggest hug she'd ever given. She didn't care about getting soaked by him or the rain.

The Coastie who'd been giving updates caught up with Tessa. He snapped a salute at Ethan.

"Sir, ma'am, Special Agent Holm has arrived at the hospital and is being prepped for surgery." He gestured over the rail to where a four-seat speedboat closed in on the cutter. "Your ride is on approach."

Tessa transferred over to the speedboat with Ethan. Now that the danger was over, she didn't want to let go. She just hoped she wouldn't have to hold him at a funeral for a friend.

38

HOLM'S PARENTS arrived in Charleston from Tampa on a private plane charter Diane arranged as soon as she got word of the severity of his injury.

Linda and Ben Holm met Tessa and me in the surgical waiting area. I'd met them before, but Tessa hadn't. If it had been under better circumstances, it would've been fun to see a reaction to Ben looking like Robbie, more like brothers than father and son. As it was, if Tessa noticed, she chose not to mention it.

"Ethan, how is he?" Linda asked in a rough voice. Her red-rimmed eyes begged for good news.

I rubbed the back of my head, unsure of how to answer. Fortunately, the surgeon walked into the room. His blue scrubs swished as he took a seat opposite Linda and Ben.

"You're Robert's parents?" he asked.

Ben nodded. Linda wrapped herself around his right arm.

"We'll be in there for a little while yet," the surgeon told them. His gentle voice somehow made it sound less bad. "That knife did some real damage." The doctor took a significant look at the Ka-Bar still strapped to my leg as if it had been the one that had hurt Holm. I leaned forward to block it from Linda's view. "The good news is that we got the worst of it. We're going through again to make sure we didn't miss anything, and then we have to close up."

"Can I get you some coffee or something?" I offered. I needed an excuse to get out of there and leave them to their privacy. "I can get that or food."

Linda sniffed and forced a smile. "Thank you, Ethan. That'd be nice. It's just..." She pointed at the combat knife. "Is that the same kind that hurt him?"

"Yes, ma'am. Near enough."

"I... I just can't—"

"Mrs. Holm, I'll find a place to put it. You won't have to see it again."

I took Tessa down to the lobby. Muñoz, Birn, and

Stark were getting their visitor stickers as we got off the elevators. Like me, they hadn't changed from their fatigues worn during the raid.

"How is he?" Birn asked. Worry lines creased the corners of his eyes.

"In surgery still," I told them. "The surgeon seems to think he'll make it." I swallowed. This was my best friend we were talking about. "We'll know more in a while."

Muñoz nodded and handed Tessa and me a Target bag each.

"I figured you two wouldn't leave the hospital for a while, so we stopped to get you something clean and dry. Birn will pick up your stuff from the field office as soon as debriefs are done."

"Thanks, Sylvia." I opened my bag to find sweats and clean socks... and an Air Force shirt. "Very funny," I told her.

"Buyer chooses." She winked but then gave me a hug. I froze. Muñoz hugged no one. "We were only going upstairs to drop that off. I guess we can go now. We'll be back after our briefing."

"I'll walk out with you," I said as I patted my leg for their attention. "I need another favor."

The rain had stopped for a while, and we all

went out to the car they'd borrowed. I removed my knife and handed it to Stark for safekeeping.

"I can't be carrying that in the hospital. I already look like Rambo in there." I took a deep breath but couldn't beat a yawn. "Will you look after it until we're done here?"

Stark held her hands out, and I laid the sheathed knife and leg strap across her palms. She handled it as if it were a samurai sword. Maybe it was, in a way.

"I won't let anything happen to it," she promised.

"Tessa, you can go back with them," I offered. "See the admiral, talk about whatever you need to talk about."

"That might be—" she began, but Birn cut her off.

"He left. As soon as we went ashore, he took a plane back to New York. Said he has deadlines to meet." He sent an apologetic look to Tessa. "Sorry. I know you wanted to see him before he left."

Tessa's lips thinned, and her eyes narrowed. Lightning arced across the sky behind her as if she'd called it. Thunder rumbled throughout the area. Without another word, she turned her back and walked inside.

"I guess she's staying with me," I said with a flat

attempt at humor. "Seriously, guys, thanks. I'll call as soon as I know something."

That call came sooner than I expected. The rest of Holm's insides looked good, and they got a plastic surgeon to tidy up the gnarly wound. He came out of anesthesia fine only to fall sound asleep with the help of some meds.

"We're going to be at a hotel," I told the Holms. "The team isn't in any shape to travel tonight, so we'll be close by. We can get you a room if you like."

"No, I want to be here with my son," Linda said with a kind smile. "You look half dead yourself, Ethan. Get that rest."

Birn picked us up soon after that. He had some updates for us on the way to the hotel. I sat in the back with Tessa because, dammit, I needed to be close to her.

"The ME finished with Kelley already. Dumas is having a shit fit, but the body's here, and she isn't." He chuckled. "Turns out this ME knows a thing or two about sharks. It was a lemon shark that got Kelley. A damned lemon shark."

"Are you kidding me?" Tessa blurted out. "They hardly ever go after people. They're not nearly as aggressive as others."

"Right," I agreed. "That's... wow. Dare Lemon's

murderer is killed by a lemon shark. Birn, you're a spiritual guy. What d'you think about it?"

"I think Kelley's rotting in hell and Dare Lemon helped send him there. Simple as that."

"I'm okay with that," Tessa said.

I laughed. "Yeah, I am too. Has anyone told Bridget Lemon?"

"Muñoz called her. She won rock, paper, scissors." Birn shook his head. "That woman beats me at that game every time."

"What about Charity Anderson?" Tessa asked. Her brow wrinkled. "Is she even alive?"

Birn was slow to nod. A mighty sigh came from his direction as he turned left into the hotel parking lot.

"I don't know if she's lucky or unlucky," he eventually said. "There's scarring, and they're going to put a plate in the side of her head once the swelling goes down. They said she can draw letters to spell things, but there's no speech yet. She'll probably survive, but they don't know how far she'll heal."

"There'll be a trial for Greer's murder," I added. Tessa turned away and watched out the window. "I know that was hard, but we need you to testify."

She nodded. "It's just that she didn't have to kill him. It was a game to her until Kelley shot her in the head." She looked up at Birn. "Do they think she'll know where to find the rest of Kelley's stash?"

"That's anybody's guess at this point," Birn rumbled. He parked the car. "In we go. Oh, and Stark has news of her own."

I never knew what to expect from younger agents having news to share. It could be anything from quitting, getting married, going to the military, or who knew what. Tessa held my hand as we went into the hotel. MBLIS had rented two rooms, and the party was in the girls' room. We went in to find a bottle of champagne had been uncorked and poured into SOLO cups. Pizza was the entrée and potato chips, the hors d'oeuvres.

"Does this have to do with Abbie's big announcement?" Tessa inquired as she scooped up a generous slice of pepperoni.

"It is," Stark told us. Her rosy cheeks and loose hair suggested she'd had quite a bit to drink so far. "I'm getting promoted!"

"You got it?" I clapped my hands once and hooted. "You got it!"

"Director Ramsey said it came through during the raid." She hiccuped. Wow, for a badass, that girl was a lightweight. "Special Agent Stark, at your service."

"Congratulations!" Tessa ran over and hugged her.

That was not a shock. The shock was when Muñoz made it a hug pile. Champagne splashed on the bed, but nobody cared. They all spoke at once, and I couldn't understand a damned thing.

"I'm going to get some shuteye," I told the women. "You all behave."

"Go away, Marston," Muñoz shouted. "Girls' night!"

"C'mon, Lamarr, I can tell when we're not wanted," I said with a laugh. Once in our own room, I had to ask him, "Is that what women seriously do? Sylvia and Abbie are so uptight at work."

Birn shook his head. "And just when I think you've learned it all, man. There are no rules for a girls' night, not other than kicking the menfolk out." He cleared his throat. "We're flying out before lunch. Ramsey wants you and Tessa on the plane."

I looked at the floor, which suddenly got a lot more interesting.

"My partner is here."

"Your best friend is here," Birn said. "He's going to be out for a few weeks at a minimum. This would be a good time to take a trainee."

I looked at the wall as if I could see through to

the other room. "Stark? Hell, she could be a trainer in no time herself."

"Maybe, but here's the interesting part. She's going to be assigned to Meisha's field office."

"Griezmann?" I asked with a raised eyebrow. "She's out in Honolulu."

"Abbie doesn't know that part yet," Birn noted. "Diane wants it to come from you. The two of you will train for a while, and then you'll deliver her to Hawaii."

I blinked. "Since when do we hand-deliver Special Agents?"

"Since the director of this particular office knows a guy with an interest in a certain pirate ship."

I blinked again. "This has what to do with Hawaii?"

"Meisha happened across an interesting display at her library. It was about pirates and the Caribbean. Obviously, she decided to check it out. Turns out the display was mostly about the *Dragon's Rogue*."

"A lot of people know about the legend," I told him. "I'd expect that to be more about Blackbeard, but Grendel made a name of his own."

Birn grabbed a tablet off of the dresser. He

pulled up a webpage and handed the tablet over to me.

"Check this out," he said with a hint of excitement.

The webpage showed the display at the library. In the middle of the case was a book that looked older than sin. The article stated that the book was the personal log or journal kept by Grendel himself and passed down from father to son for several generations. While it started in the Bahamas, the book moved to Hawaii with one of Grendel's great-grandsons almost a century later.

"I've done hundreds of online searches," I mused. Well, dozens. "I've never come across this."

"That's because the owner just found it last year."

"This is great." I looked up at Birn and grinned. "This is fantastic, man."

It felt like Gramps was leading me on in a way he never could during his life. Some people would say that the way the clues were stacking up since Gramp's death was a coincidence. Maybe, maybe not. Either way, I felt like wherever he was, he knew and was happy.

"Oh hey, one other thing." Birn took the tablet

back and put it on the dresser. "I didn't know Robbie's sister was in Hawaii."

I stilled. "What?"

"Yeah, Meisha saw her at a mall." The way Birn said it so casually meant that he didn't know what I did about the disappearance. "Ronnie didn't hear Meisha call out to her, but it was definitely her. She has that tattoo behind her ear, y'know?"

"Yeah, the one that covered that birthmark."

I'd forgotten about that. When she was old enough to get a tattoo, Ronnie marched right into a shop and had the artist turn the somewhat flower-shaped birthmark into a cute little tiger lily.

"That's the one." Birn shook his head a little. "Meisha was sure Ronnie should've heard her, but maybe she was thinking about other things."

Or maybe Ronnie didn't want Holm to find out where she was.

"Hey, do me a favor and don't mention it until he's better," I said. "I'll explain eventually, but right now, it's not a good time for him to know that. Let Meisha know, as well."

Birn frowned but nodded. "Okay, but you owe me that explanation."

"Thanks, man." I sighed, as much out of exhaustion as worry. "Honestly, I just want to see Robbie awake and himself again."

As luck would have it, Holm was plenty awake the next morning. He cracked a few bad jokes and made me swear to miss him every day that he was away from the job. I didn't have the heart to tell him right then about his sister. The guy didn't need the extra stress, especially when he was recovering. I did, however, text him a photo of a gift left at our desks from Bridget Lemon... the entwined diving masks from their home.

Tessa lingered in Miami, and she talked about the possibility of staying, and that she might get a condo. That changed three days after we got back to the houseboat.

"I have to go back to New York," she told me out of the blue.

"What?" I was toweling my hair after a great shower and had the bathroom door open. I hoped I hadn't heard her correctly. "You said something about New York."

She looked at her cooling breakfast. "I have to go back. Uncle Donald needs me. Besides, it'll be better to write up the feature without certain... influences right near me."

With a calm I did not feel, I set my towel on the

bathroom counter and pulled on my sweatpants and t-shirt. I walked over to the table.

"Why does he insist on you going?" I asked in as nonjudgmental of a way as I could manage. "I thought you didn't want him to run your life anymore."

She shook her head. "I don't, but the thing is, something is going on with him. I love him, I really do. I just—"

"There's something wrong, and you want to know what."

She nodded and bit her lip for a few seconds. "I have to know. He was the fleet admiral and a Joint Chief. I get that he knows things we will never imagine, but there's something odd about his reaction over Kelley." She looked up. "I still don't know what Mike told you, but the fact that he got spooked, also, that was creepy. If Kelley was out there with all these guys knowing, who else is and why?"

A cold lump formed in my stomach. "Tessa, be careful. Please, be careful." I took her hands. "You should let it go, but I know you won't. If I can ever help, reach out." I thought for a second. "Tell me a color and flower you hate."

"What?"

"Just do it."

"Okay. I hate the color cranberry, and I hate roses." She pulled her hands back and crossed her arms. "There."

"If you ever get in over your head, call me and ask for cranberry roses." I walked around to where she sat. "Then, give me a location."

"Okay."

"I'll ask how soon you want them," I explained with utter seriousness. "If you say 'now,' I'll send someone. I know people all across the country, and they'd bust a few asses to help any of my friends. Say 'as soon as you can,' and I'll be there within twelve hours, less if possible."

I hugged her for all I was worth, and she hugged back for all she was worth. By the next day, she was gone, and I went to Mike's for a few shots of Four Roses. Birn, Muñoz, and Stark went along to keep me from harassing Mike over the tango music. And to keep me company. Mostly to help Mike put up with me.

Tessa's feature turned out to be a hit. She talked Donald into letting her be vague about the agency involved. That was great for keeping us under the radar, but it didn't help the funding issue.

"He's right," Diane told me a few days after Tessa's article went to print. We were in her office with the door shut. "This could've helped us get funding. People are going to think this was all the Coast Guard and CGIS."

"Why'd they give us the money for the plane if they were going low on funding?" I paced her office. "It doesn't make sense."

"Yes, Ethan, it does." Diane tapped her pen on the desk. "The powers that be look at expenses. The plane hiked our expenses and annual budget. Someone is making it look like we're too big for our britches."

There wasn't much more to discuss, because we had no proof. Donald Farr's warning was the only concrete word we got, but life went on. All we could do was keep proving our worth.

Holm was on medical leave for three months. The doctors wanted four to five, but some people can't be contained. So, when Stark and I flew out to Hawaii a month after the raid, Holm tagged along for some R&R.

Funny thing about life, though. It throws screwballs at you, and that R&R ended up being a hell of an adventure.

But that was a story for another time.

EPILOGUE

THAT STORY TOOK a good three shots of Mango Fest to tell, and my mouth was dry as hell. The kids, though, looked happy. Mostly.

"Hey, you didn't say what happened with all those weapons Kelley made," Jeff pointed out. "Did you guys find them? Are they still out there?"

I licked my lips. Not enough drinks in the world could cover that answer. The group waited more patiently than I'd give them credit for.

"Some of the details are still classified."

I glanced at Mike, and he shrugged. The kids had conveniently left him alone. Yeah, that dude was a bigger badass than me, and his glower kept them off his back. Only I knew there was no menace behind that. And I hadn't told the kids that Mike Birch wasn't his real name. He didn't need that heat.

"I'll just say that Charity was helpful. She's in prison still, and she has a lot of physical challenges because of the bullet she took. Greer's family and our department got her a shorter sentence because she's taken a hell of a punishment and she's cooperated. She's a different person now."

"But did you find the weapons?" Jeff pushed.

"Charity helped. That's all I can say. I wish I could tell you more."

He shrugged and seemed to give up. I understand. If I were one of these youngsters, I'd want to know too. The truth was that we only found a few stashes. Charity hadn't been privy to all of Kelley's secrets. I didn't want to encourage treasure hunts of that nature.

"What happened in Hawaii?" Ty demanded. I silently thanked him for changing the course of that conversation. "Come on, you can't leave us hanging."

"Shut up, Ty." Charlie play-punched the guy in the shoulder. "It's hard enough to get Marston to tell one story."

I looked at Mackenzie. The swelling in her ankle hadn't gone down much, but it wasn't worse, either. Her ankle, however, wasn't what stole her attention.

She pointed to something special behind the bar and on a shelf above the liquor shelves. A hand-carved tiki took that place of honor, and it always gave me a warm feeling.

"Is that from your trip to Hawaii?" Her face softened.

"It is."

"My mom is from the big island. Dad met her when he was assigned to Pearl Harbor." The guys looked over at her, and she lifted her chin. "Yeah, I'm a Navy brat. Proud of it, too."

"You never told us that," Ty complained.

"You never asked," she countered.

"Ensign Shore," I intoned.

"Sir, yes, sir." She straightened in her seat and tried to stand, but I put a hand in the way of her leg.

"I have an offer for you."

"Sir?"

"Two things. First, for the love of God, stop calling me 'Sir.'"

"Yes... Mr. Marston."

That was the best I'd get from her, I had a feeling. She'd grown up in the life, and those manners wouldn't change.

"Mackenzie, go take care of your ankle. I'll get you tickets to see the band at your next leave. And to sweeten the pot..." I grinned at the lot of them. "If you fellas make sure she does what the doctors say, I'll tell you the Hawaii story. Without complaining." I winked.

"I can live with that," Mackenzie conceded, "but one other question."

"What's that?"

"You talked a little bit about Agent Holm's sister," she reminded everyone. "Did he ever find her?"

"Funny thing about coincidences," I told them. "The next time I tell a story, you might find out a thing or two about Ronnie Holm. And that's all I have to say."

AUTHOR'S NOTE

Hey, if you got here, I just want you to know that you're awesome! I wrote this book just for someone like you, and if you want another one, it is super important that you leave a review.

The more reviews this book gets, the more likely it is there will be a sequel to it. After all, I'm only human, and you have no idea how far a simple "your book was great!" goes to brighten my day.

Also, if you want to know when the sequel comes out, you absolutely must join my Facebook group and follow me on Amazon. Doing one won't be enough because it relies on either Facebook or Amazon telling you the book is out, and they might not do it.

You might miss out on all my books forever, if you only do one!

Here's the link to follow me through e-mail.

Here's the link to my Facebook Group.

Made in the USA
Middletown, DE
24 June 2024

56189684R10300